FLESH EATER

HOUNDSTOOTH BOOK 1

TRAVIS M. RIDDLE

www.travismriddle.com

Book Layout © 2017 BookDesignTemplates.com

Cover design by Deranged Doctor Design

Flesh Eater/Travis M. Riddle. —1st ed.

ISBN 9798692408020

Zank said, "Well, Dend acquired some…compromising photographs of the boss. Not sure who gave 'em to Dend—Nomak is pissed just thinkin' about it. He's already fired all his personal staff that could've had access to the photos wherever he kept 'em. But he's seen proof that Dend does indeed have 'em."

"What kind of photographs?"

"Photographs of a sexual nature."

Coal huffed, amused. It sounded embarrassing, perhaps, but not something worth losing a considerable amount of valuable property over. The thousands—maybe millions, more realistically—of tups that he'd be losing out on over the years. All because of some photos.

"That seems like something he could pretty easily recover from," said Coal.

Venny and Zank laughed some more.

"Well," said Venny, "the thing about Nomak is that evidently he's…not particularly well-endowed."

Coal stared ahead at the two giggling rabbits caked in the yellow glow of the Starlite's sign. Marl was still unamused by the nature of their task.

"So," Coal started, seeking clarity, "we're stealing back photos of a Vinnag City Garna that show he's got a tiny cock and balls so that the public doesn't find out he's got a tiny cock and balls?"

"Yes," Zank confirmed.

Coal rolled his eyes but laughed at the Garna's fragile pride costing the man so much money and effort.

"Given the reputation of the Garnas, it seems like just being fired is cutting the staff a lot of slack," said Coal.

For Jenna

1

THE FIRST TIME COAL Ereness spoke to his father's ghost was the night the man died. The second time was the following morning.

The specter of his father had a bluish-green tinge, his fur and clothes monochromatic. No vibrancy to them. Matching the man's personality in life.

Coal was eerily reminded of that night while sitting at a small round table watching a burlesque show in the city of Vinnag. A little more than a year had passed, and he was now on the other side of the kingdom from where he last spoke to his father. At times, though, he feared he would never be far from that moment.

There was a single dancer on stage, a pretty raccoon covered in white fur. A rarity. Her stage name was, appropriately, White Rose. Almost all her fur was exposed while she danced and gyrated on stage to the smooth tunes of the house band nearby. A group of hedgehogs tooted away on saxophones and muted trumpets. One tapped animatedly on a drum and cymbal.

Blue stage lights drenched White Rose in their cool embrace, following her every seductive move. Well, for anyone else they would have been seductive, but Coal had allegedly spoken to a ghost. So, up on that stage he did not see an exotic, sexy white raccoon—he saw a blue, drifting spirit. He saw death.

Coal shook the morbid thought from his mind. He generally tried not to think about his father too often, and tonight was definitely not the night for it. He needed to focus. He did not want to come across as distant or weird in front of Zank's associates.

He scoured the walls for a clock but found none, which was not much of a surprise in a place like this. Worrying about the time meant worrying about some far-off responsibility. Responsibilities were for the real world. This was not the real world. This was the Starlite.

Coal watched White Rose and waited for Zank. He wondered how often the raccoon received comments on her white fur.

He was no stranger to unsolicited remarks about his own unusual visage. His fur was orange and black instead of the orange and white coloring typically found in his fellow foxes. His father told him on more than one occasion that when he was born, his face looked like it was rubbed in coal, hence the name.

Coal hated that story. He was glad to no longer hear it.

The hedgehog band's song began winding down. White Rose came to a slow stop on the stage, smiling broadly and bowing deeply. Men and women in the audience hooted and hollered for her, cheering her on to do one more dance, but the raccoon laughed and tossed her hands as if to say *"Oh, stop! You know I can't!"*

She shuffled backstage as the house lights dimly lit back up and the band transitioned into a softer tune. Attendees chatted amongst themselves while waiting for the next performer to take the stage.

A waitress in a short skirt and a skimpy top stopped by Coal's table to ask if he needed another drink or something to eat. He'd already downed one glass of water and did not want to be caught needing to relieve himself later, so he declined the drink. The Starlite's air was filled with the aroma of smoke and sweat, which effectively curbed his appetite, so he turned down any food as well. The woman offered him a sweet smile and scurried over to the next table.

Nervousness jittered through his body. He tapped his nails on the tabletop uncontrollably.

He would be lying if he said part of him didn't wish Zank would abandon him tonight. Just complete the job without him, or call it off altogether. He desperately needed the money, there was no denying that, but something like this was far out of his comfort zone.

There was a sudden clap on his shoulder and a raspy shout of *"Junsuelu!"*

Zank sat himself down in the seat across from Coal, who returned the customary rabbit greeting. So much for calling off the job.

Two others accompanied Zank: another rabbit and a wolverine. Coal nodded a hello to them both, which they returned.

Zank scratched behind his tall ears while he looked Coal up and down. "How long you been waitin'?" the rabbit asked.

Even in the low light, Zank's rough, patchy fur was plain to see.

"Not long," Coal lied. No reason to introduce any friction to the group, however faint. He hadn't minded the wait anyway, aside from the creepy blue lights during the last performance.

"Great," Zank grinned.

The waitress returned to dote on her three new guests, who each ordered a shot of liquor.

"That the best idea, you think?" Coal asked, pointing the question at Zank. He didn't want to come off as accusatory toward the two others he had never met, but he and Zank went back years. The rabbit could take a soft jibe.

Zank shrugged. "Not the *worst* idea."

After a few moments of silence, it was clear that their scatterbrained mutual friend was not going to be making any introductions. "I'm Coal," he said, extending his hand toward the wolverine sitting to his right.

"Marl," the intimidating man said with a smile, exposing rows of sharp fangs.

Coal did the same for the rabbit, who introduced herself as Venny. He had heard a lot about Venny from Zank. Coal had been staying in the man's apartment since arriving in Vinnag two weeks earlier, and Venny had come up in conversation several times. She and Zank were close.

The waitress returned with the trio's order. As she sauntered away, Zank asked Coal, "Did White Rose go on already?"

"She finished right before you got here."

"Shit," Zank muttered. He knocked back his drink, something thick and brown that Coal hadn't caught the name of over the club's music. Zank went on, "Well, no need to dally, then, I s'pose. Might as well hop to it." He pushed his chair back and stood. Marl and Venny did likewise after downing their shots.

Zank nodded to Marl, and the wolverine tossed a handful of coins onto the wooden table to pay for the drinks.

It made sense that Zank had solely chosen the Starlite as their meeting place so that he could watch a dancer perform. He was by far the horniest person Coal had ever met, even reaching back to their youth.

The rabbit cocked his head toward the back of the club and said, "C'mon."

The three followed their intrepid leader toward a rear door that had a burly boar standing guard over it. Both of the man's tusks were chipped and his expression clearly stated he was unafraid of damaging them further.

"Off limits," was all he grunted at their approach.

Zank flashed him a toothy grin and said, "Onomatopoeia."

The boar cocked an eyebrow and stepped aside. Zank pushed the door open and stepped through, followed by Marl and Venny with Coal bringing up the rear.

They rounded a corner and found themselves in a narrow hallway that led to a door painted bright red. On either side of the hallway were rooms with PRIVATE signs tacked to the doors. They heard female voices behind the door on their right, which Coal assumed was the entrance to the dancers' dressing room. Zank rapped his knuckles on the door to their left.

Perhaps Zank had a utilitarian reason for meeting at the nightclub beyond general horniness.

The door swung open and a rabbit with black fur stood before them. His left ear twitched as he examined the new arrivals. "Who's the fox?" he asked.

"He's fine," was all Zank said.

That was good enough for the twitchy rabbit, who stood aside to let them into the private room.

It was a messy office with too-bright lighting and three desks all crammed into tight quarters amongst shelves of seemingly unorganized documents that spilled onto the floor. Only one desk was currently occupied. A flustered, yellow-coated marten wearing a white button-up shirt stained with sweat and possibly coffee was scribbling away at some papers on her desk. She had a hefty stack piling up in front of her, almost obscuring her entirely from view.

She glanced up at the people her coworker had brought into the room and asked, "This them?"

The black rabbit nodded.

The marten sighed dramatically and returned to the work that was giving her so much grief.

"She wants to be left out of it," the rabbit explained.

"Understandable," said Zank.

"I ain't no sympathizer," the marten piped up, not taking her beady eyes off her work. "But I ain't tryin' to be involved, neither."

"Understandable," Zank repeated.

Coal only vaguely knew what the plan was tonight, and he definitely did not know what they were doing in the back office of the Starlite. He faintly heard the girls arguing about something in the room across the hall, their voices raised and irate.

The black rabbit, who Coal figured would remain name-less, stepped behind the marten's desk and kicked a small, faded rug aside, scattering some loose pieces of paper that were on the floor. This elicited a yelp of protest from his coworker. Apparently, she had a finely-tuned organization system that included leaving papers on the floor.

Beneath the dirty rug was a trapdoor that the rabbit yanked open, revealing a cache of guns and ammunition.

Coal gulped at the sight.

"What do you need?" the rabbit asked.

"I think just a pistol each," said Zank. "Something light and simple."

"A revolver, if you've got one," Marl answered for himself. Venny remained silent, content to accept whatever she was given. Coal didn't say anything either, partially out of igno-rance when it came to weaponry and partially out of anxiety. Introducing guns to the situation came as a shock.

The day before, Zank had explicitly told Coal the Starlite inspected its guests before allowing them entry, so they would not be bringing any weapons in. For that reason, Coal thought this would be an easy, bloodless endeavor, but clearly Zank had other plans. And more connections in Vinnag than Coal realized.

They started a weapon train, with the black rabbit (whose ear had not stopped twitching) handing a gun to Zank, who handed it to Marl, who handed it to Venny, before ending with Coal, who still stood by the door. They continued this until everyone had a gun and some extra ammunition.

Then Coal was nearly knocked aside when the office door burst open and a topless doe entered, screaming that she had finally had enough with "all the bullshit."

Venny's arm swung up, aiming her gun at the intruder.

The doe stared at the four strangers wielding handguns, one of which was pointed at her chest, understanding immediately that this was not the time to bring her concerns about the bullshit to management. She swiftly backed out of the office, slamming the door shut behind her.

"Can you deal with that, please?" the rabbit asked his coworker.

The marten shook her head and said, "I told you not to schedule them together. You clean up your own mess."

The rabbit groaned, his left ear shaking more intensely than before. "The reason I needed to schedule them both tonight is that—"

"Can you maybe settle this in, like, two minutes when we're out of here?" Zank asked.

"Yes, *he* can settle it then," the marten smirked. She shoved aside the paper she'd been working on and snatched another from the towering pile.

The black rabbit groaned a second time but dropped the subject. It looked as if his ear was raring to pop off his head and bounce out of the room. He turned away from his uncooperative colleague and pressed a discreet button on the back wall.

A whirring of hidden mechanics buzzed through the room as a wide panel opened on the ceiling above the rabbit. A green metal ladder extended downward into the room.

"Ooh, secret ladder," Zank cooed. "Very fancy."

"Not so much a secret as it is just more convenient to keep it outta the way," said the rabbit. He gestured toward the ladder, which had finally come to a stop a few inches above the floor.

Zank was first to ascend, disappearing into the darkness. Coal followed behind everyone else.

As they climbed, the club's stale rank faded and gave way to warm, fresh air. The ladder led to the Starlite's roof, where Coal's associates awaited him.

The night air soothed him somewhat, but not much. The gun in his hand was a good deterrent to any calmness he felt.

"All clear!" Zank called down into the darkness from which they had emerged. A moment later, they heard the familiar whir of the ladder retracting.

They stood behind the club's yellow and blue neon sign proclaiming its name. Even behind the sign, its glow was strong enough to bask them in some of its light. Probably not enough to be visible from street level unless a person was specifically seeking out bodies, but still, Coal was uneasy.

Vinnag's entertainment district was bustling below them. There were multiple nightclubs on Harrower's Avenue, all with varying levels of debauchery. By all accounts, the Starlite was one of the more savory joints in the city.

But Coal still wasn't sure why they were on its roof.

Zank stood at attention and surveyed his three recruits, pistols in hand. There had been no revolver available, much to Marl's disappointment. The wolverine's dark brown fur bristled in the breeze.

"Okay," said the wiry gray rabbit as he inspected his gun. "Venny, please go over the plan again for our new friend here. Bring him up to speed."

"How much does he know already?" Venny asked.

"Not much," said Zank. "Almost nothin'."

Coal had known Zank since they were kids. Their friendship was one of the driving factors for Coal making his way down south to Vinnag. The rabbit had promised him lucrative job opportunities, which he needed. Having a friend to confide in and spend downtime with didn't hurt either.

They had worked a few minor jobs together, but this was the first big mission he was joining Zank on. He was aware the rabbit was connected to the city's underworld, but not to what extent or in what capacity. It didn't really matter, though; he needed money, and he needed to lay low, so proper employment wasn't viable at the moment. Regardless of how anxious it made him.

He would do what needed to be done tonight, but he hoped it was nothing too sinister.

"Okay," Venny began. "For starters, welcome to the Dripping Fang."

"The what?"

"Don't interrupt," said Marl.

Coal nodded and shut up.

"The Dripping Fang," Venny said again, and this time Zank beamed with pride at the name. "We work under secret orders from Garna Nomak."

Coal had not been in the city long enough to know who Nomak was. What he did know was that Vinnag's Garnas were a group of elite businessmen who essentially owned the city's various districts, gobbling up real estate and collecting rent from purveyors who wanted to open up shops or clubs or restaurants or whatever else.

It was Garna Dend who controlled the entertainment district, and he was immensely proud of that fact. Every club or brothel in the district had a portrait of him hanging up in it somewhere. Given he hadn't seen it in the Starlite, Coal assumed it might be displayed in the dancers' dressing room. He shuddered at the thought of the large, ugly tapir leering down at all the women as they undressed.

"Nomak thinks Dend is getting a little too big for his britches," Venny went on. "Dend's planning to extend his reach a little too far and buy up some newly-developed property that the city is about to put on sale. Nomak believes the property's rightfully his."

"Because it falls within his invisible territory marker?" Coal ventured a guess.

"Right. And who are we to disagree?" said Zank.

That meant Garna Nomak controlled either the garment district or Renning Heights, the two districts that bordered Dend's. Trying to expand one's district always caused unrest amongst the city's Garnas.

"Dend has the money to buy it, no problem. All the Garnas do, really, but he's the only one bold enough to make the move," Zank explained.

"But he's only bold because of what he's got on Nomak," Venny cut back in. "He knows that as long as he's got this hanging over Nomak's head, the boss isn't gonna put up a fight for the property."

This intrigued Coal. "What does Dend have?" he asked.

The three exchanged a look, and the rabbits chuckled. Marl remained unfazed.

"We're really not supposed to say," Zank laughed. "Well, I wasn't supposed to say, but I already say'd to these two here. I couldn't help myself."

Venny laughed harder. Marl was stoic.

Coal looked among the members of the Dripping Fang. "What is it?"

Zank said, "Well, Dend acquired some…compromising photographs of the boss. Not sure who gave 'em to Dend—Nomak is pissed just thinkin' about it. He's already fired all his personal staff that could've had access to the photos wherever he kept 'em. But he's seen proof that Dend does indeed have 'em."

"What kind of photographs?"

"Photographs of a sexual nature."

Coal huffed, amused. It sounded embarrassing, perhaps, but not something worth losing a considerable amount of valuable property over. The thousands—maybe millions, more realistically—of tups that he'd be losing out on over the years. All because of some photos.

"That seems like something he could pretty easily recover from," said Coal.

Venny and Zank laughed some more.

"Well," said Venny, "the thing about Nomak is that evidently he's…not particularly well-endowed."

Coal stared ahead at the two giggling rabbits caked in the yellow glow of the Starlite's sign. Marl was still unamused by the nature of their task.

"So," Coal started, seeking clarity, "we're stealing back photos of a Vinnag City Garna that show he's got a tiny cock and balls so that the public doesn't find out he's got a tiny cock and balls?"

"Yes," Zank confirmed.

Coal rolled his eyes but laughed at the Garna's fragile pride costing the man so much money and effort.

"Given the reputation of the Garnas, it seems like just being fired is cutting the staff a lot of slack," said Coal.

"I think he's gonna be doing an investigation into all of them and whoever the guilty party is…isn't gonna have a nice time," Venny said. "Firing them was just the fastest, cleanest punishment for now."

"Are the innocent ones gonna get their jobs back?"

"Doubtful," she replied.

Coal glanced at Marl, who still bore no expression. He stood with his arms crossed, waiting for Zank or Venny to lay out the actual plan. The wolverine was clearly uninterested in the personal affairs of his boss and simply wanted a payday. Coal was in the same boat.

"So why are we on the roof of the Starlite?" he asked.

"Because," Zank said, hopping over to the edge of the roof where the neon sign's light couldn't reach, "this is here."

Out of the dark, he held up a thick plank of wood.

"What you may or may not know is that Garna Dend's private office is across the alley here from the Starlite. I have it on good authority that he's keepin' the photos there. So we're gonna walk across the alley on this board, break in through an entryway on the roof, and rummage through his shit until we find the photographs. Sound good?"

"Sounds risky," said Coal after thinking it over a moment. "People will be able to spot us from the streets. Four people walking on a piece of wood between rooftops is pretty conspicuous."

"Walk fast, then."

"Great note. Next, won't Dend have people guarding the office if he keeps valuables there? Or possibly just normal employees still working in there? It's not very late by the entertainment district's standards."

He was not accustomed to this lifestyle, and he did not want to screw up the job or risk his life. He was trying to think through all the possibilities and voice his concerns.

"That's what the guns are for. When you aim 'em and pull the trigger, problems get solved," said Venny.

That finally garnered a laugh from Marl. More like a huff than an outright laugh, but Coal counted it.

Coal, however, found her retort unamusing. Between that remark and how quick to the draw she was when the deer interrupted them in the office, he could guess that things tended to get a bit bloody when Venny was involved.

"I'm not killing anyone," said Coal seriously.

Zank saw the grave expression on his friend's face and nodded. "No deaths unless absolutely necessary." He looked to Marl in particular and said, "Incapacitation is good enough tonight." The wolverine shrugged.

"Do we have any intel on whether there are bodies inside?" Coal decided to ask, not expecting much.

Surprisingly, Zank had at least a crumb of information. "My source who told me the photos are kept there also said Dend only employs two night guards. A fox and a macaw. Shouldn't be hard to deal with."

"That seems light," said Coal, though it was based on nothing more than his gut instinct. "Do you know this source well? You trust them?"

"Well enough," Zank nodded. "We've had a few tumbles, if you catch my drift."

"Sounds like you two have great pillow talk," said Venny.

Coal did not particularly want to know any more about Zank's sex life. He said, "I still think that sounds too good to be true. These Garnas are powerful, but their power can be taken from them at the drop of a hat, and that makes them paranoid. Shouldn't there be more guards in there protecting all his valuables?"

"All due respect, pal, but you don't have much experience with these folks," said Zank.

Coal's home city of Muta Par did not contain anything similar to Vinnag's districts and its Garnas, but his father had worked closely with the local government there, so Coal understood those types of people. They were all egomaniacs whose lives would be ruined if they lost any ounce of their control.

Still, he had to concede the point. He had a general idea but admittedly did not know a ton about the Garnas' day-to-day operations. Maybe their security really would be that light in this situation.

"Okay," he relented. "A fox and a macaw. Sounds easy enough."

"It will be." Zank smiled.

"Did your girl tell you exactly where the photographs are being held, by chance?"

"She did not," said the rabbit, "but they'll be easy to spot. They're the ones that have an anteater with a tiny dick 'n' danglies."

Venny burst out laughing at that, and Zank joined her. The two rabbits truly wound each other up. Marl shared a conspiratorial glance with Coal, but he began to giggle as well. The wolverine grunted, cracking the faintest smile.

When the hares had calmed themselves down, Zank carefully positioned the plank of wood between the two buildings. Only a few inches extended past the edge on either end, which worried Coal. The slightest wrong movement might shift the board and cause it to fall.

Zank hopped onto the plank and turned to address the three others. "Well," he said, "let's get to it!"

2

I T WAS TRUE THAT Coal was fairly inexperienced when it came to the sort of jobs that required one to walk across an unstable piece of wood several stories above a darkened alleyway. He was more accustomed to office work. Something light and simple and far from thought-provoking.

He had only been at work as a mercenary for a little under a year. And "mercenary" made it sound more official or more intense than it actually was; he was more inclined to say he did odd jobs around the kingdom. He was gravely ill-equipped for jobs such as these.

Ever since his father's death, Coal had been keeping a low profile as he worked his way south, collecting tups in exchange for menial tasks. Usually he only made enough to feed himself, shelter for a night or two, and continue onward. He had been hoping these jobs Zank lined up would provide him with a bigger safety net as far as money was concerned.

Right now, looking over the edge of the wooden plank at the Vinnag alley below, he wished for a literal safety net instead.

Several people had stopped to look up at the strange sight taking place above their heads. A few bobcats exchanged hushed whispers and pointed up at the crew creeping slowly in the night.

Marl walked ahead of Coal, who was yet again bringing up the rear. Every shift of the wolverine's hulking dark body sent a shiver of unease down Coal's back. He was sure he'd soon be plummeting into those bobcats on the street.

It felt like an hour, but the four crossed the wood without incident in a matter of seconds. It could not have been more than half a minute. But still, Coal breathed out a sigh of relief when his feet touched the roof of Garna Dend's office building.

"Step one off without a hitch," Zank declared with misplaced pride. Marl grunted his approval.

"How many steps are there?" Coal asked.

"To be determined."

The rooftop was littered with dead leaves blown in from the city's surrounding forest. At one point in time, long ago, the entire kingdom of Ruska was one enormous forest, covering nearly the entire valley tucked within the Yuluj Mountains. Less-developed areas still had plenty of greenery nowadays, but the larger technologically-advanced cities such as Vinnag were all stone and bright lights with the only trees being at their outskirts.

Stray leaves crunched underfoot as they swiftly stepped toward the rooftop door. There was a keypad attached to the handle, which Zank fruitlessly tried to turn before confirming that it was, of course, locked.

He pulled from his pocket a scrap of paper with a series of numbers written messily on it. Glancing back at the paper after every single number, he typed in the code, his long fingernails clacking against the pads. There was a light *click* as he pressed the final number, and he was able to turn the handle with ease.

"Step two," he whispered.

"Was meeting at the club not step one?" Coal asked.

"And then going in the back? And getting on the roof?" Venny smirked, wanting to annoy Zank.

"The steps are murky," said Zank, waving the two of them off. "Doesn't matter how many steps. Quit focusin' on the steps. It's about the destination, not the journey."

Coal would have chuckled if he weren't already so nervous. The payday at the end of this job seemed worthwhile when Zank had first brought it to him, but now he was growing more unsure by the minute. He was still unconvinced that things would go as smoothly as the rabbit promised.

What choice do I have, though? he asked himself. It was certainly a great deal more dangerous than harvesting vegetables for weary farmers or painting signs for shopkeepers, but he couldn't make a living off that. And there was no way to lock down a real job, not with his record.

Zank was a childhood friend, the both of them growing up in Muta Par, near the capital and not too far from the Houndstooth. Zank's family moved away to a village in central Ruska when the boys were ten years old, but they got together over summers when Zank and his parents would return to visit relatives who still lived in the city. They kept in touch over the years, and so when Coal needed a place to go, he figured Zank's new residence of Vinnag was as good a choice as any.

The rabbit looked at each of them in turn, ending with Coal. "Ready?" he asked.

They all nodded.

The others slunk through the doorway. Coal took a second to close his eyes, take a deep breath, and steel himself. It mildly worked.

His footsteps echoed lightly in the stairwell but sounded to him like gunshots in the silence.

He couldn't stop thinking about the fox and macaw that were apparently somewhere in the office. Coal hoped Marl would deftly handle them without him having to get involved.

They went one by one through the doorway at the bottom of the stairs, entering a typical office space. There were a few partitions set up, with roughly five desks and chairs. Not too big. This was likely not Garna Dend's primary base of operations, but rather something small for when he wanted to avoid the public eye.

There were two other doors in the room. One led out, presumably to a hallway or another set of stairs going down to street level, while the other was for a private office.

Zank pointed to the door leading out. "One of the guards should be on the other side," he whispered. "The other's outside, standing at the entrance to the building."

"Which is which?" Marl asked in a low growl.

"Who cares?"

"I do."

Zank groaned, uninterested in the minutiae. "Bird's the one inside, I think," he answered.

Marl crept toward the doorway that supposedly had a macaw on the other side, positioning himself in case the guard decided to pop into the office for whatever reason.

Meanwhile, Zank headed over to the private office, which seemed like the safest bet for finding the incriminating photos. Coal decided to tag along to help look and cut down on the time they'd need to spend in Dend's domain.

Venny kept to herself and initiated a search throughout the rest of the office's desks and cabinets. For a brief moment, Coal thought it might be more logical to help her scour the larger area, but then reconsidered. The photos simply *had* to be in Dend's office, and his efforts were best put toward that.

There was another keypad on Dend's private door. Zank extracted a second piece of paper from his other pants pocket and input the code. With another satisfying *click*, they were in.

Zank edged the door open slowly. There was not even the slightest creak from its hinges. Somehow that fact alone spelled out "wealth" to Coal.

On the other side was a much more modest office than Coal had expected, given what he'd heard about the city's Garnas. They were men of extreme wealth and ego, who yearned for extravagance. The office, however, was humbly decorated with simple furniture. A plain redwood desk with a small lamp atop it, two half-filled bookshelves, and a couple filing cabinets. There was also a door that probably housed a private bathroom, which was seemingly the one luxury Dend allowed himself here. Otherwise, he apparently did not want to bring much attention to this place.

The two did not speak as they began their search of the room. Coal circled around the desk, setting his gun down atop it and quietly pulling open each drawer.

In the topmost drawer was a collection of documents that seemed to list real estate holdings of Dend's, along with the names of the establishments on those properties, the monthly rent costs, and the renters' names. None of the pages included much detail beyond that; Dend could afford to employ a trained accountant to handle all the more complicated tasks and these pages were likely just for his reference. More importantly, there were no illicit photographs alongside the sheets, so Coal gently closed the drawer and moved down to the next one.

It held nothing more than a canister of chewing tobacco and a mostly-empty bottle of rum with a label Coal recognized from Baoa, a treetop village in central Ruska that Coal had stayed in for a week on his way south. The thought flittered through his mind to drink the last of Dend's bottle out of spite—there was only enough left for half a glass, maybe—but he dismissed it for the same reason he declined to drink in the Starlite, wanting to remain alert. He shut the drawer, listening to the bottle smoothly rolling around inside.

His hand was already wrapped around the handle of the next and final drawer (on the left side of the desk, anyway) when he heard the flush of a toilet.

He glanced up and saw that Zank was indeed still in the room. The rabbit was rifling through the Garna's meager collection of books, checking for photographs hidden between the pages, but he had stopped to turn and stare at the bathroom door.

Their eyes locked with each other then back toward the door, which swung open to reveal a macaw yawning while he buckled his belt. He stopped to stare at the fox and rabbit before him.

Zank was fast. In a split second his pistol was aimed and cocked, filling Coal with dread. The macaw leapt backward into the bathroom, ducking around the corner. Zank's bullets burst through the door in a shower of splinters.

"What happened to no—"

Before Coal could say "deaths," there were confused yelps of alarm from Venny and Marl in the other room. They could be heard scrambling around the desks, knocking over chairs, trying to reach the Garna's office.

Coal shoved himself against the wall the office shared with the bathroom. It only took him a couple moments to realize it was the worst position he could have chosen if the bird started firing through the wall, but he also had no idea if the wall was too thick for bullets to burrow through.

He felt woefully out of his depth.

Instinctively he ducked down, as if that would protect him from a spray of bullets. At that point, he realized his own firearm was still resting on the desk several feet away. He swore softly.

Venny then appeared in the doorway almost instantaneously with Marl, who evidently had much more speed in that bulky body than Coal would have predicted. The two shoved themselves through the doorway at the same time, effectively stopping either of them from breaching the room.

Which turned out to be a good thing, as the macaw peeked out from the bathroom and commenced firing on the office doorway. Still, Venny let loose a harsh shout of pain as she disappeared back out into the main room.

Zank ducked behind Dend's desk and yelled, "V! You okay?"

"Just a graze," she called back. "Fine."

Marl cautiously rounded the doorway, which elicited more gunshots from the cornered macaw, so he immediately retreated. Coal saw Zank peering over the top of the desk, but he did not act. The bird must have had a line of sight with the office door without needing to move.

"You're fucked," Zank taunted the bird. "There's four of us and we've got you backed into the shitter."

"I've got backup," said the macaw with a cough.

As if on cue, there came more shouts from Marl and Venny, followed closely by gunfire. Zank and Coal looked to the doorway, but could not see any of the action. Coal assumed the fox guard from downstairs had joined them. Hopefully there were not in fact more guards with him that Zank's informant had left out.

The gunfire ceased, followed by grunts and thumps, and Marl's voice shouted out, "No more backup."

"Okay, *now* you're fucked," said Zank.

On the other side of the wall, Coal heard the bird curse to himself.

Suddenly something small and round flew through the air from the bathroom, out into the area where Venny and Marl had just taken out a fox (hopefully by knocking them out rather than killing them). Then another careened toward Zank's position.

The rabbit stood and sprung forward, slamming into Coal and knocking both their heads into the wall as the item exploded in a controlled ball of flame that miraculously did not catch any of the Dend's furniture or carpet on fire. The scorch marks would be tough to deal with later, though.

Coal clutched his pounding head, his eyelids fluttering. Zank lay prone on the floor next to Coal's gun, which had been propelled off the desk by the explosion and had thankfully not fired.

But he did not have a chance to grab the weapon before the macaw took a confident step out of the bathroom.

Without thinking, Coal rushed the bird's body and sent him sprawling, knocking his head into a vase sitting in the corner of the room. The swirly purple-and-blue ceramic shattered on the macaw's black beak, momentarily stunning him.

All of Coal's weight was on the bird's body. He felt the guard start to shift underneath him, so he grasped the bird's arms in either hand, pinning them to the ground. Stray feathers fluttered to the floor and the bird's gun tumbled a couple feet away. Not very far, but out of reach for the moment.

"Some help!" Coal yelled to his companions.

Venny and Marl entered the room, the latter kicking aside the abandoned handgun. "Get up," he ordered Coal.

Coal did as the wolverine instructed, pushing himself up off the macaw. The bird stood shakily, brushing himself off, and opened his beak to say something when Marl shot him in his right knee.

"Vyru above!" the bird screamed.

Marl closed the distance between them, only a few steps with his long stride, and slammed the butt of his gun into the bird's head. He crumpled like a paper doll. Coal took a second to check and noted that the bird was still breathing.

With both guards out of commission, Venny rushed to Zank's side.

She shook him and his eyelids fluttered open, his pointy ears twitching. He sat up, his eyes instantly looking over the bird.

"Good," he said.

"You alright?" Venny asked him.

Zank nodded. "Mighta got a little singed from his Fireball, but I'm fine."

Coal looked at the spot where the round object had blown up in the office. Unfortunately, he'd had a few run-ins with Fireballs before, so he knew a little about them. They were specially crafted using technology developed by the Palace and caused very limited explosions (their radius depending on the model) that somehow did not spread fire. Larger ones had a much more visceral impact, splattering bodies and destroying buildings; the one the macaw used had to be the smallest and least deadly variety, a Fireball-S, given how little damage it had actually done to the desk and wall.

Which was not to say it couldn't have seriously hurt Zank if there had been direct impact, but no use worrying over something that hadn't happened.

Once he caught his breath, Zank asked, "Either of you find the photos out there?" Both Marl and Venny shook their heads. "Alright, let's get back to it. I'm not sure if the commotion was heard outside or if one of these chuckleheads called in more backup, but regardless, we should beat feet."

He hated the expression, but Coal agreed with the sentiment. He retrieved his gun from the floor, just in case—all the good it had done him during the last *in case*—and moved to check the drawer he had been opening before being interrupted. Zank resumed his book inspection.

Coal kneeled down and yanked open the bottom drawer and grinned. He grabbed the plain, unmarked envelope and looked inside to find six revealing photographs of an anteater who he could only assume was Garna Nomak.

"Got 'em," he said, standing. He slipped the photos back into the envelope and tossed it over to Zank, who caught it deftly.

The rabbit flipped through the pictures, whispering as he counted them out loud. "This is all of 'em," he said, returning them to the envelope. "Good job."

"I'm well-trained in opening drawers," said Coal. It was a joke, but also quite possibly the only real skill he brought to the table in this operation.

They exited into the main area. Over by the door Coal saw the fox guard face-down on the floor, but from this distance, he couldn't tell what condition the guy was in.

Zank waved the envelope at the others. Venny grinned toothily while Marl remained mostly expressionless, but Coal thought he saw the slightest hint of a smile on the wolverine's face.

"Let's scoot," said their leader.

That sounded great to Coal.

Like before, they all followed Zank. Envelope in hand, he skipped through the doorway back up the stairwell toward the roof. Coal followed directly behind him.

He said to the rabbit, "That got a lot messier than I expected."

"Me too," said Zank. "To tell the truth, I really did think these guns would just be a precaution. Didn't think one of the guards would leave their post to drop a shit in the boss's bathroom. Sorry to get you wrapped up in it."

It had been more than he'd bargained for, but Coal couldn't be picky at this juncture. "It's fine," he assured his friend. "I'm thankful you brought me on. Really. I need the tups."

"You and me both, pal," Zank laughed.

They reached the top of the staircase a few moments later, rushing into the night air's warm embrace. Across the way, the yellow glow of the Starlite flickered in its neon tubes.

Zank hopped two or three bounds toward their plank of wood before a booming voice ordered him to halt.

All four of them stopped in their tracks. To their left were two menacing bobcats who were each strapped into HM-3s. Or, as the machines were more commonly referred to throughout the kingdom, robotic scorpions.

The bobcats lay prone, strapped onto the top of the HM-3s with a sheet of metal plating covering the majority of their backs. Their faces were still exposed to allow visibility, while their arms and hands were attached to the machine's enormous pincers. One of the scorpions was a metallic black while the other had been painted red.

It was difficult to know for sure in the dark, but Coal squinted as he looked in the bobcats' faces and could swear they were the two he'd seen watching them from the alley earlier.

Coal's stomach dropped.

"Remain calm and do not attempt to move," said the bobcat in the red HM-3. He was the one who ordered them to stop in the first place.

Zank craned his neck to look at his crew over his shoulder.

No, no, no, Coal pleaded internally.

"Dend's got more boys, do he?" Zank scoffed.

Without warning, Venny fired on the bobcats. Their scorpions roared to life.

3

COAL'S INSTINCT WAS TO leap backward, putting as much distance as possible between himself and the two HM-3s. He knew from experience that you did not want to mess with one of those robotic exoskeletons. Better to get far away. Far, far, *far* away.

But the rest of the group was either unaware or uncaring. Venny continued firing on the bobcats, who easily shielded from her fire with their machines' bulky claws. Bullets pinged off the metal, not even denting it, and scattered uselessly to the ground.

At the very least, the Dripping Fang had the sense to keep a fair amount of space between themselves and the scorpions. If they remained out of reach of the claws, they would be in good shape. Coal knew that wasn't the only thing the HM-3s had in their arsenal, but it would be foolish to employ such tactics on top of a building.

"Zank!" he yelled to his friend. The rabbit fired off a few meaningless rounds before risking a glance toward him. "We need to *go!*"

But Marl had not heard Coal's plea over the two rabbits' gunfire. That, or he was uninterested in backing down from a fight.

Whatever the case, the wolverine charged toward the black HM-3, the one nearest him, and jumped forward onto its back. The bobcat inside was largely protected by the metal plate covering, but there were a few parts of his body left vulnerable.

Marl grasped the edge of the metal plating with one hand to keep himself on board, and with the other he dug the barrel of his gun into the bobcat's shoulder.

The cat instantly knew what was about to transpire but had no time to react. Marl pulled the trigger and the man's shoulder burst, splattering blood all over the HM-3 as well as Marl.

While screaming in agony, the bobcat still had enough sense to try dislodging his attacker. He reached with his unhurt arm to maneuver the scorpion's claw around to grab Marl, but the wolverine dropped down off the machine and temporarily retreated back toward the rooftop door.

His plan had worked, though. With the bobcat's shoulder ruined, he was in too much pain to operate the scorpion's right arm.

If he could do the same to the other, all that left in their arsenal were the long-range attacks, which would be unwise. Coal had seen the damage these HM-3s could do, and he was not eager to see it again.

The red scorpion scuttled forward, aiming to take out Zank. If he got caught in its claws, not only would he be in a world of hurt, but there would be absolutely no way for any of them to free him.

Zank was clever enough to realize that, even if he'd never encountered these machines before. He waited until the scorpion had reached him, its claws only a foot or two away, before jumping into the air and landing on the left claw, propelling himself off of it and wrapping his arms and legs around the tail.

Its handler let out an irritable grunt, waving the tail back and forth to throw off the parasite, even if it meant he'd careen off the side of the building. Losing Zank would clearly be of no concern to the bobcats.

Venny was now shooting at the red scorpion while Zank flailed about on its tail. She seemed to be trying to shoot the bobcat in the head, but it was not going very well on account of the man shielding his face with the scorpion's massive claws.

Coal had absolutely no idea what Zank's next plan of action would be.

Marl, meanwhile, was attempting to circle around the injured black scorpion to take out that bobcat's other arm. His plan was more achievable than Venny's or Zank's, but still nearly impossible. The scorpion's mechanical legs were too fast for the wolverine; he would not be able to run around the machine quicker than it could turn with him, nor would he be able to jump high and far enough to land on the other side. Especially not with the bobcat's guard up after the first assault.

Coal wanted nothing to do with this.

There was nothing he felt he could contribute anyway.

He was going to make a run for it.

The others would follow if they were smart, which he doubted more and more by the second.

He took off to his right, heading for the wooden plank connecting the two rooftops.

The red scorpion had a bead on him, though. With Zank still wailing away on the tail, it rushed forward past Venny, knocking her aside with its claw, and bounded toward Coal.

Venny flew backward and crashed into the other machine's side as it turned to keep its eye on Marl. She rolled on the ground, trying to avoid getting trampled by one of its feet, but was unsuccessful. One of them crushed her left arm and she screamed.

It lifted up only a second later to continue turning, but the damage was done. Venny's arm was a mangled mess.

"V!" Zank cried.

Both he and Marl stopped what they were doing and leapt to their comrade's aid. Zank flung himself off the red scorpion's tail, landing in a rough roll on the rooftop and stumbling as he righted himself to run for her. Marl was already at her side, picking her up off the ground, when Zank arrived.

Coal was careful getting up onto the wooden plank and managed to get halfway across it before the red HM-3 ruined things. Its claw came crashing down on the wood, destroying the side propped up on the office roof.

Feeling the makeshift bridge collapsing at his feet, Coal took a chance and leapt forward, stretching his arms out as far as he could to grasp the Starlite's ledge.

His fingers brushed against the building's ledge and he gripped tight, his body slamming into the side of it. He was distressingly out of shape, which had never been more obvious to him than in this moment. He huffed and sputtered, trying to pull his body up onto the club's roof.

Behind him, he could hear the HM-3 pacing back and forth. Waiting to see if he succeeded or not before making its next move.

Coal's boots scraped against the building as he tried scrambling up its side, using whatever small amount of upper body strength he possessed to hoist himself up onto the roof. His muscles strained and his lungs were fit to burst, but eventually he threw himself over the ledge and breathed with heavy relief as he lay on his back.

There was no time to celebrate his victory, however. The bobcat had decided on what to do.

And Coal was now on a different roof.

Farther away.

He suddenly realized what that meant.

Given that he was laying on his back, he did not actually see it happen this time, but he had witnessed it during his previous run-in with these machines. He knew that the tip of this HM-3's tail had opened up, spitting out a round mechanical device nearly identical to the Fireball-S used in Dend's office. This one, though, would have a yellow stripe rather than red.

The ball landed with a clunk fifteen feet away from Coal, who turned to look at it but could not muster the strength to stand and run. Not that there was anywhere to run to—the only non-lethal way off the roof was the ladder on the other side of the device.

So he braced himself.

The round device exploded in a flurry of lightning bolts. They shot outward, reaching for anything they could touch, which in this case was the Starlite's huge neon sign.

Electricity crackled fiercely and blew out the sign's neon tubes, enveloping the entire rooftop in darkness. The only remaining light came from the lightning bolts that were still whipping around in search of targets.

Luckily for Coal, it seemed the bobcat had only employed a Lightning-M. If he'd gone for the L, Coal would either be unconscious or dead, and given what these bobcats intended to do to him he felt he was dead either way.

He needed to act fast if he was going to get out of there. But he hadn't been in Vinnag long, and he had no idea where he could realistically hide from these people. It was obvious he couldn't stay in the city anymore. He might not even be able to collect the payment for this job.

Coal sat up and saw the scorpion was readying to lob another ball of lightning at him. He also saw that Marl had moved Venny to the other side of the roof while Zank was firing on the black scorpion, which was pressing in on them.

Marl had seemingly lost his gun at some point, and so was simply watching Zank shoot at the bobcat while he stood guard in front of Venny. She had since passed out from the pain and lay limp on the rooftop.

The wolverine's attention shifted to the red HM-3, which was stepping up onto the roof's ledge to position its tail at a better angle for its next volley.

Marl saw this as an opportunity. He ran forward.

Oh, shit, Coal thought, not anticipating this to go well at all.

The bobcat was still aiming his scorpion's tail and unable to see the wolverine charging behind him. The tail's tip opened just as Marl collided with the back of the machine.

Its footing was precarious, and with its heavy weight, even the slightest unexpected shift was enough to throw it off-balance. The HM-3 tipped forward, the front of it now pointing downward at the alleyway below.

The bobcat tried readjusting the feet to get a better grip on the roof, but Marl gave one more powerful shove, and that was enough to send it hurtling over the edge.

Coal grinned as the red scorpion plunged, shooting out another Lightning-M as it did so.

The ball's ruined trajectory sent it flying into the side of the Starlite, erupting in a spray of sparks on the stone building.

Marl and Coal both watched as the HM-3 careened toward the earth, crashing into the alley in a fiery explosion. The machines seemed difficult enough to disengage from under normal circumstances; Coal saw no way that the bobcat would be able to escape the wreckage in time. If he had even survived the fall in the first place.

Suddenly the black rabbit who managed the Starlite popped his head out from the panel that housed the ladder. Spotting Coal, he shouted, "What the fuck is going on out here?"

"No time," said Coal, running toward the man, tripping over himself and nearly falling flat on his face. "Is there another board?" he spat out, slurring his words.

The rabbit hadn't processed the question, instead looking up at his broken sign and asking, "What in all the fucking hells happened to my sign?" His left ear was twitching uncontrollably.

"No time!" Coal shouted again. He grabbed the rabbit's face and forcefully turned it to look him in the eye. "Is there another piece of wood up here? Or in your office?"

But the man ignored him yet again when his eyes trailed to the other roof and he saw what was going on. The black HM-3 was snapping at Zank, who still couldn't get the upper hand on the bobcat driving it.

"Hey!" Coal screamed.

Still twitching, the rabbit nodded mindlessly. He pulled himself up onto the roof and ran away from Coal into the dark. There was a scraping sound punctuated by Zank's continued gunfire before the rabbit returned with a length of wood.

"This long enough?" he asked.

"You tell me," said Coal.

The rabbit shrugged. "All I've got."

Now the marten poked her yellow head out from the ladder. "What's going on?" she asked.

The rabbit had no patience for her right now. He turned and shouted, *"Go back inside and calm the girls down!"*

Her head disappeared in a flash.

Coal picked up the other end of the long board and helped the rabbit carry it over to the roof's edge. Marl was still near the edge on the opposite roof, watching them.

They reached the ledge and the rabbit started setting up the plank, but Coal stopped him. "Wait," he said. "Not yet."

He worried that the remaining bobcat might smash it like the other one had, or that even if Zank and the others managed to cross safely, they'd still need to contend with the scorpion.

He didn't see a clean way out of this. Disposing of the other bobcat was the only path forward.

"Help Zank!" Coal yelled to Marl across the divide.

To his credit, the wolverine did not question the command or offer any resistance. He simply nodded and ran toward

Zank, who had to be running out of ammunition sooner rather than later.

Marl whisked right past the rabbit and the scorpion and knelt down to grab something near the other side of the roof. Coal couldn't see the object at all, but he knew it had to be the previously-discarded handgun.

The bobcat couldn't contend with both Zank and Marl at the same time. Not with one arm out of the picture. He already knew how much of a threat Marl posed, so he rotated the machine to follow him, leaving himself vulnerable to an attack from Zank.

Zank bent his knees then sprang into the air, grabbing onto the HM-3's tail yet again before dropping down onto its back with ease.

All the while, Marl was firing distraction shots at the bobcat, who was too busy blocking them with his one functional claw to pay any attention to the rabbit on his back.

Unfortunately for him, that meant it was only a few moments before Zank lodged a bullet in his head.

The scorpion halted immediately with no one controlling it anymore. It stood lifelessly on the rooftop, a black statue silhouetted against the moon.

Zank slid down off the machine, panting heavily. Marl circled around and gave his friend a brotherly pat on the back. The two then returned to Venny, who was still unconscious.

Coal and the black rabbit positioned the new piece of wood so that the others could safely cross the alleyway. Zank came over first, followed by Marl cautiously carrying Venny.

The black rabbit was still demanding to know what happened to his sign, but everyone was too exhausted and irritable to bother explaining everything to him. Instead, they descended the ladder and navigated through the empty club, which must have evacuated once everyone started hearing explosions outside.

"Where are we going?" Marl asked once they were back on the street.

Zank pondered the question for a moment. "Wherever we go, we need to take alleys. More of Dend's goons will be congregatin' here any minute now. We can set up in my apartment, let Venny rest there."

Marl and Coal both nodded, not offering any better ideas of their own. Zank's place was as good as any now that the scorpions were dealt with, as far as Coal was concerned. Or so he hoped.

The streets surrounding the Starlite were in a frenzy. Coal peered out at the main streets as the group ducked through the alleyways. People shoved past each other, screaming about an attack, trying to track down friends and loved ones. In reality, there had been very little damage done to any of the buildings, and as far as he knew the only casualties were the two bobcats. But the public didn't know that, so maybe their bombastic reactions were justified.

While they walked, he looked out to the mountain range in the east. In the night, one could sometimes see the glowing eyes of some massive creature peering out over the tops of the mountains, gazing down into the valley below. The sight never failed to creep out Coal. Thankfully the skies were clear of unsettling eyes tonight.

They slipped from the entertainment district into Renning Heights. It was in a much calmer state than its neighboring district. The group snaked through neighborhoods until they reached the poorer side of the district where Zank lived.

His apartment was a four-story building called the Fairpaw. Its façade was a sky blue that had long since faded, never repainted since the building had first opened however many years before. Every unit was accessed from the outside, granting the complex more of a motel feel than the nicer apartment buildings found elsewhere throughout the city.

Zank's unit faced an inner courtyard and was on the third floor. Marl, growing sore from the combination of the rooftop battle and carrying Venny for such a great distance, was lethargic in getting her up the stairs. They finally reached Zank's front door, which he unlocked and slipped through quickly with the others close behind.

The apartment was small, consisting of a single bedroom, a bathroom, and a kitchen/living room area, which was where Coal had been sleeping for the past two weeks. It was sparsely decorated, only containing the bare essentials as far as furniture went, and hardly any decorations. There was a fake plant in one corner of the room, and a stack of albums with a record player in another. Most of Zank's disposable income went toward outside entertainment rather than sprucing up his apartment.

Marl laid Venny down comfortably on the couch and confirmed there was nothing else he needed to do. He then took his leave, not before promising Zank he would avoid busy streets.

Coal sat at Zank's kitchen table, adorned with a yellow tablecloth sporting myriad stains. He watched Venny sleeping across the room. Zank plopped himself down in a chair opposite Coal and asked him, "Want a drink now?"

"Hmm?" Coal mumbled, only half-listening. His mind was still up on that roof, staring down the robotic scorpions.

"You didn't want one back in the club," said Zank. "You want a celebratory one now?"

"Oh," said Coal. "No, I'm fine. Thanks."

Zank said nothing and did not get up to grab himself a drink. He remained at the table, tapping his nails on the dirty cloth.

They both watched Venny for a couple minutes. Coal didn't know the woman at all, having not met her before tonight, but he was struck with guilt for getting her wrapped up in his mess.

"Well, that was fucked," Zank finally said, letting out an awkward laugh.

"Yeah," Coal agreed. He felt sick.

"I'm gonna have words with my source," Zank said. "I thought we had somethin' special. I didn't think she would leave out somethin' as important as gigantic robot bugs. I don't even know how Dend got those. He's gonna be fucking furious when he sees his roof and his office."

Coal had to tell his friend. The guilt over Venny was gnawing at him.

He said meekly, "They weren't with Dend."

Zank, in spite of his utter exhaustion, perked up at this. "What do you mean? Who else would they be with?"

"Dend wouldn't have access to tech like that," said Coal. "HM-3s come straight from the Palace."

The rabbit blinked, still not understanding.

Coal sighed. "They were after me," he said. "Those were bounty hunters, and they wanted me."

4

W HAT ARE YOU TALKIN' about?" Zank
asked, furrowing his brow. His ears folded
back in concern.

Coal bit his lower lip. He almost blurted everything out, but
stopped short. His sharp ears flicked anxiously.

"I don't wanna involve you," he said. "It's complicated."
He had instantly regretted mentioning anything at all. Zank
was already assuming the scorpions belonged to Dend. Why
did he contradict that?

Zank rolled his eyes. "You shouldn't've said shit, then," he
said, echoing Coal's own thoughts. "And let's be real, man.
You already got us involved. My best friend is passed out over
there with an arm that might be fucked for life."

Coal sighed. He hadn't wanted to burden Zank, one of his
few friends—maybe his only actual friend—with this information. This monumental mess of his. Upon his arrival in Vinnag, he had explained to Zank that he'd run into some trouble

up in Muta Par and needed to lay low for a while, but did not elaborate any further.

Before he could explain, Zank stood and fetched himself a bottle of beer from the cooler. He pointed it toward Coal, but he declined again. Zank stood by the table and said, "Let's go outside. I don't wanna disturb V."

Coal looked at her over on the couch, her arm wrapped up as best they could manage, and sympathized.

"I don't want to either," he said, "but this isn't really something that I would want out in the open air, you know?"

Zank thought it over for a moment. He then popped the top off his bottle and took a pull, licking his lips as he swallowed.

"We'll just have to keep quiet then, huh?" he said, heading for the door. He paused, then said quietly, "Last chance for a beer."

Coal shook his head and followed the rabbit outside. His stomach twisted.

Crickets chirruped outside, intermingling with the buzz of nearby streetlamps. Coal followed Zank down a staircase into the apartment courtyard, where Zank sat himself down at a community table. He tapped the bottom of his glass bottle on the table as he waited for Coal to take a seat.

"Kinda out in the open," said Coal uneasily. His eyes darted back and forth in search of anyone else who happened to be out for a nighttime stroll. It was pretty late, so it seemed unlikely, but still better to practice caution.

Zank shrugged. "It's fine. Whisper and no one'll hear you but me."

His tone was grave. Coal had never seen the rabbit act so serious before. He wondered precisely what sort of history Zank and Venny shared.

Coal took one last look around the empty courtyard before relenting and sitting down at the table. Zank had set his bottle down and was drumming his fingernails against the bare, label-less side of it, the soft *clink* joining the cacophony of crickets and lightbulbs.

It was difficult to find a place to start. The situation was daunting, and messy, and impossible.

Zank sat staring at him expectantly, tapping away on his glass. Coal wished he'd stop and take a drink instead. Give his ears some peace.

He scratched the bridge of his snout and sighed.

"Go on, then," said Zank. He took a swig of the beer.

Coal pushed himself to take that momentary silence as an opening. "So, when I got here, I told you that I needed some low-profile work. Nothing official, nothing on the books. Nothing that required paperwork of any sort."

"Mhm," Zank grumbled, licking his lips again. "Garna-type work."

"Yes," Coal nodded. "I wouldn't be surprised to learn that between all the city's Garnas, I could stay employed for as long as I needed."

"Until you were dead, probably," Zank said with a smirk. "Very few of the Garnas would take kindly to you working with the others against their own interests. Hell, I'm not sure if there's even *one* who'd be okay with that. Nomak certainly wouldn't."

"Right, well, I wasn't being literal," said Coal.

He took a breath, recognizing that he was stalling. He still didn't know exactly how much of the truth he should reveal to his friend.

He said, "I was still living in Muta Par before this. I never left. You know I was never the biggest fan of my father, we were never particularly close or anything. But he was getting up there in age, then with his injury and all, even when I had opportunities to leave I stuck around to help him out."

"Von Ereness was not my biggest fan," Zank grinned. "Your dad hated me."

Coal laughed. "That's true," he said.

"Ah! So you finally admit it."

"Well, you were always causing trouble when you visited! Stealing, vandalizing, just generally causing a ruckus—and you always got his sweet, beautiful boy wrapped up in it."

Zank guffawed. Coal was glad to see him loosening up a bit.

"Yeah, yeah," said the rabbit. "His sweet, beautiful boy was the one coming up with the designs we were painting on the sides of those buildings."

"Those designs were all just some swear words or two people fucking or someone taking a shit or something," said Coal. "As fellow teenagers, I think one of you would've gotten there eventually. Even without me."

"Whatever. Innocent you were not."

"Hey, all my troublemaking stopped once you were gone…" He trailed off, letting the insinuation linger.

Zank was still grinning, but he said, "Get on with the story."

Coal tried to go on, but stopped. "I…" He struggled with what to omit. He said, "There was…an accident. My father and I were both involved. It was a huge deal, and…he died."

Zank's ears flattened. "Shit," he said. "Sorry."

Coal's heart started racing as he imagined himself back there in Muta Par. Seeing his father with his—

"Long story short," he blurted out, wanting to erase the image from his mind, "it looked like I killed him." His voice hitched as he said it. "Which is untrue, obviously, but that's what it looked like."

That was as much detail as Zank was going to get. Coal couldn't find it in himself to say any more, nor did he want Zank wrapped up in this more than he needed to be. He was already doing Coal an enormous favor by hooking him up with jobs to earn enough money to sustain himself. He didn't want to repay that by getting his friend in deep trouble with the Palace.

His friend remained silent, processing the information. His long ears slowly perked back up.

"I tried explaining myself to the officers who found us, but they wouldn't listen," Coal continued. "They didn't care. In their eyes, they had orders from the Dirt King, a job they had to do, circumstances be damned. So I bolted. Ran straight out of Muta Par, couldn't even stop to grab anything from my apartment. Just kept running all through the night. Nearly died of exhaustion out in the forest."

It wasn't far from the truth. In fact, none of it was a lie, but it was only the broad strokes version of the story.

And no mention of the ghost.

The ghost was definitely a complication he did not want to burden Zank with.

That was all in his head, anyway. He was better now, he assured himself.

"Shit," Zank muttered again. "When was this?"

"A little over a year ago. Brightmonth last year," Coal answered. "I've just been making my way south the entire time. I knew you were here and that maybe you could help me out."

"Because you knew I was a shady bastard."

"Well, I mean," Coal grinned. "My father had a feeling about you."

Zank jokingly rolled his eyes before his expression turned serious. "That's fucked," was all he said, and Coal was thankful the man did not want him to expand on the story. "So the guys with those robots were trying to arrest you?"

Coal nodded. "They're called Stingers. The Palace sends them out for people they consider to be highly dangerous."

"Highly dangerous?" He choked out a laugh. "I saw your ass in a fight back there. It's a shame they didn't see you with Dend's guards. If they had, maybe they'd realize you ain't worth shit and would drop your case."

Coal had to laugh at that. While he was admittedly pretty worthless in a fight, he had not realized the extent to which he was worthless until tonight.

"That's true," he said. "I've encountered Stingers twice on my way down here. This was the third set of them—they're always in pairs. The others I got away from, obviously, but I don't know how they keep finding me in the first place. I've been using different fake names in every town I visit, but it's been useless."

"You've got a pretty distinctive face," said Zank.

"I guess so, but how do they know what city or village to check for my distinctive face?"

Zank shrugged. "The Palace is sendin' 'em out, right? Dirt King's resources are pretty limitless. Maybe they're just sendin' people out everywhere."

"You might be right," Coal conceded. "But however they're doing it, I'm sure they'll be on me even harder now that two of them actually died. Which still astounds me, by the way."

It was true the current iteration of the HMs left something to be desired defense-wise for its operator, but in Coal's brief run-ins with the machines he had never seen a Stinger take much damage. Not that he had ever really put up a fight, though; whenever he spotted one, he instantly took off out of town, just as he had in Muta Par.

"Did what we had to do to get outta there," Zank said softly. "I wish I could say it was the first time I'd had to resort to that, but…well, Marl and Venny didn't kill Dend's men in the office, so our consciences can be clear at that, at least."

After a few seconds, Coal asked, "How much of this are you gonna tell Venny and Marl?"

Zank thought it over, clacking his long, chipped nails on the side of his glass bottle. "You don't want 'em to know, I take it?" Coal nodded. "They won't know, then. Maybe Venny deserves to, since she's the one who was hurt by it, but it wouldn't do her no good anyway. And it'd just make Marl pissed at you for not warning us that people were on your tail. Marl ain't someone you want pissed at you."

Coal could positively believe that.

"As far as they're concerned, Dend got some extra funding from somewhere, I guess. Garna Nomak might need to know the truth, though. Otherwise he might react in unnecessary ways, you know?"

It was far from ideal, but Coal understood his point. He nodded.

Seeing the worried look on his friend's face, Zank said, "Well, I'll see how he takes the news first. And if I need to tell him, I'll tell him in private."

"Thanks." Coal smiled weakly.

With that, Zank downed the last of his beer. There had to be little more than backwash left in the bottle, but he gulped it heartily anyway, topping it off with a smack of his lips.

Placing the bottle back down, he said, "I think it's probably best if you don't stay here after all."

Coal said nothing. He'd feel more secure staying with Zank for the night, but he couldn't fault the man's decision.

"There might be more—what'd you call 'em? Stingers?—in town lookin' for you, and no offense, but I don't need no robot bugs knockin' down my door. I want V to rest and heal."

"I understand," said Coal. "I should've warned you ahead of time anyway."

"Yeah, you should've," said Zank, "but it's fine. Don't worry about it." He rose and tossed the beer bottle into a trash can a few feet away from the table. "I've got a buddy who can give you a place to stay for the night. Maybe a few days. Maybe even longer, if you scrounge up some money. It's a shithole, though."

"A shithole is fine," said Coal, though he dreaded seeing the place in question. Zank's apartment wasn't exactly the cleanest he'd ever been in, so if even *he* thought his friend's place was a shithole...

"Guy's name is Fanaleese," Zank told him. "He's a marten who runs a dumpy bar called the Uncut Gem a few blocks from here. It's got a couple spare rooms for supplies and shit upstairs. Tell him I asked for a place for you and you should be good to go. He owes me for gettin' him in good with Nomak. Otherwise, his collection money would be double."

Coal thanked him profusely, and Zank then proceeded to explain how to reach the Uncut Gem. It sounded easy enough to find, and should only take around ten or fifteen minutes of walking to reach it.

They returned to the staircase and stopped at the bottom to say their goodbyes. Coal did not have many possessions in Zank's apartment anyway, so they decided that rather than risk disturbing Venny, he would gather his things the following day.

"We're meeting Nomak tomorrow afternoon," Zank said. "I'll come and get you on our way over there. Sound good?"

"Sounds good," Coal affirmed.

Zank leaned in and hugged him before heading back up the stairs to his apartment.

The streets of Renning Heights were quiet as Coal followed the rabbit's directions toward the bar. He thought he might have recalled Zank mentioning Fanaleese at some point, but he wasn't sure. The bar's name was unfamiliar too.

This district was where Coal had spent a majority of his time. It was not an especially flashy part of town, even outside of the more run-down neighborhood in which Zank lived. Many, if not all, of its buildings were constructed of stone rather than the new fancily-named metals that the Palace had developed in recent years.

In many ways, Renning Heights seemed to be the forgotten district of Vinnag. It was located on the eastern edge of the city, its perimeter wall running up against the forest rather than mountains like in the western districts. That led to most of the district's population consisting of men and women who would venture into the forest to gather various supplies—plants, fruits, meat—but with the Dirt King's ban on hunting, a third of those already low-paying jobs disappeared. After the switch to insect-based diets across Ruska, many hunters tried to adapt, but it wasn't long before insect farmers in the inner city outpaced them.

As a result, Renning Heights was largely abandoned by those who secured jobs in other districts or who could no longer pay their rent. The people who remained were mostly farmers and criminals, the latter of whom found an opportunity to do their business in a less-trafficked area and could afford housing with their profits. But that still left slightly less than half of the district's buildings abandoned and falling apart after years and years of disuse.

From what Coal had gleaned, Garna Nomak was one such lowly criminal way back when, but he had risen in the ranks and was now doing what he could to build up the district he'd called home for so many years. In a way, it was admirable, though Coal knew the man's means to accomplish his goals were not entirely pure.

He rounded a corner into an alleyway that Zank assured him was a shortcut. Propped up against the building wall was a vending machine lit up with the enticing words BUY NOW, CHEAP flashing above its keypad.

Seeing the machine made Coal realize he had skipped dinner and not even eaten a snack at the Starlite. He approached and peered behind the glass at the five rows of prepackaged snacks. His stomach gurgled with intense desire.

It held several varieties of dried, seasoned bugs—beetles, ants, crickets, anything he could dream of. There were also some fruit pastries that he could not imagine being anything less than extremely old and stale, and anyway he was not in the mood for something sweet.

For an extra tup more than any of the bugs, he could purchase a bag of dehydrated vegetable chips, which sounded pretty appetizing. He didn't have much money to spare, but...

Hey, I'm getting paid tomorrow.

He popped the requisite coins into the machine and input the corresponding number. The bright green bag of vegetable chips plummeted to the bottom of the machine and he retrieved it merrily.

The chips were indeed a delightful, nourishing snack as he walked the remaining ten minutes to his destination.

When he stepped around the corner of another nondescript and possibly long-empty building, he spied the illuminated sign for the Uncut Gem. Across the street was a trash can in which he deposited his emptied bag of chips before entering the establishment.

Just as Zank had claimed, the place was a shithole. Which was to be expected for this part of town, he supposed.

Inside, there were only three guests who, based on how they swayed in their chairs, would certainly be regretting their choices tonight once they woke up later. Behind the bar stood a bored-looking marten with amber fur who was mindlessly reading liquor bottle labels for what was surely the thousandth time in his life.

The entire bar was painted green, which Coal thought might have been an attempt at making it look like a gem somehow, though if that were the case it was incredibly off the mark. There were no other colors accenting the green—just green all over. It was the most off-putting establishment he could remember ever seeing, though he had to admit there was a sort of charm to how unbearably ugly it was.

The marten glanced up at the sound of his new guest's footsteps and said, "Welcome in."

"Hi," said Coal, approaching the bar. He placed his hands awkwardly on the countertop, not sure how to broach the subject at hand. Would it be polite to order a drink first? Or just dive right into asking the man for a room?

He thought a drink might make him sick, and he was desperately tired already. As a child, he was nocturnal, as were all foxes. But at his father's insistence, he had partaken in a stimulant called Noctgone, a very literally-named drug produced in pill form that many bats, raccoons, beavers, and other generally nocturnal races took to keep themselves energized during the day. Eventually, if they took the medicine frequently enough, their body would acclimate to the new hours and they would no longer require it, but there were many who chose to remain nocturnal and only use it when necessary. A large portion of the bat population in Yagos still kept nocturnal schedules and only stimulated when they had to conduct outside business, but his father had long since adjusted to a daytime lifestyle and wanted the same for his son. It was, in most aspects, easier.

Now, though, he wanted to get to bed more than anything. It then occurred to him that wherever he slept tonight would probably not actually have a bed in it, but still he was undeterred.

"What'n I get for ya?" Fanaleese asked.

Diving right in. "My name's Coal," he said, his drowsiness barring him from the idea to use a false name. "I'm a friend of

Zank's. He sent me over here, said you might have a place for me to stay the night."

Fanaleese huffed. More in affirmation than annoyance, Coal thought. Or hoped, rather.

"Been a couple weeks since I seen Zank," he said. "How he's doin'?" He had an undeniable northeastern twang in his voice.

"He's good," said Coal. "I'm an old childhood friend of his, just passing through."

Fanaleese grunted but said nothing.

"So…yes, he said you might be able to help me out with some lodging," Coal said again, now mumbling sheepishly.

The marten nodded, setting down the bottle of thick dark liquid whose label he had been reading. Coal had the passing thought to inform the man about the existence of books.

"I's got a room you could use. For a couple days, anyhow."

Coal beamed. "That would be fantastic. I really appreciate it."

Fanaleese grunted again and cocked his head toward some stairs behind the bar. Coal circled around and followed him up, leaving the three inebriated guests behind. They were all so deep in their drinks they didn't seem to pose any threat being left unattended for a few minutes.

The room Fanaleese brought him to was one of two upstairs from the bar. The other he thought might be where Fanaleese lived, because the room he showed Coal contained countless crates of booze. Unless the marten needed two rooms to store his supplies, Coal didn't know what else could lay behind the other door besides the old marten's home.

"Hope Zank didn't lie an' say it'd be comf'table," Fanaleese said with what sounded like a laugh.

He certainly did not.

"This is perfectly fine," Coal told the man. It would not be the best night of sleep he'd ever gotten, but at least it was indoors and hopefully off the Stingers' radar.

For now, that was all he required.

He thanked Fanaleese, who simply nodded and returned to his mind-numbing work downstairs.

The man had allowed him to stay, no questions asked, so Coal did not want to press his luck by requesting a pillow and blanket. He settled down into the far corner of the room, nestled between two tall stacks of boxes labeled with the names of some central Ruskan villages where the alcohol had been brewed.

He inhaled deeply and let it out slow, trying to banish thoughts of tonight from his mind. If he thought about the rooftop fight too much, his heart would never slow enough to let him drift to sleep.

Instead, he thought about the forest just over the city wall. About the grass underfoot, the breeze rustling tree leaves. A stream babbling, dipping his feet in the ice cold water.

He thought about having nothing. Being nothing. No responsibilities, no expectations.

Being unburdened.

5

COAL WAS DREAMING OF the Muta Par library when a rapid knock at the supply room door jostled him from his slumber. He was thrust from a world basking in the smell of yellowed pages and the warmth of natural light into one of musty wood and darkness.

"Wake up, sumshine!" Fanaleese's croaky voice called from the other side of the door. Coal couldn't tell if he was mishearing the old marten due to grogginess or if he was misspeaking. "Y'got a visitor!"

A visitor?

Who would be visiting him? Had the Palace already dispatched more Stingers after last night's incident?

"Did they say who it is?" he asked, pushing himself up off the uncomfortable floor. His body ached. He'd gotten a full night's rest, but only because he'd been so exhausted and passed out.

"Zank," said Fanaleese.

Oh. Of course.

Coal breathed a relieved sigh. He looked around the room for a clock to see how early it was, but naturally the walls were bare. No real need to know the time when you're just grabbing a box of liquor. It wasn't exactly a hotel.

He opened up the door and found Fanaleese still standing in the hall with a grimace.

"Do you know what time it is?" Coal ventured.

"D'*you* know what time it is?" Fanaleese asked. "Too early fer me to be up fieldin' guests, is what my answer'd be. I only went to bed three hours ago, fer Lalen's sake..." He grumbled more about how much of an inconvenience Coal was while shuffling back into his own room.

Coal rubbed the sleep from his eyes, his ears twitching as they perked themselves up. He then headed down the stairs into the bar, where he found Zank sitting at the counter with his head in his hands. His ears drooped down over his face and he looked just as tired as Fanaleese.

"Hey," Coal greeted him, taking a seat beside the rabbit. "You're up early."

"Mhm," Zank mumbled, still staring ahead at the rows of glass bottles behind the bar. His ears flopped over to the back of his head. "I didn't get much sleep, really. I was too worried about V." He looked at Coal. "While I was awake, though, a thought occurred to me."

"Yeah?"

Zank nodded, now turning his whole body to face Coal's. His ears bobbed at his shoulders. He said, "I know someone who might be able to help you with your problem."

"It seems like you know a lot of people with problem-solving skills."

"I've developed quite a retinue here over the years."

"Which problem of mine is it that they can solve?" Coal asked. It felt like his life had consisted of one problem after another for the past year.

Zank breathed in deep. He was clearly worn out. It'd be best for him to get some rest before their meeting with Garna Nomak later. Coal made a mental note to offer to look after Venny for a while so that his friend could sleep.

"Your problem with the Palace bein' after you," Zank specified.

Coal blinked. That did not seem like the sort of problem a random person in Vinnag could handle.

"You're sure about that?" he asked.

Zank nodded. "Stuff like that's her specialty. It'll cost you, of course—she don't owe me a favor like Fanaleese—but expunging records is her whole thing."

It sounded too good to be true. It probably was.

But it was an intriguing notion.

"How does she do it?" Coal wanted to know. Was it a reliable process? Or would the Palace catch on to what had happened after a week and send more goons after him once he'd already paid this stranger however many tups?

"I dunno," Zank shrugged. "That's her game, not mine. I just know she's legitimate, and I trust her. If anyone can get the job done, it's her. You pay her, she erases any bad marks on your record, and the Palace ain't got no reason to send no one after you anymore."

"I could finally live in peace," Coal blurted out.

Zank smiled warmly, his ears perking up a little. "Yep," he said.

That sounded nice. It was something Coal had not thought would even be possible. Deep down, he had resigned to being on the run for the rest of his life.

Until now, he did not know how much that had been weighing on him. Even just hearing that this woman could potentially help him had lightened the burden on his shoulders.

"Who's this friend of yours?" he asked.

"Her name is Netraj. She's up in Mountainside."

Three districts in Vinnag were adjacent to the mountains, but only the northernmost one incorporated that fact into its name. Coal had not spent much time there. Now that he thought about it, he wasn't sure if he'd been there at all.

"She keeps pretty early hours," Zank continued. "She closes up shop around ten. Don't know why. Don't know what she gets up to in her personal time. But that's why I wanted to get to you early, so you had time to go see her."

That reminded Coal to check the time again, only to discover there was no clock anywhere inside the Uncut Gem. Was there one in Fanaleese's living quarters? Or had the man progressed beyond the need for time?

"How much time does that give me?" Coal asked.

"Should be about three hours, give or take a couple minutes."

"We can go now. Maybe grab something to eat on the way." His stomach had been rumbling for most of the conversation.

But Zank shook his head. "I'm not goin'," he said. "I wanna get back to Venny. She was kinda stirring when I was fixin' to leave, so I wanted to make this a quick visit."

He then detailed where to find Netraj's shop in Mountainside. Evidently she ran an apothecary as her day job while assisting unsavory types such as Zank in her spare time. He also mentioned that her shop was located at the end of a street filled with food stalls of all sorts, so Coal should have no issue finding some grub. He was practically drooling listening to Zank's descriptions of the various cuisines available.

"Have you tried jonwek yet?" Zank asked him.

Coal shook his head. It wasn't strictly true, though; the Vinnag delicacy had traveled up through Ruska and he'd eaten versions of it, but from what he heard, nothing touched the quality of the authentic version here in the city.

Jonweks were a simple dish, but packed with flavor. They consisted of crickets and mealworms ground up, mixed with a binder and a spice blend, which seemed to change in each region. Everyone wanted to put their own stamp on it. The mixture was then formed into hefty spheres big enough for one hand, battered with seasoned flour (again differing based on region), and deep-fried.

Coal loved the jonweks he'd tried before, and it shocked him to realize he had yet to try the real thing in the two weeks he'd been here. His mind had been otherwise preoccupied. No time for fried treats.

"There's a great jonwek stall on her street," said Zank. "I wouldn't say it's the *best* in the city, but it's very good. The best is probably a few blocks over from the Starlite, actually. The entertainment district's got all the best food. Drunk people stumbling around need late-night snacks, naturally." He stood from the counter and walked toward the exit. "Do you have any other plans today?" he asked.

"Nope."

"Alright. I'll come by and get you this afternoon around…three, I guess? That should give us enough time to get over there. Hopefully V's up and movin' by then."

"She needs real medical treatment," said Coal, worry creeping into his voice.

"I know," said Zank. "Nomak will get it paid for since it happened on the job. He doesn't need to know the people who did it weren't part of Dend's crew."

So he had decided against telling Nomak. Even if it was for Venny's benefit and nothing to do with him, Coal was grateful.

"No point complicating matters," he said.

"Exactly," Zank nodded. Then he left, his ears still floppy with fatigue.

Coal returned upstairs with the intention of informing Fanaleese he was headed out for a while, but he could hear the marten's belabored snores through the closed door and decided against it. He crept back down into the bar and poured himself a glass of water, not realizing how dry his throat was until the liquid shot down his gullet. He emptied the glass and immediately poured himself another, which he downed just as fast. He took a minute to rinse the glass and set it on the drying rack before departing.

The sun was already shining brightly upon Vinnag.

While a great majority of Ruska was still covered in forest, the kingdom's great cities had done away with the pesky greenery (except for decoration in certain places) and opened themselves up to the harsh sunlight.

Growing up in a similarly large city, Coal was used to it. But he had grown fond of some of the smaller towns he had passed through on his journey southward, still hidden under the forest's canopy, light filtering through the leaves. It made the world seem so much smaller, so much cozier.

In his hometown of Muta Par and here in Vinnag, the world felt vast and uncaring. It was never an impression he got when he had been living in Muta Par, only in retrospect after spending some time in places like Baoa and Pontosk and elsewhere. He could see himself retiring in Baoa or one of the other two treetop villages connected to it.

The thought was absurd, though. Retirement. He didn't even have a job, nor any realistic prospects for one as long as the Palace was after him.

But maybe Netraj would change all that. Give him his future back.

If she did, he wouldn't even need to wait for retirement to move to Baoa or wherever else he fancied. With his father dead, there was nothing left tying him to Muta Par. In fact, for the sake of not needlessly kicking up any dirt, it would probably be best for him to *not* return to the city.

The idea of never returning to his home pained him somewhat, but he buried that pain for another day. Right now, he had other matters on which to focus.

Like getting some breakfast, he told himself. *Getting some authentic jonwek. And also clearing my name so the Palace doesn't try to capture me for the rest of my days.*

The streets of Renning Heights were never very busy. Coal only ran into a few people as he walked west in the direction of Mountainside. It was just as well; the fewer people who saw him, the less likely word could get back to one of the Palace's envoys.

Between Renning Heights and Mountainside, he had to cut diagonally across a district called Skipsbarrow. It was a strange name, and he didn't have the faintest clue where it had originated. Perhaps it was named after some old frog or bat nicknamed Skip who had made their mark on the city somehow.

Skipsbarrow was home to a lot of residential neighborhoods, the most of any other district in the city. There were a couple areas with houses, most one or two stories, but primarily it was populated with tall-standing apartment buildings that could pack in hundreds of residents. Many of those who moved out of Renning Heights in the past had moved into Skipsbarrow which, in addition to all its apartments, housed Vinnag's biggest insect farm, where many worked.

With the Dirt King's ban on consumption of any meat due to dwindling wildlife, insects and plants were now the only sources of food in Ruska. As a result, insect farming had grown immensely popular and profitable. The meat ban had been put into effect around thirty or thirty-five years ago, so Coal was too young to have ever consumed any meat.

His father had regularly grumbled about missing his ventem steaks, though. Losing ventem steaks, he always said, was the biggest tragedy of his life.

Many of Skipsbarrow's residents were already out and about despite the relatively early hour. There were people suited up in uniforms on their way to work, parents walking their children to school; Coal even spotted some slimes already out making their daily deliveries.

The sunshine was improving his mood. After such an unexpectedly horrific night followed by being crammed into a dank, dark room until morning, Coal appreciated the warmth and vibrancy of the lively district. He smiled and nodded greetings to people as he passed, though still taking care not to draw too much unwanted attention to himself.

He milled past the insect farm at the district's center. It towered high above every other building in the vicinity. The company's name was stamped across the side of the building in blocky letters: NYERS FOODS. The brand was well-known across the lower regions of Ruska. Coal watched as workers filed in through the front door, saying downtrodden hellos to each other. He briefly wondered what working conditions were like inside. Very few of the individuals entering Nyers Foods appeared to be looking forward to their day.

It was not long before Coal found himself in Mountainside. The district looked much like Skipsbarrow, with the exception that its westernmost buildings were carved directly into the mountains that bordered Vinnag and the rest of the valley.

He took Barnes Street down to Yulue and turned left, which dead-ended into Killow, the street he was looking for. The moment he turned onto Killow, his nostrils were filled with the rich smells of Zank's promised street foods.

There were tons of stalls lined up and down both sides of the street with vendors toiling away at their craft. Coal wandered down the street, eyes wide and tongue practically lolling out of his mouth as he eyed each stall's offerings.

A portly beaver was selling blueberry jam-stuffed bark. Coal knew that many people had a taste for tree bark (most of those being beavers), but he had never acquired the taste no matter how many different preparations he tried. He did not figure combining it with fruit jams would quite do the trick.

Another served roasted vegetables on a stick, everything from onions to bell peppers to carrots and more. Bright rainbows of delicious-smelling seasoned veggies, steam billowing into the sky.

They were tempting, but Coal stayed the course for his sought-after jonwek. Near the end of the street, he finally found the stall.

It was manned by an elderly marten with a smattering of gray in her hair. She smiled at Coal with kind eyes as he approached and asked him, "Can I get you something good to eat today?"

"I would love that," said Coal, feeling genuine excitement for the first time in weeks. Possibly months.

Food was one of the things that gave him the most joy in life, and it had been a long while since he'd eaten anything truly fantastic. He had high hopes for this woman's jonwek.

The woman gave him a gap-toothed grin and grabbed a paper basket, into which she tossed two freshly-fried jonweks.

Coal paid and then eagerly took the basket from her. "My buddy told me great things about your food," he told her, which lit up her face in delight.

He picked up one of the golden brown balls, which was still hot but not scalding. He gave it a light blow before taking a bite, and he nearly passed out from the blast of flavor in his mouth. It was at once spicy and sweet with a touch of vinegar, with a crunchy exterior from the batter but a delectably creamy interior.

His expression must have betrayed how he was feeling, because the woman clapped her hands in triumph.

"Your friend must have been telling the truth!" she said.

"Absolutely," he said, his mouth stuffed. He swallowed and said, "It's delicious. Thank you so much."

"My pleasure," said the marten with another wide smile.

Coal stepped away from the stall to make room for other customers and finished up his food on the sidewalk out of everyone's way. Both jonweks were equally delicious, and he had half a mind to walk back over to the stall and order ten more.

But instead he tossed the paper basket into the trash and set out for the end of the street in search of Netraj's apothecary.

Just as Zank had described, the woman's storefront was easy to spot with its blue walls and yellow trim. On the bright red front door, painted in curly script, was DALIANCA'S DELIGHTS. Zank had explained to him that *Dalianca* was a fake name that Netraj used for her regular business.

Coal entered the shop and a blast of scents even more powerful than those of the food stalls out on the street struck him. The walls were lined with shelves full of bottled potions, candles, bundles of herbs, and much more that intermingled in the air.

The food had made him feel better, but now that he was in the store, his nerves were rattled. He felt uncomfortable explaining his situation to this stranger, and he was extra uncomfortable trying to skirt the law, even if it was actively working against him.

A pretty, young bat poked her head up out from the counter near the back of the store. "Can I help you?" she asked. "Looking for anything in particular?"

"Uh…" Coal mumbled. "Just looking for rotten soap," he said, hoping he didn't sound like a complete moron or a psychopath. Zank had told him that was a code phrase used to indicate he wanted to partake in the woman's side business, but it was entirely possible his friend had been screwing with him. Zank had a weird sense of humor.

Thankfully, that was not the case. "Come around here," the bat said, gesturing toward a door behind the counter. "I'll just be a minute," she told another bat who was stocking a shelf nearby. She then disappeared behind the door, and Coal followed.

She was already sitting behind a desk and flicking on her lamp when he entered. Behind her, mounted on the wall, was a landscape painting of the northeastern cave system Yagos, where many bat tribes lived.

Coal took a seat and she extended her hand toward him. "Netraj." He shook her hand and introduced himself.

"Zank Redeia suggested I get in touch with you," he said next. "I've got a problem that he thinks you could help solve."

"Is that so?" said Netraj, leaning back in her chair, batting her long, dark eyelashes. "Lay it on me."

Her casualness put him at ease. In his mind, he had been imagining her as some sinister, intimidating figure like the Garnas. But she seemed normal, by most standards. Just someone with an abnormal job.

It was difficult to start, but he needed to be totally truthful with her. It was possible to omit some aspects of his story when reciting it to Zank, especially to spare himself any judgments. But if this woman was going to put herself at great risk for him, she needed to know precisely what the job entailed. For all he knew, it might involve more highly-guarded records than she was used to.

"My father and I were in an accident last year," he began. "We were both working in—"

"I don't mean to be rude," Netraj cut him off, "but today's kind of a busy day for me. I've got other clients who need some work done. I'm sure you understand."

"Sure."

"So I don't really need to know the finer details of your life. No offense, but please just cut to what your issue is and what you need me to do."

"Sure," he said again, embarrassed. He swallowed. "I...well, I'm marked as a Flesh Eater."

Netraj stared at him, her mouth slightly agape.

Long before the Dirt King's ban on meat consumption—hundreds and hundreds of years before that, in fact—the immortal king had implemented a ban on cannibalism. Offenders were sent to one of three prisons specially built to house Flesh Eaters.

Those prisons were originally claimed to be built for the purpose of punishing the kingdom's most deranged criminals, murderers who ate their victims, but it trickled down throughout all of Ruskan society. Not to say that the denizens of Ruska were running around devouring each other, but it wasn't out of the ordinary for certain cultures to practice rituals—typically upon death—that involved eating the remains of loved ones.

When there inevitably came some pushback, the Dirt King deemed these traditions too barbaric for the society he was shaping, and declared a kingdom-wide ban on the practice. Absolutely no exceptions. No culture and no tradition was exempt.

The boars in particular were said to have had many rituals involving the eating of flesh way back then. There used to be celebration feasts during which attendees would eat the deceased, and similarly it was tradition to devour a child if it was stillborn. These practices were believed to help the individual's spirit live on in this world through the bodies of their loved ones.

Coal did not know if these peoples, such as the boars, no longer believed in the old traditions or if they simply had to live with the idea of their loved ones not passing on properly.

Those who disobeyed the order and ate the flesh of another sapient being were marked as Flesh Eaters and sent to one of the three designated prisons, which were officially labeled as "villages" rather than prisons, but everyone knew the truth. There, the Flesh Eaters would be under constant surveillance by guards trained at the Palace. The prisoners carried out manual labor for the surrounding cities and towns, whether that meant farming, raising racing spiders, or whatever else the general populace needed done, while paying very little for their involuntary service.

"How?" Netraj asked him. "How are you here?"

"With great difficulty," he replied.

"Yeah, I bet," she laughed. "There must be Stingers after you."

"Yes."

"How have you slipped past them so far?"

"Like I said: with great difficulty."

"So you want your record cleared of that mark to get the Palace off your ass," she said.

"The way it hap—"

"Don't care," Netraj interrupted him again. "You said you're marked. That's all that matters." She paused a moment, then said, "It's not gonna be cheap."

Coal nodded. "I figured as much." All the joy he had felt from eating the jonweks had drained from his body. Maybe he would grab some more after this, get his spirits back up.

"I've never actually cleared a Flesh Eater before," Netraj admitted. "I can do it, it's similar to shit I've done before, but..." She chuckled. "This is neat. This'll be fun." She started to write something down, but Coal could not see what.

He asked her, "So how much will it cost?" That was all that truly mattered. He waited for the shoe to drop.

And it did indeed drop. "Eight thousand tups," she said, still scribbling away nonchalantly. As if she had not just asked him for eight thousand tups.

He felt like he might vomit up the dough balls he'd eaten a few minutes prior.

His jaw was on the floor. "I..." He struggled to find the words. All hope had evaporated. "I don't have that kind of money," he finally said. His stomach twisted.

Netraj stopped writing and looked up at him.

"Oh," she said. "Well, I guess that's that, then." She balled up the paper she'd been writing on and went to toss it in a bin at her feet.

"Wait," he said.

Her hand hovered over the trash can, but she held onto the ball of paper.

Coal said, "I'll...come up with some way to get the money." He couldn't believe the words coming out of his mouth.

Right now he could not begin to imagine possessing eight thousand tups, let alone handing them over to this woman. There were days he could barely afford food. The payout from last night's job for Garna Nomak would be good, but "good" to him had meant three hundred tups.

Knowing now how much he needed to scrounge up to secure himself a real future, his definition of "good" had shifted drastically.

"You sure?" Netraj asked, an eyebrow raised.

He nodded, his breathing shallow.

The bat un-crinkled the paper and smoothed it out on her desk. She said, "Okay then. I've got no real timeline on this; I can start whenever you've got the funds. No worries on my end. I guess you just gotta worry about not getting arrested." She cracked a smile as she said it, but it was not as amusing to Coal.

"Okay," was all he said. He could not think of anything else.

He had to obtain eight thousand tups. There was nothing else to say or do. That was his new reality.

Netraj stood and held out her hand to shake again. The hand that had been holding the paper moments ago.

"I look forward to doing business with you," she said, and he took her hand. As they shook, she said, "I really do think it'll be fun."

Loads of fun.

Coal left the apothecary not knowing what his next move would be. Without being able to secure a real paying job, his best option was to continue doing work for Garna Nomak, but the Palace already knew he was here in Vinnag. Laying low wasn't much of an option anymore. He had only eluded them thus far because he kept on the move.

"Fuck," he sighed heavily, the sun beating down on his head. He ran his fingers through his orange fur, pulling at it, yanking out a few stray strands. He let them momentarily dance on the breeze and then land without fanfare on the street a few feet away.

He tore his gaze from the ground and looked up.

He then knew what his next move would be. It was the only thing he *could* do, really.

He walked back over to the elderly marten at her jonwek stall.

"Hello," he greeted her with a smile.

"Back for more?" she said, reciprocating.

Coal nodded. "You've got it." He placed his tups on the table.

He needed to rid the taste of his father's flesh from his mouth.

6

THE EXTRA JONWEKS HELPED a little, but not for long.

There was still a fair bit of time before their planned meeting with Garna Nomak, so Coal took the opportunity to walk around the city some more.

More specifically, he went back to Skipsbarrow. He had found the district exceedingly pleasant, aside from the looming Nyers Foods factory at its center. The district felt homey, much more so than any other district in Vinnag, which all had a layer of grime. Walking through the residential neighborhoods and seeing normal people living normal lives did a lot to clear his head. Even if it somewhat saddened him.

He grabbed lunch at a café that was advertising a soup and sandwich special. Despite the discounted price, it was a little costlier than Coal was anticipating (though surely nothing out of the ordinary for a Skipsbarrow resident), but he indulged anyway. He was going to get paid in a couple hours. Both the soup and sandwich were vegetarian with nary a bug in sight, and the vegetables on the sandwich were crisp and delicious. It was dripping with a thin orange sauce that Coal had to stop himself from licking up off his plate.

Once again, the food improved his mood, but only for a short while.

Maybe getting paid will make me feel better, he jokingly thought to himself.

Soon after, he returned to the Uncut Gem to await Zank and the others. It was only an hour or so past midday and Fanaleese was now awake on his own terms, reading a book at one of the tables downstairs.

An old, dusty, red-and-yellow jukebox in the corner of the room was playing a relaxed number, something Coal would never expect to hear in a bar. It was interesting that the song was an option on the jukebox.

As soon as Fanaleese peered over the top of his paperback and saw Coal, the marten said, "Ya didn' lock me door."

Coal stopped dead in his tracks, thinking back to that morning. It was true. He had left without securing the place at all.

"Shit," he muttered, panicking. "Shit! I'm so sorry. What was stolen? I'll work to replace it, I'll—"

"Nuffin' happened," said Fanaleese, still holding up his book to obscure his face. All Coal could see were the man's beady eyes. "I'm just givin' you a hard time, is all. It's me own fault. I shoulda gave you a spare key or somethin' while you's here."

He set his book down, a tatty and faded paperback with a fox knight adorning its cover, and dug into his pocket to retrieve a small iron key. He placed it on the table, then picked up his book and resumed reading.

"Oh," said Coal, walking over to the table. He pocketed the key and said, "Thank you. I'm glad nothing bad happened. Sorry again. I didn't even think—"

"S'okay," Fanaleese said, now starting to sound annoyed. Coal left him to enjoy his novel.

Coal wandered over to the jukebox to investigate what song was playing. He squinted through the cloudy, cracked glass and could make out the name of the musician as Wallar Noyeu. He recognized the name; the man was a famous artist who wrote moody, soulful instrumental music.

He was positive the Uncut Gem was the sole bar in Ruska with an album by Wallar Noyeu on its jukebox.

"My father liked this guy," he said to Fanaleese, momentarily forgetting the man was trying to read in peace. He looked over to the marten, who was once more glaring at him over the top of his paperback. "Sorry, I'll leave you alone." He moved to retreat to his supply room.

"Nah," said Fanaleese. "S'okay. Yer pap has good taste. There ain't many out there who's better'n Wallar. Only two I can think of's Mal Dala and Zoj."

Coal had heard of Mal Dala, which was a well-known (albeit old and no longer active) jazz band. The name Zoj eluded him.

"I haven't listened to much Mal Dala," said Coal.

"Maybe yer pap's taste ain't as good as I thought."

Coal shuddered at the man's phrasing.

He tried to ignore it and said, "Strange choice for bar music. Wallar doesn't really set the sort of tone I would think a bar in Renning Heights is going for."

Fanaleese put his book down again, looking stern. "You think my bar ain't classy enough fer Wallar?"

If he kept stepping on this man's toes, favor or no he was going to be kicked to the curb sooner or later. He stumbled over himself apologizing until Fanaleese cracked a smile.

"I'm only jokin'," the marten chortled. Coal let out a relieved laugh as well. "I gotta keep the 'box stocked with shit I ackshly like so's I can listen to it durin' the day. I'm not crazy nuff to buy another player just for me room."

"Makes sense to me," Coal conceded.

They proceeded to discuss Wallar Noyeu's albums for a little while before transitioning into which of Mal Dala's offerings Coal needed to check out. Eventually, Fanaleese declared he wanted to read another chapter or two before readying the bar for the evening.

Coal left the old man to his pleasures and went upstairs to wait for Zank. He flipped on the supply room's light and sat on the floor, leaning his back against a wall to stare at some crates. He closed his eyes and wondered what Garna Nomak was like.

Before he knew it, he had fallen asleep. It was not long before Fanaleese came knocking at the door.

Downstairs, Zank and Venny stood by the front door waiting for him. Venny's arm was in a sling and the look on her face was one of outright misery. Zank didn't appear too jolly himself, but his expression was at least a little brighter.

"Hey," Coal greeted them both. "How're you feeling?" he asked Venny.

"Not great," she replied. "Arm hurts."

"I can imagine," Coal said unhelpfully. Feeling stupid for saying it, he shifted the topic to Marl's whereabouts.

"He had some other business to deal with this afternoon. He'll meet us there," Zank answered. "Let's go."

Their walk through Renning Heights was largely silent. Coal was too uncomfortable about the role he played in ruining Venny's arm to initiate any conversation. The other two seemed uninterested in discussing anything either.

As they were passing by Zank's apartment, though, the rabbit asked, "How did things go with Netraj?"

The question piqued Venny's interest. She must've known who Netraj was. Coal was beginning to assume everyone in the city's underbelly knew everyone else.

"It went fine," Coal answered halfheartedly. He still did not want to go into too much detail around Venny, and would prefer if Zank did not know his status as a Flesh Eater. "The cost for her service is pretty high."

"What she does ain't easy," said Zank.

You don't know the half of it.

"Yeah. Still, it's more than I expected," Coal sighed.

"Are you gonna do it anyway?"

He shrugged and said, "I don't really have a choice. I just need to figure out a way to get the money somehow."

"Unfortunate news on that front. I know Nomak's about to be out of town for a couple weeks, so I doubt he'll have anything lined up for us. I bet we can find some work around town, though."

It didn't sound especially promising to Coal, but he would dutifully tag along on whatever jobs Zank could arrange. He'd accumulate every single tup he possibly could.

Conversation died out quickly after that, but it was only about ten minutes before they made it to their destination.

It was a nondescript building on one of the district's many abandoned streets. Probably not the Garna's official meeting spot, but rather a space to carry out more private meetings, much like the office they had broken into. This place was definitely more of a dump on the outside than Dend's, but it fit in amongst the rest of the buildings on the street.

Nothing about it stood out, which was what Nomak surely wanted.

Zank held the door open for them, and Coal was surprised to find just how much nicer the inside was than out.

The lobby was small, but decorated nicely. Paintings hung in thick, extravagantly carved golden frames along the walls, depicting cityscapes and portraits of the Garna. The walls were green and bore an intricate design which Coal could not tell whether it was wallpaper or painted by hand. It all seemed over-the-top for a place that moments ago he had assumed few people visited, but then again, maybe the Garna wanted to impress people no matter where they met him.

Marl was waiting for them when they arrived, standing a few feet inside the entrance. He was barefoot and nodded a greeting at the trio as they settled in.

Plush red carpeting covered the floors except for the entryway. A meek woodpecker wearing wiry glasses with a shock of red feathers on the top of his head insisted they remove their shoes to keep the carpet clean.

"The Garna likes the feel of it on his feet," Zank offered as an explanation.

The four of them followed the woodpecker's order and were then led down a side hallway with a closed door at the end. The man knocked twice, then opened the door without waiting for a response.

Garna Nomak's voice filled the room as they shuffled in. His assistant remained outside and shut the door behind them.

"Zankaras! *Junsuelu*, my friend!" the anteater boomed. It had been years since Coal heard someone use Zank's full name. Nomak rose out of his chair but remained stationary behind his desk.

The Garna was a rotund individual. His chest was as wide as Coal and Zank standing side by side, with arms that were thicker than Marl's neck. He wore a flashy orange suit with a jacket that seemed not long enough for his arms. The color was a nice complement to his fur, which was light brown with a black stripe near his neck and shoulders that just barely peeked out from underneath his clothes. His snout extended from his thin head and was easily as long as Coal's arms. The relative smallness of his head was at great odds with the rest of his body.

Coal could not help but think about the man's toes sinking into the thick carpet, his bare feet touching every inch of floor in this building. And then he could not help but think about how he had seen photographs of the man's genitalia. The latter was another thing of a size at odds with the Garna's body.

Nomak's snout bobbed up and down with excited anticipation. "I trust you were successful?" he asked, taking a seat.

There were only two other chairs available in the room, so Zank and Venny sat while Coal and Marl stood behind them. Nomak's eyes scanned Venny's arm and he frowned deeply.

"What happened here?" he then asked before they could answer his first question.

"More guards than we were expecting," Zank answered quickly, keeping the answer vague.

Nomak nodded. "I've seen the news. How the fuck did Dend get those things?" he asked rhetorically, leaning back in his chair. It squeaked—practically screamed—in protest as he did so. "But first, did you get it?" he asked again.

In response, Zank pulled a sealed envelope from his jacket pocket and pushed it across the hardwood desk. The Garna snatched it up eagerly and broke the seal with one of his long, curved nails.

They watched him pull the photos from the envelope and check them over. His thin, pink tongue slithered out from his snout and dangled a few inches from the photos before starting to wiggle back and forth. Saliva dripped from its fleshy pink tip. He quickly slurped his tongue back into his mouth and placed the delicate images back in the envelope, looking more than satisfied.

"I knew I could trust you with this," he said to Zank. "And I assume you practiced discretion as well?"

This question pertained to everyone in the room. All four of them affirmed without hesitation.

"Excellent." With that out of the way, Nomak stuffed the envelope into a desk drawer. Coal wondered if the man was going to keep the photos for his own pleasure or burn them so that something like this did not happen again. Probably the former, if he had to wager.

The anteater then swiped a jar of pickled scorpion eggs that was sitting on his desk. He unscrewed the lid and thrust his hand into the viscous yellow liquid, pulling out a handful of gelatinous eggs. His tongue shot out, wrapping tightly around one of the eggs before yanking it into his mouth, gnashing delightedly. Liquid dribbled from his lips and dripped from between his fingers, still holding three or four of the eggs.

"Sir," Zank began, "we were hoping to garner some additional wages for Venny's medical costs since her injury was incurred on the job."

Coal had never heard Zank use such vocabulary.

"Right, right, the arm," said Nomak, swallowing. He leaned back further in his chair and Coal was sure the thing was going to shatter before their eyes. "One of Dend's goons did this to you?" He slurped up another egg. Coal cringed.

Venny nodded. "Scorpion stepped right on it," she said matter-of-factly.

The anteater's eyebrows shot up. "Fuck me," he moaned, which Coal found unsettling. "That must've been quite a shitshow."

"Yes," said Venny. Clearly "shitshow" would not be how she'd choose to describe the horrific incident, but better not to contradict the Garna.

"I still don't understand how Dend would have access to Palace tech," said Nomak, scratching his snout in thought.

Please do not connect any dots, Coal pleaded internally.

But the Garna went on, "We're gonna have to keep a closer eye on his movements. Someone must have slipped up." With his free hand, he grabbed a notepad on his desk and wrote something down. "A bit extra to pay the doctor won't be a problem, though. I appreciate your service. Matter of fact, I think all of you deserve a little extra for having to deal with those fucking robots." He shoved the remaining eggs into his mouth and wiped the residue off on a handkerchief lain carelessly atop the desk.

"Thank you," Zank and Venny both said. Marl and Coal were silent.

It was then that Nomak finally comprehended Coal's presence in the room. "Who is this?" he asked. He finished writing on the pad, then tore off the slip of paper and handed it to Zank.

"He's the new guy I was telling you about," the rabbit replied. "My childhood friend. He's reliable. I don't think we would've gotten away as cleanly as we did last night without his help."

Coal was thankful that neither Venny nor Marl refuted the lie. Venny had been passed out for the last part of the confrontation, so for all she knew Coal had singlehandedly taken down both HM-3s with all of his special, advanced combat training in the Muta Par library.

"That so?" said Nomak, intrigued by this unknown fox standing before him. "What's your name, friend?" he asked.

He took a moment considering whether or not to use an alias, but figured if he lied to the Garna it would come to light at some point and screw him over in some way. "Coal," he said.

Nomak blinked. "The hell kind of name is 'Coal'?"

"When I was born, my father thought it looked like I'd had coal rubbed all over my face. Sir."

The anteater grinned at the use of an honorific. It was easy to get on the man's good side, it seemed. Coal just needed to be sure to stay on it.

"And here I am just named after my grandfather. Maybe I should've been called Lightbulb instead!" Nomak laughed.

The rest of them, Coal included, laughed lightly out of politeness.

Staying on his good side.

"Well," said Nomak, wearing himself out with his own joke, "I think that should just about do it for us today. Thank you again for your help with this, Zankaras. Might be a little more effort on our part to mitigate Dend's response given how much I hear you fucked shit up over there, but this mission was a success, so I'm happy."

The Garna smiled wide, and the four of them made for the exit.

"Thank you, sir. Enjoy your trip to Soponunga," Zank said. He held the slip of paper Nomak had given him in his hand.

Nomak let out a pained groan at that. He said, "I will if this fuckbrained moron I invested in can get his shit together. Sometimes I wonder if he even knows how to saddle a spider."

Zank laughed and said, "Well, I hope he figures it out, for your sake."

"He better hope he does too," Nomak grimaced. "I can tell you now, it will not be a pleasant time for him if he's not at *least* in the top three."

"Best of luck to you and your racer. And safe travels," Zank said as they filed out of the room.

Nomak's woodpecker assistant escorted them back to the lobby, where Zank spoke with a receptionist and handed her the paper Nomak had written on. She read over the note and got to work gathering their payment.

Coal approached Zank while they waited. "Nomak is going to a spiderback race?"

The rabbit nodded. "He sponsored a racer from here, paid for all his gear and the spider and everything. He's got a lot riding on it, reputation-wise. Probably money-wise too, if I had to guess."

"It's in Soponunga?"

Another nod. "The Soponunga Spiderback Showdown, they call it. A real mouthful. This is the...third year they've done it, I think? Lots of people travel from all over for it. You haven't heard of it?"

Coal shook his head. Word hadn't reached him up north. It had been a while since he'd been a part of the spiderback racing scene, to be fair.

Back in Muta Par, spiderback racing was a common hobby amongst the city's richer families. Coal and his father were far from affluent, but his grandparents had worked at a farm on the outskirts of the city and in his youth Coal had gotten the chance to learn spiderback riding from the owners.

He was no professional, and it had been several years since he'd ridden, but he knew how to saddle a spider. It sounded like he had a leg up on at least Nomak's racer.

"Do you know what the prize is?" he asked.

Zank cocked an eyebrow. "You thinkin' of gettin' in on that?"

Coal shrugged. "These things usually have big cash prizes, don't they? And I know my way around a spider." He had entered in a few local races and usually placed in the top five spots, even winning once.

"They do. This one's three thousand tups. It's a big one. But that's not the only prize." He took a second to grab their money from the receptionist, thanking her. As he doled out the payments to everyone, he continued. "There's also some rare anteater artifact up for grabs. That's why Nomak is so invested in the race, honestly."

The bigger cities in Ruska were home to a varied mix of people, but there were certain regions in the kingdom that were primarily populated by one, though of course some others were sprinkled amongst them. Soponunga was a beaver city, so it was peculiar that they would have an anteater artifact as a prize for their race.

Zank could tell by Coal's expression that he was confused. "The local government of Eorpu Naro was apparently not doing great, so they went around to some other cities offering up this thing. I think it's some kind of diamond claw or somethin', I dunno. Some old-ass thing that had been passed down for years and years. They were just trying to pawn it off for some quick money to fund something else in the city."

"If it's that valuable and old, weren't the people in Eorpu Naro upset about their government getting rid of it?"

Zank shrugged. "I dunno. I dunno if anyone really knew about it. I only know about it 'cause Nomak made an offer on it himself, but the beavers outbid him."

"So now he's trying to win it in the race."

"Yup."

They exited the Garna's offices to finish their conversation on the street. Now that he had his money, Marl took off with hardly a goodbye.

"Do you know how much the claw is worth?" Coal asked.

Zank shook his head. "I mean, how do you apply a real value to that? All I know is that Nomak offered to pay twelve thousand tups for it, but the beavers offered more. They wanted something truly grandiose as the grand prize for their race."

Coal swore. "That's a lot to pay for some old claw."

"The man likes nice things," said Zank. "And the rarer, the better. It'll grant him higher status or whatever. Anyway, we're off. Gotta get this arm looked at."

Zank and Venny left, and Coal sauntered slowly down the littered street back in the general direction of the Uncut Gem.

Coal's mind spun with thoughts of that anteater claw.

Twelve thousand tups.

If he could somehow win that race, he could turn around and sell the claw to Nomak and easily pay off Netraj in exchange for cleaning up his record. Not to mention the three thousand of winnings on top of that.

But that would be crazy. He hadn't raced in years, and even at his prime he wasn't the best in Muta Par. It would take a miracle to win. And he didn't even have a spider to ride.

He looked down at the wad of bills Zank had given him. He counted out how much extra Nomak had decided to pay them.

Double.

He was holding six hundred tups. Far from a fortune, but not an inconsiderable amount of money.

I might be able to rent a spider with this.

With such a bombastic grand prize, second and third place had to be pretty substantial as well. Coal knew he had *some* skills. The other racers would probably be professionals, or at least much more seasoned than him, but…

…third place might not be unrealistic.

And whatever third place's prize was, it would probably get him a lot closer to affording Netraj's fee.

Am I really gonna do this? he asked himself. *Am I gonna go to Soponunga?*

Zank had said it himself: it was unlikely they would have any big paydays in the next couple weeks while Nomak was away for the race. This could be his shot to make some big, fast money.

And if it didn't work out, then he would just return to Vinnag at the same time as Nomak and resume taking jobs for the man. It was a gamble, but placing top three wasn't out of the realm of possibility for him. A Palace Stinger could be lurking around any corner, so the sooner he could pay Netraj, the better. It would take months of working for Nomak to scrounge up that kind of cash, and Coal was not entirely comfortable with the sorts of jobs the anteater might task him with.

Being seen outside of Vinnag might work to my advantage anyway, he pondered. *Make the Stingers think I left here for good so they're not waiting for me when I come back.*

While he walked back to the bar, Coal kept running through the scenario in his head. Playing out the race, reminding himself of the knowledge and techniques he'd accrued a decade ago.

Again he asked himself, *Am I really gonna do this?*

7

IT TOOK A LONG time for Coal to fall asleep that night. This time, however, it wasn't due to the unideal conditions; his mind was aflutter with thoughts of spiderback racing.

He recalled the spider's bristles tickling him as he rode, his legs secured tight around the creature's abdomen. Watching with awe as all eight legs worked in tandem to gain speed and deftly maneuver around obstacles.

If it were a simpler race, done on land only, a racer could get by with a speedy spider. In advanced races it took more than speed, though. Most spiderback races were carried out both in the treetops and on soil, the racer moving back and forth between the two whenever necessary, whether that was due to the route's limitations or their own strategy. To win, one's spider needed to not only be fast, but able to jump highly and precisely while navigating the winding branches. Sometimes the spider's spinnerets would be involved, but high-speed weaving was difficult to control and not used very often. Webs were more likely to be implemented to slow down racers behind you since it was easier to fire off some webbing that way.

The spider Coal used to train and race with was a massive, beautiful orb weaver named Voorluresk. Young Coal had been transfixed by the beast's white, semi-translucent body. Voorluresk's abdomen was huge and rounded, making him slightly harder to ride than other spiders, but Coal had gotten the hang of it fairly easily given it was his first experience riding at all. He was able to quickly master securing himself atop the spider without pressing in too hard with his heels and causing it pain, which would not only be cruel but also slow it down. When he tried riding other spiders after, he found it to be much simpler with their smaller abdomens.

Voorluresk was who Coal earned his only win with, although that was not during his first race. There were a handful of failures at the start, due to the routes being much trickier than Coal ever anticipated (in spite of his father's insistence that he was unprepared). But those failures pushed him to train harder, much to his father's delight, and soon he was moving up in the ranks with each race.

He steadily achieved rankings in the first five slots for a while, so Coal felt confident in his abilities. When he finally won, it was more out of luck than anything else. He was in a close second for a majority of the race, and it was only in the last curve of the track that his first place opponent screwed up.

There were pitfalls set up ahead of them. They were easy to spot, and any racer who wasn't a novice would know they were there. The route required the racer to leap into the air, dart through the trees for several strides, then jump back down once they cleared the pitfalls—or just stay in the trees until the finish line.

But the organizers were clever. The hanging branches were slightly out of reach of most spiders' leaps—there were maybe some that could achieve such distance, but Coal's opponent was not one of them.

The racer's spider bound through the air but just barely came up short, and both racer and spider plummeted into one of the pits.

The spider was fast, though, and Coal had known it would only be a few seconds before they scrambled out of the pit, regardless of how deep it was. But he also knew that his spider could not make the jump either. Something he would definitely not have known if he'd not seen someone else fumble the jump first.

So he acted fast. He had yanked on the spider's reins, indicating for it to rise up onto its front four legs only, raising its abdomen into the air. This slowed it down considerably, but allowed the spider to shoot off some webbing in front of it.

Coal pushed in with both of his heels multiple times, and Voorluresk shot webbing out in front of them, enough to cover the top of the first pitfall on their path. He then brought the spider back down onto its eight legs and leapt forward, onto the fresh web, using the silk's elasticity to then propel them even higher in the air.

The web fell apart almost immediately since there had obviously been no time to properly secure it along the entire edge of the hole. Coal's trainer would have strongly advised against the tactic should he have been there.

But it worked.

Coal and Voorluresk latched onto the branches above, skittering all the way to the end of the track with a healthy lead.

He and his father had celebrated the win that night by dining at Coal's favorite restaurant with some family friends, as well as Zank. The rabbit had been cheering him on from the sidelines and was the first to congratulate him when he dismounted his spider, having hopped straight past his father and trainer.

Spiderback racing was the only real thing Coal and his father Von bonded over while the man was alive. Coal spent a good portion of his youth angry with his father, mostly in regard to his mother, but eventually he grew past that. Not past the resentment, but past acting on it. They settled into a familiar, if not slightly awkward, rhythm with their relationship.

They never really fought or came to any disagreements, but Coal and Von were vastly different people and had trouble connecting on any real level. They got along fine, but Coal could not say that he really knew his father.

Thoughts of the man inevitably brought Coal to his father's final days, which he fought to cast out of his mind. Eventually, he was able to stop thinking about those days—the water trickling, his father's stench, the gaminess of his arm—and sleep finally came to him. He did not dream.

HAVING FALLEN ASLEEP SO late, kept awake first by thoughts of excitement and then of disgust, Coal woke late in the morning and found Fanaleese was already downstairs eating breakfast.

He greeted the old marten, who informed him that there was still some bread and jam left if he was hungry. Usually he did not have much of an appetite when he woke up, but maybe sleeping in so much later than he was accustomed to had him hungrier than usual.

The two made small talk while Coal spread some black-berry jam onto two pieces of bread. Music was playing in the jukebox, but he couldn't place who the artist was. As much as he had enjoyed their musical discussion the day before, his mind was buzzing too much with thoughts of spiderback racing to delve into the topic again. There was only one thing he wanted to talk about at the moment, and he did not think Fanaleese was the person to talk to.

After finishing up his breakfast, he strolled out onto the sunny streets of Renning Heights and headed toward Zank's apartment.

The rabbit answered the door promptly, looking more disheveled than usual. "Hey," he said before letting him in.

Venny was situated on the couch still, her arm now in a proper cast. She looked less irritable and pained than yesterday, which alleviated Coal's guilt some. Her knees were pulled to her chest and she had a book propped open on them.

"You allowed a book to enter your home?" Coal joked with Zank. He could not recall a single time he had ever seen the rabbit reading something.

Zank laughed. "There was a lot of paperwork involved, but she was persistent and we got the permits all worked out."

"If he's intent on helping take care of me while my shit heals, then I'm not gonna just leave my books at home, wondering how they end," said Venny. "I only had a hundred pages left in this one."

Coal didn't blame her. It didn't seem like there was much else to entertain herself with cooped up in Zank's place.

"Seems like you're doing better," he said.

Venny nodded. "Not too bad," she said. "It's broken in several places, and it's gonna take a while to heal, but the doctor said I'll be alright. The physical therapy is gonna be shitty, but the pills I got for the pain are pretty nice."

"Plus, you've got the best nurse in the city," Zank chimed in from the kitchen. He then asked Coal, "You want anything to drink?"

"Nah," Coal shook his head, taking a seat on the opposite end of the couch from Venny.

Zank returned and said, "We were gonna pop out to grab some lunch soon, if you wanna join."

"Maybe." It sounded tempting, but Coal had something he needed to discuss, and he wasn't sure what sort of timetable he would be on by the end of the conversation. He said, "I think I'm gonna enter that race after all."

The rabbit grinned, enthused by his friend's bravado. Venny looked up from her book. Zank asked, "You think you've got a shot?"

"I don't know," Coal admitted, "but I don't think I'd totally fuck it up, you know? You've seen me race."

"You're no amateur. But you're no pro, neither."

"That's true. But those winnings would go a long way in paying Netraj. The sooner I can pay her and get those Stingers off my tail, the better. Aren't the jobs gonna dry up while Nomak is gone?"

His friend nodded. "We'll be making some money, but yeah, nothin' too substantial until he's back. Definitely no pay-days like what we got yesterday."

Which led Coal to his question. "Do you know what the best way for me to get to Soponunga would be? Is it possible I could ride with Nomak?" He knew it was a longshot, but traveling with the Garna would offer him some layer of protection.

Zank shook his head. "Nope. I know he liked you, but I don't think he liked you enough to ride with you all the way to Soponunga," he sniggered. "And besides, he already left this morning. He wanted to get there a few days before the opening festival to indulge in whatever nasty shit he likes to indulge in."

"'Whatever nasty shit.' You know exactly what types of nasty shit," Venny teased him with a smirk.

"Yes, I do," said Zank, "and I am trying not to think about it, thank you."

The last thing Coal wanted to do was imagine Garna Nomak "indulging" in anything, so he could relate. He said, "Well, if Nomak's already gone, do you know any other…less-traveled routes?"

"Places where the Palace is less likely to be sniffin' around," Zank clarified.

Coal nodded.

Zank pondered the question for a minute. He scratched at his fuzzy chin, trying to come up with a good solution. But it was Venny who spoke up first.

"There's always the dung tunnels."

"Excuse me?" said Zank.

"Not the most appealing name," Coal added.

Venny looked back and forth between the two. "The Houndsvein," she said, as if they were morons.

"Oh," said Coal.

The Houndsvein was an enormous series of interconnected tunnels. It started at the northern tip of the kingdom, at the Houndstooth, and spanned all of Ruska. There were tunnels leading to every major city and most towns and landmarks. Hulking beetles navigated the tunnels, crawling along the ceiling with carriages dangling from their shells to carry loads of passengers.

"So your suggestion to avoid detection and the Palace's men is to pile onto a crowded carriage and use routes that literally directly connect back to the Palace?" said Zank.

Venny rolled her eyes. "The Palace's officers don't use the Houndsvein much," she said, nudging him with her uninjured arm. "Especially not the elite ones who're after him. The dung tunnels are for 'poor people' who can't afford any other travel than those dank, smelly underground routes, crammed into tiny carriages. Why else do you think they're called the dung tunnels?"

"I have never heard them called dung tunnels," Zank said. Coal concurred with him.

"Fancy northern boys," Venny scoffed. "There are *some* luxury lines, but I'm not saying he should ride a beetle anyway. There are offshoots in the tunnels that were dug up and used by maintenance workers and smugglers that he could travel through instead. It'll take a little more time than a direct route, but he'll still get where he's going."

The dung tunnels were beginning to sound like a more reasonable option. Coal asked, "Do you know your way around down there? Seems like it'd be very easy to get lost."

He had only ridden a Houndsvein carriage once before, but he remembered how dimly lit the maze-like tunnels were. He imagined the offshoots would be even darker and more confusing.

"I know 'em a bit, but my brother knows them pretty well. When are you trying to leave?"

Coal looked to Zank for guidance. "When's the race start?" he asked, realizing how very little he knew about this whole endeavor. Things were starting to move fast.

"The opening ceremony festival thing is in four days, I think," Zank replied.

"Tight schedule," said Coal. "I know Soponunga's not *too* far, but…"

"Walking there will probably take two or three days," Venny said. "I'd count on three. You should probably get going today." She folded down the corner of a page and closed her book, setting it on the end table. She hoisted herself up off the couch and said, "I can go to my brother's place and have him draw up a map. You gather up whatever shit you need and then I'll meet you over at the Gem, yeah?"

"I'll go with you," Zank said to her.

She laughed. "I'm not falling apart over here. My arm's busted, not my legs or my damn head. I can manage walking to my brother's apartment."

"I'd still—"

"I'm only even staying here while my arm heals because I know you'd flip out if I didn't. I'll be fine, I swear. Go with him and help him pack."

"Fine," Zank grumbled, defeated.

Venny smiled and gave Zank a quick peck on the cheek. "See you soon!"

GATHERING SUPPLIES DID NOT eat up much time, and the irony was not lost on Coal that he was packing them up in a supply room.

He and Zank bought some packages of dried fruit and dried insects to eat while he was underground, as well as a flask that they filled with water. Besides that, he stuffed his meager amount of possessions into the bag he'd already been traveling with and was good to go. He wasn't sure where he would be able to refill the flask underground, but he'd had to ration water before and could do it again for a couple days if necessary.

As Coal packed and Zank sat bored on the supply room floor, Coal asked him, "How long's that been going on with Venny?"

"What?"

"That kiss on the cheek. Did you think it was somehow undetectable by anyone but you two?"

"Oh." He gathered his thoughts before speaking. "It's…I dunno, it's been sort of an on-again-off-again thing," he said. "It's been going on for a couple months now."

"Was it 'off again' because of your tryst with the unnamed source in Dend's office, or the other way around?"

"Other way around," Zank said defensively.

"So you behave yourself when you're together."

"Of course. I've always been a good boy," Zank laughed.

"Yeah, yeah," Coal grinned. "I guess this injury has brought you back to 'on again.'"

Zank shook his head. "We sorta unofficially got back together a week ago. I guess we're just settling into it more now that we're in the same apartment together."

"So *that's* why she's letting you take care of her."

"Maybe. But who doesn't wanna be doted on anyway? She acts tough but I know she's enjoyin' her time laid up on the couch reading."

"Sounds like the dream, honestly," Coal sighed.

It had been so long since he truly *relaxed*. Spending a year constantly on high alert was wearing him thin.

Venny showed up at the bar a short while later, cheerily greeting Fanaleese as she marched through the unlocked front door.

The marten was still meandering around with a few hours to spare before needing to get the bar ready. His eyes widened at the sight of her arm.

"Who banged you up?" the old man asked her, stumbling over to where she stood to take a closer look at her cast. "I 'spect you gave whoever it was a good bangin' of their own."

"I wouldn't exactly put it that way, but yes, they were taken care of," Venny said with a chuckle.

"Good. Piece of shit oughta be put in his place for tanglin' with a lady!" he declared. Venny laughed again. Clearly the marten had no idea what sort of damage she was capable of.

Zank gave her a casual greeting, which amused Coal given what he knew now about their relationship. She returned it, waving with her unhurt arm, which held a folded-up yellowed piece of paper that Coal presumed was her brother's map.

She approached the two while Fanaleese wandered over to the jukebox to switch up the tunes to something snazzier and more fun. What he landed on was a brassy number Coal thought the band might have actually been playing in the Starlite the other night. Certainly a toe-tapper.

Venny handed Coal the map, which he unfolded to inspect in case he had any questions.

Her brother had put a surprising amount of detail into the map. His lines were neat and his notes were clear, lending it more the appearance of a blueprint than a drawing some random guy had hastily scribbled down.

The map was kept as simple as possible, only fully sketching out the tunnels that he was meant to travel through. The other passages were designated by circles on the edges of the tunnels, only so that he knew how many passageways to pass before actually venturing down one.

The path looked easy enough to follow, though admittedly there was no way of telling how long each tunnel was. He hoped it would not take the full three days Venny had estimated.

And there was one other thing causing Coal some concern. "You said these routes are used by smugglers, right?"

"Yeah. And maintenance."

"I'm more concerned about the smugglers. Am I gonna run into smugglers?" He'd had enough trouble attempting to subdue Garna Dend's guards. He would rather avoid any further confrontations if he could. And then another thought occurred to him. "Or am I gonna run into maintenance guys who think *I'm* a smuggler?"

Venny shrugged. "I asked the same thing, actually. Dahl doesn't *think* you'll see anyone, since his encounters down there have been pretty rare. But it's been a while since he's been in the tunnels at all, let alone these specific ones."

"So maybe."

"Maybe."

Great.

Still, smugglers and handymen were better than Palace Stingers with their colossal robotic scorpions.

"You should maybe take a gun," Zank said. Weaponry was not something they had considered while gathering his supplies.

Killing someone was far down on the list of things he wanted to do, but if it came down to defending himself, he saw no other choice. At the very least he could shoot the person in the kneecaps and run away.

That was something people did, right? Shoot kneecaps? He was sure he'd read it in a book somewhere.

"I don't have a gun," he pointed out. He'd left the firearm he used during their infiltration back at Zank's apartment.

Fanaleese piped up from over by the jukebox, where he'd been dancing to the music by himself. He was still kicking and gyrating when he said, "I've got guns for ya."

Coal laughed at the old marten's moves. "I think I only need the one."

"Well, let's us go take a look." He stopped dancing and traipsed up the stairs, Coal folding up the map to pocket it and following him. Zank and Venny trailed close behind.

Upstairs, Fanaleese told them to wait in the hall while he fetched the aforementioned firearms from his room. The man valued his privacy. He reappeared a couple minutes later with three pistols, a shotgun, and a rifle with a scope attached.

"I don't think he's gonna need the rifle, you old, crazy bastard," Zank laughed.

"Well, it's an option," Fanaleese mumbled, waving his insult away.

The shotgun would obviously deter attackers in the tunnels' close quarters, but Coal was already uncomfortable with guns in general and did not feel great about blasting the hell out of someone with it. If he went for the kneecap with that, he was liable to blow their leg off.

He took one of the pistols and told Fanaleese, "This should be fine. Thank you. Are you sure, though? Isn't this, like, valuable?"

"I got plenty," said Fanaleese. "I don't e'en know where all 'em's at. What's one more missin', eh?"

"You should probably find your missing guns," said Zank.

The old marten grumbled gibberish and waved his hand in Zank's face. Coal laughed and thanked him again.

Fanaleese scurried back into his room with the unwanted guns. He emerged another minute later with an appropriate holster and some extra ammunition, both of which Coal tucked into his bag along with the gun (after ensuring the safety was on). He did not want to draw attention to himself walking through the city with a holster strapped to his waist, whether there was a gun in it or not. He'd get properly set up when he was down in the dung tunnels, as Venny so affectionately referred to them.

With that, there was only one question remaining.

They all returned to the bar downstairs, where Coal pulled out the map again and pointed at the tunnel opening marked as the entrance. The place where he would begin his journey. He knew it couldn't be in the Vinnag station, because there would only be beetle carriages loading and unloading there.

He asked Venny, "Where is this?"

8

THE SECRET DUNG TUNNEL entrance was located just outside the city walls, about a twenty-minute walk from the crumbling exit in Renning Heights. Venny led Coal to the designated spot with Zank tagging along, of course. Fanaleese had opted to say his farewells back at the bar and told Coal he could stop by any time.

The trio came to a halt at an enormously wide tree.

"So the tunnel is under the tree or something?" Coal ventured a guess, pointing at a sizeable hole near the base of the tree trunk. "Climb in there and drop down?" He had read his fair share of adventure novels.

"Right on the money," said Venny. "Ah, there's one more thing I just remembered—pull out the map."

He did so, and she pointed at one of the tunnels. None of them had a pen or pencil to physically mark the page, so Coal made a mental note of it.

"This one's a main thoroughfare. Meaning that it'll have beetles crawling along the ceiling, and people riding those beetles. Be careful and stay out of sight as much as possible here. There'll be a good amount of space between you on the ground and the carriages, so it'll probably be hard for anyone to spot you, especially since they have no real reason to be looking down there in the first place. But still. The tunnels are lit, so it's a possibility."

"Aren't they lit closer to the ceiling, though?" Coal thought he remembered that from the one time he rode the Houndsvein.

She nodded. "Yeah, but it's not like everything in the lower half is pitch black or nothin'. Just be careful."

"Got it." He folded up the map again and slotted it in his pocket.

As their last order of business, Zank informed him of what hotel Nomak and his crew would be staying in, just in case Coal wanted to link up with the Garna for any reason. "If he's so unhappy with the racer he's already with, maybe he'll sponsor you too, I dunno," he said. "Either way, it's good to know someone there. Even if that someone's him." He cracked a smile.

It wasn't a bad idea. Being perceived as part of Garna Nomak's circle could offer him an extra layer of protection. Not that the Palace would particularly care when it came down to it, but maybe the man's reputation would at least give them pause and buy him some time. Perhaps Nomak would even have his men protect him.

Coal hugged Zank goodbye and thanked him for all his help. He didn't think that he and Venny were close enough for a hug, especially not with her injured arm, but he thanked her as well and said he was looking forward to seeing them both again in a couple weeks.

The two rabbits watched as Coal clumsily ducked into the tree hole, feeling around with his foot for some sort of ladder or incline or whatever would be easing his way underground.

It was the latter. The ground was at a very shallow incline, probably to make it easier on the smugglers who were transporting goods. The ceiling was low, though, and the dirt ramp was not steep enough to simply slide down, so Coal had to walk on his hands and feet all the way down, with his bag scraping against the ground.

He looked like a complete fool, and he was thankful that neither Zank nor Venny could see him. He reconsidered how useful this would be for smugglers with their cargo.

After twenty minutes of this slow, awkward movement, he finally reached the wider tunnel opening and was able to stand. His arms, legs, and back ached as he stretched.

First things first, he strapped the holster around his waist and slipped Fanaleese's gun into it. It felt strange.

Strutting around with a gun at his side was not Coal Ereness. He felt like a fraud. Like someone playing dress-up.

Next, he extracted the map from his pocket and checked it over yet again. By now he was far past double-checking; this was closer to quintuple- or sextuple-checking. But he wanted to be absolutely positive that he did not screw this up and find himself emerging in Janaroosh or even in the middle of the Dirt King's chambers somehow.

He counted the number of tunnels that he should be passing on his right before turning down the correct pathway. Once he counted them three times, he felt confident enough to set out.

The dung tunnels—*Houndsvein,* he corrected himself, though Venny's colloquial name was catchy—were spacious underground caverns, with enough space between the floor and ceiling for vast carriages to hang from the beetles' backs as they crawled along their designated routes.

These smugglers' offshoots, however, were no bigger than five men wide and perhaps seven feet tall. If anyone had been traveling with him, Coal would feel claustrophobic.

It also meant that if he did happen to encounter somebody down here, there would be no avoiding them. They would either have to cordially saunter past one another or engage in a confrontation. Fleeing would not be a viable option. Not only would it be simple for his pursuer to catch him, but if he wandered down the wrong path in a panic, he'd never find his way back.

Coal walked down the tunnel for a long time without incident. There was more space in between each tunnel opening than he expected—it was close to three hours before he reached the second tunnel he was meant to enter. The sun would be starting to set soon.

Or that is what he guessed, anyway. He did not own a watch and it was impossible to keep track of time in the dim tunnels.

Another difference between the official Houndsvein routes and these were that there was very little lighting set up. His vision had adjusted to the dark, but he was grateful for any sliver of light he could get down there. It made the whole affair feel less crushingly bleak. Like he wasn't some spirit wandering through underground graves.

He shuddered at that image, not knowing why it had come to mind. In his head, his father's blue ghost was looking at him expectantly.

He tried to think of something else. He thought of the Starlite's dancer, White Rose, basked in that blue light. The music stirring her hips, coursing through her entire body. The club pulsing with her energy.

It worked. For a while, at least.

As he traveled down the second tunnel, he thought of nothing else but that white-furred raccoon. The music she danced to then led him to the conversation he'd had with Fanaleese. Maybe he would get the chance to listen to some Mal Dala when he was in Soponunga.

If this is a big enough event, maybe they'll play the opening festival, he thought. But Mal Dala hadn't been active in a long time. *Maybe a reunion show. The beavers are going all-out with the grand prize, maybe they're doing the same with the entertainment.*

It was unlikely, but it kept his mind occupied as he stared at the dirt walls monotonously passing by.

Another couple hours later, he came to an opening in the side of the tunnel that was not another pathway, but rather a circular area seemingly meant for camping.

Coal referred to his map and was dismayed to find this area was not marked by Venny's brother. Or was it meant to be this third opening? Or were the marked openings only supposed to indicate other passages?

The uncertainty was crippling him, and either way, if this was a place to sleep then he felt he should probably sleep. He wasn't sure what the exact time was, but his eyelids were heavy and his body was sore from several hours of uninterrupted walking. He had only paused once to pee on the ground, which felt barbaric, but he had seen no other option.

He backtracked several dozen feet and relieved himself again before returning to the circular opening to make camp.

There was an unlit torch attached to the wall, but Coal had no way of lighting it, so he remained in uncaring darkness. He set his bag down, which was a shockingly great relief.

He plopped his ass on the dirt and leaned his head back against the wall. The holster dug into his side uncomfortably, reminding him that he was wearing it. A fact that had slipped his mind at some point in the intervening hours. He unbuckled it and scooted it away from him, though still within reach.

From his bag he pulled out some of the dried insects he'd packed. He snatched a handful and tossed them in his mouth. The salty crunchiness soothed him a little, but not much.

The ground was warmer than he thought it'd be, but it was nowhere near comfortable. Coal shockingly found himself yearning for the mild comforts of Fanaleese's supply room. At least there he didn't feel like an intruder could shoot him in the gut at any moment.

Claustrophobia began to sink in deeper. He closed his eyes in an effort to make his brain forget where he was.

But he could feel the walls around him. Closing in. The weight of the world above collapsing the tunnels. Trapping him.

He unavoidably thought back to the incident with his father.

Coal and Von used to work at one of Muta Par's libraries, in the city's biggest and nicest branch. It was set into the cliffside directly by the waterfall at the city's epicenter. Just across the river was city hall, and at the top of the waterfall was a beautiful view of the Palace and the Houndstooth in the distance.

The Houndstooth was a massive tree, far older and bigger than any other tree in the forests of Ruska. Maybe even the entire world. It towered thousands of feet tall and hundreds of feet wide.

Its branches grew no leaves, leading many to believe the tree was long dead. The tree's girth blocked the only way out of the valley where they all lived. No one in Ruska had left the kingdom in countless years. Hundreds. Thousands, possibly. Its bark was black and sharp, more akin to rock than wood. No blade nor bullet could penetrate it.

The Houndstooth was immutable.

Looking at it always creeped Coal out. A grotesque, jagged thing reaching out into the sky. Trapping them.

Von performed janitorial work in the library. Before that, he was a construction worker, and had actually built the newest section of the library many years earlier. But after an accident left one of his legs permanently injured, he had to cease strenuous manual labor. Coal was able to secure his father a job with a light workload in the library where he was employed. He wasn't thrilled about it, but his father had to earn money somehow.

Coal enjoyed his quiet, simple life as a librarian. He found pleasure in the organization and in helping others track down books they were specifically searching for or leading them to the perfect recommendation. The job also came with plenty of downtime, during which he could relax and read. He would often be found near the library's entrance in one of their plush chairs, reading a novel, awaiting someone who needed assistance.

Working together was awkward at first. Von's first day on the job was only a few weeks after engaging in a heated argument with Coal about his mother. The fight was initiated at a point after they'd both grown irritable being around each other so much, with Von laid up at home in recovery. The tension had boiled over.

The biggest source of discontent between the men had always been the subject of Coal's mother.

He had never known the woman. The only thing he knew about her was that she was around for the first couple years of his life, but was gone before he could form any real memories of her.

But Von refused to ever speak about her as Coal grew up. Even now that he was thirty years old, he could not pry any information about the woman from his father.

Coal did not know his mother's name.

He did not know what she looked like.

He did not know what she had done for a living.

He did not even know if she had left them or if she had died.

Von would not divulge anything about her. Not the smallest detail. Coal asked about the color of her eyes once, testing the waters to see if his father would crack at all, but the man clammed up and clumsily changed the subject.

By the time of the accident, Von had been working at the library for close to three years. They went in to work together and left together, but generally kept their distance during the day.

On the day of the accident, Coal had stepped into one of the back rooms to sort through some paperwork that his boss had given him. He needed to isolate himself to focus and get it done quickly so that he could get back to reading *The Suns of Daranakla*.

But he had found Von in the room, emptying out a trash can. The old fox looked up at his son, his ragged fur graying. He muttered a quick hello.

"I'm just about done in here," he then said.

"It's fine," Coal told him. "Take your time."

Coal took a seat at one of the tables and spread out the set of papers he'd been given. He was only beginning to read through them when a soft rumble reverberated through the floor, shaking the table at which he sat.

He looked up at Von, who had stopped moving and was looking over at his son.

"What's—"

Before Coal could finish, the shaking intensified, and the walls began to crack.

Fissures snaked up the wall and onto the ceiling, which began to crumble and fall to the floor.

Coal didn't know what to do. He sat frozen at the table while the room was practically disintegrating around him.

"Get under!" his father roared, diving underneath the table nearest him and letting out a yelp of pain with the strain of his leg. Coal scrambled under his own table and curled up with his knees to his chest. He watched his father several feet away, rubbing his leg.

He could hear others screaming out in the library. They were quickly drowned out by the earth's rumbles and by stone crashing down from above.

Coal closed his eyes and welcomed the darkness. If he was going to die, then he was going to die. Nothing to be done about it now.

As suddenly as it had begun, the earthquake ceased.

He opened his eyes, surprised to discover that he was not dead. He looked over at the other table and saw that his father was alright too.

They both crawled out from under their respective tables and embraced each other.

"You're okay?" Von asked as he pulled away. Coal nodded, still too stunned to speak.

It was then he turned to exit the room and saw that rubble blocked their means of escape. In fact, half of the room was blocked off from them, the ceiling having collapsed. The ceiling from the second floor had fallen too and was preventing them from moving upward. They were trapped in the back half of the room with no food or water.

"What are we gonna do?" Coal desperately asked his father once he regained his voice. "We're fucked."

"Do not say that," said Von, who had always discouraged Coal's use of foul language despite him being an adult now and in spite of how often he himself used it. "For now, we wait. There will be rescue parties."

"When?"

Von furrowed his brow. "I do not know," he replied. "I suppose it depends on how much of the city was affected, and how badly. I would think that city hall was definitely affected and that would be a high priority."

"So then they'd cross the river and get to us, right?"

"Maybe. Or maybe there are other places hit worse that need help sooner. Or buildings that offer more important, vital services that have to be tended to. It is impossible to know from our position. It is entirely possible it may take a few days."

Coal then panicked for several hours. He screamed for help, banged on the stone walls, tried and failed to move debris. Anything he moved just caused the pile to shift and more to tumble down from above. He felt useless and helpless.

As it turned out, Von's estimate of a few days was incorrect.

After a week, still no one had come to their aid.

The two were sustaining themselves on water from the nearby waterfall. One of the larger cracks in the exterior wall was large enough for them to slip an arm through and get some splashes from the waterfall on their palm to lick up. It took a long time and a lot of licks to quench their thirst, but they had nothing better to do—Coal's novel had unfortunately been left out at a desk in the lobby—and it was keeping them alive. They also periodically waved their arm around outside the crack, in hopes that someone would spot them and come to their rescue.

A few more days passed and Von was growing weaker. Coal's stomach was wrenched with hunger pangs, but he could fight through them as long as he got some water. His father was nearly twice his age, though. The lack of food was taking a much larger and visible toll on him.

Von sat in the corner of the room, too weak to move. Each day, Coal struggled more and more to get the man up and over to the crack in the wall to fetch himself some water. Eventually Coal had to do it himself, having his father lick the droplets off his palm.

He died waiting for the rescue party.

Coal sat in that ruined room with his father's corpse for a day before the idea started creeping in.

It was a horrible thought, the worst he'd ever had.

But it had been nearly two weeks since the earthquake now, and he had no idea when help was going to finally come. If it ever would.

If he was going to survive, he needed to eat.

And so one day, after thinking it over for an hour or two while continually licking meager droplets of water off his palm, Coal crawled over to his father's body and began to unbutton the man's shirt.

He stared down at his father's orange arm, speckled with the black and gray fur of age.

At that point, he retched. Then retched again, and again, and probably would have thrown up if there was anything at all in his stomach.

But he convinced himself it had to be done.

He lifted his father's arm and bit down on the flesh.

His fangs sunk into the tender meat and pulled away a chunk. He chewed on the piece of arm, gnashing up the raw meat with the strands of hair.

The taste was vile. Coal had never eaten meat before.

Once he started, he couldn't stop. Hunger overtook him, infecting his mind, banishing the thought of anything else but eating. Consuming.

When his head finally cleared and he returned to reality, he was horrified to discover he had stripped his father's arm down to the bone.

He pushed himself away from the body, slamming himself into the library wall, and then realized he was no longer alone in the room.

A translucent blue figure stood over by the pile of rubble.

It was his father.

"What in the fuck?" he blurted out, half-screaming.

The ghostly Von frowned. "Please restrain yourself," he said. He then looked down at his own corpse and said, "Although I know this must be a troubling experience for you."

"Yeah, no shit it is," said Coal.

His father let that one slip.

"What's going on?" Coal then asked. "Am I hallucinating? Am I losing my mind?"

He knew that Flesh Eaters were sometimes those who had been deemed rabid. Ravenous individuals who had lost all control of themselves. Maybe that was happening to him now. His mind was slipping away.

"I do not know," the blue figure said. The blue figure that was quite possibly the ghost of his father.

Assuming he wasn't going rabid.

"Are you feeling okay?" his father then asked.

Coal shrugged. He was once more losing his ability to speak. His throat felt dry. The acrid taste of his father was still fresh on his tongue. He had short, orange hairs stuck between his teeth.

"I do not think you are ill," said Von. "But I cannot say I know why we are able to speak. Perhaps—"

"No," Coal said, suddenly able to form a word, albeit only a one-syllable word. After a few moments mustering his strength, he said, "You need to stop talking. This…this is fucked." He didn't know how else to describe it.

But, amazingly, his father listened. He stood on the other side of the room, glowing that eerie blue color, for almost half an hour before fading away without another word.

Coal blinked, closely watching the spot where his father's spirit had been a second ago. When Von did not reappear, he slumped over and breathed deeply, trying to relax.

He wanted to force himself to go to sleep, to erase the day from his mind, but sunlight still shone through the wall's cracks and the meat had reenergized his body.

For the rest of the evening, Coal distracted himself by imagining what was going to happen in part three of *The Suns of Daranakla*. He had about two hundred pages left in the book—it was a meaty volume—and he spent the night writing an ending in his head. He gave it a more romantic bent than the actual book would probably contain.

The next morning, he awoke and gasped at the sight of his father's fleshless arm. Part of him had thought (or hoped) that everything had been a dream and that his father was still alive.

Much to his regret, he was also hungry.

He consumed some water first, drinking for half an hour and attempting to gather the courage to eat another meal.

Then he crept over to Von's slack body, moving around to the other, untouched arm.

After taking a deep breath to steel himself, he bit down.

At the conclusion of the meal, in which he limited himself to only half the arm, Von's ghost again entered his vision.

"Hello, son," said Von.

Coal was not any more prepared for the encounter than he was the first time. Again he scrambled away and demanded the ghost not speak, which he obliged.

It went on like this for another four days. Coal would eat some of his father, and immediately afterward Von's ghost would appear and attempt to speak with him, which he'd decline.

Soon Coal accepted that he was losing his mind, driven to madness by the act of consuming his father's flesh. The delusion seemed to last longer the more he ate, the more he digested.

Coal tested this theory one day by only eating a small sliver of meat. The blue ghost appeared after he swallowed, though this time it only remained for a couple minutes.

A day later, Coal was starting to lose hope. Three full weeks had passed since the earthquake. But then a burst of sunlight shot through the room and someone began to clear away the rubble.

Any joy and gratitude he felt was swiftly washed away by fear and regret.

The officers who were working with the crews to clean up Muta Par's destroyed buildings restrained him upon seeing his father's marred corpse. Both arms and one leg were eaten down to the bone, only tiny bits of flesh and sinew left dangling from the pale white.

He pleaded with the officers to let him go free. They all knew what had happened, it was plain as day. He had only done it to survive. Surely they could make an exception. He knew the law, but he wasn't *really* a Flesh Eater.

But there were no exceptions under the Dirt King's rule.

All that mattered was that he had eaten flesh. The context was irrelevant.

He was officially deemed a Flesh Eater, and he had to be taken away.

After three weeks of being confined to that half a room, the thought of being hauled away to some other miserable place where he'd be stuck for the rest of his life opened up a pit in Coal's stomach.

By some stroke of luck, one of the arresting officers was Monol Rened, an old friend of his father's. The two men had worked construction together before Monol had decided to apply his brute strength as an officer of the law instead.

Monol told his associates that he would handle transporting Coal. He ushered him far from the scene of Von's body, far from the eyes of the other officers, and told Coal to run.

He told Coal there would be no avoiding documenting the offense, that he would be registered as a Flesh Eater. But Monol was sympathetic to the reason, and he cared about both Coal and Von. He would tell the others that Coal escaped his custody and accept whatever punishment was doled out.

Coal did not have to think twice about the offer. He thanked his father's friend and fled Muta Par with haste. No time to even stop by his home and gather clothes or food or money. Those were things he'd have to worry about when he could slow down.

Coal's eyes shot open in the dung tunnels, his heart racing and his breaths staccato. For a second he had thought he was back in that library room with his father's rotting body. With his father's ghost.

But he was in the Houndsvein.

And he was alone.

9

COAL WOKE FROM HIS fitful sleep with a start. Someone was in the tunnel with him.

He sat there frozen, listening for the footsteps again. It took him several seconds to come to his senses and grab the gun by his side. He aimed it at the dark opening, waiting for the person to reveal themselves.

Minutes passed in silence. All he could hear were his own shallow breaths. His ears perked up, flicking in each direction trying to locate the source of the sound.

Nothing.

He relaxed, lowering the gun. The dream he'd been having about the earthquake in Muta Par must have put his whole body on edge. Made him imagine danger was afoot.

For what was probably the hundredth time, he wished that Zank was here underground with him. Venny and Marl, too. The wolverine could certainly handle some stupid smuggler.

Coal tried to fall back to sleep, but he was too restless. His mind spun with thoughts of marauders and earthquakes and blue spirits.

It might already be morning, but it was entirely possible that he had only been asleep for an hour or two. The tiny area he'd camped out in looked exactly the same as it had when he arrived. No brighter, no darker.

In any case, he was energized. More out of fear than restfulness, sure, but energized all the same. He could bear walking for a few hours.

He stuffed his few possessions into the knapsack and referred to the map one more time before setting off. It was still unclear to him whether this area had been marked on the map, but the hastily-drawn legend in the bottom right corner clearly stated that the circles were "Tunnels," and there was no way to argue that this small round room was a tunnel. He'd have to take his chances and assume it was not included. Maybe it was a new addition to the tunnel system since Venny's brother had last traveled through it.

Coal trundled down the pathway, ears still on high alert for any subtle sound in the distance before or behind him.

Soon he came to the main thoroughfare that Venny had pointed out. At the moment it was empty, and Coal appreciated the wide open space and the comparatively bright light it provided.

Without knowing what time of day it was, he was not sure whether any beetle carriages would currently be in operation. There were a few that ran during late hours, but those were rare and not during the wee hours of the morning. If they were running, though, that could possibly explain the noises that had awoken him. He did not realize how close he had been to the tracks.

The next tunnel he needed to go down was at the other end of this one, and it was in the opposite wall than the one from which he'd emerged. He crossed the wide tunnel, looking up at the railway fastened to the ceiling, wondering what material it was built from and why the beetles needed to stay on a specific track. Or how the handlers even enforced it.

While he pondered this pointless musing, he kept close to the wall, counting each tunnel offshoot as he passed it, wondering which of them had been officially dug by the workers who created the Houndsvein and which were dug by criminals looking to avoid detection.

Like himself.

He dragged his claws along the dirt wall, scraping tiny chunks of dry earth off onto the ground.

Etched into the wall were unrecognizable symbols. He almost hadn't noticed them, and at first mistook them for plain nail-scratches like what he was creating, but they had distinct patterns and were carved much deeper into the dirt.

Coal took a minute to stop and more closely examine the markings. Each one was roughly half the size of his palm. None were any letters that he was familiar with, and in fact they looked more like drawings than writing. There were triangles with varied amounts of slashes in the sides, squiggly lines, overlapping rectangles—but as he moved down the line of symbols, Coal started to find common lettering.

Someone had scrawled underneath a collection of symbols "The moon dims," and elsewhere was written "The child is trapped."

He had no idea what the writing meant, but it was effectively creeping him out. Further down the wall, someone had simply written the word "Recedes" over and over, written so many times that the letters sometimes overlapped each other and created a dizzying mess of markings.

It was then he heard a great rumbling ahead and above. The clacking of colossal insect feet against the railway's sturdy material, whatever it may be.

Coal watched the ceiling and after a few seconds, the beetle appeared.

Beetles were the second-largest known creatures in Ruska, behind snails. Its body was immense, easily the size of his father's house back in Muta Par. The exoskeleton was dark brown, nearly black, allowing the insect to blend in with the dirt ceiling. Two thick antennae poked out from the curved shell of its head, their tips a dull orange color. Its six meaty legs skittered along the ceiling, clinging tightly to the rails.

Maybe the rails are easier to grip than the dirt, especially with a carriage hanging from their back, he thought as he watched the beetle move.

The carriage that hung from the beetle was roughly the same size as its body. It was a brilliant white with gold trim, contrasting with the shell of the creature that carried it. There was a door on either side of the carriage, which could hold around fifty people, though it was slightly cramped at full capacity. It hung suspended from the beetle by a thick rectangle of metal (painted gold to match the trim), which attached to a black metallic harness strapped around the beetle's thorax.

It had been many years since Coal rode one, but this carriage appeared distinctly nicer than the one he and his father traveled in. That carriage had consisted simply of a few rows of seats, four people to a row, with an aisle in the middle dividing them. Not especially fancy, but comfortable. Plush seating, drink service, food for longer trips. Not the cramped, horrible conditions that Venny described, though maybe the cheaper ones had devolved in the intervening years. The beetle scuttling above him now looked like a larger, more expensive one that had private rooms available for rent. The beetles that could carry those were some of the biggest things Coal had ever seen in his life. They always left him gawking when he watched them loading at the station.

He stopped walking and pressed his body flat against the wall, hoping to remain unseen by any onlookers passing by. His fingertips brushed against the mysterious writing, sinking into the divots.

They don't know how lucky they have it, he thought as he observed the people overhead. Standing still had caused the soreness in his feet to set in. He would give anything to be able to sit down and be pulled the rest of the way to Soponunga.

Before too long, the beetle was once more out of sight and Coal continued his trek down the tunnel, listening for any other incoming travelers either by carriage or on foot.

No others showed up by the time he reached the next tunnel. Part of him was glad he'd gotten the chance to see one of those beetles again. He was always awestruck by their size.

Plus, it had banished the strange messages from his mind and livened up his excruciatingly boring journey.

He was close to halfway done by now according to the map, making good time (he assumed), but he'd have to throw a party once he saw real sunlight again.

Once he was in the next offshoot, he found himself deeply missing the illumination in the main thoroughfare.

It had taken a while to affect him yesterday, but today it only took around forty minutes down the next tunnel before the unending dark started to frustrate him. His night vision helped him to see farther ahead than most, but still he walked into darkness, the only thing visible being dirt walls on either side of him. It was making him anxious, twisting his stomach in knots.

If Father were here, he'd at least be able to provide some light, Coal thought, imagining the blue glow of Von's spirit form lighting up the path ahead.

He was tickled by the morbid image, surprised it had come to him. It was the first time he had thought about the ghost without freaking himself out. He had even almost chuckled!

Just as he was congratulating himself, he heard it again.

Some sort of clomping. A heavy footfall.

He was too far from the main beetle route now for it to be the rumbles of their track.

A bear? Or a tapir?

It also sounded like it could have been a boar or a moose, if any of them could even comfortably fit in the cramped tunnels. Both the bears and moose largely kept to themselves in the east, and hardly any boars ever left the Mudlands; Coal could not think of a logical reason they would be using secret tunnels on this side of the kingdom.

Whatever it was, it was ahead of him. And it was coming closer.

Coal halted and fumbled to pull the gun from its holster. He aimed it straight ahead, his arms trembling. Then he remembered to click the safety off and aimed it again, his entire body now trembling.

Kneecaps. He had to take out the kneecaps.

Kneecaps are so fucking small, he whined. *How am I gonna be that accurate?*

He then hoped that the smuggler was a boar. Boars at least had larger kneecaps than most others. If they were a boar, they could easily pummel him to death, but at least he'd have a marginally better chance of shooting the person's kneecap.

I guess this is the tunnel I am going to die in.

The stomping was loud now and gaining speed. They would be upon him in only a few seconds.

His finger was on the trigger. His fur stood on edge.

When the figure materialized from the darkness, Coal could not find it within himself to fire. Mostly because he had no idea what in the hell the thing was.

The creature before him was like nothing he had ever seen before. It was most assuredly not a boar or a tapir. It looked familiar, yet wrong.

It walked on six legs, causing Coal to think for a second that perhaps it was a baby beetle, but the amount of legs was all it shared in common. At the end of each leg was a three-pronged hoof that clomped in the dirt. The animal's skin was slick with a sickly sheen to it, smooth except for areas where the flesh raised up in malformed bubbles that jiggled as it moved, as if they were full of liquid.

The animal's face was hardly a face. Its head extended into a long, thick snout that snarled with jagged fangs, though it seemed like half its teeth were missing. It had one single large eyeball in the center of its head with a pupil that floated around, looking in every direction mindlessly.

But then its drifting pupil finally landed on Coal and the animal realized it had company.

And so it wanted to greet him. By leaping at him.

Coal was knocked out of his daze by the creature's sudden movement and dove to the side just before it headbutted him. He slammed into the wall, dirtying his fur.

The creature careened head-first into the ground, letting out a gargled screech. Blood erupted from the place of impact, and Coal saw that it had knocked one of its own teeth loose.

It stood, stumbled into the opposite wall, and barked in surprise. Coal had no clue if its range of vision was improved or worsened by having one big eye in the middle of its head.

He was raising his gun to shoot at it, no longer worrying about kneecaps, when the thing leapt sideways without even so much as glancing in his direction. They collided, smashing Coal into the wall again and loosening his grip on the pistol. It fell to the ground and was incidentally kicked further away by the animal when it landed and scrambled to its feet.

Coal clutched his stomach and tried to catch his breath. The wind had been knocked out of him. He gasped for air and staggered toward the gun, but the grotesque animal stood between him and the weapon.

It screeched in rage again, an irritatingly high-pitched scream that was wet and throaty. It now faced him head-on and he stopped moving, waiting to see what it was going to do next.

While they stared each other down, Coal was able to get another good look at it despite the dimness of the tunnel.

When it had crashed onto the ground, some of the bubbles on its face had popped. There were now splotches of green and yellow on the animal's face as well as staining the ground a few feet away, mixing with its blood. Coal noted that it bled red just like everything else in the world.

It was then he understood why the monstrosity looked familiar at first. The animal reminded him of a ventem, the source of his father's favorite steaks back when eating animals was not outlawed.

A normal ventem had only four legs, no weird bubbly skin, and two normal-sized eyes, but he could spot the similarities beyond that. This creature was like some deformed ventem that had made its way underground.

He may have deduced what animal the creature brought to mind, but that did not explain why it was so nasty, and it did not mean that he knew how to properly confront it. Meat was banned before he was born; he had never gone ventem hunting with his father.

The abnormal ventem propelled itself forward again, and Coal once more dove to the side, sprawling out on the ground and reaching for the pistol. He landed with a thud, as did the creature behind him, and he scrambled forward a couple feet to grab the firearm, panting heavily.

He rolled over onto his back, holding the grip with both shaky hands. The safety was still off, naturally, and it was lucky that the gun hadn't fired when it clattered to the ground moments earlier.

Here we go.

He pulled the trigger.

He flinched as the gunshot blared in his ears.

The bullet whizzed right over the monster. Not even close to grazing the top of its head.

"Shit."

He cocked the gun again.

But the not-ventem rotated quickly with its six legs and pounced without hesitation. The thing was either super reckless or half braindead. Coal couldn't tell which was true.

It landed on top of him, all six legs straddling his squirming body. The muzzle of the gun pressed firmly into its throat as it barked and snapped at Coal's face.

He fired.

The creature's throat exploded in liquids of varying color and viscosity. Red blood spattered across Coal's face, as well as whatever the green and yellow stuff its skin sacs were filled with.

"Shit," he spluttered again, spitting out some of the rancid gunk that had landed in his mouth. His ears were still ringing from the first gunshot and only grew worse with the second.

Having its throat blown open did not stop the animal from continuing to thrash on top of him. If anything, it only intensified the thrashing.

The thing was blinking wildly, its pupil bouncing listlessly in the white of its eye. It bit down on Coal's throat. The sensation was unpleasant, but none of its teeth were sharp enough to puncture the skin. One actually broke off when pressed against his neck.

It was clear the animal was in bad shape even before Coal encountered it.

Was it born this way? Or had something even bigger and meaner down the way fucked it up?

Coal was having a hard enough time with this thing. If something else had done this much damage to it, he didn't stand a chance.

But that was a problem for later.

He shoved the animal off his neck, bashing it in the head with the butt of his gun and tossing it into the wall. It yelped but swiftly regained its footing, throwing its head back and forth as if trying to shake something off.

Coal couldn't help but feel sympathy for the animal, but it needed to be put down. Both because it was a threat to his own life and because there was something very wrong with it and should be put out of its misery.

He stood and took a few steps back in case it leapt again. The gun was still loaded, so he aimed it carefully at the animal's head, and fired—

—once again missing completely. Although at least this time he could reasonably blame it on the thing swinging its head so erratically. That was what Coal told himself, anyway.

The bullet lodged itself in the wall behind the animal, and the gunshot re-alerted it to his presence. For a moment, he wondered if the creature was as disoriented by a ringing in its ears as he was.

If so, it exhibited no additional signs of disorientation than it already was. It lurched toward him, tripping over its own spindly legs, cutting the distance between them quickly.

Coal fired again, hitting it in the shoulder blade and halting its progress for a few seconds. As it continued to move he squeezed the trigger again, and this time the thing's eyeball exploded in a spray of gore.

The creature's body collapsed to the ground, its many limbs twitching in light spasms.

Coal inhaled deeply, waiting a second before exhaling loudly from his mouth. Some of the monster's liquids dribbled from his chin.

"Did I do it?" he asked himself aloud. "I killed it? I killed a thing with a gun?"

He took a tentative step forward, still pointing the gun at its inert body just in case it could regenerate itself somehow. There was no actual way to magically regenerate body parts— especially not a head presumably carrying a brain—but then again, he had no idea what this unknown creature truly was or what it was capable of.

He bashed the mushy remains of its head with the gun for good measure before determining that it was indeed dead. Dead as can be. He had killed it with a gun.

Remembering his theory that something else had potentially beaten the hell out of this thing, Coal decided he needed to get out of the Houndsvein as soon as possible. As quickly as his weary legs could carry him.

Which was not very quickly, as it turned out. He was sore from walking, and the previous aches in his body were not aided by being tossed around and attacked by the beefy, disgusting animal.

But he soldiered on (not before checking to ensure nothing had been dislodged from his bag and left behind), navigating through the tunnels with extra caution. He took more frequent breaks to rest and regain his strength, and after several hours he came upon another of the circular camping areas. It was carved into the side of the second-to-last tunnel he was meant to travel, according to his map.

The amount of time it had taken him to traverse each tunnel had varied. The second half of this tunnel might take him ten more minutes or it could take him four hours. There was no sense of scale to what Venny's brother had drawn.

It could very well be just one more hour before he was out of the Houndsvein and a short walk to a comfy hotel bed in Soponunga, but it could also be another half a day's travel.

He made the choice to stop and get some sleep, especially since he still had no idea what time it was. It had been an exceedingly rough day, and he was grateful for no more interruptions after the scuffle. The ringing in his ears had mercifully subsided.

After eating a light dinner and downing another small portion of his water, Coal curled up next to the wall and lightly dozed halfway between sleep and wakefulness. Enough to be aware of any stray sounds in the tunnels, but still resting.

The Houndsvein was silent. He took deep, relieved breaths. He shivered. He had killed a thing with a gun.

It did not bother him as much as he thought it would. Not for the same reason, anyway. Mostly he felt pity for the creature.

What the hell was wrong with it? he wondered. *How did it even get down here?*

The silence provided no answers.

10

COAL EMERGED ABOVEGROUND IN a part of the valley that was thick with trees. If sunlight had been blaring down like it did in Vinnag, it would have blinded him. Still, he wanted to throw his sunlight party.

As it were, he took some cautious steps from the hollowed-out tree trunk and turned his head to each side, searching for any sign of life. There was a lone curious retno nearby, poking its head up from the bush it was eating from to see what the sudden movement was, but that was all. Its antlers were long and twisted, an adult male. Coal smiled at the animal and gave it a polite wave, but it remained absolutely still as if doing so would keep it unseen by him.

The remainder of his journey through the Houndsvein had been mercifully uneventful. He had woken up that morning feeling oddly refreshed, though his body ached immediately upon beginning to walk. But he navigated the tunnels as hastily as he could, all the while listening for any other not-ventems or smugglers, and only a few hours later found himself hiking up a shallow incline back into the world above.

He needed to orient himself. Most of Ruska looked the same, just trees and grass and bushes. Sometimes the area around a city or town would be landscaped in a different fashion, and there were certainly some geographical anomalies spread out—like the bats' cave system in the northeast, or the Mudlands where the boars preferred to dwell—but for the most part, Ruska was forest.

The map said that if he headed north, he would hit Soponunga. Evidently Coal was not as resourceful as Venny and her brother, because he did not know how to tell which direction was north unless there was a sign planted in the ground stating "North Is This Way" with an arrow pointing.

How the hell...? He tried to think back to his school days, attempting to remember if they had ever learned such a thing as how to determine the cardinal directions. Surely they had.

He could hear water flowing not far off. He knew that Soponunga was built entirely on docks over the Lunsk River, so if he followed it he should eventually reach the city. Assuming he followed it in the correct direction.

Standing around like an idiot trying to deduce how to tell east from west was getting him nowhere.

With his hooked claws he was a somewhat adept climber, so he set his pack down, kicked off his boots, and latched onto the nearest tree, digging his nails into the bark and scurrying up its side. The faster he moved, the less likely he was to fall. He knew other foxes who could somehow hold onto the side of a tree without issue, but he was not one of them.

Using his momentum, he swiftly made his way up the tree, dirtying his clothes in the process, and sat himself down on the topmost branch. From there, he could see far out into the distance, but all he saw were trees.

He carefully turned himself around, tightly gripping the thick branch that was holding him, and grinned at what he saw. Piercing through the forest canopy was a tall wooden structure which Coal knew to be the Soponunga city hall.

The building was constructed of wood and mud, just like every building there. In spite of the relatively primitive construction techniques compared to similarly-sized cities such as Vinnag or Muta Par (his father Von would never dream of using mud in his building plans), Soponunga was still a fairly advanced city. It was nowhere near as flashy as something like Vinnag's entertainment district, with its neon signs illuminating every street corner, but it had luxuries that many smaller towns lacked.

City hall was by far the tallest and most impressive structure in the city, lending to the importance the beavers placed on their leaders. The mayor of Soponunga was a much more well-regarded figure by his residents than was the one in Vinnag, where it was unspoken but widely recognized that the Garnas called the shots.

The building rose into the sky in rectangular tiers, which grew narrower the farther up you went, finally culminating in a wooden mast boasting the city's flag. It waved lazily in the breeze now, dyed a calming blue with a green circle in the middle.

Coal did not know what the flag was meant to represent, but he was glad to see it all the same. It didn't look far, and now he knew which way was north.

He gingerly made his way back down the tree, pulled on his boots and bag, and set out for the city.

While traipsing through the forest, he encountered a few more retnos. There was an entire family (an incredibly rare sight with the animals' population decrease) grazing by the river, which Coal had found and began to follow upstream.

He made a mental note: *Following the Lunsk upstream is north.* The river zig-zagged a bit, but was generally pretty straight. It could be a decent marker if he found himself lost in the wilderness someday, which was not unlikely.

His legs were killing him. He hoped for some time to rest before the race in a couple days so that he would be in prime condition.

Renting a spider should not be too difficult in a city as large as Soponunga. Once he signed up for the competition and secured a mount, he could go off and relax until it was time to race.

Maybe should get some test laps in to shake the dust off, though.

The remainder of his walk was devoid of any other fauna, which was a mild disappointment, but it was great to finally reach the entry archway of Soponunga.

At this juncture, the Lunsk River curved westward before again turning north, then east, then northward again, essentially making a C-shape. It was an enormous river, large enough to fit an entire city within its width. Soponunga sat above the river on labyrinthine docks, each varying in width to support rows of buildings, with short bridges connecting from one major dock to the next.

There was a wide, plain wooden bridge that jutted out over the Lunsk, allowing entry into Soponunga. Extending skyward from the middle point of the bridge was a thick, intricately-carved arch with the city's name as well as a phrase in the language of the beavers that Coal could not translate: BUHN LASAK MON'TO NI.

Several people were milling in and out of the city across the bridge, either by foot or by wagon. Coal joined them.

As he crossed the bridge, being around people for the first time in a couple days and brushing elbows with them, he grew paranoid about somebody being a Palace operative and spotting him in the crowd. Not for the first time in his life, he lamented the abnormal coloring of his fur. Hard to disguise yourself as a typical fox when you looked markedly different from most of them.

Coal felt more eyes on him than ever before, and every pair could potentially belong to a Stinger. His skin crawled with the thought of some unknown entity cataloging his every movement, waiting for their moment to strike.

But his last confirmed sighting was in Vinnag, and up to this point he had been reliably traveling south, so he had some hope that they would assume he was staying consistent and would not have backtracked northward. It was possible he would have a few days, enough to power through the race, before anyone from the Palace caught the faintest whiff of him in Soponunga.

He pushed the thought from his mind as he took his first step onto the docks, the city proper, and breathed in some fresh river air.

Soponunga was noticeably more vibrant than Vinnag. While the latter had many run-down, abandoned, dead areas, by contrast Soponunga was brimming with life. It helped that the city looked much more naturalistic with all its wood buildings, as well as being surrounded by water with no ugly perimeter wall blocking the view of forest on either side of the river. The sounds of rushing water being audible everywhere also lent a soothing melody to the air.

Decorations adorned every building, every streetlamp—practically every inch of the city. Between colorful posters, beautiful potted plants and flowers, and mesmerizing water features which were the beavers' specialty, there was always something to catch one's eye while traversing the city's wooden streets.

All he'd had to eat for nearly seventy-two hours was dried fruit and insects, so the impulse to stop at a restaurant and munch on something substantial was at the forefront of his mind. With his limited funds, though, it would be smarter to see how much a spider rental was going to set him back first. If he blew his chance at competing in the race because he bought a sandwich, he would feel extraordinarily foolish.

Maybe if I can find Nomak, he'd be willing to buy me a lunch…

It was a selfish thought, but Coal hoped for it nonetheless. Garna Nomak was not lacking in money to throw around, anyway. He could spare a sandwich.

So Coal commenced his search for the Longowosk Hotel.

Every store and restaurant he passed had handwritten signs propped up next to their doors advertising some sort of Soponunga Spiderback Showdown Special they were offering. Some restaurants had discounted lunch specials, while others offered limited-time appetizers themed around the race (though regardless of what the food literally was, calling it a "glazed spider egg" sounded highly unappetizing to Coal). A

candle shop was having a two-for-one sale on their large candles, while a weapons shop had twenty percent off bulk pur-
chases of bullets. No matter what the establishment was
selling, they were trying to capitalize on the increased foot
traffic the race was bringing in.

Coal's stomach rumbled as he traversed the docks. An impressive building a few blocks ahead towered high above the
others. He could not see any signage on it, but he suspected it
might be the Longowosk.

The hotel was painted a pastel yellow with stripes of orange
in varying thickness running down its side. It was positioned
on the very edge of the city, with one side of it overlooking the
river while the other looked out onto Soponunga's docks.
There were six rows of wide, floor-to-ceiling windows leading
up the building with most of their drapes drawn to conceal the
guests inside. Rooms with a view of the river all had spacious
balconies with weather-worn furniture. It was one of the biggest hotels Coal had ever seen, and seemed like the type of
extravagance Garna Nomak would enjoy. A deck extended out
further onto the river on the hotel's bottom floor. On the deck
was a circular bar and plenty of tables and lounge chairs. It
was covered in people sunbathing, drinking, and merrily eating food together.

Maybe Nomak will buy me lunch out on that deck.

His two greatest dreams in life were for his criminal record
to be expunged so that he may finally maintain some sem-
blance of peace in his life again, and for someone to buy him
lunch right now.

He sauntered up to the entrance, which was located on the
side of the building opposite the river deck. Thick, heavy doors

gave way to an elegantly-decorated interior. Coal's first, un-wanted thought was that Nomak would love to get this carpet between his meaty toes.

The check-in desk was directly in front of the entryway, staffed by slim beavers in slick yellow suits to match the ho-tel's exterior. As Coal approached, one of them asked, "Can I help you with something?" She wore a pleasant smile on her face, which Coal was compelled to return.

"I'm supposed to meet some friends of mine here," he said. It was not strictly true, but close enough. The truth's cousin. "I was wondering if you could tell me where to find them?"

Still smiling, the beaver said, "I can't divulge information such as a guest's room number, but if you tell me their name I can look them up and get a message to them."

That was reasonable, but Coal was not itching to put his real name out there. That was all Nomak knew him by, though, if the man even remembered him at all.

Then an idea came to him.

"My friend's name is Nomak," he told the woman. "Could you just let him know that Lightbulb is here to see him?" Her smile faltered and gave way to an odd look, to which he said, "It's just a joke between us. He'll understand."

"Right away, sir. Feel free to wait in the lobby if you'd like, or out on our deck. We have a fully-stocked bar and a restau-rant menu."

Even if he couldn't afford to order anything, waiting on the deck sounded nice. "I'll be out there," he told her, and she said she would inform his friend of his arrival.

He exited out the back side of the hotel and stepped onto the deck, immersing himself in the din of the contented guests, many of whom had to be visiting for the race. He wondered if any of them were racers, or if they were all just wealthy spectators.

He did not even grant the bar a passing glance, rushing past it to avoid temptation. He did not trust himself with the menu. There was a railing at the end of the deck devoid of anyone else, as they were all preoccupied eating and drinking at their tables.

But Coal stepped up to it and leaned against the sturdy wood, gazing down at the water below. It splashed against the deck's support posts as it rushed by, spraying stray droplets up into the wind.

The flowing water reminded him of the river that cut through Muta Par, the one whose waterfall had kept him alive after the earthquake. He found himself yearning for home, as he often did. He caught himself daydreaming, thinking that perhaps Soponunga would make a nice home once all this blew over. Right now the multitudes of people gave him anxiety, but he could see himself enjoying the city's vivacity under better circumstances.

Looking up at the sun starting to dip, he realized it was growing closer to dinner than lunchtime. He was about to pull out the last of his dried insects when there came a tap on his shoulder.

He turned and faced a smartly-dressed woodpecker who wore thin, red-framed glasses that matched the slicked-back red feathers on his head. His face had white feathers with stripes of black over his orange eyes, and red feathers covering his cheeks. Coal instantly recognized him from Nomak's office.

The bird took one look at Coal's face, clearly recognizing him as well. Still he asked, "Excuse me, sir, but are you—"

clearly he felt uncomfortable asking the question "—Light-bulb?"

Coal laughed and nodded. "Well, my name's actually Coal, but...well, it's just a joke between me and Nomak."

The woodpecker smiled meekly. "Okay. The Garna is seated at a table near the bar, if you would like to join us." Glancing over the bird's shoulder, Coal could easily spot the anteater in another dazzling suit, laughing boisterously at a table with a few others.

They all had menus in front of them.

"That sounds great, thanks," he said, trying not to sound too eager.

The bird turned and led the way.

He said, "My name is Ilio, by the way. I am the Garna's personal assistant."

"Nice to meet you," said Coal.

Ilio already seemed much more mild-mannered than Nomak or anyone else in his immediate circle. It was a mystery how such a man would end up in the Garna's employ. Maybe he would have a chance to ask about it sometime if they hit it off. They seemed like they might be kindred spirits.

Nomak's face lit up when he spotted Coal.

"Lightbulb!" the hefty man boomed, spreading his arms out like he expected a hug, though he remained seated.

Coal wasn't sure if Nomak remembered his real name or if he was simply *Lightbulb* to him. He wasn't going to press his luck by asking and inviting irritation. "Hey there," he greeted the Garna. "Mind if I join you?"

"By all means!" said Nomak with cheer. He gestured around the table and introduced his companions in turn.

Seated with the Garna was Ilio, a rotund shirtless beaver named Mungrus, and a deer named Hiji whose antlers were shaved down nearly all the way to his scalp.

Nomak clapped the deer on the back and said, "Hiji here's my racer. Gonna bring home that claw, ain't that right?" He smacked the man on the back again, and this time Coal noted a hint of menace to the action.

Hiji smiled weakly and nodded his confirmation. Then he said, "No doubt about it." His tone of voice was not in the least bit convincing.

Mungrus cheered and raised his glass of beer to that sentiment, pouring the entire thing down his gullet in one long swig. He burped and muttered something incomprehensible.

"What brings you here?" Nomak asked Coal, taking a sip of his own drink, some sort of pink but muddled cocktail.

There was not a single plate of food on the table, much to Coal's disappointment. The guys were just indulging in happy hour.

Coal said, "I was planning to compete in the race, actually."

Nomak's eyes widened. "Is that so?" he said.

"I used to race back in the day," Coal said with a nod. "I wasn't bad. Even won a couple times." It wouldn't hurt to fudge the truth a little to make himself sound more appealing to the man. Encourage him to open up his wallet.

"That so?" said Nomak again. "Well, best of luck to you. Not the *best*, maybe, since I need my boy here to win"—he clapped Hiji on the back again—"but *some* luck to you."

The Garna laughed at his own cleverness, and Coal joined in, thinking about his plan to win the claw himself then turn around and sell it to the man for an exorbitant price.

"Thanks," Coal said, watching the Garna take another swig of his muddy drink.

"I'm still thirsty," Mungrus interjected.

"Let's get you quenched," said Nomak. He snapped his fingers in the air to attract a waiter. He pointed at Coal and asked, "You want anything to drink?"

Coal wanted to firmly position himself on the Garna's good side, so he said, "If you're offering, I'll take whatever you're having."

The anteater grinned. "Good choice." When a waiter scurried over, Nomak ordered Mungrus another tall glass of local beer and a drink called a Rosaceous Rivulet for Coal. Ilio was only drinking water.

When everybody had their drinks, Nomak held up his own and they all clinked their glasses together. Coal had no idea what ingredients comprised a Rosaceous Rivulet, but he kicked it back with enthusiasm. When it hit the tongue it was delightfully sweet, but it burned on the way down his throat. It had been a while since he'd had any alcohol.

Nomak circled back around to Coal's presence. "Zankaras didn't tell me I'd find you here."

"He didn't know," Coal said. "It was kind of a last-minute decision, really. I only recently heard about the event and thought it sounded like a good time."

"It certainly will be!" Nomak roared. A woman at the table behind theirs jumped in surprise at his voice. The man was incapable of speaking at a normal volume.

Mungrus yelled something too with a dopey grin on his face, but his words were too slurred for Coal to parse any of it. He couldn't tell if the man was already insanely drunk this early in the afternoon or if that was how he regularly spoke.

Apparently Nomak could understand the beaver, because he nodded and said, "I'm right there with you, my friend. Would you like to join us, Lightbulb?"

Coal blinked. "Uh…" he mumbled. Mungrus looked at him eagerly. Ilio seemed uninterested in the conversation and was no help deciphering what was going on.

"Have you ever been?" Nomak asked.

Coal took a chance. "I'm not sure what it is," he said, hoping that whatever Mungrus had said involved a proper noun about which he could feign ignorance.

"First time in Soponunga, eh? Must be, if you've never heard of the Lodge," said Nomak. "It's a restaurant over by city hall. Best in the city. My treat. Think of it as a welcome present."

Free dinner.

"That sounds fantastic," said Coal, nearly spitting the words out.

Nomak clapped his hands together, then downed the rest of his second Rivulet. "Perfect! Oh, did you just get into town?" Coal nodded. "I take it you still need to sign up for the race, then?"

He did. It had kind of slipped his mind while he'd been focusing on squeezing a free meal out of the Garna.

"Yeah, actually," he said. To Hiji, he asked, "Where is it that I sign up?"

Nomak answered for the deer. "He doesn't know shit about that. Ilio signed him up. Come to think of it, I've got an idea." To the woodpecker, he said, "Take him to the signups then bring him to the Lodge later. Help him get acquainted with the city."

"Yes, sir," said Ilio dutifully.

Coal felt weird about having an assistant escort him around, but he had to admit it would be a huge help. "Thank you," he said. "I really appreciate it."

Nomak waved his words away as if he was the one being thanked. He then said, "I am now buzzed enough to spend some time in the spa. How does that sound to you?"

Mungrus said something akin to affirmation.

The two hefty men stood from the table, leaving the other three without so much as another word. Coal looked to Hiji, who sipped from his straw while looking deeply uncomfortable.

"Would you like to come with us?" Coal asked him. "It'll probably be boring, but it's something to do, I guess."

"No thank you," said Hiji, rising as well. "I will see you both at dinner." He nodded in farewell, leaving his beverage half-finished.

Coal turned and asked Ilio, "Did I do something to offend him?"

The woodpecker shook his head. "He is not usually like this, but I believe he is feeling a lot of nerves about the race. He has been anxious for the past week."

"Nomak mentioned he was having some trouble," Coal said, though he was unsure if that was meant to be private information. There was probably nothing in the world too private for the Garna's personal assistant to know. He had likely lain eyes on those photographs more times than Nomak himself had. Poor soul.

"Yes. The Garna has been somewhat hard on him in recent weeks and I think that may be affecting his confidence as well." Suddenly Ilio realized he was saying too much and he took a nervous sip of water. He then asked, "Are you ready to go?"

Coal took one more swig of his cocktail, ice clinking in the now-empty glass as he set it on the table. "Sure," he said.

"Okay," said Ilio, standing. "Let's go get you signed up for the race."

11

ILIO WAS A CHEERFUL yet not very talkative fellow. Anything said between the two of them had to be initiated by Coal. Which was fine, though Coal was not accustomed to being the person driving a conversation. Usually he was in Ilio's shoes.

They were heading toward the center of Soponunga. To their left, many blocks away, was city hall, standing tall and proud. With the famous Lodge next door, evidently.

"Where are signups?" Coal asked, as if he knew anything about the layout of the city anyway.

"Tucarumong Street," Ilio answered.

He almost didn't say anything further, but decided to mention, "I am not familiar."

"Oh. Sorry. Tucarumong is essentially 'Main Street' here. It is where the opening ceremony festival for the race will be held tomorrow. The race officials have set up a stall there for competitors to sign up and receive information about the race.

Tucarumong also has one of the city's biggest hotels, which the stall is set up near, and where most racers stay when they are here for the event."

Coal was impressed by the woodpecker's lengthy answer.

"You know a lot about how things are done here," he said. "Are you from here?"

While it was true that Soponunga was built by the beavers way back when, nowadays many different species resided there, as was the case with almost everywhere in Ruska. All of the valley's species had their own territories throughout the kingdom where their oldest lineages tended to live without any other species, such as the Mudlands for the boars or Yagos for the bats, but for the most part they all intermingled in Ruska's many townships.

But Ilio shook his head, turning down another street. Coal quick-stepped to catch up.

"No," said the bird, "I am from Varoosh. But I have worked as Garna Nomak's personal assistant for many years now, and the Garna partakes in monthly trips to Soponunga, on which I always accompany him."

It was hard to imagine someone as shy and seemingly tightly-wound as Ilio working for Garna Nomak for multiple years. Maybe he was the one who had leaked the illicit photographs. A way to ruin his boss and tear down the whole operation, give himself an excuse to scram.

Far-fetched, maybe, and completely unfounded, but fun to think about.

It had been months since Coal spent such a long period of time near a river. He loved the smell of the water on the air, the crisp freshness of it, and he basked in the smell as they navigated to Tucarumong Street. If the hotel there was where the other racers were staying, then he would probably end up booking a room as well. Or someplace cheaper, depending on their rates.

Probably the latter.

"That hotel on Tucarumong not really Nomak's scene, I assume?" Coal asked. He desperately wanted to inquire about whether Ilio leaked the photos or not, but he knew he shouldn't broach that topic. But it was just so *tantalizing*.

"No. It is one of the nicer hotels here, but the Garna prefers the Longowosk."

"One of the nicer hotels." Probably not in my price range. Figures.

"He likes the view of the river there?" That was one—probably the sole—thing that he and Nomak shared in common.

But Ilio was quick to deny that. "No, he does not care about the view where he stays. It is simply more expensive, with higher quality food and furnishings."

"Ah." Naturally.

"Where are you staying?" Ilio then asked.

Coal was shocked by the man asking a question. Taking charge.

"Uhh…nowhere yet," he replied. "I only got here a little while ago. I went straight to the hotel to meet with Nomak. I haven't looked into anything."

And it was something he was dreading. Renting a spider would surely eat up a large amount of his funds. A piece of him felt immensely foolish for investing everything into this race with no guarantee of a return.

He had not ridden spiderback in years. What were the chances of him realistically winning the race? He had already come this far, nearly killed by some strange monster in the

Houndsvein, but it was not too late to back out. His name was not yet on that signup sheet.

For now, he ignored the negative thoughts and pressed onward. He asked Ilio, "You have any places in mind? Any good recommendations?"

"Unfortunately, I am unfamiliar with a majority of the city's accommodations," said Ilio with a curt shake of the head. His glasses slid a little down his smooth beak and his red feathers ruffled in the light breeze. "I have only ever stayed at the Longowosk with the Garna."

"Oh well."

They walked to the end of the street and reached an intersection when Ilio stopped and turned to face Coal. There was no expression on his face whatsoever. He asked, "Do you mind if we make one quick stop?"

Coal shook his head, and Ilio seemed to slightly relax.

"Thank you."

He set off again, turning right onto the next street, and Coal followed. Ilio led them past a couple buildings before turning into a short, narrow alleyway. After a few strides they rounded a corner and were in a small enclosure surrounded by buildings with a single door in front of them. The tiny lot was littered with bits of trash.

At least it hasn't fallen into the water, Coal thought at the sight of the debris.

The door was unmarked, no signage on or above it. Not the type of place Coal would typically find himself. And not the type of place he would imagine Ilio finding himself, either, except when running errands for Nomak.

As if reading his thoughts, Ilio then explained, "I need to pick something up for the Garna. It will only take a minute."

He pulled open the door with a noisy creak and stepped inside. Coal entered behind him, not needing to wonder for long what kind of establishment this was.

Inside the darkened shop were shelves lined with potions and herbs of assorted colors, with names that Coal did not recognize—those of which he could read, anyway, given the proprietor's messy scrawl. It was not hard to guess that these were maybe not the most legal of substances. Myriad scents combined in the air to grant the place a stale, faintly rotten stench.

The shelves containing the multitude of bottles, jars, and baggies were all positioned safely behind a counter manned by a rough-looking sloth with a thick, jagged scar running down the side of his face and numerous patches of missing hair. He wore a scowl that Coal suspected was permanent.

There were only a few feet between the door and the sloth's counter, not much space to move around in. It was practically like a stall set up on the street, but much more cramped and uncomfortable.

"Hullo," said the sloth. Only the left side of his mouth moved, and Coal realized that the scarred side of his face was paralyzed. "What can I get you?" he growled.

Ilio was calm and collected. This was surely not an uncommon experience for him, shopping in nasty, dubious storefronts. This was like popping down to the local bakery for him.

"Three packets of hoswit," the bird requested. He then began counting tups from his pocket and placing them on the counter before the sloth.

"Fun night ahead for the two of you, eh?" the shopkeeper said with a half-grin. He tapped a long, yellowed nail on each tup and scraped it along the uneven countertop toward himself, counting them out loud in a whisper.

Ilio glanced backward at Coal with a look of embarrassment. He actually stumbled over his words when he said, "No,
no, no, not for us. It is for my boss." He swallowed loudly.

That was a lot of no's.

"My mistake," said the sloth, shrugging. He finished counting up the money and, satisfied, grabbed the product from a
tilted shelf behind him.

The man picked up a jar of some crushed yellow and brown
herb concoction (which had been sitting behind one of the labels Coal failed to read) and placed it on the counter. He
fetched a small wooden scoop and poured some of the hoswit
into three separate bags that were each only around an inch
and a half tall and wide. Not a ton of product for the amount
Ilio had just paid for it.

The sloth handed over the herb, which Ilio accepted and
hastily stuffed into his jacket pocket. "Thank you," he said,
still sounding anxious.

"Pleasure doing business."

Ilio nodded then turned and stepped past Coal back out into
the lot.

"Bye," Coal muttered, his first and last word to the shopkeeper. He exited.

Outside, Ilio was tapping his foot nervously. "Ready to
go?" he asked.

Coal chuckled. "I mean, I don't have anything to buy here,
so yeah," he said.

"Right. Of course." The bird gulped again and composed
himself. "I appreciate your patience."

"It's really fine," Coal assured him. "It only took, like, two
minutes anyway. Don't worry about it."

Ilio was on edge now, clearly not used to entertaining guests. Garna Nomak was who he spent most of his time around, and the Garna probably did not take kindly to having his time wasted.

They left through the alleyway and continued toward Tucarumong Street.

Coal took Ilio's embarrassment as a chance to pry a little. Maybe the man would be more willing to divulge some juicy details if he was feeling like he needed to make up for the errand. He asked, "So, what does hoswit do?"

For a few moments, Ilio didn't answer. But eventually, he said, "It is a performance-enhancing drug that one brews a drink with to consume, much like tea."

"So he's going to have Hiji cheat to win the race?" Maybe he needed to run back there and spend some tups on a packet of hoswit too. If others were using it and getting an edge on him…

"Not that kind of performance," said Ilio, leaving it at that.

Coal processed what he said for several seconds before it dawned on him.

"Oh," he said. "Oh. Gross."

"Yes," said Ilio. And did Coal hear a chuckle? Or at the very least an amused snort? He was making progress breaking through the bird's shell.

Ilio had seen Coal at that meeting back in Vinnag, and he had to know what they were there to deliver. So Coal said, "I've seen what the guy's working with, and I don't blame him for getting some extra help."

That did it.

Ilio burst out laughing, even stopping on the sidewalk to get ahold of himself. Coal couldn't help but laugh at the sight of the woodpecker losing it.

"It is true," Ilio sputtered when he finally caught his breath. "It is a recent development in the past couple months, though. I think someone made an unkind comment about it and now he makes sure to brew himself a cup of hoswit before meeting with his women. Which means I have to go to shops like that in every city we visit due to his predilection for—" He stopped himself before he said too much.

"For brothels," Coal finished for him. "You were gonna say brothels. C'mon, Ilio, there aren't many other words that sentence would end with," he grinned.

Ilio chuckled. "I did not say that."

"Yeah, yeah, okay." Coal then asked, "If he's so self-conscious, then why's he taking photos of it?"

"I do not have an answer for you," said Ilio. "The Garna is a complicated man."

He tickled himself with that one. Coal joined in on the laughter.

Ilio truly was a delight.

The woodpecker did not want to gossip any more about his boss, fearful that he would reveal something he shouldn't, but the conversation was now flowing much more naturally while they walked. The two discussed what Ilio's hometown of Varoosh was like (Coal had never visited a bird-built town and was fascinated by the architectural designs), as well as some of the best places to eat in Soponunga, which included the restaurant at which they would be dining later that evening.

"They have an appetizer that is bread topped with…I am not really sure what," said Ilio, "but the Garna orders a few of them every time we eat there, and it is absolutely divine. It is some mixture of cheese, seasoning, and sweet but spicy diced peppers."

It sounded pretty tasty to Coal. Walking around the city had distracted him for a while, but now that they were conversing about food, it reminded him how desperately hungry he was. But he did not want to tell Ilio that.

They soon turned onto Tucarumong Street, and it was beyond obvious that this was the epicenter of the event. A banner hung suspended over the street, strung up between two buildings, with vivid silver-painted letters spelling out THIRD ANNUAL SOPONUNGA SPIDERBACK SHOWDOWN set against the banner's light blue background. It was a gigantic sign, and yet the lettering still had to be pretty small to fit the absurd number of characters.

Colorful pennants hung from streetlamps, on the sides of buildings, and in shop windows. Some were plain, solid colors, while others bore the logos of businesses that were sponsoring racers. A select few had little representations of the racers themselves. Coal looked around and spotted one he thought might be for Hiji. It was simple enough: a green gradient with iconographic antlers.

Though Hiji's were shorn off...

Maybe it was inaccurate, or maybe it wasn't Hiji's pennant. But if it wasn't, there had to be one for him somewhere. Garna Nomak seemed the type to go all-out on an investment such as sponsoring a racer. He would want a pennant.

The registration stall was built of wood (like basically everything in Soponunga) and painted the same shade of light blue as the banner overlooking them. The event's extremely long title was also painted onto the top plank of the stall, with two gleeful beavers sitting behind it, discussing something with a raccoon and a bat.

As he and Ilio approached the table, Coal overheard some of the conversation taking place. The raccoon sounded exasperated, but the beavers were maintaining a polite, jovial demeanor.

One of the beavers, a woman wearing a wide-brimmed sun hat with blue ribbon wrapped around it (the same shade as the race's official color, of course), was telling the raccoon, "I understand that, but it's not a matter of monetary value. It is the value of the item itself, and that is one of the biggest drivers of the competition!"

The raccoon sighed, slapping a palm to her face and rubbing her forehead in frustration. "I get that. I do. I understand the concept. But it's—look, it's complicated, and I can't explain, but—okay, we need it. We can offer…" She looked to her associate and gestured at him to offer a figure.

"Triple," he said.

"Really?" the raccoon asked.

The bat nodded, then began rubbing his head like it hurt.

"Triple the value," said the raccoon. "You'd be out of your mind to pass it up. Just truly out of your gourd."

The beaver gave them an apologetic frown. "I'm sorry, I truly am, but to obtain the claw, you will have to win the race. That is the only way. It's not for sale. Would you like me to get you signed up?"

Evidently the raccoon did not want to get signed up, given the grimace and groan she then emitted.

She said, "What I'd *like* is to speak to someone who actually has the authority to negotiate a deal. Someone who's *not* out of their fucking gourd."

"There is no need to be vulgar," said the other beaver, his congenial smile faltering in the face of profanity.

"There is no need to be a moron," said the raccoon.

Coal laughed at that, capturing the attention of everyone involved.

All four turned to look at him, and Coal could feel Ilio shrink back in embarrassment at the unwelcome attention.

The bat, still rubbing his head vigorously, looked at Coal with a cocked eyebrow. His eyelids then began to flutter and his eyes rolled back in his head before he fainted, crashing onto the cobbled sidewalk.

"Shit," the raccoon muttered, kneeling down to help her friend. She glared at the beavers and then Coal in turn. "We'll be back later," she said to the beavers, though she was still looking at Coal with suspicion, as if he were the cause of her friend fainting. The heat had probably been too much for him and he was dehydrated. That wasn't Coal's fault.

Luckily, the bat's head didn't appear to be bleeding. The raccoon hoisted her friend up and began to stagger away toward the hotel two blocks away, which Coal presumed to be the one Ilio had mentioned.

"Do you require any assistance?" the beaver woman called out to the duo, a hand cupped to her mouth, but the raccoon ignored her. She sighed, but then quickly reapplied her happy face to address the newcomers. "How can I help you?" she asked Coal and Ilio.

This was it.

No backing down after this.

"I want to sign up for the race," Coal told her.

She smiled and got her papers and writing utensil at the ready. "Excellent. Coming in just under the wire! Signups close in just about an hour."

If I had dallied in the tunnels or at the hotel much longer, I would've screwed myself, he thought.

The other beaver said, "All's we need's your name, the name of your spider, and the entry fee."

"Entry fee?"

Zank had not mentioned an entry fee. Why would he, though? Why would he have had any idea there was one? Coal was an idiot for not already assuming there would be a fee to enter.

"Yes. The entry fee's four hundred tups."

"Fuck," Coal blurted out. Seeing the looks on the beavers' faces, he immediately apologized for his language. "Sorry, I just wasn't, uh…made aware of an entry fee."

That was a hefty portion of what he made off the photograph job, some of which he had already spent preparing for this trip and would need to spend on a spider and lodging. The fee would substantially eat into those costs and determine what quality of mount he could afford. Would it even be worthwhile at that point, if he was stuck with a lousy spider?

"Is there any sort of refund option available? Just in case I, for whatever reason, can't participate in the race?"

"If you sustain a serious injury or if your spider expires before commencement of the race, you can make a request to receive your fee back," the woman said.

"What if my spider sustains a serious injury?"

The two beavers looked at each other. Then the man said, "We will have to look into that."

"Okay." He did not know why that made a difference.

It hurt, but he pulled the tups from his belongings and handed them over to the beavers. The man took them gladly while the woman readied her pen.

"Name?"

"Mine or the spider's?" He was stalling, trying to conjure up an alias to use.

"Yours."

"Oh. I'm Von Rened."

She wrote that down then said, "Now the spider's."

He had no spider yet, but he couldn't freely admit that to these people. Racers didn't typically sign up for races before even having an animal on which to race.

So he said, "White Rose." He had no idea if there would be any consequence to bringing a spider with a different name than what he signed up, or if anyone officially involved in the race would even know, but he had to take the risk. He also found it odd that the first name that had come to mind for his imaginary spider was that of a burlesque dancer he'd watched.

The woman wrote that down as well and looked up at him with a smile. "You are all set." She wrote something else on a separate piece of paper, then hastily filled out a short form, which she handed over to Coal upon completion. She said, "Bring your spider to the city's stables and house it there. On the day of the race, come back here and hand that form to the person working. They will verify your information and escort you to the starting line, where your spider will be waiting."

Easy enough, assuming he had a spider by then. If not, he would tell them it died. Or he would break his own leg. Whatever he needed to do to reclaim his four hundred tups.

He thanked the beavers for their service and stepped away, walking down the colorful street with Ilio at his side.

The woodpecker said, "White Rose is a very pretty name. I look forward to seeing what your spider looks like."

"So do I," said Coal.

"What?"

Coal stopped walking and faced Ilio. The bird looked wildly confused.

"Do you know where I can rent a spider in this city?" he asked.

Ilio looked even more confused.

"Preferably for very cheap," said Coal. "I'm running low on funds and still need to book a hotel room."

"Um…" Ilio groaned, at a loss for the first time. He said, "Let me think about that."

12

EVENTUALLY ILIO CAME TO the (in hindsight obvious) conclusion that the first place they should check for spider rentals was the stable that the beavers had mentioned.

Ilio knew from assisting Hiji with his check-in that the stables were in the northeast quadrant of the city, not terribly far from the northern bridge exit.

I'd be wandering like a lost buffoon without him, Coal thought. The man really was a wealth of information.

As they headed that way, Ilio asked the inevitable question pertaining to a detail Coal hoped he'd missed.

"So, why 'Von Rened'? Is 'Lightbulb' an alias for Coal and 'Coal' is one for Von? Or is Coal a nickname?"

Coal was having such a good time with Ilio, he did not want to spoil it with talks of his sordid, unfortunate past. He was also worried that the truth would paint him in an unflattering light. At the end of the day, he *was* technically a Flesh Eater, regardless of the circumstances—and that could be a difficult truth for anyone to wrangle.

Still, Ilio *was* familiar with the criminal underworld. Far more so than Coal was. He should be able handle a little bit of shadiness just fine, if he dedicated his whole career to it.

"It's kind of complicated," Coal began, "so I won't get into the details, but there are...people after me." Better not to specify it was Palace Stingers. That would set off some alarm bells. "But no, Coal is my real name. Not a nickname or an alias. You've got the real thing. I just need to keep it out of the public sphere, if you know what I mean."

"Of course," said Ilio, sounding even more understanding than Coal expected him to. "I will not pry," he added.

"Thanks," Coal smiled. "It really is a huge misunderstanding, but...yeah, not the lightest topic of conversation."

"Believe me, I understand complicated," Ilio told him. "A person does not end up on Garna Nomak's payroll without a smidge of complication in their life."

"I guess we've got that in common, then."

Ilio glanced back at him, and Coal would have sworn he was smiling. He liked this new, more open version of Ilio that was unimaginable merely an hour ago. It was probably a side of himself that he rarely showed while working, if ever.

They had to cross a narrow bridge back out onto solid land, technically outside the city limits, in order to reach the stables. Like every spider stable, the beasts were corralled in a tangle of trees that encroached on the modest shack in which the stable's employees worked. Their green leaves were smothered by wispy white webs woven by the spiders themselves to act as their housing. There were special perimeter fences built both on the ground and in the trees to keep the huge insects from escaping. But aside from that, they were allowed to freely roam the treetops and underbrush. Typically, when a spider was stabled, a colored band was wrapped around one of its legs that corresponded to a master list kept by the stablemaster. This indicated which spider it was and to whom it belonged.

Soponunga's stablemaster was a stout frog wearing the dirtiest pair of overalls Coal had ever laid eyes on, caked head to toe in mud and webbing.

The frog did not hide his exhaustion as the two approached him. "Hello," he croaked. The man sounded at the end of his rope. This had to be the busiest week of the year for him, and Coal saw no other staff to speak of. Possibly they were among the trees back behind him, tending to spiders.

"Hi," Coal greeted him with a wide smile, trying to inject some cheer into the man's day. Deep down, he knew it would not work, but he felt the need to try anyway. "How are you doing today?"

"Y'don't have a spider wit'ya and I don't recognize ya so y'ain't pickin' one up." The stablemaster was skipping pleasantries and getting right down to business. "Whatcha want?"

Coal's smile faded and he cut to the chase. "I was hoping to rent a spider for the race," he explained. "I will be upfront with you: I do not have a large amount of money."

"And I ain't got a large amount o' spiders," said the frog. He started reading over the clipboard he held, already uninterested in the conversation. He said, "Y'know the race is in two days, don'tcha?"

Coal nodded, but the frog was looking down at the clipboard and did not see. The lack of vocal response did not deter him from continuing, though.

"I'm all out of spiders to rent. None to sell, neither, and I ain't plannin' to inspect and buy no more 'til after the race is over and done."

That makes sense, Coal admitted, but it was not ideal.

He asked, "Is there anywhere else that rents them?"

"There's the Sculio Brothers, but they're gonna fuck ya with the price. That's their specialty: fuckin' people with the price."

That did not sound good, but it was better than nothing. "Where can I find these brothers?"

The stablemaster glanced up from his clipboard and furrowed his brow.

"Ya wanna go get fucked?" he asked.

Behind Coal, Ilio suppressed a laugh.

"I don't *want* to," said Coal, cracking a smile at Ilio's reaction, "but I'm kind of in a bind here."

The frog nodded, then said, "Who'm I to judge ya for wantin' t'get fucked?" He then went on to provide directions to the Sculio Brothers' storefront, which was set up on the southeastern outskirts of the city.

"Do we have time to go out there before the dinner reservation?" Coal asked Ilio. The woodpecker nodded, then Coal asked, "Do you mind coming with me?" He was enjoying the man's company.

Ilio's cheeks puffed up, the way birds expressed smiling since they couldn't with their beaks. He said that of course he would come.

Coal thanked the frog for his assistance, then set off across the bridge back into Soponunga. He then veered toward the southern bridge out of the city, with Ilio in tow.

"That man was insane, right?" asked Coal, once they were out of earshot.

"Oh, absolutely," Ilio nodded. "He is undoubtedly having a terrible week with all the racers stabling there. I am sure many of them are high maintenance, requiring a very specific set of instructions about how to best care for their precious spider."

"Even so, I'm surprised by the amount of expletives he felt comfortable using with a customer."

"Are you uncomfortable with vulgarity now?" Ilio teased.

"No!" Coal denied. "But I'll admit I was a little shocked by how many times a stranger was talking about me getting fucked." They both laughed.

As the sun began to set, Soponunga's streetlights flicked on and cast a warm, pleasant glow on the wooden docks below. The persistent buzzing of their bulbs was like insects. Water gently slapped against the docks' support beams. The streets were still crowded, with many people shuffling into restaurants or sitting at tables outside cafés. There were many who sauntered down the street with drinks in hand, talking and laughing boisterously with their groups. Coal was unaware whether the city had much of a nightlife to speak about, or if it was a result of the influx of tourists there for the race. Surely in a city of this size there were cabaret clubs and dancehalls and hidden gambling dens. He grinned, amused by the idea of Ilio entering a nightclub like the Starlite.

"Can I ask you something?" said Coal. "It maybe sounds kind of rude, but I do not mean it that way, I promise."

"Sure," said Ilio, sounding more intrigued than put-off by the caveat.

"What do you do for fun?"

Ilio laughed. "Do I seem like the type of person who does not have fun?" he asked. "Is that why the question might sound rude?"

"Yes," Coal nodded. "I mean—shit. I mean that yes, that is why the question might come across rude, but no, you do not seem like someone who's never had fun before." Suddenly he was stumbling over himself and feeling nervous about offending this guy.

"Well, I haven't." There was silence between them for at least five full seconds before Ilio said, "That was a joke."

Coal laughed at that and was immediately put at ease once more.

"In all honesty, I do not get much time to myself," Ilio answered. "Being the Garna's assistant is a very demanding, all-hours type of job."

"That sounds shitty."

"It took me a while to get used to, but it is my 'normal' now. And the pay is good, so I cannot complain."

"I would."

"Yes, well...like I said, one does not fall under Garna Nomak's employ without some sort of complication leading them there. I am thankful for the opportunity the Garna gave me."

Coal couldn't refute that. He had only obtained this miniscule chance of buying his freedom due to his recent association with Nomak.

And the man was buying him dinner. He couldn't complain about that.

They came to the city's southern entrance and crossed the bridge. Men and women smiled cordially at them as they passed each other. Coal's boots clomped against the sturdy wood.

"So you haven't had any fun since you started working for Nomak," he said.

"That is not true!" Ilio declared. "I have had time to enjoy myself now and again."

"Doing...?"

Ilio mulled it over for a moment. Coal did not think it was a particularly difficult question, being asked what sorts of activities one enjoyed, but Ilio was a peculiar man.

"I suppose it is a fairly mundane answer, one that most people would say, but I like to read."

"I used to work in a library!" Coal said excitedly.

"Is reading a hobby of yours as well?"

"Yeah, of course. I just said I worked in a library."

"Working in a library does not automatically equate to a love of reading," said Ilio.

He supposed that was true. His father came to mind. Coal did not have a single memory of the man cracking open a book.

They veered to the left, toward a patch of webby trees spotted in the distance. Coal was surprised he had not noticed it on his way into the city earlier.

"Well, yeah, I like to read too. I haven't had a chance to in a long time, though," Coal said, which had not actually occurred to him before now. That fact saddened him. He asked, "Do you have a certain genre you like? Or a favorite series or anything?"

"I am most interested in historical fiction. There is a series I am a big fan of called *Masters of Mud* that takes place in the Mudlands six hundred years ago."

Coal laughed. "That is a terrible name for a series," he said.

Ilio chuckled as well. "That may be, but the prose is excellent and I love the characters. Come to think of it, I know for certain that another entry in the series came out that I have not yet read. There may even be two by now. The last one I read was the fifth volume." His tone was downtrodden.

"The *fifth*?" Coal blurted out. "So there might be *seven* books in the series now? That is too many books for a series with such a bad title."

Ilio looked mock-offended. "Do not disparage the *Masters of Mud* name!" he said, giving Coal a playful shove. They both laughed. "You would enjoy it."

"What makes you say that? You think you've pinned down my taste in books?"

"No, but anyone would enjoy it, because it is excellent."

Coal snickered. "Yeah, alright. I've never read any historical fiction, it always sounded too dry to me. I'm more a mystery type of guy. I always try to solve the case before the characters do, but I am never right."

"Well, you can be sure *Masters of Mud* is not the slightest bit dry."

"Not with a name like that."

Ilio practically screamed with laughter, causing Coal to jump in alarm. The bird's laughter was contagious. Evidently that was the funniest joke he had ever heard in his life.

Once he could speak again, Ilio said, "I also—it may sound stuffy after the 'historical fiction' answer, but I also quite like attending plays at the theater. Vinnag does not have much of a theater culture to speak of, however, so it has been a long while since I have seen anything."

Muta Par had a renowned theater, but Coal had never watched any of the plays put on there. Tickets were usually pricier than what he wanted to spend, given his interest level. If they were cheaper, he would have gladly checked them out on a lark. Some of their stories sounded pretty interesting to him. He told Ilio as much.

"It is a delightful experience," the woodpecker said. "You must save up for it. Especially if you are somewhere that is putting on *The Gangs of Hesh*. That one is my favorite. It has plenty of violence and intrigue for you." He grinned.

"I'll make a note of that," said Coal, returning the smile.

"I wish we had time to go see something here," Ilio said. "Soponunga's theater is breathtaking. I have never seen such an ornate stage anywhere else. Maybe on your next visit."

"That sounds like a good time to me."

By now they were coming up on a meager shack with a sign hanging on its door proclaiming it to be the storefront of the Sculio Brothers. The unimpressive building backed up against a thicket of trees, and Coal could make out some spider fencing on the ground and among the branches.

If he was being honest, the place looked shitty enough to offer him a spider for the price he could afford. Maybe the stablemaster back in the city had just meant he would be fucked by the price in comparison to the quality of the spiders.

Which was bad in its own way, but still. He would need to inspect the bugs to determine if they would even be worth riding. With his experience, he should easily be able to mark the difference between a lame spider and a winner.

They entered the shop and were greeted by two deer chanting in unison. "Welcome to Sculio Brothers' one-stop shop for all things spider and slop!"

He felt compelled to ask what exactly they meant by "slop," but he was already immensely turned off by these weird men and wanted to end the interaction as soon as he could. Ilio also refrained from inquiring further, thankfully.

Coal said, "I'm looking to rent a spider."

"Perfect!" said one of the Sculio Brothers. The men were twins and wore the exact same blue pinstripe suit with the jacket unbuttoned. A far cry from the shop's exterior appearance.

The other said, "Do you have a breed in mind?"

"An orb weaver, if you have one," Coal said. He was most familiar with orb weavers. "Any would be fine, though, if not."

Both brothers grinned toothily and knocked their antlers together. Coal had no idea what the hell they were doing, but he thought they might accidentally get tangled up in each other if they weren't careful.

One of them said, "Lucky for you, we have a few orb weavers available! We just got one in from Faranap the day before yesterday."

The name struck Coal. A shiver coursed through him.

Faranap was one of the three Flesh Eater encampments throughout Ruska, the southernmost one. Come to think of it, he remembered now that it was not very far from Soponunga. Possibly only an hour's walk.

"Do you get many spiders from Faranap?" he asked timidly.

The brothers nodded. The one on the right said, "Almost exclusively. They breed and raise the spiders there and we buy them for low, low prices to pass the savings on to you, the customer!"

Flesh Eaters were used for all sorts of cheap labor, including the breeding of spiders. It made sense that a city so close to Faranap would purchase a majority of its spiders from them.

The cost savings must be extraordinary buying from there rather than the more traditional breeders found elsewhere in the kingdom.

"That sounds wonderful," Coal said flatly. He liked to think that overall he was a cheery person, but these men's extreme, unearned enthusiasm was grating. "How much are they?"

The left brother hauled a thick binder out from beneath the counter and heaved it onto the wood with a loud *thud*. He flipped through the pages until he found what he was searching for.

He planted a fingertip on the page and read, "Our orb weavers currently range between six hundred and nine hundred tups."

Coal was sure he had misheard the man. "No, I was looking to rent, not buy," he said, just in case there had been some miscommunication.

The deer looked up from his binder and nodded. "Yes, those are our rental prices per two days with a two-day minimum."

"That's absurd," said Coal, laughing because he didn't know how else to react. That price was outrageous for a two-day rental of *any* spider breed, let alone the less-popular orb weavers.

Getting fucked was right. The stablemaster had not been exaggerating. Coal was expecting to reluctantly pay three hundred tups max.

"Do you have anything cheaper?" he asked. It was plain to see that these men would not be open to negotiations. An orb weaver was out of the question.

The Sculio Brothers nodded in tandem. Coal and Ilio both shuddered, immensely creeped out by the deer.

Flipping through the binder, the deer on the left said, "I have the perfect spider in mind for you. One moment…" Near the back of the binder he stopped and pointed his finger on the page again. His nails were neatly trimmed. "Our last hacklemesh weaver."

Coal had never ridden a hacklemesh before, but he was familiar with the breed. They were small and brown, with a smaller abdomen than an orb weaver, similar in size to its thorax. Easier to ride, but the breed had a tendency to get tripped up on itself due to a lack of coordination. Not the best spider for racing, more for casual riding.

It was not his first choice, but he could maybe make it work in a pinch, and this was certainly the tightest pinch he had ever been in.

"How much?" he asked, still yearning for a good orb weaver.

"Five hundred tups for two days with a two-day minimum."

"Are you kidding me?" Coal half-shouted, having to restrain himself. The prices were ludicrous. "No one who knows anything about spiderback racing would pay that much for a hacklemesh. That's insane."

The deer brothers were unbothered by his outburst. "Unfortunately, that is the lowest price we have available for a spider, sir," the one with the binder said, offering Coal his fakest frown. "There are many people in town for the race, trying to obtain that oh-so-tantalizing prize. It's a matter of supply and demand, you see?"

"It's insane," Coal repeated.

The binderless Sculio Brother shrugged. "Would you like to proceed with the rental?" he asked.

Coal shook his head and promptly stormed out of the shack.

He was kneeling down several feet away, staring at the grass, when Ilio caught up to him.

Ilio crouched as well, looking concerned. "Are you okay?" he asked.

"No," Coal sighed.

The plan, as uncertain as it had been to start with, was shot.

Without a spider, there was no race. Without a race, no prize. No prize, no money. No money, no future.

"Is there anything I can do to help?" Ilio asked. He placed a friendly hand on Coal's shoulder.

But there was nothing to be done. Not unless he could somehow convince Nomak to sponsor him for the race too, which was unlikely.

He said, "No. I'm just..." He trailed off, feeling ashamed to tell Ilio. But it spilled out. "I'm just fucking broke. I can't afford the spider. If the entry fee wasn't so damn high and if I didn't need to pay for a hotel room, I could get that shitty hack-lemesh, but..."

There was nothing else to say. Ilio rubbed his shoulder, searching for any words of encouragement. Coal knew he would come up short. Nothing would pull him out of this.

But then, miraculously, Ilio found the perfect words.

"Do you want to head to dinner?" he asked.

Coal looked at him and smiled. Ilio smiled back at him, his hand still on his shoulder. He felt comforted by the man's presence.

"That's exactly what I need right now," said Coal. "A free meal. A free expensive meal."

Ilio stood, and Coal followed suit.

"Then we shall get you one," Ilio said.

"Lead the way."

"I was planning on it. I have been all day," the bird joked.

Before they set off, Coal looked him in the eye and said, "Thank you."

For a moment Ilio broke eye contact, bashfully looking toward the ground and readjusting his glasses. But then he smiled at Coal, his red cheeks puffed. "You're welcome," he said.

Together, they leisurely walked back to the bridge leading into Soponunga. The sun was halfway obscured beneath the horizon and the sky was a brilliant purple. As they crossed the bridge, Coal's anxiety and anger began to fade away and he simply appreciated the sight of the city's skyline set against the purple, with blue clouds drifting lazily by.

13

THE LODGE WAS FLOATING on its own little mass not far from city hall. That was the surest indicator that it was a place for the wealthy: it could afford to separate itself from the city's larger planks. Purchasing the materials and paying for construction—of the foundation, the proper support beams, the building itself and all the necessary restaurant equipment—was no easy (or inexpensive) feat.

Coal followed Ilio across the suspended bridge over to the restaurant, which was a dome two stories high. Circling the upper level was an elegant terrace, already full of guests chowing down on appetizers and kicking back tall drinks.

The hostess greeted them inside and asked for a name. Apparently they did not accept walk-ins. The place was probably booked weeks, if not months, in advance.

Ilio provided her with the necessary information, adding that an extra guest would be joining the party. She smiled cordially and led them to their table.

As they navigated through the restaurant, Coal tapped Ilio on the shoulder and asked, "How long ago did you have to make this reservation?"

Ilio chuckled and said, "The same day the Garna decided to attend the race. So, about…nine months ago?"

The hostess brought them to a spiral staircase at the center of the restaurant and they followed her up. Of course Garna Nomak had requested a table on the terrace. Upstairs, she brought them to a large table positioned against the railing. It could comfortably seat five people: one on each end and three sitting opposite the railing, looking out over the water.

"Thank you," Ilio said. The woman gave them a polite nod and returned to her station. He took his place in the middle of the three seats and began to flip through the drink menu.

"You don't wanna sit by Nomak?" Coal asked him.

"I am his assistant, but he does not need me to feed him," Ilio joked.

"Fair enough." Coal pulled out the chair to Ilio's right and plopped himself down. He too began to read about the Lodge's specialty cocktails. His Rosaceous Rivulet had been delicious, and he would not pass up the opportunity for another free drink.

Their table was around the back side of the dome building, looking out over the river rather than the city. The Lunsk's water was dark, the moon barely yet risen in the sky. In the distance, Coal could faintly make out more forest on the other side of the river. It would be a pretty view, once the moonlight shone down brighter.

A minute or two later, a thin lynx stopped by the table and introduced herself as their waitress. She asked if they wanted any drinks while they waited for the rest of the party.

Ilio ordered three drinks with flowery, vague names, and Coal asked for a Bombshell. Based on the description, it seemed like the closest thing to the hotel's Rivulet, a taste which he was craving.

The waitress smiled and scooted off to fetch their beverages.

"The Garna likes to have his drink waiting when he arrives," Ilio explained.

"Of course," said Coal. "Who wouldn't?"

The lynx soon returned with their drinks. Ilio placed one at the seat to his left, and the other on the end by an empty chair. Coal assumed Nomak would be the one at the head of the table, and that their other companion was probably Hiji. The deer must have had to tell Ilio his alcohol preferences earlier.

Or it might be for Mungrus. Coal shuddered.

He took a sip of his Bombshell. While it had even more of an alcoholic bite to it than the Rivulet, it was still nice and fruity.

"Good evening, boys!" came a booming voice from behind them.

They turned in their chairs to see Garna Nomak approaching, whipping his long tongue around hungrily, with Hiji trailing behind. Ilio rose from his chair out of respect, which in Coal's opinion was excessive, but still, he did the same.

He felt a tinge of disappointment; he found himself yearning for more time to chat with Ilio before the Garna dominated the conversation.

Nomak assumed his place at the head of the table while Hiji sat beside Ilio, who returned to his seat. Coal was the last to settle back in.

The Garna's tongue slithered out from his mouth and dipped into his glass sitting on the table. It swished around the blue liquid for a few seconds before snapping back into his mouth in an instant. He giddily smacked his lips and declared, "Delicious!" He then picked up the glass and drank from it, like how a normal person would.

Half the glass was emptied and slammed back down on the table before Nomak asked, "How was your traipse about town? Get all your shit sorted?"

"Uh...it was alright," said Coal. "Got it half-sorted, I guess."

"I actually wanted to speak with you about that," Ilio said. Both Nomak and Coal raised an eyebrow at his interruption.

Nomak said, "First, we need food. I'm starved."

Coal's protesting stomach suspected the Garna might be speaking hyperbolically, but he was more than ready to get some food on the table. He snatched up a menu and started to browse.

"What's that shit I like here, Ilio?" Nomak asked, scanning the menu himself. Every so often, he greedily flicked his tongue into his glass.

"The bread boat," Ilio answered after taking a second to scour the menu and locate the proper name.

"That's the ticket. We'll need two of those. Or make it three, actually. I'm starved."

In addition to the three bread boats, they ordered a couple more items. Two servings of a cheesy dip accompanied by battered, fried caterpillars and eggplant, as well as a cheese platter. Between the three different appetizers, they would not be left wanting for dairy.

It was more than enough food to satiate Coal, even split four ways. He could not fathom ordering an entrée after the incoming feast, but he was thrilled to engorge himself.

He quickly learned why the dish was called a bread boat, though it was a generous moniker. On each plate was a loaf of bread nearly a foot long, with its top sliced off and the middle scraped out to make a dip in the loaf, granting the bread the appearance (somewhat) of a kayak or other small boating vessel. Sprinkled atop the bread was everything Ilio had described earlier that day: melted cheese, seasonings, and some variety of diced red peppers.

It was unbelievably delicious. Coal could easily understand why Garna Nomak went crazy for the stuff. Perhaps three orders of it was a little much, but he did end up cutting off multiple slices for himself, so who was he to judge?

The other two appetizers were just as scrumptious. Especially the batter on the caterpillars and sticks of eggplant, which was wildly flavorful with just a little heat and a fantastic crunch. Somehow through the process of frying, the eggplant also grew incredibly tender, almost creamy. Coal scarfed down more caterpillars and eggplant than anything else.

Nomak ravenously grabbed at each of the plates, rubbing his meaty hands all over everything before shoveling the food into his face. Rather than cut the bread boats with a knife, he was tearing pieces off himself. Every single time he dipped his fried bugs and vegetables into the bowl of melted cheese, he overextended and got some of the sauce on his fingertips, which he proceeded to suck off (so maybe it was not an accident and he simply wanted more cheese). And the cheese plate was seemingly meant just for him, because once again, rather than cutting off chunks with a knife, he instead grabbed the various pieces of cheese and bit into them. No one else ventured near that platter, and Coal counted himself lucky that he was able to eat off the boat and dip that were on the opposite end of the table from the messy anteater.

"How was your time at the spa?" Ilio asked the Garna.

"It was good," Hiji answered. He was attacking the appetizers with much less gusto than his sponsor.

"Oh, you attended as well?" asked Ilio. The deer did not sound any more well-rested after going to the spa than he had before.

Nomak's fingers were dripping with cheese sauce. His tongue once again emerged from his thin lips and wrapped itself around each finger one by one, licking up the cheese and carrying it back to his mouth before moving on to the next. Now his fingers dripped with glistening saliva.

"Can you believe he'd never been to a spa?" he then roared. "When I heard that, I told him he had to come. It was better than good. It was fantastic. Those ladies know how to work a shoulder." He shifted his shoulders to emphasize, as if the three of them might have forgotten what part of the body shoulders were.

"I did enjoy the heated rock massage," Hiji admitted, a brightness to his voice Coal had not yet heard.

Nomak nodded. "We're gonna need to get you another one of those fucking things tomorrow night before the big race. Maybe even one the morning of. You're way too tense." He smacked the man on the back, nearly causing him to spit out his eggplant. "Either that, or some time in the sauna. I invited him in there with me today, but he turned me down!"

Coal would not have wanted to share a steamy confined space with a nude Garna Nomak either, so he couldn't blame

Hiji for his decision. The massage—heated rock or other-wise—sounded appealing, though.

"I was already feeling a little dehydrated," Hiji said. "I thought the sauna might exacerbate things."

"Well, Mungrus and I had a grand old time in there. Ha!" the anteater grinned stupidly, tearing off another chunk of bread. One of the boats was already fully depleted.

A sauna with both Nomak and Mungrus. Hiji had made the correct choice.

There was more idle chitchat about the spa while they shared the appetizers. Over the course of the meal, Coal learned far more about Mungrus's body than he ever wished to know about the beaver.

Coal was already stuffed when it came time to order their main courses, but there were so many dishes that looked de-lectable. He couldn't resist. It was hard to choose just one.

And Nomak didn't, naturally. He ordered three different entrees while everyone else more reasonably picked a single one.

With their bellies sufficiently full for the time being, Ilio attempted once more to broach the earlier topic of conversa-tion while they awaited their dishes.

He said to the Garna, "I wanted to discuss with you some of the complications we encountered today."

So businesslike. Was Ilio about to tell Nomak he couldn't afford to rent a spider? Coal slumped down in his chair and popped another caterpillar in his mouth, eating his shame.

"Complications? What, you forget how to spell 'Lightbulb' on the signup sheet?" The Garna guffawed heartily at his own quip.

"Not quite," said Ilio, moving right along.

Coal kept his mouth shut. While he had internally wanted Nomak to fund his racing venture, in reality he did not have it in him to request such a thing. And either way, he felt it best to let the man's assistant steer the conversation. Ilio would know how to properly finesse him.

"You see, the city's proprietors of the two spider rental facilities have either already exhausted their full stock or are hiking up the prices to unreasonable levels. Coal was relying on renting a spider here, but as a result of the price gouging, they have become unaffordable and therefore his participation in the race is in question."

His explanation sounded a lot more elegant than how Coal would have put it. Maybe the man's vocabulary could be attributed to all the fancy historical fiction he was reading.

"That doesn't surprise me," said Nomak, followed by a disgusting smack of the lips. "Everybody's gotta make money. If you see an opportunity to make it, you gotta grasp it."

Coal couldn't disagree. That sentiment was the whole reason he was trying to compete in this race.

"I was wondering if you might be interested in sponsoring him in the race," Ilio then said.

There it was. Coal knew he had wished for Ilio to request Nomak's assistance outside the Sculio Brothers' shack, but had he accidentally expressed it out loud? Surely not.

Hiji looked more tense than ever, thinking that his free ride with Nomak might come to an end. But the Garna laughed at the idea, dismissing it immediately.

"No can do. Dumb idea, Ilio. Wouldn't make any sense." He bit down on a piece of soft white cheese from the platter and it squished between his fingers. Still gnashing on it, he said, "I had a budget for this, you know? I know you know, because you're the one who handles it. I already put the amount of money I was comfortable with into Hiji here."

The deer sighed in relief.

"That, plus I put a hefty bet on him. I put down *win*, *place*, and *show* bets—though I did that three weeks ago, and now I'm not feeling so sure about the *win*," he said with a pointed glare toward Hiji. "But anyways, it doesn't make any sense for me to spread my funds out and bet on multiple spiders to win. That's a fool's bet. I could try for an *exacta*, but no offense, kid—I don't know how well you race. And like I said, I'm already unsure about my odds with this guy in first now, let alone claiming you'll be in second."

Coal wasn't disappointed. You could only really be disappointed if you were expecting something, and he hadn't been. Not realistically. He had never thought of Nomak funneling any money into him as more than a passing daydream.

Ilio appeared as if he was about to object, but Nomak cut him off.

"I'm not gonna consider it any more than I already have. Sorry, Lightbulb."

"It's fine," said Coal softly with a shrug.

He was resigning to the fact that he would need to inform the beavers his spider died overnight somehow. He tried to formulate a convincing lie, something that would guarantee they refunded his money. Maybe he was taking it for a ride and he careened into the river? Or into a tree? Those wouldn't work. Perhaps he was doing target practice and accidentally shot it in the head?

That was a problem for tomorrow. He'd come up with something. Hopefully.

An idea came to Nomak. His wrinkly brown face lit up and he said, "Hey, how's about instead of giving you a handout, I give you a chance to earn some cash yourself?"

"What do you mean?" Coal asked.

"I am not sure he would be interested in that," said Ilio, clearly on the same page as his boss.

"No, what is it?" said Coal. He wanted to hear the man out. If he could avoid dropping out of the race, he was willing to field some ideas, no matter how outlandish.

Nomak grinned. "We're going out tonight," he said.

Ilio's body tensed almost imperceptibly, but sitting next to him, Coal had picked up on it.

The anteater continued. "It's something of a tradition for me and Mungrus whenever I'm in town. Hiji's coming out too, aren't you?" He gave the deer a look and swiftly received a nod of affirmation. "He's never been to one of these neither."

"One of what?" Coal asked, thinking about his earlier conversation with Ilio about how much Nomak loved brothels. He failed to see how such a tryst would earn him any money.

"It's a gambling den," Ilio answered before Nomak could.

"A casino?"

Both Ilio and Nomak shook their heads.

"It is in the basement of a confectionary shop," said Ilio. His feathers were ruffled. "A private affair."

"Higher stakes there," said Nomak, "and less prying eyes. You get what I'm saying?"

Coal did not, but he would not admit that to the Garna.

"I'm not gonna lie to you. The buy-in is big, but not the biggest I've ever played. A couple hundred tups, usually. But you can make that back, plus a ton more, if you play your cards right. Literally." Another laugh. Nomak cracked himself and nobody else up. "You seem like the clever sort. I'd think you could make enough to go get yourself a nice spider tomorrow morning."

Ilio gave Coal a silent look, but one that he instantly understood. The woodpecker did not think it would be a wise idea for Coal to play with these people. There were probably dangerous men involved, ones with vastly deeper pockets than his own. Coal also had much less confidence in his card-playing abilities than Nomak did. He would likely be wiped clean in a hand or two.

It's either this or drop out, though.

At that point, the lynx returned with their trays of food. She placed Coal's plate in front of him. It held a steaming cauliflower steak smothered in a creamy red sauce made from tomatoes and red bell peppers. The aroma floating up into his nostrils made him forget that he had been full to the point of vomiting only ten minutes ago.

The woman handed over Ilio and Hiji's food, but she had to make a second trip to fetch all three of Nomak's plates.

When everyone had their food, Coal finally responded to the Garna's invitation.

"You might be right," he told the man, a sentence he never dreamed he would say to Garna Nomak. "It sounds like it could be a good opportunity. Thanks."

"So you'll be joining us?"

"I will," Coal nodded. He exchanged a look with Ilio, who at once looked disappointed yet happy about him tagging along.

"Are we able to grab some sweets from the shop on our way downstairs?" Coal asked jokingly.

"Ha!" Nomak boomed. "As if we'll need to. Don't worry, we'll be taking a look at the dessert menu."

That did not surprise him.

Coal cut off a bite of his steak and popped it into his mouth. He stopped himself from moaning in delight. Everything on the menu was ridiculously priced, nothing he would ever pay himself, but the Lodge had rightfully earned its reputation for being delicious.

After swallowing another bite, he asked, "Are we going after dinner?"

Nomak's mouth was stuffed with one bite from each of his plates all at once, so Ilio stepped in before the Garna could answer and spray food all over the table.

"No, it will not open up for a little while. We will have some time between dessert and then."

"Great," said Coal. "I need to find a place to stay." The idea of trying to track down a hotel room in the early hours of the morning after a drunken night of gambling sounded like a fate worse than death.

Ilio told him he could help with that, and Coal thanked him.

Soon their waitress returned to ask if they would like to take a look at the dessert menu.

Coal was taken aback when Nomak contradicted himself and told the woman, "No, no need for that." But it was quickly amended with, "Just bring one of everything."

Somehow, Coal had managed to consume all of his cauliflower steak and now there were who knew how many desserts on the way.

This is how I die, he thought.

But he licked his lips in anticipation, trying not to mimic Nomak too much.

It sounded like a great way to go.

14

C OAL AND ILIO WERE walking side by side on the lit Soponunga streets, taking in the starlight and the gentle sway of the water beneath their feet.

He did not know where the hell he was going to sleep that night. And he did not know what exactly a night of gambling with Garna Nomak entailed.

And while he was listing things he didn't know, he remembered that Ilio mentioned not knowing any cheap places to stay.

"I appreciate you offering to help," he told Ilio earnestly. In all honesty, a big part of why he accepted Nomak's invitation was so that he could spend more time with Ilio. But he did not want to say that out loud and make things weird between them. He went on, "But I think I recall you specifically telling me that you don't know anything about hotels here except for the Longowosk and that one where all the racers are."

"You are right," Ilio said, walking with purpose. Coal had been following the man blindly, trusting his sense of direction in the floating city. He was sure each of the huge, weathered dock sections had some sort of name akin to Vinnag's various districts, but at this point every street and connecting bridge looked exactly the same to him.

"Well…" muttered Coal, not having anything to add.

Ilio remained quiet after that, which was typical for his behavior when they first met earlier that afternoon, but Coal thought he had breached the man's defenses. He had to admit he was a little disappointed. Maybe Ilio was just full from the meal and not in the mood to speak.

The Longowosk was visible amongst the skyline, its yellow, orange-striped façade brightly lit so that no one would miss it. It was then that Coal realized Ilio was leading him there.

Probably needs to grab something from his room, he figured.

They reached the hotel and Ilio brought them up to the sixth floor. Once there, Ilio explained, "The Garna rented out a block of rooms. The entire floor, actually."

This did not shock Coal in the slightest. Garna Nomak had proven to be a man who needed to flaunt his wealth, or else what was the point of being wealthy?

"As you have no doubt learned by now, the Garna is not traveling with a large group of people at this time," Ilio continued. "Therefore, several of the already-rented rooms are currently unoccupied." He allowed a slight puff in his cheeks, proud of his little surprise.

Coal blinked. He tried to process the concept of him staying in the top floor of a hotel such as this. It was something that would have never happened even when he was financially stable. The Muta Par library did not exactly pay as well as Garna Nomak's innumerable business ventures.

"Are you serious?" he asked, blinking himself out of his momentary stupor.

Ilio nodded. "I know things have been rough for you, so I would like to help ease the burden as much as possible."

You don't know the half of it.

"The Garna will not care, I am sure of it. Even if he did not already like you as much as he clearly does."

Coal couldn't stop himself. "Thank you," he said, wrapping his arms around Ilio.

The woodpecker seemed in awe for a moment, his arms dangling limp at his side, but he then wrapped himself around Coal as well and hugged him tight.

"You are most welcome," Ilio said. His beak brushed lightly against Coal's shoulder.

Coal pulled away and asked, "So, where's my room?"

"You can take the one next to mine," Ilio said, walking down the hall. He came to a stop a few doors down, at room 604. "I am in 603. Everyone else is on the other side of the hall." He jerked his head back at the rooms behind him. "I tend to keep my distance whenever possible."

"Smart," Coal grinned.

Ilio extracted a few silver keys from his pocket, fingering through them to find the right one. He then unlocked the door and pushed it open, gesturing for Coal to enter first.

Thin, soft carpet lined the floor, blue with white stripes zigzagging all over the room to create an abstract design. The walls were painted a spotless white, pristine as if the staff had applied a fresh coat only yesterday. Billowing blue drapes hung from the windows, open now to reveal the hotel's deck bar below.

The room was nicer than any he had ever stayed in and would ever stay in again.

It was divided into two parts, separated by a freestanding wall against which was a desk, presumably for fancy business-men to conduct business at. On one side of the room was a sitting area with a short sofa and an armchair. There was also a counter topped with a minibar, a bowl of bagged snacks, and a pitcher in which to brew coffee. The other half of the room was the sleeping area, with an enormous bed that could easily fit four of him in it and the silkiest sheets he had ever felt.

He lay sprawled on top of the bed, rubbing his fingers along the sheets and exclaiming how fantastic the room was. He pro-fusely thanked Ilio again for hooking him up with the one and only luxury of his life.

"It really is no problem," said Ilio, taking a seat in the plush armchair. He laughed at Coal bouncing up and down on the bed like a child. "There was something I wanted to say, though."

"Oh no," said Coal, sitting up. "The room comes with a 'but.'"

"No, no," Ilio shook his head. "It is about tonight."

Coal could see where this was going. This was why Ilio had kept to himself on their walk to the hotel. Girding himself for this conversation. "I take it you don't mean about dinner," he said with a weak smile.

"No," Ilio said again.

"I know it's not the best idea," Coal said, heading him off. "I just…I can't think of any other options. It's either this, or I leave empty-handed. I mean, I'll maybe be leaving empty-handed even if I *do* race, but I'd like to at least *try* to win. To not even have the opportunity would be..." He searched for the right word. He came up short.

Ilio nodded. "I understand," he said, rising from the chair. He began to pace through the room's lounging area. "I do not blame you. I would probably do the same in your shoes. I just wanted you to be fully aware of the types of people the Garna associates with."

"I'm pretty aware at this point," said Coal, thinking back to the job he completed with Zank, Venny, and Marl. Garna Nomak's lifestyle was no secret to him.

"These men are different than what you may have dealt with in Vinnag. They are not criminals; they are not dangerous in that sense—they are simply high rollers. Men with more money than they know what to do with. Willing to blow large sums on every whim."

That was a fair description of Nomak, too, based on what Coal had seen.

"They will not take pity on you. They will take every tup you have, with absolutely no regard, and leave you with nothing. They are rich, and they want to become richer. They are there to win."

"I get it," said Coal. "I'm out of my depth."

"Maybe you are, I do not know," Ilio shrugged. "Are you an experienced gambler?"

"Nope."

"Well, okay, then. Yes, you are out of your depth."

Coal nodded. He figured that was the case. Ilio was not exactly telling him new information.

But he had to try.

And he wanted to go with Ilio.

As if reading his mind, Ilio then asked, "Do you still wish to attend?"

Coal pushed himself up off the bed, briefly fantasizing about throwing himself into those sheets later that night. Rubbing them against his fur. He couldn't wait for that moment.

"Yep," he replied.

And so they left.

THERE WAS STILL A bit of time before the game started. They opted to walk the riverside streets, letting the massive amount of food they had eaten settle in their stomachs.

As they passed a cute-looking bookshop that was unfortunately already closed for the night, Ilio said, "There was something I was wondering."

"Hmm?"

"Where did the name 'Von Rened' come from? You pulled that one out pretty fast. Is that your usual alias? If I do some digging, will I find records of a *Von Rened* wreaking havoc across Ruska?"

Coal chuckled. "No," he said. "First time I've used that." He was employing a new fake name in every place he ended up. Somehow this one had not occurred to him until today. "Von was my father's name, and Rened is the surname of a friend of his."

"Ahh. Your use of past tense makes me think I should offer you condolences."

"Picking up on tenses. You really are a reader." Ilio laughed at the dumb joke. He went on, "Yeah, he passed away about a year ago."

"I am sorry."

"It's fine," Coal said, despite the staggering untruthfulness of the sentence. But he felt it was what one usually said in a situation such as this.

"I know how difficult that must have been for yourself and your other parent," said Ilio. "When my mother passed, my father was a wreck for many years. I was not much better, of course, but it truly broke his heart."

"It has not been the best year," Coal said, the biggest understatement ever uttered. "I don't know if my mother would really care, though. I haven't seen her since I was a kid."

There was genuine despair in Ilio's voice. "I apologize," he said. "I do not mean to keep bringing up depressing subjects, I swear."

Coal chuckled and once more told him that it was fine.

"So we both grew up with just our fathers," he then said.

Ilio took a moment to respond. "Not exactly," he said. "My mother died when I was already grown up and moved away. I was living in a small village called Menta at the time."

"Where's that?"

"It is in the northeast, not terribly far from Yagos. But I had to put my life on hold and moved back to Varoosh to assist my father in the aftermath. I stayed there for a long while."

Coal could relate to putting his life on hold. He wanted to ask if this disruption was the complication that started him down the path to Garna Nomak's employ, but he refrained for now. He did not want to dredge up more painful memories.

For the remainder of their walk, they discussed lighter things. Coal brought up the bookstore they had passed, and Ilio said that he frequented it whenever he visited Soponunga.

There was always something in stock that interested him, though he could not speak to its mystery selection.

It felt like they were walking in circles, but Coal didn't mind. He had a hard time believing how much had happened in a single day. It seemed like he had been in Soponunga for a week already.

Somehow his legs were aching less than they were that morning in spite of how much ground he had covered with Ilio. If they never went to Nomak's weird, secret gambling den and instead walked the streets all night talking, he would be completely satisfied. There was something about the bird that made him feel at ease. Like he could finally exhale after holding his breath for the past year. He desperately wanted to hold on to that feeling.

But eventually it came time to meet up with Nomak, Mungrus, and Hiji. The confectionary shop was located only a few blocks from the Lodge, and Coal began to suspect this section of the city was where its wealthier denizens resided.

The storefront was pink with white-trimmed windows. A bit predictable, in Coal's opinion. None of the lights were on inside, but Ilio turned the doorknob and it swung right open.

Inside were countless shelves of multicolored bags and boxes. The powerful aroma of sugar struck Coal with staggering force, and he nearly retched. If it was somehow not obvious to him before that he had overeaten at dinner, it was now. Getting drunk would be a disastrous idea. Nomak must have a steel stomach.

"Code," came a low voice from the back of the store.

Coal jumped. In the dark, he had not seen the woman sitting bored at the counter. He peered in the back of the store and saw she was a fox with her head propped up on her hand, doodling on a piece of paper to entertain herself.

"Rotswallow," said Ilio.

"Go on back," said the woman, pointing her pencil toward a door behind her. She did not seem like the best guard, but Coal had no room to talk. He could probably be easily bested by her in a fight.

They stepped behind the counter and entered the back room. It was stocked with even more sugary inventory and a staircase leading to the basement. Coal followed Ilio down and was relieved to leave behind the sickeningly sweet smell, though its replacement—smoke and sweat—was not any better.

The basement was much what Coal had expected, like it had been plucked out of one of his mystery novels. It was a typical gambling den, a faintly-lit bare room filled with a layer of smoke and the din of men grumbling and laughing. A man walked from person to person with a tray, handing out drinks to the ungrateful patrons.

There were three tables set up, each with their own card game. Nomak sat with Mungrus at the table furthest from the entryway, with Hiji standing stern and cross-armed behind the Garna.

Nomak spotted them at the entrance and waved them over. Coal and Ilio filed past the other two full tables, filled with men eager to commence their night of debauchery. The fox upstairs was seemingly the only woman in the building.

Coal felt gross being in the room, like entering it had caked a layer of grime on his fur that an hour of scrubbing in the bath wouldn't clean off. Spending the next few hours walking around the city with Ilio was sounding more appealing by the second.

"Grab a seat!" roared Nomak, yanking the empty chair beside him from the table. He had evidently saved it for Coal.

He sat down beside the anteater, who was already slurping up a cloudy beverage. Mungrus leaned over and slapped a hand on the table, making direct eye contact with Coal.

"Hello, old pup!" the beaver beamed, slurring his words even more severely than he had that afternoon out on the deck. Coal did not anticipate ever interacting with the man while he was sober.

"Hi," said Coal, not sure what the slap was all about. He gingerly tapped the top of the beaver's hand in greeting, and that seemed to do the trick. Mungrus removed his hand from the table with a wide grin and chugged more of his own drink.

Ilio assumed a position standing behind Coal, next to Hiji. "Not playing?" he asked the deer.

"Not yet," Nomak answered for his racer. "He ain't too versed in the game, so he's gonna stand back and learn the ropes first. Ain't that right?"

"Yes," said Hiji.

At that, Coal looked around the table to try to determine what game they were going to be playing, but there was no indicator whatsoever. He asked Nomak.

"Slapstick," the man said with a foul smile. At this proximity, Coal could taste the man's stale breath, tinged with the sting of alcohol.

It was a popular card game, but Coal had never played it himself. Around once a month, his father would go to a friend's house after dinner to play some hands, but Coal had either been too young to join or too uninterested when he was older.

"I might be as inexperienced as Hiji here," he confessed.

For whatever reason, Nomak looked shocked. Coal had no idea what made the man believe he was a skilled card player. *What could I have possibly said to give him that impression?*

"Maybe you should sit out the first hand," Ilio suggested.

Nomak grinned. "You and Hiji just watch how it's done. I'll take these old bastards' money right quick and then we'll get you a hand."

The dealer, a gangly rabbit with coarse brown fur, asked the men at the table for their initial buy-ins. Coal gaped as Nomak tossed three hundred tups into the middle of the table along with everyone else.

The rabbit then dealt each of the players their cards. In addition to Nomak and Mungrus, there was a sloth named Runo and a macaw named Uyu. The latter was gravely serious as he inspected his cards, while Runo seemed to be there to have fun.

"Take a look here," Nomak said, and Coal leaned over while Hiji peered over the man's shoulder to catch a peek at the cards.

Each man had been dealt five cards. Scanning Nomak's cards, Coal had no idea what to make of his hand. He had two with illustrations of bats, though one of them had a green square at its center and the other had a green triangle. Another card bore a picture of a wolf with a green triangle, and the last two had a circle and a triangle with no drawings.

It was a typical deck of cards, but Coal could assign no meaning to the cards in the context of this particular game. He checked Nomak's expression, but the anteater's face betrayed

198 • Travis M. Riddle

no emotion. He shuffled the cards around so that all of the illustrations were together, which Coal thought looked more or-
ganized, but he failed to ascertain its function.

The dealer looked to Mungrus for his move.

Mungrus grunted, but it was hard to tell whether he did so
out of disdain or drunkenness. Regardless, he threw twenty
more tups into the pot and placed three of his cards face down
on the table. He crossed his arms and sat back in his creaking
chair with a satisfied smirk.

Nomak gave Coal and Hiji a knowing look, as if they
should already be aware of what he was going to do. He
matched his buddy's bet and placed his three triangle cards on
the table. "You're a fool," he told Mungrus as he did so.

Mungrus mumbled something that no one could understand.

Next up was Uyu, who folded angrily. Runo raised the bet
and placed two cards on the table.

The three men all looked at each other. Mungrus decided
to fold, but Nomak further raised the bet. Runo matched, and
the dealer instructed them to reveal their cards.

Nomak flipped over his three triangle cards: one bare, one
with a bat, and one with a triangle. Runo's two cards had illustrations of boars with matching red squares.

"You dipshitted fuck!" Nomak cursed, slamming a fist on
the table.

The dealer collected the cards and slid Runo's earnings
over to him.

Coal sat dumbfounded, no more illuminated on the rules of
the game than he had been before arriving. He looked to Hiji,
his companion in ignorance, and the deer gave him a shrug,
pouting his lips.

Next, Coal turned to Ilio standing behind him and whispered, "The hell happened?"

He opened his beak to answer, but before he could, the dealer yelped for the men to buy in if they wanted to play another hand.

Coal turned himself back around and saw Nomak staring at him expectantly. There was no way he would come close to beating any of these guys.

"I'll watch one more hand," he said. Hiji was eager to join him.

"Suit yourselves," Nomak shrugged. He carelessly threw his three hundred tups onto the pile. The last to join in was Mungrus, who was having immense trouble counting out the money in his drunken state.

Coal observed Nomak again. This time, none of his five cards were alike in any way, and yet he raised the bet by a hefty amount and placed the entire hand down. He was not shy about expressing his pleasure, emitting a delighted giggle before sucking up more of his drink.

Nobody folded and they raised the bet a couple times. When the dealer asked them to reveal their cards, they all shouted in disgust at Nomak's cards while the anteater belly-laughed and snatched up all his winnings.

What in the fuck does any of this mean? Coal asked himself, knowing full well he could not ask for a detailed lesson on the game here and now.

The buy-in would eat up almost all his funds, so he would need an absolutely guaranteed win for it to be worthwhile.

It was a folly to think he could waltz into this place and expect to learn the games and instantly win enough money to earn his spot in the spiderback race. What had given him that notion? Had it been drunken hubris back at the dinner table? He hadn't even had that much alcohol.

He was about to excuse himself from the table and ask Ilio for that walk (if he was even allowed to leave his boss's side) when Nomak said, "Let me buy your first hand for you. Get your feet wet."

"That's very generous of you, but it's *too* generous, I think," said Coal. Three hundred tups wasn't nothing.

"Nonsense!" Nomak waved his words away. "I owe you for how you helped me with my little situation." Coal almost chuckled at the choice of words. "I mean, I already paid you for it so I guess I don't *owe* you anything, but I like you, Light-bulb. Play a hand with me." He placed the necessary tups on the table in front of Coal with a smirk. "After that, you'll be hooked."

Coal wasn't so sure of that.

"It'll definitely be a waste," he told the Garna. "I, uh...I still have very little idea of what the rules are."

"'Very little' sounds to me like you've got a good start!" said the man.

Coal wholeheartedly disagreed with that sentiment, but the Garna was not taking no for an answer, so he would happily waste the man's money. It was his only real chance at winning anything tonight. He couldn't risk losing his own money with the buy-in.

Nomak pushed the tups into the middle of the table, and the rest of the men followed suit. Hiji was still sitting out for now, though he assured the Garna he would join in on the next round.

Coal's heart pounded in his chest as the rabbit dealt him his cards. He lifted them up to take a look at what he was working with.

Bat with a red square.

Green triangle.

Green circle.

Rabbit with a green circle.

Red circle.

He stared at the hand with a blank expression.

He did not know what the fuck to do.

He had three circle cards. That was probably a good thing. But one of them was red. Should the red circle not be put with the green ones? Did the rabbit or bat have anything to do with each other? Should the red and green bare circles be paired together?

For fuck's sake, Coal thought with a heavy sigh. He could tell that Ilio was examining his cards, and he wished he could ask the bird for some guidance.

Before he knew it, it was his turn. He had been so flustered over deciding what to do with his cards, he did not notice what Mungrus or Nomak had done. It seemed both men added a little bit to the pot.

"What's, uh…what's the bet?" he asked stupidly.

"Thirty tups," the dealer replied.

Anything else he put into the game would come from his own pocket. It was a much smaller risk than three hundred tups, of course, but it made him uneasy nonetheless.

He looked over his cards again, all too aware that it was taking him substantially longer to come to a decision than anyone else at the table.

With three circle cards, he felt confident that they could potentially bring him a win. Well, not exactly *confident*, perhaps, but—

Well, there was no but.

Three circles has *to be something.*

Coal counted out thirty of his own tups and threw them into the pot. He then set down his three circle cards and hoped for the best. A pit opened up in his stomach and he suddenly felt the urge to shit or puke.

Uyu matched and Runo raised slightly, then Mungrus raised considerably. Coal nearly groaned. Nomak raised further and gave him a devious look.

He would have to put down an extra hundred tups on top of the thirty he'd already placed in the pot. It was still meager compared to what Nomak had donated to his cause, but it was not a small amount of money to him.

Folding was inevitable.

Then Nomak said, "Let me give you one piece of advice, Lightbulb. It's obvious, but sometimes a man's gotta hear it. There's only one rule to cards: you gotta bet big to win big. Like I said, obvious. But you want that fuckin' spider, don'tcha? You feel good about those cards you got there?" He flicked his tongue downward at the three circle cards Coal had placed face-down on the table. "Bet big and win big. Make a bold move."

It was impossible to deny the logic, but it still left him feeling unsure. He was, at best, mildly confident in his cards.

Three circles just absolutely has got *to be something, right?*

He looked to Ilio, who shrugged. Just as clueless about Slapstick as he was. Come to think of it, he did not even understand why the game was titled Slapstick. Another mystery.

"Fuck," he groaned, yanking out the money and tossing it onto the table.

Nomak and Mungrus hollered and cheered, congratulating him on his aplomb. Uyu and Runo were unmoved. The latter folded.

Coal once again turned back to Ilio and asked him, "I fucked up, didn't I?"

Ilio had to laugh, but his expression quickly turned serious. "Maybe," he said. "It is certainly not what I would have done."

He was right, back in the hotel room. These men were all hungry for Coal's money with no regard for him as a person. Even Nomak. Coal then pictured Nomak at the dinner table shouting "I'm starved!"

Of course he'd encourage you to bet big, you fucking moron, Coal chided himself. He fully regretted placing the bet.

The dealer then went around the table, asking each player to flip their cards.

Coal did not know the first thing about how to play Slapstick, but Mungrus's cards looked wholly unimpressive. The man was making rash decisions, more concerned about his drinks than his cards.

Suddenly Coal was lit with hope. Maybe his three circles were good enough. They had to be better than Mungrus's bare red triangle and bare red circle. What could that even be?

Nomak appeared pleased with what he'd laid down, though, and Coal's hope diminished. The Garna clearly knew what he was doing. Uyu seemed to know his way around the game as well, and who knew what he had played.

It was now Coal's turn. His stomach twisted as he revealed his three circle cards and he awaited a reaction.

But there wasn't one. Nothing at all from any player nor the dealer.

Coal still had no idea if he had played anything at all. A vulgar word came to his lips, but he suppressed it.

Uyu showed his hand with a disgruntled tut, practically throwing them at the dealer. He scowled at Coal.

Coal's eyebrows raised. His breathing intensified.

Uyu was mad at him.

Had he just won?

Had he just won over two thousand tups?

Holy shit.

His mouth hung open in disbelief.

He was going to leave the table after this. There was no way he would risk losing it all again. He needed to make the most of that money, and he did not intend to give it all away to Garna Nomak or Mungrus.

But then the dealer said, "Congratulations," and pushed the pot in front of Nomak's spot. Not Coal's.

Coal's mouth was still agape, trying to process what had happened. Angry and embarrassed that he had tricked himself into thinking he had won.

His money was gone.

"Fuck," he said again.

Nomak bellowed with laughter. "Thank you!" he said.

Ilio placed a sympathetic hand on Coal's shoulder and squeezed.

"I think I'm out," Coal then said. He stood and pushed his chair out from the table.

"Oh, come on now! We've only played a few hands. The night is young! Don't be a sore loser!" said Nomak, not bothering to even look at Coal. He was too preoccupied with tapping his claws on all the money he had just won.

Coal tried to maintain his composure. He said, "It's not that. I just…the table's too hot for me." He blurted out the words, not sure if what he said was even a real phrase.

But it got the point across to everyone else.

To Ilio, Coal asked, "You wanna come with?"

Like he had before with Hiji, Nomak answered in Ilio's stead. "He's gotta stay and help me lug all this fuckin' money back to the hotel," he grinned. "Ain't that right?"

And like Hiji before him, Ilio said, "Yes."

Coal frowned, and he could see the deflated disappointment in Ilio's face as well. "Alright," he said. He moved out of the way and Hiji took his place at the table.

Upstairs, as he moved past the counter, the bored fox asked him, "Heading out already?"

"Afraid so."

"Quitting while you're ahead? Or quitting while you're behind?"

"Behind."

"Oh well. Better luck next time."

"Right."

Coal exited the shop and made his way back to the Longowosk, reflecting on the insanely long day that was now finally winding down.

He thought about signing up for the race with his fictionalized spider named White Rose.

He thought about visiting the two stables, being priced out, all hope lost.

He thought about losing a fourth of his money in that stupid game of Slapstick, at Nomak's insistence.

Tomorrow, he would have to find those beavers and offer an explanation as to how White Rose died. He needed to think up a believable story.

He fantasized about how nice it would've felt to be riding spiderback again. How freeing. Clutching on to White Rose, darting through the forest.

He then thought about the Sculio Brothers getting orb weavers from Faranap, not too far from the city.

He could still hear Nomak in his head stating, *"Bet big and win big. Make a bold move."*

A bold move.

Bold moves were all that could get him out of the immense, fucked up mess he was in.

Doing jobs for Nomak month after month wasn't going to cut it. The Stingers would track him down again by then. There was no doubt in his mind.

To win big, he needed to bet big.

And a big bet suddenly came to mind.

It didn't make any sense. Not really. Nothing about how the last few days had gone indicated that he was skilled enough to pull off the plan.

But he was tired of living in fear. Of being stressed out every waking moment, worried that around every corner a Stinger would be waiting to snatch him up and haul him away. Imprisoned for the rest of his life.

In the end, his yearning to feel safe again—at whatever cost—outweighed any amount of trepidation.

He was resolute. It was a ridiculous idea, but it was the only card he had left to play. The only thing he could think of to ensure his freedom.

Ironically, that meant he was going to go to Faranap.

He was going to the prison of the Flesh Eaters to steal himself an orb weaver, and he was going to enter the race.

And then he was going to win the race.

He had to.

His stomach churned with nerves and he leaned over the railing of the bridge he was crossing, vomiting into the Lunsk River.

15

HE DID NOT KNOW where exactly Faranap was.

And he could not exactly ask the hotel concierge for directions to the Flesh Eater encampment, because that would make him look like a crazy person. So instead, he told her that he wanted to go on a long walk outside the city so please tell me where Faranap is so that I can avoid going in that direction thank you.

She happily obliged.

Coal did not know what he required for this ludicrous plan of his to work. He still had the gun from Fanaleese, and aside from that, he could not think of anything else he might need. There should be proper riding equipment to use somewhere within Faranap's stable; and besides, every store in Soponunga was closed this time of night, so he couldn't buy any even if he wanted to.

Using the gun would be an absolute last resort. No part of him wished to fatally harm anyone within Faranap's walls. The Flesh Eaters captured and brought there might be rabid, or genuine criminals, but they also might be people put in impossible situations like himself. Or those who had simply wanted to honor their cultures' ancient traditions and were punished severely for doing so.

No matter the case, he did not feel right hurting them.

Maybe he could knock one of them out if necessary (if he could even pull that much off), but he would prefer to avoid that too. He was unsure how many guards Faranap employed, or if there were any other surprises lurking.

Far too many unknowns for his liking.

By the time he finally set out, it was a little over an hour since he'd left the confectionary shop.

Soponunga's nightlife had begun dying down an hour or two before, not nearly as vivacious as Vinnag's. It was entering the early hours of the morning now, and it would take roughly an hour to walk to Faranap, which Coal hoped would be the perfect time to sneak in undetected and triumphantly ride a spider out.

He crossed the southern bridge out of the city and began to formulate a concrete plan in his head.

The first thing he needed to figure out was how he would even enter Faranap. From what he had learned since being marked as a Flesh Eater, each of the three prisons was surrounded by thick stone walls towering at least thirty feet high. Prisoners' nails were filed down every few days, so that fact combined with the stone made it highly unlikely that anyone could scale the walls and escape.

210 • *Travis M. Riddle*

But that also meant it would be difficult for him to get in. His own nails were long and hooked, but that helped him climb tree bark, not stone. And asking nicely at the front door was not an option.

Or is it? he asked himself. *Would they just let me in and have a spider? What do they care?*

He shook the naïve idea. It was his slight leftover inebriation talking. It should wear off by the time he got to Faranap. Throwing up had done him wonders on that front.

Grass and leaves crunched underfoot as he ventured into the copse of trees near the Sculio Brothers' shack. For a moment, Coal felt the impulse to steal a spider from *them*, but he was sure that would not end well for him. Their stock was probably tagged in some way that would be obvious come time to race and then he'd just be arrested for a different crime.

He wandered in the direction the Longowosk concierge had told him to avoid, double- and triple-checking before committing to his route. There was no way to differentiate between anything once he was in the thick of the trees. The already faint light of the moon and stars was obscured underneath the looming treetop canopy. His vision adjusted to the dark, but there was nothing to see anyway except tree trunks and bushes.

There were no animals out tonight. Not even the rustling of a geigex in the treetops overhead. Only the mere buzzing of insects.

Spotting animals out in the wild was somewhat rare in the first place; he had been too exhausted from his tunnel trek earlier in the day to fully appreciate the retno he'd caught grazing. The dwindling amount of wildlife throughout the valley was the primary reason behind the Dirt King's ban of meat consumption all those years ago. It was an attempt to curb the decline, though some species had gone extinct since then and the matter did not seem to be improving, as far as Coal was aware.

It would still be a few hours yet until the sun started rising. He would not mind having it light his way back to Soponunga, but he could not imagine how poorly things would need to go to result in this trip taking that long. Plus, he was already incredibly tired from the day's events and from simply being awake for so long.

Tomorrow was the race's opening ceremony festival. He needed to sleep before then.

While he walked, he took out the pistol, checked the safety was on, and practiced twirling it on his finger. The action looked awkward and amateurish, yet he felt cool each time he (clumsily) did it. Like a Palace Stinger, trained in the art of killing. Not that he had any desire to be a killer, but it was fun to imagine himself as one of the characters in the books he loved.

Half an hour passed without incident, and doubt crept into Coal's mind. He knew not to expect any sort of landmarks, but still he worried that he had gone the wrong way. He thought he was keeping a steady, straight path, but it was hard to be sure.

Nothing to do but keep going.

He kept himself busy thinking about what Ilio was doing right now. Whether he was still standing in that stale basement trying not to choke on smoke, or if he was laying in the comfort of his hotel bed, drifting into dreams of...

What would Ilio dream of? he wondered.

Ilio dreamed of travel, he decided. The most concrete detail he knew about the man was his love of books, but that would be too simplistic. Too obvious. And really, who dreamed of reading?

So Coal decided that tonight, Ilio would be dreaming about visiting somewhere he had never been before. Perhaps Jaq Yul, in the eastern mountains. It was a tiny but scenic village carved into the mountainside, famous for its hot springs that attracted tourists from all over the kingdom. Coal had not been there either, though he had heard a lot about it and always wanted to take a dip in those springs. They could go together.

He was still daydreaming about relaxing in those warm waters when he spied an imposing white stone wall through the trees.

It had to be Faranap.

That second half hour had passed by in a flash. He raced forward, stopping at the edge of the treeline, keeping himself hidden behind a thick trunk while he observed. His heart started beating frantically, trying to warn him that this was a foolish endeavor. He did his best to ignore it.

Whichever side of the encampment he was looking at, it wasn't the main entrance. All he saw stretching down the length of the wall was white. No way in or out.

He cautiously approached the wall, then made his way over to the corner and peeked around. More white. No guards. He sniffed the air, but couldn't pick up on any person's scent. There was no one close by.

Maybe they were in fact patrolling the perimeter, but he wasn't sure what exactly the protocol was here. Right now, though, he was in the clear.

Deep down he knew it wouldn't work, but he had to try. He hopped upward and dug his claws into the stone and tried scrambling up like he would the side of a tree, but he failed to get a good grip on it. His nails and boots scraped noisily against the wall as he dumbly slid back down to the earth.

He cursed to himself in a hushed whisper and tried to concoct an alternate plan. He paced back and forth, growing more and more anxious about a guard popping around the corner at any moment. He took another cautious whiff of the air, and smelled nothing but flora, stone, and wood.

Maybe I should not have acted so rashly and done some fucking research into this place before I came here.

Berating himself wasn't going to solve anything. He needed to either act or leave. And right now, he was desperate, and did not intend to leave without a spider.

Climbing the wall would clearly not work, but maybe he could climb the nearest tree and leap over. He had enough trust in his legs to propel him that distance. Though as he looked up at the treetops, seeing the space between them and the wall, that trust slowly slipped away.

He circled around to the side that he already confirmed was not the front and examined the trees over there. Near the opposite end were a couple that were closer to the wall, which might be suitable.

With as much grace as his tired body could muster, he darted quietly across the expanse of grass and scrambled up one of the trees before a guard could appear. He looked down at the ground from the safety of the branches and saw that no one had come around on patrol. He could not spot anyone anywhere.

He then stared ahead at the length between the tree and the wall and gulped. This was the closest tree to the wall, and still it was farther than it seemed from the ground. Much farther.

Act or leave, he told himself again. *You can still climb down this tree and walk your sorry ass back to the hotel and go to bed. You can just hang out at the festival tomorrow and watch the race then go back to Vinnag and try to lay low again until you earn enough money to pay that bat.*

Neither option was desirable.

Nothing about his life had been desirable ever since that fucking earthquake.

He had decided to take matters into his own hands and try to alter his situation for the better, and at every step of the way, he faced horrible obstacles. But he was realizing that would never change. The situation was too bad for the solution to be simple.

One way or another, he was getting into Faranap.

Either by jumping onto its walls and sneaking in, or being dragged through the gates kicking and screaming by a Stinger.

Neither option was desirable.

Do not fuck me, he ordered his legs.

He braced himself on the branch as far out as he could manage while maintaining balance. Then he crouched down and leapt forward out into the open air.

Time stood still while he was in mid-air, his arms outstretched, reaching toward Faranap's rough, white wall. The tip of his tail brushed the tree branch's outermost leaf.

An obtrusive image entered his mind: him grasping the top of the wall and his nails not finding purchase, sending him careening down the side to splatter on the earth below.

The real Coal then slammed into the wall, his upper body draped over the top, clawing at the stone. A shockwave of pain rippled through him, but he quickly regained focus and kicked with his legs to push the lower half of himself up onto the wall.

He lay on his back with his arms and legs splayed, the wall thick enough to fit two of him. He panted heavily, trying to catch his breath after being winded from the impact.

I did it?

Every time he accomplished anything with a minimal amount of success, he shocked himself. It was easy to be impressed when he expected so little.

It took a full minute before he felt okay enough to sit up. When he did, he looked over the other side of the wall into Faranap and realized he had a whole new problem to contend with.

How the fuck am I gonna get down?

His shortsightedness was continuing to bite him in the ass.

Below, Faranap was asleep.

It was the size of a small village, and within its walls were several shoddily-constructed wood buildings that looked as if they would crumble with the push of a light breeze. The walls were thin and the planks of wood used were not pressed tight together; even from this distance, Coal could peer between them to spy sleeping figures inside.

The gate was on the wall opposite him, so it was good he had not gone around that side to check things out when he was on the ground. Two guards stood at attention there, armed with rifles.

Coal pressed his body down flat against the stone to hopefully remain unseen by them. He was pretty high up, though, and did not expect the guards would be scanning the skies for intruders, but rather making sure no inmates were attempting to sneak out.

He couldn't tell which buildings were meant for lodging and which were for work. Flesh Eaters were put to task with various jobs during the day. In addition to breeding spiders, Coal knew that some places had them sewing clothes, some were maintaining insect farms (though much lower quality than a company like Nyers Foods, but as a result much cheaper), and in some cases crafting furniture, under strict supervision with the tools required. Anything that the typical workforce did not actually want to do could be done by Flesh Eaters for almost nil.

Hardly any trees poked out over the top of the wall. The barest hint of greenery. Everyone there had to be miserable, constantly bombarded by the sight of only plain, white stone day in and day out with nothing else going on in their lives but working and sleeping.

Coal shuddered, trying not to picture himself in their shoes. He felt a pang of sympathy and wished there was something he could do for them.

One building in particular stood out to him as he squinted in the dark. It was twice the size lengthwise of every other building in the compound, and Coal would swear he could see glimpses of white between the cracks of the walls. But this building was much better built than the others, the gaps in its walls kept at a minimum, a fact which further lent itself to Coal's suspicion that it was where they were housing the spiders.

A lot of the night's events had been built upon reckless momentum, but Coal recognized that he needed to take a minute and think through a legitimate plan of action if he stood any chance of succeeding.

If his assumption was correct and the long building was where all the spiders were stabled, then he needed to either cross all of Faranap or walk along the top of the wall to that side of the compound. Both scenarios invited unwanted attention from the guards. They might not be watching the top of the perimeter walls now, but a silhouette moving such a great distance for that amount of time would surely pop up in their periphery. There was nowhere to hide up there, standing stark against the moonlight.

There would be more opportunities to hide within Faranap itself. So that was what he would do. It was simply a matter of getting down there.

I can hop onto one of the roofs and then jump down onto the ground.

It was the most logical idea he had. Hopefully doing so would not cause the entire flimsy building to collapse, which did not seem out of the realm of possibility.

Once he made his way back onto the ground, he would have to slip between the buildings and make his way around the outside perimeter until he reached the stable. Saving time by cutting across the open expanse of dirt in the middle of all the buildings would be suicide.

Then he would quietly enter the stable, through a back entrance if possible.

Why would there be a back entrance? he immediately questioned himself.

He needed to expect the worst. He would probably have to go in through the front, in plain view of the two entryway guards. They stood only fifty or so feet from the stable.

And that was discounting any other guards milling about the compound or within any of the buildings. Possibly inside the stables themselves. It would be lunacy to expect that only two people were guarding all of Faranap, with all its allegedly "dangerous" inmates.

Once inside the stable, he'd choose a spider as fast as he could—preferably an orb weaver, but he would take any full-grown spider that looked like a decent racer—and...

And then what? he wondered. *How am I supposed to get out of here with a huge spider without anyone noticing?*

An unrealistic expectation. The spider was not going to be silent or subtle. If no one was alerted to his presence by that point, which was already a huge *if*, they definitely would be then.

He would need to just embrace the chaos and ride the spider out, praying that neither he nor the spider got shot by the guards' rifles. He could attempt some suppressing fire with his own pistol, but his encounter in the Houndsvein proved he was a horrible shot while standing still and at close range, let alone bucking wildly on the back of a moving spider.

But next would come the easiest part, which would be directing the spider to scurry up the walls and leap into the trees.

Any spider here would not be tagged in any way; that part of the process would come later, when they were making sales to stables in other cities. So even if they decided to go looking for their stolen animal, there would be nothing definitive linking him and his spider to Faranap. And there was no possibility of any guards here catching up to a spider at full speed.

As long as he cleared those walls on spiderback, he was home free.

It was not the best plan, but it was not the worst plan, either.

It was adequate.

Adequacy could get him far if he had a bit of luck on his side, although maybe his performance during Slapstick was proof that he did not.

No time like the present, he thought, psyching himself up.

Coal pushed himself to his feet, still crouching low, and swiftly crept across the wall to the tallest building he could jump to while still maintaining a good distance from the gate.

Things would move fast once he started.

You can still leave, he told himself, knowing it was untrue. He was in too deep now. His heart was already in it. And his heart was pounding, fit to burst from his chest.

He jumped, landing on the wooden rooftop with a heavy thump.

From inside came confused, muffled murmurings.

He had awoken the sleeping Flesh Eaters.

Off to a solid start.

16

COAL REMAINED COMPLETELY STILL
under the shroud of night, listening to the rustling of
the Flesh Eaters beneath his feet.

There came more mumbling, words that he could not pick
out at all but were clearly people speaking to each other.

*It was just a branch falling onto the roof, it's nothing, go
back to sleep,* he silently willed them. If they were rabid,
though, they could be constantly on edge and ready to charge
at a moment's notice.

Just then the thought occurred to Coal that it seemed the
compound had a surprising lack of guardsmen, if the majority
of its prisoners were meant to be so wild and dangerous.

But that was something to unpack at a later time. The prisoners were stirring.

Coal looked over at the gate to see if the noise alerted the
guards, but they weren't visible from his vantage point. Another building blocked his view.

He heard the creak of a door opening. Then footsteps. Slow, apprehensive, bare feet scuffling in the dirt.

There was no grass whatsoever in Faranap. Just dirt. The hopelessness of the entire place was overwhelming.

The person who had wandered out mumbled something to the others, and then a guard shouted from the gate, *"Get back inside!"* They immediately obeyed, a few footfalls followed by the door closing. Inside, the Flesh Eaters spoke amongst themselves for a minute or two before quieting down.

The guard's outburst solidified Coal's plan. He knew for sure now that he would be completely visible if he tried cutting across the small village. The place was almost totally dark, with no external lighting at all, only a hint of moonlight. Yet the guards had been able to spot the curious Flesh Eater; their night vision was impeccable.

They had to be foxes or raccoons, he guessed. Though a fox probably would have heard the bang of his entrance. Regardless, he would be sticking to the perimeter, staying in the shadows.

He still had not moved an inch since landing on top of the building. Once it sounded like the prisoners had calmed down and were drifting back to sleep, he slinked across the rooftop and peered over its edge.

The building was only two stories tall, able to fit a good amount of Flesh Eaters inside. It was not the tallest building in the world, but Coal did not feel fantastic about jumping off it. He looked around for anything to break his fall or to grab onto and slide down, like some sort of pole or gutter, but there was nothing of use.

Just gotta do it. Tuck and roll. That's something people do to make falls not hurt, right?

He felt woefully inept.

He took a deep breath, braced himself, and jumped. He curled his body in on itself, pulling his knees to his chest. There was an attempt to position himself so that he would land on his upper body and use his arms to push and roll safely, and he was immediately unsure if he was doing any of it correctly.

But he did not have long to find out, because the ground was hurtling toward him with no regard or mercy.

Something obviously went very wrong, as he crashed to the ground shoulder-first, coming to a complete halt and not rolling at all. There was a crack like lightning and a sharp pain in his left arm. It took all his willpower not to scream.

He lay prone in the dirt, gasping for air, the pain in his arm immense. It burned in his flesh.

He thought about that bed back in the hotel room and how much he would prefer to be laying in it, wrapped in soundless sleep.

"I have fucked up," he whispered to himself.

He rolled over onto his back, taking the weight off his injured arm. He took another deep, shuddering breath, attempting to center himself. The sky above was black.

Off to an exceptionally solid start.

Coal lifted his left arm, testing it. The limb trembled uncontrollably as he held it aloft, and it hurt like hell, but it did not seem broken. That was something, at least. He rotated it a bit, biting back a yelp. There was something wrong, but nothing that couldn't be fixed with a bit of rest and some painkillers.

He could not hear the guards moving, nor were the Flesh Eaters coming outside to investigate.

Either he had been quieter than he thought, or the prisoners feared reprimands. That was fine by him. Let fear be on his side for once.

Coal sat up, flexing his arm a bit more, and deemed it okay for now. He would have to try using it as little as possible. Riding spiderback would be tough, but figuring out a way to recover before the race was a problem for later.

For now, he stood and reassessed the situation. He was on the opposite side of the village from the spider stable. He would need to circle around the back and slowly make his way over there. Slow and quiet was the way to go; he needed to have some patience, as difficult as that tended to be for him.

He commenced moving around the wall, behind the decrepit wooden buildings. It was shameful how poor the living conditions were here. With such large, careless gaps in the walls, a night with even the slightest breeze could be bone-chilling for those trying to sleep.

Coal peeked through the gaps in the slats with each building he passed, his curiosity getting the better of him.

Some of the structures held equipment for various jobs, none of which looked familiar. If he was brought here, would he be put to work on day one and simply be expected to know what to do with this machinery? Was someone there whose job it was to train new workers? He had trouble believing Faranap or the other two Flesh Eater compounds had employee training protocols like Nyers Foods or any of Ruska's major companies.

Others held more sleeping prisoners. He could only clearly make out a few—there was a hefty bear, a fellow fox, even a rabbit. The latter surprised him. There had to be an interesting story there.

They all slept curled up on the floor. There were some paper-thin blankets and a few flat pillows to share amongst them, but no real beds to speak of. Just lying in the dirt, shivering in the night air.

But something else caught Coal's eye and he leaned in closer, just shy of slipping his snout through the gap. His eyes widened.

Everyone inside was muzzled.

Their mouths were clamped shut with a metal contraption that locked together on the back of their heads. Each muzzle was specially crafted for the race it was covering, to accommodate their differing facial features and mouth shapes.

It was not as if Coal was expecting the living conditions in a Flesh Eater prison to be anything resembling pleasant, but it was so much worse than he had imagined, and it was growing more horrific with each new aspect he learned.

That was why their speech had been so difficult to understand when they heard him up on the roof. They were speaking to each other through their muzzles.

If they even had to sleep with them on, Coal could not picture any scenario where they were allowed to remove them. Mealtimes had to be quite an ordeal.

Do they even get to eat meals? he started to wonder. At this point, it would not surprise him if the answer was no.

This glimpse into his potential future filled Coal with an overwhelming dread that threatened to crush him. Paired with the dull ache in his arm, he needed to get out of here fast.

Slow and quiet was sounding less and less appealing.

Every minute in here was another blow to his spirit. He wished he could help these people somehow. Given his track record, though, he could barely manage to help himself.

He resolved to not look inside any more of the buildings. Doing so would only distract him, and he needed to focus on the task at hand.

No additional obstacles had popped up thus far, and he was already halfway across the back wall. It seemed too good to be true, but he took a break to sit against the wall. The pain in his arm was clouding his mind, giving him a headache. He was dizzying and needed to rest a minute to recuperate.

While he sat there with his head pressed into the wall, eyes clamped shut, his ears flicked to his left at the sound of someone walking. He sniffed at the air. The scent was unfamiliar. Rotten. Acrid.

It came from the direction he was headed toward, so this was not good news. He opened his eyes and squinted, trying to focus and find out what exactly he was dealing with.

Please just be some guy coming outside to take a piss.

He knew the wish was unrealistic, but he put it out there anyway. Maybe some sort of deity was listening and feeling generous tonight.

But obviously no one was listening, for what Coal discovered as he peered down the walkway was a horrifying sight.

It was a creature like no animal he had ever heard of, which instantly reminded him of the not-ventem in the Houndsvein, but he could not even conjure up a regular beast to compare it to. The thing was covered in unnaturally smooth flesh that appeared to be a sickly yellow when it caught in the moonlight. It was bipedal, lumbering on thick legs with cloven hooves. Its arms were long, gangly, hanging down to the ground and dragging its hands in the dirt as it walked. Though it was a stretch to call them hands; what Coal saw on the end of its arms were more akin to daggers than hands. Blades the same foul color as its flesh, coming to a sharp point. The thing's head was on the end of a long neck that stretched and curved in the air, swaying mindlessly like a worm, its face devoid of features except for a round mouth that did not close. Short tendrils hung from its chin, swaying in the air just like its neck, as if they were billowing underwater. The tendrils reached out, searching for something.

So this was why Faranap did not need very many normal guards.

It had monsters lurking about.

Coal could not see any eyes or ears on its face, so it was possible that he remained undetected for now. Something told him its tendrils were how it moved through the world. Whether they were sensing smell or vibrations or whatever the fuck else, he did not care to find out.

He stood and scrambled back the way he'd come, away from the abomination. Away was good. He risked a glance over his shoulder and saw the creature had paused, craning its neck in his direction with all its tendrils flailing madly.

That can't be good.

It wasn't. The monster charged toward him, silent but for its clomping footsteps.

A small, frightened bark loosed from Coal's lips, unable to contain himself.

He ran, cutting half the distance he had previously covered. The thing would chase him all the way round to the front gate if he let it.

There was more disturbed rustling from inside one of the structures housing Flesh Eaters. Coal ducked out of the pathway and pressed his body tight against the side of the building, hoping that the monster would be unable to differentiate his scent or movements or whatever else from those who were inside, only a few feet away.

He held his breath as the monster came to a halt, its tendrils dancing in the air, searching him out.

It turned toward the building, its head directly facing him. He stared into its eyeless face, watching the tendrils tangle with each other as they tried to deduce where he was.

Tears streamed silently down Coal's face, wetting the fur of his cheeks. His body shuddered, holding back sobs as he stared at the monstrosity.

Much to his relief, the thing started to veer closer toward the building itself rather than him, picking up on the movement and muffled murmurs inside. If nothing else, this could put less suspicion on him; if the prisoners heard him sneaking around, they might just assume their monstrous warden was making the rounds.

Coal watched the abomination consider what it was sensing. Then it reached out toward a gap in the wall. The smooth, yellow flesh suddenly bubbled, its blade morphing into a three-pronged claw with which to grasp the plank's edge, tapping its claws on the building's inner wall.

He had to suppress another yelp at the sight of this thing shapeshifting before his eyes. He tried to blink away his tears, but they kept coming. He wiped them from his eyes to clear his vision.

What the hell is this?

It was like magic. Coal could not comprehend how the monster had just changed its physical body. Though, to be fair, he could not comprehend how the thing existed in the first place.

He gaped at the thing's rounded face, staring into its perfectly circular mouth hole. It had no teeth, but a whip-like tongue suddenly lashed out and the creature emitted a piercing shriek.

His instinct was to bolt, but fear immobilized him.

The abomination stood completely still. A few seconds later, another shriek came from elsewhere in the compound.

It removed its claw from the gap (Coal could hear a collective sigh of relief from the muzzled people within) and it transformed back into a blade, though one much longer this time. Its other blade extended in turn.

Then it took a few steps back, the tendrils still surveying the area, before turning to continue down the pathway on the route it had been on before catching wind of him.

Coal was incredibly torn on whether "slow and quiet" was truly the best way to proceed, because more and more he wanted to get out of here.

Once the monster had rounded the corner and was patrolling the other wall, Coal wiped more tears from his face and pushed himself from the building, steadying himself. He then continued proceeding the way he had been going. Not quite running, but not taking it as slow as he had before. Keeping on the tips of his toes to go unheard.

That thing had come out of nowhere, absolutely no sign of it when he'd been gazing down from above, so there was no telling how many of them were prowling around Faranap. There was clearly at least one other, given the call and response. He saw no reason why the others would not have responded to the monster's call if they were around, but he'd count himself lucky if there were just the two.

It did not seem like anything of the natural world. Especially not with its bizarre ability to transform itself.

The Dirt King had lived for hundreds of years and was capable of crafting unimaginable wonders. He was the reason why Ruska had electricity, why medicine had reached such potency, why architecture and infrastructure had some such a long way. The Dirt King, unknowable as he was, was solely responsible for every technological breakthrough in the valley. It wasn't out of the question that he could create a creature of that nature, though Coal was hard-pressed to think of a justifiable reason as to why he would do such a thing. Making it only for patrolling Flesh Eater compounds and instilling fear in them seemed unusually cruel, but...

Well, everything about this place seemed unusually cruel.

He came to the next corner and cautiously leaned over to inspect the path. The part of it he could see was clear, but farther along where the stable sat was not visible from this distance.

When the second abomination had screamed, it was from the direction of the gate and stable. It could not be far off, hidden in the darkness, waiting for him. Perhaps what the first one had communicated was a warning: look out for a bumbling, idiot fox.

He skulked forward, pausing at the opening between each building to ensure an abomination was not lying in wait. The stable was now in sight, only three buildings away, though he could still not determine whether it contained a convenient back entrance.

There then came another of the monstrous screams. Did the residents have to constantly put up with these check-ins every night? Coal had to assume it was a regular occurrence, since the first yell had not kicked the guards into action.

The response was close by. Coal's ears flicked and he pinpointed it in front of the next building over.

Close, but far enough away to stay under cover.

He assumed.

Coal inched forward, testing the waters. His boots scraped against the dirt, kicking up tiny clouds of dust, but he heard no movement from the abomination. It was standing still in front of whatever building this was. There were no gaps in its backside through which he could sneak a peek at what it contained.

He moved past that building, and then the next, and only when he reached the one before the spider stable did he hear the unsteady tread of the monster.

It was moving in the same direction as him, spitting out another scream-click to its partner.

Coal rushed ahead with the intense need to enter that stable before the monster reached it.

As he ran, the abomination's footsteps quickened in kind.

Shit.

He stopped cold, as did the creature.

He was standing behind the stable, and he guessed that the abomination was in front of the building, sniffing him out with its tendrils. Likewise, he could smell its putrid stench on the air.

It would be easier to determine his location here, amongst the spiders rather than other foxes and the rest of the Flesh Eaters. He would not remain hidden for long.

Standing still would get him captured or killed. He couldn't leave, so he needed to act.

There was already a high risk of being seen by the guards if he navigated around to the front of the stable, seeing as there was no back entrance after all. With some hulking abomination thrown into the mix, it would not be a smart move. He needed a distraction.

All he had with him was the gun. Firing it would be stupid, revealing his location instantly.

I could throw it.

It was another boneheaded idea, but nothing else was coming to mind. He could throw a boot instead, but having to make a quick getaway without proper footwear could be tricky. His arm was already injured; he did not need to add a foot or leg to the list.

Fuck it, he thought. Might as well build on that reckless momentum.

He unholstered the gun and checked that the safety was on. The last thing he wanted was for it to fire when it landed and possibly harm one of the prisoners. Then he reared back and chucked it as hard as he could in the direction from which he'd come.

It bashed against a rooftop, skittering across the wood before plummeting to the ground.

The abomination let out another click, which the other responded to, and then set off toward the sound. So that was the monster taken care of. For a couple minutes, at least.

"Hell was that?" asked one of the guards, now only about fifty feet away from Coal's current location.

"Go look," said the other.

Coal heard the first guard scoff before saying, "The ugly fucker'll take care of it. Probably just a rock or a branch or something."

But the other guard was insistent. "That thing ain't even got any eyes," he said.

"No, but it's got hooks for hands and shit. It'll take care of whatever's over there."

"It ain't got eyes and it don't speak same as us so it can't tell us whether it was a rock or not. Go look. You ain't gettin' paid to sit around on your ass all night while those things do all the work for you."

"I'm not gonna go near the fuckin' thing," said the first guard.

Coal was getting antsy. He was wasting time listening to the men argue. The abomination could saunter back over any second.

"For fuck's sake," the other guard muttered. "You're such a baby. Come on, then."

Coal heard one pair of footsteps start toward where the gun had landed, shortly followed by a second. He silently thanked the deity that had earlier forsaken him.

He scurried over to the other side of the stable, looking around the corner at the two guards. They were indeed raccoons, as he had predicted. He watched their white-and-black tails swish as they walked. They were taking their time crossing the open yard, but soon they were out of sight behind the building. He hurried forward, peeking around the next corner to watch them continue on. Once he determined they were out of earshot, he stepped forward and slipped through the stable doors.

The long, rectangular building was covered top to bottom in spiderwebs. Sticky webbing clung to Coal's boots as he traipsed through, examining the sleeping insects.

Nearest the door were the babies, dozens of them cramped in each diminutive stall, huddled together in a corner as they slept. The adolescent spiders were each at least the size of his head, if not slightly larger. A plaque adorned each stall stating what breed of baby spider it held. Their stalls were covered with glass that had been drilled with breathing holes so that they could be observed but not run loose.

The adult spiders, on the other hand, had free reign of the building, just like they did in normal forested stables. Right now they were all asleep, save for two or three that scuttled around the topmost corners of the building.

Coal scanned the large room in search of an orb weaver. He would settle for a different breed if he couldn't find one, but he grinned when he spotted one sleeping on its web over in the back corner, only a few feet from the floor.

The spider was large, easily two or three times bigger than Coal. It had a thick, round abdomen colored white with splotches of yellow and brown that mirrored on each side, eventually coming together at the tip near its spinnerets. Its thorax and head were white, with a tinge of grey to them. The long, spindly legs matched the coloring on its abdomen, alternating stripes of yellow and brown, giving way to black at the ends.

He tiptoed over to the insect and gently cooed it awake. The spider's eyes blinked open and its body tensed, black fangs shivering, but Coal clicked his tongue to soothe it.

"It's okay," he whispered. *"Wanna go for a ride with me, White Rose?"*

The spider relaxed, embracing his calming energy. It knew he was a stranger but that he was not there to hurt it. He could be trusted.

He lightly tugged on one of its legs, indicating that it should climb down off its web. It did so obediently and with haste. The Flesh Eaters were doing a swell job of training these spiders.

Another click.

But this one was not from him.

Coal turned slowly and saw one of the abomination's frames filling the doorway. Its bladed arms scratched into the dirt floor, its tendrils tasting the air.

A reply click came, and the other abomination was just outside the door.

"Looks like they found 'em," he heard one of the guards say distantly. "Come on out!" he then yelled.

As of yet, the abomination had still not moved. He wondered what information it was gleaning from its nasty, worm-like appendages.

Coal warily slipped onto the orb weaver's back. Regrettably, there was no time to search the stable for proper riding tack. He tightly gripped its abdomen with his legs and held on to the sides of its thorax.

It was not the ideal situation, but he was about to receive the biggest possible test of White Rose's mettle.

"Time to go," he whispered.

He dug in with his heels and White Rose shot forward. The abomination screamed and raised its bladed arms.

17

THE ORB WEAVER CUT across the length of the stable in a flash. Coal would have been more impressed with its speed in the moment if they had not been barreling toward two outstretched flesh-blades.

He steered the spider to the right and it heeded him with no hesitation. The spider's spindly legs did not miss a step transferring from the dirt floor to the wood wall, skittering onto its side and narrowly avoiding the abomination altogether.

Coal clung to the insect's abdomen and clenched his fists in its thick strands of hair, using all his strength to maintain his grip now that he was horizontal. Sharp pain shot through his left arm as gravity pushed him down. He was able to resist for a few seconds, but he had to give in and let go. In turn, he tightened his legs, taking care not to squeeze the spider's abdomen too hard and either hurt it or give it an unintended command.

The abomination a few feet behind them screamed in irritation. Its partner, just outside, screamed in return.

With great difficulty at their current angle, Coal lifted up his right leg and tapped one of White Rose's leg. The spider immediately did what he wanted, which was leap off the wall and land safely on the ground. His face slammed into the thorax and the awful taste of dirty hair filled his mouth, but he took another moment to appreciate how well the prisoners had trained their spiders.

They were facing the wrong way, but Coal could hear the abomination running toward them.

There was only a small bit of distance between them and the door now, but the second abomination was hunkering down and blocking their exit.

All the commotion had awoken the other spiders in the stable. The babies, of which there were four or five dozen, were now scuttling all over their little stalls. Climbing up onto the glass, tripping over each other, making agitated chirps and hisses.

The adults were climbing down off their webs to see what was going on. At the sight of the abominations, they all began to hiss in warning as well.

Coal grinned. It felt good to have some backup.

"Come out and we can resolve this peacefully!" one of the guards shouted, unaware of the chaos that was set to erupt inside. Coal then heard the raccoon yell, "Get back inside! No one told you to come out! No, I wasn't talkin' to you!"

The Flesh Eaters were joining the confusion. Faranap was waking up.

White Rose pushed forward, rushing past the door and climbing up the far wall instead. The abomination came to a halt, letting out another horrible screech. The second one re-mained outside, waiting in case Coal somehow made it out there, demonstrating a surprising amount of intelligence.

"Good spider!" Coal praised White Rose, patting it on the thorax with his left hand. He could fight through the pain for that much.

He then learned that a pat on the left side of the thorax was a command of which he was previously unaware.

White Rose hissed angrily and propelled itself off the wall straight toward the abomination, all the while shooting web-bing from its spinnerets, which attached to the wall and trailed behind them as the spider flew across the room. It landed on the ground and skittered past the abomination, which swung a blade and nicked Coal's already-injured arm.

He barked in pain, his arm hanging limp at his side.

The spider almost accidentally flung him off its back as it skidded to a halt ten feet from the abomination, circling around and running back toward the wall from which they had come, still trailing webbing.

It was trying to wrap up the monster.

Coal tapped White Rose again, and the spider once again jumped left, in the direction he had tapped. It landed atop the glass lids of the baby spiders' stalls and darted across them until Coal tapped its thorax again and it leapt leftward, scarcely avoiding a collision with the abomination.

But White Rose moved past it and Coal continued tapping precisely, the spider's leaps growing more and more frequent so that they wrapped the monster in tight webbing.

It struggled within the strong strands of white, screaming for its ally.

238 • *Travis M. Riddle*

By now the other distressed spiders had left their respective webs and were crawling the walls, some heading toward the cocooned abomination in the middle of their stable while others went to the door where they could hear further disturbances.

Coal brought White Rose to a halt on the ground with the webbed abomination between them and the exit.

"Good spider," he said again, this time not giving it any stray touches that might set it off again.

After all the terrible conditions he had observed tonight, it made Coal laugh seeing a dozen fully-grown spiders crawl out of the stable toward the unsuspecting guards. He figured that even though the beasts had free reign of the stable, that door was never opened except for a couple seconds while someone entered or exited. They were finally getting a taste of freedom.

Predictably, the guards let out high-pitched screams as the spiders emerged from the stable. Coal could also hear muffled reactions from the muzzled Flesh Eaters, though it was hard to discern whether they were reacting with fear or triumph.

The abomination in the stable quickly shredded its bonds. The blades on its arms tore through the shimmering white web, which cascaded dreamily to the ground. Its tendrils pointed straight and stiff toward Coal and his mount, which did not seem to him like a good thing.

Coal waited to see what the monster's next move was before instructing White Rose to do anything.

He watched as the thing's bladed arms began to shift, the oddly smooth yellow skin bubbling and pulsating like boiling water. They thinned out and curved into pointed hooks with barbs at the ends.

Again, this did not seem like a good thing to him.

His body went rigid, and he could feel White Rose's do the same.

But the abomination remained in place. It arced its arm back and then swung, the flesh stretching forward at an incredible speed, fixed for their position.

"Fuck!" Coal swore, instinctively tapping White Rose on the side again.

The spider jumped to the left, spraying more web behind it, and smashed through the glass plate covering the stall full of baby funnel weavers. They scurried out of their confinements, knocking shards of glass everywhere and climbing all over the stable with no regard for what was happening.

Another shriek from the abomination as it retracted its hooked arm. That was a nasty trick Coal had not been expecting. Nothing like this creature had ever been documented in the world. Not in any of the books he had read, anyway.

The adult spiders that had remained indoors now all leapt at once toward the abomination, seeing it as a threat to the freed babies.

It had no time to morph its hooks into weapons more suited for close-quarters combat, but that unfortunately did not seem to deter the thing too much.

Coal watched with horror as it hacked away at the spiders. Funnel weavers, tarantulas, dome weavers, orb weavers, jumping spiders—none stood a chance against the abomination.

The hooks dug into the spiders' thoraxes, ripping through and slicing their bodies apart. It gained the opportunity to turn one hook back into a blade, which it used to slice off limbs and pierce eyes in between cutting up webbing that the spiders were attempting to contain it with.

There were only so many spiders in the stable, over half of them having gone outside, and those that remained would clearly not last long. It was a sobering look at how White Rose would fare if Coal made any attempt to tackle the thing head-on.

He knew he needed to seize this chance while the abomination was occupied with the others. He dug his heels into White Rose's abdomen and the spider lunged forward, scuttling past its brethren and out the door into Faranap.

The spiders outside were doing much better than their indoor counterparts, seeing as they had much more space to maneuver around. A few large insect corpses littered the ground, but it seemed the beasts had learned a lesson from their fallen allies. They were not all attacking the second abomination at once, but had instead surrounded it, keeping a safe distance and emitting warning hisses.

Apparently they did not know that the creature could extend its flesh, and frankly Coal did not know why it had not yet employed the tactic, but for now it stood in the center of the circle, its tendrils flailing in every direction.

The raccoon guards opted to not deal with the spider outbreak, instead trying to usher their wards back indoors.

Flesh Eaters from every sleeping structure had filed outside to catch a glimpse at the unfolding events. He supposed this was the most excitement Faranap had ever seen. Muzzled faces of every sort crowded around the hubbub, hoping to get the best view. Some were smiling and laughing (as much as they could through their iron clamps) at the guards' dismayed efforts.

Coal's heart swelled seeing such joy brought to his fellow Flesh Eaters. At least one good thing had come out of this botched heist. Now he just needed to get out of there unscathed.

Well, he was already fairly scathed, so just not any more scathed than he currently was. That wasn't too much to ask for.

Just then the abomination burst through the door of the stable, its body covered in blood and other juices, none of which was its own. The thing had no more than some light scratches marring its otherwise perfect flesh. It loosed a howl, much different than any other sound it had made previously, which was returned with a vicious roar from the other surrounded by spiders.

It must have been some sort of battle cry, because the surrounded abomination then shot its bladed arms outward toward the edges of the circle and began to twirl in place, slicing through all the spiders which were too shocked and slow to move out of the way. All of them crumpled to the ground in tattered heaps.

The abomination's arms fell limp to the ground, looking like twenty-foot strands of cooked noodles, before slithering back toward its body. It turned to face Coal and White Rose, the only remaining spider aside from the babies in the stable.

Coal looked over his shoulder at the monster behind him and saw it rearing to throw its hooks forward. A moment before it did so, he took a leap of faith and tapped both his hands on White Rose's thorax simultaneously.

It accomplished what he wanted. The spider jumped straight up into the air, shooting out webbing behind it, and the abomination's hooks dug into the dirt where they had been standing mere seconds before.

The webbing sprayed onto the monster, covering its head and all its tendrils. White Rose landed on top of the hooks and scurried forward in the direction of the guards.

They only covered a few strides before the abomination was able to remove the web from its head. Coal wished he still had his gun and could blast the thing in the face.

In hindsight, perhaps it was an outrageously foolish move to throw his one and only weapon into the night. Maybe he should have thrown his boot after all. There was always next time.

Coal refused to believe these creatures could catch up to a spider running at top speed. There was simply no way. The only thing that might derail him and White Rose was the things' ability to extend their limbs, but surely even that had its limits.

White Rose barreled into the guards, who did not have time to even fully turn around before the spider tossed them aside like dolls. They both flew through the air and crashed into the dirt, eliciting cheers and jeers from the onlookers.

Coal did not glance back at the two monsters. He did not want to know how far away they were or see blades and hooks and whatever else they turned their nasty arms into flying toward him.

Instead he focused on steering White Rose forward and in between the shoddy buildings, headed straight for the perimeter wall.

The spider picked up speed as it ran, building on that reckless momentum just like its rider. The Flesh Eaters in its path were smart enough to duck out of the way before they were carelessly thrown aside like the raccoons.

More screeches sounded off behind them. The abominations were furious. He could hear their hooves pounding in the dirt, frantically trying to match their speed and utterly failing.

Coal steered White Rose toward a slightly wider opening between two buildings that the spider could hopefully fit through. It raced through the narrow alley, its legs nearly brushing against the sides of the buildings, and they were coming up on the wall fast.

He gave White Rose the command to jump (without spraying any web) and the spider sprung forward, turning its body in the air to cling to the wall. Coal had to hold on tight as they ran straight up the stone wall.

They crested the top and White Rose intuitively jumped into the branches of the nearest tree, leaving its life in Faranap behind.

Coal knew the guards would not bother giving chase, but he could not be sure about the abominations. He wouldn't put scaling a wall past them, given how adaptable he'd seen they could be.

He told White Rose to stop a moment, cognizant that the monsters might be in pursuit, but needing to take a beat to get his bearings. He had to make sure they were traveling toward Soponunga and not the mountains or deeper into the forest to be lost and forgotten.

Monstrous screams echoed through the woods, and Coal took that as his cue to get moving. White Rose shot forward in the direction he indicated, which he was *mostly* sure was the correct way.

With the spider's unmatched speed, it would take far less time to return to Soponunga than the hour it had taken him to reach Faranap. Even as far as spiders went, White Rose was

244 • Travis M. Riddle

surprisingly quick on its feet. Coal was impressed. He had chosen well.

I might pull this off after all.

That mildly hopeful thought also shook him from his daze, and he realized that he had actually pulled off the night's mission. He was darting through the forest on spiderback.

And on top of that, he was not dead. Not even a little bit.

He congratulated himself on a job well done, thinking that maybe he was cut out for a life of crime after all. Zank would be proud of his wild success.

How will Ilio react?

The sudden question cut him.

Part of him still found it hard to get a clear read on the woodpecker. Ilio did not shy away from life's underbelly, considering his day-to-day dealings with Garna Nomak, but at the same time he did not seem to fully embrace the lifestyle. Coal worried about telling him what he'd done, but he also didn't want to lie to the man. And him finding out was unavoidable, since Coal would be competing in the race now. He couldn't say he conjured a spider out of thin air.

These were dire circumstances. Surely Ilio would understand. He said he could relate to the complications of life, hadn't he? This was just another in a long string of complications Coal had faced. Hell, he might even be impressed. Coal was like an action hero now, escaping from a prison and the clutches of ghastly monsters by the skin of his teeth.

The abominations' screams faded away after a few minutes. Coal was right about them being unable to match the spider's speed, especially amongst the various natural obstacles a forest floor presented.

For the first time in hours—in days, really—Coal felt relief.

Exhaustion hit him all at once and he had to prop himself up on White Rose's back, nearly slumping over asleep. He could not wait to hit that hotel bed. It might even keep him from attending the festival.

Twenty minutes later they were approaching the tree line, and Coal spied the outline of Soponunga through the trees. He could hear the Lunsk River flowing in the distance. It was a beautiful, welcoming sound.

The sun was starting to crest the horizon, but neither of the stables would be open yet and he could not exactly stroll into the Longowosk with an adult spider.

Coal slowed White Rose and they stood for a moment in the grassy clearing between the forest and the entryway bridge. He looked back over his shoulder at the mass of trees and an idea came to him.

He brought the spider back to the trees and climbed up, having it craft a thick, solid web among the branches for them both to relax in.

White Rose settled down quickly, pulling all its legs tight to its body as it nestled on the webbing, which was so tightly wound it was more like a nest than a typical spiderweb. Coal lay down nearby, not wanting to intrude on the spider's space too much since they had only met not even an hour ago.

His eyelids drooped and he could not muster the strength to keep them open. Rather than fight the tiredness, he gave in, figuring he had at least an hour or two before the stables would let him house his newly-acquired mount.

So the two lay up in the tree together in the soft web.

Only a minute passed before Coal passed out, finally able to sleep for the first time in nearly a full day.

His slumber was heavy, but not dreamless. He dreamed of Jaq Yul, with its cozy, kitschy inns and the famous hot springs. Ilio was with him.

18

KNOCK SOUNDED ON Coal's door and jolted him from sleep. He could have continued for several more hours, maybe several more days. He had been enveloped in those silky Longowosk sheets, now tangled around his legs and pulled up to his fuzzy black chin. It was a feeling he was not keen to dismiss.

Forget the race, forget the prize, forget the Stingers who were after him. He wanted to lay in bed.

It was a touch better than sleeping on a web in a tree, if Coal wanted to understate it. He and White Rose had slept up in the treetops for a little over an hour before the spider awoke and grew antsy, waking him up as well with the subtle shifts of its legs jiggling the web. They then climbed down out of the tree and entered the city, making their way back to Soponunga's stablemaster (the Sculio Brothers had left a bad taste in Coal's mouth). The owner was still setting up shop when they arrived, so Coal waited a few minutes before getting

White Rose stabled. The old frog questioned where Coal found such a spider, but he kept his answer vague, implying that it came from the Sculio Brothers while not outright stating as such. Then he trudged back to the hotel, his feet dragging on the docks the entire way, before collapsing in bed.

And now someone wanted to see him.

He glanced at the clock and saw that it was a little more than an hour until midday. The race's opening festival was to commence an hour past then.

Without thinking, he yanked the sheets away with his left arm and winced at the pain. In the intervening hours his arm had not improved, but at the very least it had not gotten any worse. He would gladly take that. But riding White Rose had been a struggle one-handed, and he did not anticipate the Spiderback Showdown route being any less strenuous. Something needed to be done.

Before heading to the festival, he would track down some painkillers. Ilio would probably know where to buy medicine here. His back alley sloth friend might actually have some stronger stuff.

And speaking of which, Ilio was standing on the other side of the door, looking vastly more put-together than Coal.

The red feathers on top of his head were perfectly coiffed, contrasting with the black-and-white feathers of his face and bright orange eyes. He was wearing a more casual outfit than the previous day, though he still looked professional in the simple attire: a white button-up long-sleeve tucked into black trousers. The flashiest thing about the outfit was his belt buckle, which was a small, silver depiction of billowing clouds.

The man pushed his glasses up his beak and puffed his cheeks at the sight of Coal before letting out a soft chuckle.

"That was rude," Coal said with a smirk.

"It was but a laugh," said Ilio. "May I come in?"

Coal nodded and stood aside. As Ilio strode into the room, Coal said, "Yes, but it was a laugh at my appearance. Am I wrong?"

"That is putting it a bit harshly," Ilio objected. "I was merely amused by your level of dishevelment, not your specific appearance."

"Ah, of course. My level of dishevelment."

"Of course." He puffed his cheeks again. Then he said, "Good morning."

"Good morning," said Coal. "Want some coffee?" He walked over to the brewer, not quite sure how to work the appliance, but willing to give it a shot.

Ilio shook his head. "I am fine for now. And I was actually coming to invite you to a meal."

"Oh, great. So I don't have to flounder like a fool trying to get this thing to work," Coal grinned, taking a step away from the mysterious brewer. "Nomak treating everyone to a big lunch before the festival?"

Ilio's cheeks deflated a bit. "No. I was actually just inviting you myself." He sounded hurt.

Coal raised his eyebrows. "Oh! That sounds even better," he said sincerely. Very little of him ever actually wanted to interact with Garna Nomak, but dining with Ilio, on the other hand, would be a treat.

The puff returned to Ilio's brilliant red cheeks. "Excellent," he said. "I know just the place. I will leave you to get ready and wait for you downstairs in the lobby." His voice was tinged with eagerness.

"Is there some sort of dress code there?" Coal asked, looking the bird's outfit up and down. "I don't think I can match that."

"No, no, anything is fine," Ilio assured him.

Coal agreed to the plan, and Ilio took his leave.

He quickly bathed and clothed himself, grabbing whatever crumpled outfit was atop the pile inside his traveling bag and throwing it on. Looking at himself in the mirror, he decided he was not a *complete* mess, though as he had predicted, he was no match for Ilio. The bird may once more laugh at his level of dishevelment. His fur was looking nice and soft, the orange pleasantly bright, but the wrinkles in his dark green shirt were the biggest offenders. He spent a minute trying to smooth them out before relenting.

Downstairs, he found Ilio sitting in a lounge chair with his legs crossed, flipping through a tiny notebook.

Coal stopped a few feet away, staring at him until he noticed. It took almost a full minute before Ilio finally glanced up and realized it was him. He laughed and closed the notebook, slipping it into his pocket.

"You look better," he said.

"Thanks. You look the same," Coal replied. "Interesting reading?" he asked as Ilio stood.

"Not particularly. Just my day planner."

"Any more virility errands to run for Nomak today?"

"Thankfully not. He should be satiated for the time being."

"Gross."

"Poor choice of words. Sorry. Are you ready to depart?"

"Yes, I am *ready to depart*," Coal smiled, mocking him but without any edge.

Ilio did not seem to notice regardless. He puffed his cheeks and led the way outside.

It was a beautiful Highmonth day in Soponunga. Warm and bright, with a gentle cooling breeze. A nearly cloudless sky above the calming flow of the Lunsk. Perfect for a festival.

Everyone on the streets seemed poised for the festivities to begin. Many people were rushing to and fro, hauling supplies or hanging up decorations or scribbling on signs. Coal assumed the event was confined to Tucarumong Street, but based on what he saw, it seemed the celebration would engulf the entire city.

"So, where we goin'?" Coal asked, breathing in the fresh air. He had only slept a handful of hours, but the luxurious bed and the crisp river air made him feel refreshed.

Ilio pondered the question a moment before answering, "I am not sure I want to say. It might be more fun to keep it a secret."

"I must remind you," Coal said, "that I know nothing about this city. Less than nothing. You could say the name of any restaurant and it would mean nothing to me. Less than nothing. Except for the Lodge, I guess. And the Longowosk deck, if that place even has a name. But if that's where we're going, then I would say you've chosen a pretty inefficient route to get there. No offense."

The jape made Ilio laugh. "No, it is neither of those places. It is an establishment called the Crookery."

"Weird name. Seems like it fits that sloth's store better than it does a restaurant." It could have worked as a smooth segue, but Coal was giddy about being invited to a meal with Ilio and did not want to bring up his sore arm yet.

"It is meant to be clever," Ilio explained. "The conceit is that the restaurant specializes in lighter, healthier fare but is just as flavorful and filling as any other place, so there must be something suspicious going on behind the scenes in order to achieve that."

"You say it's 'meant' to be clever as if you don't think it actually is clever."

Ilio shrugged. "It is a fine name. But I think they simply incorporate more vegetables into their recipes than most other primarily insect-based restaurants around the city in order to trick you into believing it is healthier, but still cook it all in loads of butter. That is my theory."

"I hope your theory is right," Coal told him. "That sounds tasty to me. A load of butter is just what I need this morning."

The Crookery was on the next platform over, which pleased Coal to see since his stomach was starting to rumble. His late-night escapade evidently worked off the massive amount of food he'd eaten with the Garna. It was the only explanation that made sense as to why he could possibly be hungry again after consuming what felt like three times his weight at dinner.

It was a modest wooden building, painted pastel orange with a cute yellow roof. A hand-painted oval sign hung above the doorway with the restaurant's name written in swooping red letters, accompanied by an illustration of a stereotypical thief's mask with the eyeholes acting as the two O's in its name. It was nestled between a toy store and a plant shop. Nothing in the plant shop's window display interested him, but there were some colorful oddities at the toy store that caught his eye.

Ilio held the door open for him and they entered the Crookery. There was only room for around ten tables, with four people being the largest party size that could fit without combining them. The place was half full; they were arriving right between breakfast and lunch, and Coal expected it probably had a waiting list during those busier hours. It was too charming to not be a hit, as long as the food was good too.

A kind macaw showed them to their table, a circular iron table that was a faded green in the back of the restaurant. Ilio made a passing comment about how it sort of matched Coal's shirt.

"That's what I was going for," Coal told him with a laugh. "I wanted to match a table."

They flipped through the simple menu, covering only one two-sided sheet of paper. Not nearly extravagant enough for a man such as Garna Nomak, but perfect for the two of them, in Coal's opinion.

He asked what Ilio liked to get there, and the woodpecker informed him of a few favorite dishes. One consisted of thick pieces of toast topped with a large, meaty mushroom cap and smothered in a green sauce made of thinly-diced cilantro and kale mixed into oil and grated cheese.

Another, which Ilio was ordering today, was a hash with black beans, sweet potatoes, bell peppers, and onions cooked in butter and seasoned with a special house blend of spices. It also came with a cup of hot sauce on the side for the customer to drizzle on top themselves. Coal thought he might order the same, but he continued browsing the menu in case something else popped out.

Everything sounded good, but nothing stood out to him like the hash. That was what he wanted. "Would it look insane if we ordered the same thing?" he asked.

"I would accuse you of blatantly copying me due to my intelligence and impeccable ordering skills, but I do not think our waiter would call you insane."

"Well, I don't think they'd *call* me insane either, but they might *think* it."

"I am afraid that is the risk you will have to run if you want to eat the potato hash."

"You wouldn't share yours if I got something else?"

Ilio shook his head, sporting a theatrically apologetic expression. "I am afraid not, sorry. It is too delicious to let even a single bite slip away."

"Wow." Coal grinned and gave the menu one last look-over. He firmly decided on the hash.

After they placed their order, Ilio said, "It seemed like you had a rough night."

"Because of my level of dishevelment?"

"That, and because you were not in your room when I got back to the hotel."

Coal blinked. "You came to my room?"

Ilio choked on his water, suddenly flustered. He coughed several times, regained his composure, and said, "Well, yes. I wanted to make sure you were okay. You were slightly inebriated, as well as distraught, when you excused yourself from the game."

"I wouldn't say I was *distraught*," Coal objected, "but that's sweet of you. Yes, I would describe it as a rough, late night."

Ilio just looked at him expectantly, waiting for an interesting story to go along with what he had said. Coal was still anxious about laying out the details for Ilio, but it had to be done eventually. The man would know about White Rose at some point today anyway.

Coal said, "I got a spider last night."

Ilio's eyes lit up. "That is great news," he said. "I am pleased to hear that. Though I admit I am unsure where you would retrieve such a thing at a late hour."

"Yeah, that's the thing," Coal said. He sighed, then dove into the story. He explained how the idea came to him, and his messy infiltration of the compound. Ilio's eyes widened with shock, but Coal had not even gotten to the most disturbing part. The woodpecker sat motionless as Coal described the monstrosities lurking around Faranap, knowing that his descriptions were not doing the abominations justice. "Do you have any idea what the hell those could be?" he asked. Ilio shook his head, saying nothing, and so Coal went on to explain how he busted White Rose out of the stable, as well as the unfortunate spider massacre. He concluded the tale with his daring leap over the wall just as the waiter placed their plates on the table.

"Can I get you anything else?" they asked with a smile despite Ilio's horrified expression.

Ilio shook his head no, still at a loss for words.

"That..." he finally started once the waiter left, "...that is quite a story."

Coal nodded, stabbing his fork into a potato and bell pepper. He wanted to taste the seasoning on its own before adding any hot sauce. It was smoky and delicious. The potatoes had the perfect crisp on the outside while still being fluffy on the inside. He kept quiet, unsure of what Ilio's reaction was going to be.

"I am quite impressed by your ingenuity and fortitude," the man finally said, once he fully found his voice again.

Coal had gone through several different scenarios in his mind for how Ilio might react to the information, but not a single one included being complimented on his "ingenuity and fortitude."

"Uh…thanks," he said, now at a loss himself.

Ilio puffed his cheeks. There was a glimmer in his eye as he looked at Coal, who returned the smile.

A weight lifted from his shoulders. He took another bite of his hash, and it tasted even better than before. He poured a heaping helping of hot sauce over the entire plate. The spicier the better. His mouth was watering as the creamy orange sauce oozed over the vegetables.

"It sounds like quite the adventure you had," Ilio said, taking the news that his friend had broken into and stolen from a Flesh Eater prison in surprising stride.

"You're taking this better than I thought, if I'm being honest."

Ilio chuckled. "I know I seem tightly wound," he said.

"That's not—"

"No, I am not offended, believe me. But I like excitement too. I have *fun*," he teased. "Plus, I have always found the implementation of these Flesh Eater compounds to be barbaric. The conditions you spoke of are even worse than I imagined."

Coal tensed and hoped that Ilio hadn't noticed. The man was busy digging into his hash, looking down at his food as he shoveled it around and pierced it with his fork. He said, "You disagree with the treatment of them?"

"With what you told me about Faranap? Absolutely," Ilio replied. "It sounds demeaning and inhumane. But I also do not think they should be imprisoned at all. The Dirt King's unbending law on the matter is unreasonable, as is the government's enforcement of it. If the act is done in a criminal manner, then sure, arrest the offenders and send them to one of the kingdom's many prisons. But do not condemn those who are simply trying to practice their cultural traditions and throw them in with criminals and the mentally ill and force all of them into slave labor."

It was a huge relief to Coal hearing that Ilio was against the concept of a "Flesh Eater" at all, as defined by the Dirt King. He tried to hide his smile as he kept eating.

Ilio said, "I am glad to hear you caused some mayhem for those guards and stole their property. I am less thrilled about the many spiders that were killed, but that is no fault of yours. That can be blamed on the Dirt King as well, as I am sure those monsters were creations of his."

"The guards weren't fans of them either," Coal said. "They kept calling them 'ugly fuckers.' I'm in agreement." But he wanted to change the subject, not spend their entire meal discussing such grim topics. He nodded toward Ilio and asked, "What's the symbol on your belt buckle, by the way?"

Ilio glanced down at his lap to double-check which belt he was wearing. "Ah," he said, "this cloud formation is the symbol of Varoosh."

"You guys have your own town symbol? Fun."

"Every bird city does. They are all cloud formations, though the differentiations can be quite subtle to the untrained eye."

258 • *Travis M. Riddle*

"Are you required to wear that?" Coal asked. He was unfamiliar with the concept. He had lived his whole life in Muta Par, which was a blend of races and cultures. The kingdom's fox territory and their customs were a total mystery to him.

Ilio shook his head and poured half his sauce onto his hash. "No, not a requirement. Simply pride for where I come from, that is all."

"I like it," Coal said with a smile. "Makes me think of the sky," he said stupidly.

"I would think so," Ilio chuckled.

"No, I mean—it makes me think of…freedom, I guess? Exploration? I don't know. Adventure, maybe." Then he asked, "Do birds ever fly up that high, into the clouds? Is that rude to ask?" He did not know why it would be, but he had no real idea.

"Some do," Ilio nodded. "Not often, though. It is enormously tiring."

The answer led Coal to another question. "Why don't any of you fly over the mountains? Out of Ruska?"

The mountain ranges flanking the valley were insurmountable even for the most skilled climbers, and the only actual opening in them was blocked by the immutable Houndstooth. No one without wings had any way of leaving the kingdom.

"Some do," Ilio said.

Coal wasn't expecting that. "Really?"

Ilio nodded.

He had never heard of someone leaving Ruska before. He nearly spat, "What's out there?"

Ilio shrugged but said nothing.

Coal was confused. "But you just said that people have left."

"Yes," Ilio nodded. "None have returned."

Coal thought of the massive glowing eyes peering out at the kingdom over the mountaintops. Had the birds who tried to leave been killed by whatever colossal creature those eyes belonged to?

Or was whatever lay outside the valley vastly superior to Ruska? Was there no reason to come back?

"Do you know anyone who's flown over the mountains?" he asked.

"No," Ilio replied. "It is not a common occurrence. As I said, flying to such heights plus the distance involved would be exhausting for anyone. Few attempt it."

Coal sighed. "Well, that got kinda weird and dark," he groaned. "I was trying to get away from weirdness and dark-ness."

Ilio's red cheeks puffed. "That would be good. Perhaps there is something else we can discuss." After mulling it over for a few seconds, he asked, "What do people usually talk about in situations like this?"

Coal wasn't sure what the man meant, but he said, "I dunno. Maybe…places we've been? That seems normal. Have you ever visited Jaq Yul?"

"No, I have not," said Ilio. "I hear the hot springs are a dream, though. I would enjoy taking a dip in them, I think."

Coal grinned. "I thought that you might," he said.

"Why?"

"You seem like a hot dip sort of guy," Coal told him. "Is that what you were known as back in Varoosh? The hot dip guy?"

Ilio bellowed with laughter. It was the most animated Coal had ever seen him.

"I was indeed *not* the hot dip guy," he said. "But I like the title. I may have to adopt it."

"That can be on your business card right under Nomak's assistant. Hot Dip Dandy."

Ilio was still fighting through laughter as he said, "I am a dandy now as well? And I need to state so on my business card?"

"If it's on your business card, everyone will know it's official," said Coal.

"Fair point. I need to get some new cards printed up." He took a bite of onion and potato that was dripping with orange sauce.

Coal smiled.

He continued asking questions, and Ilio asked his own in turn. Before they knew it, their plates were empty and an hour had whittled away. But still they continued to talk and joke, and another hour was passing them by, though they did not notice. Nor would they have cared if they did.

19

TUCARUMONG STREET MOVED LIKE a living organism.

People flooded the street, jostling about, chatting and shouting excitedly, smashed together like one large mass.

It looked like a nightmare to Coal.

He and Ilio stood on one of the smaller streets that intersected with Tucarumong, gazing out at the throng of people. Many were wearing handcrafted spider masks, which were ovals that covered their faces with two of the eight eyeholes cut out for them to see through. Fuzzy fangs protruded from the bottom while noodly legs made of yarn dangled from either side.

"Gross," Coal muttered to himself, watching a woman whip her head back and forth while conversing with two of her friends. The limp fake legs slapped against the front and back of her head with every quick turn. It reminded him of Faranap's monsters with their squirming tendrils.

In addition to too many people, the street was lined with stalls set up to house festival games or sell street foods. There was even one with an alleged psychic who was telling fortunes. Down the way a bit, past a ton of furry heads, Coal could make out a small wooden stage set up to host a performance of some kind, whether it be a live band or a physical feat such as juggling or whatever else people enjoyed watching at festivals. He did not gain much enjoyment watching a person throwing multiple balls in the air, but he did not begrudge others who did.

"What do you want to do first?" Ilio asked him.

Coal was knocked from his stupor. He had been so transfixed by the street's liveliness he had forgotten Ilio was standing beside him.

Entering the mass did not seem appealing, but grabbing a sweet treat from one of the food stalls did. The breakfast hash still sat heavily in his stomach, but suddenly he craved a pastry dusted with sugar on top.

But first he asked, "Do you not need to meet up with Nomak?" He assumed that Ilio was always at the Garna's beck and call, especially at official events.

"No," Ilio shook his head. "Not yet, anyway. We will meet up with him later, I think, but for now we can follow our own whims and chase our own desires."

Coal laughed at the man's turn of phrase. He enjoyed how oddly Ilio spoke sometimes. "Okay," he said. "Dessert is my desire, then."

"Let us chase it." Ilio's cheeks puffed.

Their arms brushed against each other as they pressed into the crowd. Neither of them knew exactly where to find Coal's desire, but Ilio stood a touch taller than him and was peering over other festivalgoers' heads in search of a dessert vendor.

"We're by a caramel apple place," Ilio told him, half-shouting to be heard over the din.

"Hell no. We're in search of pastries," Coal said. "Fried, if possible." Fruit was not on the menu right now, no matter how much sugar it was covered with.

They scooted passed people giddily waving their arms and smearing their own foods onto their clothes. Coal grimaced as someone squirted the juices from their hand pie onto his shoulder, leaving a bright red stain on his shirt that he would surely never wash out. It would join the rest of his stain collection that he'd been accruing in his travels over the past year.

Music was blaring from behind them. Coal craned his neck to investigate, and saw that a second stage was set up on the opposite end of the street with musicians bouncing around on it blowing into horns and plucking at strings. A microphone was positioned front and center, but the only woman not playing an instrument was backed away from it, grooving to the tunes.

He was still distracted by the band when Ilio grabbed his hand and yanked him along. He pulled him toward a stall that was surrounded by patrons clamoring for fried sweetbread.

"Is the line too long?" Ilio asked him. There were at least twenty others waiting to buy.

Coal shrugged. "We're here to eat and hang out, right? We can do one of those while we wait to do the other." He smiled.

They stood at what they believed to be the back of the line, though it was an amorphous shape that congealed with the rest of the festival crowd, so it was hard to be sure. But they were inching closer to the stall every couple minutes, so at least there was some form of progress.

"You know, we now share something in common," Ilio said. "I think, anyway."

"What's that?"

"A festival such as this was the first real big event my father and I attended after my mother's passing."

"Ahh," Coal nodded. "Yeah, I haven't really…attended *anything* since my father died, so I guess I'd call this the first event."

"I hope you enjoy it," Ilio said with sincerity. "For my father and I, it was an attempt to recalibrate ourselves and return to normalcy. As much as possible, in any case. But it was not a spiderback race. It was an arts and crafts festival that is held annually in Menta. I always went while I was living there, so I suggested to my father that we go check it out. He was always interested in art. Sculptures, in particular."

"I have no idea what mine was into," Coal confessed.

Despite being raised by only his father and spending his entire life with him, he had to admit he knew very little about the man's inner world. If someone put a gun to his head and told him to name five of his father's interests, or even one single hope or dream he had possessed, Coal would be shot dead.

"Oh?" said Ilio.

"He and I didn't really talk much, even when we lived together. He was always kinda reserved, and I'm kinda reserved, so we just never really spoke about anything other than, like…what we were gonna eat for dinner, or stuff that needed to be done around the house, shit like that. Some updates on our personal lives every so often, but nothing too deep. And it's not like I can blame him, I never offered him anything either, it was mutual. I never talked to him about the books I liked, or what music I enjoyed, or anything at all."

"Your relationship was pleasant, but always at arm's reach."

"I guess that's an accurate way of putting it."

"It sounds as if you two at least did not have a *bad* relationship. Or even one that was strained."

Coal nodded. "Yeah, I don't think 'strained' would be the right word. Maybe just…" He searched for the word he'd best use to describe his relationship with his father, but nothing was coming to mind. Which felt oddly appropriate. "I dunno," he finally said.

Surprisingly, he did not feel uncomfortable revealing any of this to Ilio. It was never a secret, really, but he had never opened up to anyone about it. He never felt the need or saw any reason to.

"I suppose *no* relationship is better than a *bad* one," Ilio said softly. Coal barely heard him over the crowd. They stepped forward as the line shortened.

"You and yours didn't get along?"

"We were cordial most of the time, but it did not take much for our discussions to devolve into arguments. We have many differences of opinion when it comes to most matters in life. We always recover, but without ever actually resolving what the argument stemmed from. It is easier to simply jump back into the familiar patterns and act as if there never was an argument at all."

"I get the sense that maybe your mother was a good buffer," said Coal.

Ilio nodded. "She had a keen sense for how to defuse situations when our talks started to simmer," he said. "A big part of why I moved to Menta was so that I did not have to put up with the arguments anymore."

"Did they continue when you moved back?"

"No, actually. My mother's death seems to have taken all the fight out of him. Which is…I do not know. It is hard to put into words." Coal gave him a moment to articulate his thoughts. "It is at once disheartening to see my father as a shell of who he once was, but I would be lying if I said it was not also a…relief."

The word sounded heavy on his tongue. It was tinged with guilt. Dripping with it, more accurately.

"Her passing brought us together, I suppose, in the sense that we no longer fight. But I do feel as if I know him less now. Or that rather he has changed in some way that I cannot know now. The relationship between us feels hollow."

"Hollow," Coal echoed. "That's maybe the perfect word to describe me and my father. Or the closest thing to it." He then asked, "Did it work? Bringing him to the art festival, I mean. Did it make anything better?"

"I think so," Ilio replied. "He seemed to enjoy himself. It was the first time I saw him smile since the funeral. There was one artist whose work he especially liked. I do not recall her name, but she sculpted the lifecycles of animals—ventems, retnos, bollies, she had a ton of different subjects. But what she did was…hmm, it is hard to put into words. It was like each stage of the animal's life was flowing into the next, in one fluid piece of white stone. My favorite was her rendition of a vey, which had four parts: an egg, a hatchling, an adolescent, and then a full-grown adult, and it was carved in such a way that it…it looked like there was movement to it, like the vey was taking flight. Each depiction of every animal in every form was incredibly lifelike, with amazingly detailed texture etched in. I could scarcely believe what she had accomplished. Alas, her work was far out of our price range, but my father and I spent a long time marveling."

"That sounds pretty wild," said Coal. "Sculptures are totally beyond me. I cannot fathom how you even approach doing something like that. Where do you start? Same with paintings. My mind just does not operate the same way; I can't comprehend how to make something like that."

Ilio chuckled. "I dabbled in painting a bit," he said.

"Really?"

"Yes. I have hobbies."

"What sort of stuff did you paint?"

He hesitated to answer. "My subjects were perhaps slightly strange."

"Go on," Coal grinned.

Ilio said, "I played with scale a lot. So I would depict normal people scaled down to the size of a grape, for instance. I would paint them in various settings, such as a kitchen counter, or trying to perform tasks like tending to a plant."

"That is not *quite* as weird as I was expecting," said Coal. "I thought you were gonna say…I don't even know what. That sounds weird, but in a cool way and not a weird way."

"Weird in a weird way," Ilio chuckled.

"Why was that your style?" Coal asked him.

"I cannot say. It was simply what came to me when I sat down at the easel. I suppose I was fascinated by the reversal, by the idea of things that are so common and mundane to us suddenly becoming untenable or fully unknowable."

"Like the eyes over the mountaintops."

Ilio nodded. "Precisely."

Hearing that explanation, in a strange way it made sense to him that a bird would fixate on that idea, given that they technically could go exploring over the mountains to see what those colossal beasts were, if they were so inclined.

"Did you ever show anything off at that festival?" he asked Ilio.

The woodpecker shook his head and moved forward. They were almost at the front of the line.

"I was never skilled enough," he answered.

"I'm sure that's not true!"

Ilio laughed and said, "Oh, but it is! One had to submit their work to the festival and be approved as a showcase artist. I was rejected three years in a row."

Coal scowled dramatically. "Fuck 'em!" he declared. "They don't know shit about art, I bet."

"Of course not," Ilio agreed with a smirk. "They are just professional art curators."

"Exactly. Don't know a thing." The two shared a companionable grin.

Finally, they reached the stall and placed their order. Coal bought a sugarcoated fried sweetbread, which was essentially a ball of dough that was fried and dusted with large sugar crystals. Ilio refrained from getting anything, but offered to pay for Coal's. He tried to deny him, given that Ilio had also paid for breakfast, but the bird insisted. Coal had no choice but to relent.

Coal took a bite of the bread, reveling in the sweet crunch of its crust and the fluffiness within. He offered Ilio a bite, which he accepted. His eyes lit up as he swallowed.

"Bet you're full of regret, huh?" Coal asked him.

"Not *full*, but there is some regret, yes."

"We can go wait in line again. We can spend the time reflecting on how foolish you were. It could be fun."

"I will instead take more bites of yours," Ilio said.

"Oh, you think?"

"Perhaps, if you are kind. And in the meantime, we can have fun in a different way than reflecting on my—"

"Dumb choice?" Coal cut in.

"I was going to say *unwise* choice."

"I think mine works better."

"We can go with dumb, if that makes you feel better. But would you like to play a game?"

"Let's do it. Let's chase those desires." He took another chunk out of the sweetbread, making a real show of it in front of Ilio, who laughed at the display then pretended to be upset.

The festival crowd had definitely not thinned out at all and was only getting rowdier as time went on. Someone somewhere had to be selling alcohol, with how much hooting and hollering was going on. Plus, it was an obvious moneymaker for an event such as this. Coal followed Ilio through the crowded sidewalk to a booth that was set up with four large tanks of water on its counter, each of them with a narrow-spouted glass resting at the bottom, surrounded by red metal tokens. People stood before the tanks, dropping more tokens into the water and watching them float downward, screaming at their metal to go the way they wanted.

Ilio brought them over to the lone unmanned tank. A large beaver with a missing front tooth welcomed them to his game.

"What is this?" Coal asked around a mouthful of pastry.

Ilio opened his mouth to answer, but the beaver beat him to it. The man said, "What we's got here is a classic water drop!" When Coal made no indication that he knew what that meant, the man continued, "The rules is simple: drop a token into the water and try to get it to land inside the glass. If ya do, yer a winner!"

"And what do winners get?" Coal asked.

The beaver grinned, exposing even more holes in his rows of teeth. "Winners get they pick of either a bubble wand, a folding fan, or a colorful bracelet!"

"Wow," Coal gaped, much to the beaver's amusement. The prizes sounded exceptionally cheap considering how difficult the game seemed to be (which he ascertained by listening to the players cursing at his side), but that was the way of a festival, he supposed.

"Want to play?" Ilio asked. Coal nodded.

The beaver took Ilio's meager payment and scurried over to retrieve their allotted tokens. He came back and slammed fifteen of the rounded red pieces on the table and boomed, "Good luck!"

Coal had not caught how much fifteen tokens cost, but he hoped it wasn't much, because he did not foresee them winning.

Ilio scooted the pieces so they sat between them and said, "We can take turns. I am confident one of us has the skills to claim victory."

"We *need* a fan or a bracelet or a bubble wand."

"We *need* it," Ilio agreed with a puff. Then he picked up one of the tokens, hovered his hand over the water, and let it fall with a plop.

They watched it waver in the water, drifting lackadaisically downward and landing silently at the bottom of the tank, a good distance away from the target glass.

"That was awful," said Coal. "Were you even trying?"

"I thought it would be best not to try with the first one," Ilio replied.

"Good strategy."

Coal grabbed a token and dropped it into the water. It clinked off the rim of the glass, eliciting a shout of dismay from both men as it fell to the bottom.

While Ilio planned his next move, Coal looked over at the others playing the game. He noticed that at the far end of the table was the bat and raccoon duo he'd seen the previous day when signing up for the race. The bat appeared to be in much better shape now after his fainting spell and was looking gleeful as he played the game.

The raccoon woman noticed Coal watching them and raised her eyebrows in alarm. He saw her subtly tap the bat on the shoulder, and the bat looked his way just as Coal averted his eyes. He felt awkward, staring so rudely.

With his attention drawn back to the game, he mocked Ilio's latest attempt, telling him he would never make it to the big leagues of dropping tokens in water. Ilio told him he was filled with intense shame.

When they were down to just two more tokens, Ilio told Coal he could do both. "Are you sure?" Coal asked him. "I don't want you to feel like you didn't get your money's worth, after all."

"I am positive. And I think you are our best bet at winning, so in truth, I am not being altruistic here."

"Whatever you say."

Coal readied the first token, taking great care to aim it above the tiny opening in the glass, and let it drop. It slipped into the water, breaking the surface on its thin side without a sound. They leaned in close together, watching it slowly sway back and forth down the tank, coming to a rest on top of the glass where it sat still, neither falling off nor in.

"What is this!" Coal roared. "What's going on here?"

"Oooh, so close," the beaver purveyor groaned, giving the tank a gentle nudge. The token tipped over and drifted to the bottom.

"That was basically in!" Coal protested. "That counts as a win!"

"Nah, I'm afraid not," said the beaver.

"Wow," Coal muttered as the man walked away to deal with another customer. He turned to face Ilio, who was laughing. He said, "This thing is rigged. We won, right? That should've absolutely—"

He was going to say "counted," but he was abruptly cut off by Ilio leaning forward and nuzzling his cheek against Coal's, stunned to silence by the action. It was the way in which birds kissed, given they had beaks and no lips.

Ilio pulled away and slightly frowned at Coal's dumbfounded expression.

"Oh," he mumbled. "I am sorry. I—"

But he was cut off as well by Coal pulling him back over and nuzzling him. They stood that way for a few seconds, Coal still holding the final red token between his fingers, before they separated. As their faces parted, Coal gave Ilio a quick peck on the cheek.

"Oh," Ilio said again.

"Sorry," Coal apologized this time. "I...was just not expecting that."

Then he smiled. Ilio puffed his cheeks in return.

There was a buzzing in Coal's chest as he and Ilio locked eyes. He had been taken aback by the kiss, but the warmth in his body was nice. It felt like something had suddenly *clicked*, like all the emotions he'd been feeling while hanging out with Ilio made sense now.

It was like an unburdening, somehow. Finally, he could recognize what those feelings meant. Why he was so compelled to spend time with the man. Why he wanted to edge closer and closer to him. Part of him felt stupid for not coming to the realization sooner.

His body tingled and he tried to blink away his infatuation, but it didn't work. He wanted a third kiss, but at the same time did not want to appear overeager.

So instead, Coal turned and held the last token over the top of the tank. "This is gonna be it," he said. "I have been recharged. It's gonna happen this time." He let go of the token and it floated listlessly to the bottom of the tank, not even flirting with the idea of entering the glass. "Shit," he muttered.

To be fair, his whole body had been buzzing since the kiss and he could not be bothered to line up the token properly.

This was a completely new experience for him, and he did not know how to act. Nothing at all could have prepared him for a kiss from Ilio. The idea had not occurred to him whatsoever, in spite of how much he had been enjoying spending his time with the man.

Now it made sense to him why Ilio was paying for everything. Coal had been on a date the entire time.

He felt like an idiot.

He looked back at Ilio, who was still smiling. Coal realized he had not stopped smiling either.

There came a tap on his shoulder that shook him from his lovesick daze.

It was the bat and raccoon.

"Hi," the woman said to him. "My name is Noswen. This is Yurzu." She gestured toward the bat, who waved meekly. He cringed a bit, as if a headache was coming on. Was he going to faint again?

"…hi," Coal said, not knowing what was going on. But he held out a hand, which Noswen accepted and shook. "I'm Coal." Then it hit him. "Oh, you two are competing tomorrow, right?"

"Yes," Noswen nodded.

That was it. Fellow racers wanting to meet. Probably to size him up, get a handle on him before the race.

Yurzu roughly rubbed his forehead like he was trying to push something out.

"You alright?" Coal asked.

"I'm fine," said Yurzu. "Just a dang headache." He looked and sounded young, much younger than Noswen. Probably in his early or mid-twenties, while the raccoon looked to be forty or so. Coal wondered what the nature of their relationship was.

Noswen was done with the pleasantries. "Can we speak to you a moment? In private?" Her eyes flashed toward Ilio, who stood silent at Coal's side.

The two seemed nice enough, but Coal was not in the mood to discuss the race or anything else with them. His heart was pounding in his chest, and all he wanted to do was keep spending time with Ilio before they had to link up with Nomak later. No wasted moments.

"Maybe later," Coal answered. "I'm kind of busy."

"We would really like to speak with you now," said Noswen, glancing at Ilio again. Yurzu stood behind her, rubbing his head.

Coal looked at Ilio, who shrugged. He then looked back at the two racers, who were growing more impatient.

Whatever they wanted to talk to him about could wait. There was plenty of time left in the day.

"Find me later. Maybe after the festival," he told her. "I'm staying at the Longowosk."

And with that, he took Ilio's hand in his and pulled him away from the game booth, leaving Noswen and Yurzu behind. Noswen was saying something else, but he let her words fade into the crowd.

"She seemed awfully serious," Ilio said.

"Yeah. That's fine, though. I can talk to her later." He squeezed Ilio's hand. "Is there another game you want to play?"

"I am sure there is," Ilio said. Then, "But do you require another sweet first?"

Coal laughed. "You know what? I might."

They trudged through the crowd in search of another delicious-looking dessert. The sun seemed brighter and the crowd was less grating. It felt good, holding Ilio's hand as they navigated the busyness of Tucarumong Street.

It did not take them long to find something else they wanted to devour. A short way down the street, past another few game booths, was a stall selling both sweet and savory hand pies (which Coal guessed was the source of the one that had stained his shirt earlier). They both agreed that they wanted some berry-and-cream pies. This time, though, Ilio made sure to buy himself one as well.

"I am not even going to try stealing bites off yours," he told Coal. "My previous gambit did not pay off at all."

"I'm glad you learned your lesson," said Coal. They both laughed and dug into their pies.

Coal felt it was too corny to tell Ilio, but he had specifically chosen the hand pie stall because it was something they could easily eat one-handed, leaving their other hands free to mesh together as they walked through the festival.

His pie was sweet, filled with luscious cream and tart berries. He grasped Ilio's hand in his own and noted that he had still not stopped smiling.

20

COAL DID NOT KNOW what was going on. Inundated as he was by the dizzying sights, sounds, and smells of the Spiderback Showdown festival, still the thing that most occupied his mind was Ilio's kiss. The rest was a blur. Background noise.

They played a few more games together after eating their hand pies, then situated themselves on a bench a short distance away from the main festivities so that they could observe people and chat amongst themselves. This time around, with both their moods so bubbly, they discussed much lighter topics than absentee parents.

After a while, the latest band to play quietened and a beaver in a trailing silver coat took the stage. He wore thick-rimmed square glasses and a blue, diamond-patterned tie that draped over a protruding belly.

That belly was where the man's body ended, however. The beaver sat strapped into a mechanical device, dark red metal that was chipped and tarnished in places, gears turning and pistons firing. It had a shallow circular bowl that the beaver's torso fit perfectly into, as if custom made for him, held aloft by four clawed legs that carried the man across the stage.

"Hoya!" he bellowed into the microphone.

"Hoya!" the crowd chanted back.

From their bench, Coal and Ilio had an obscured but decent view of the man. The mechanical lower half of him reminded Coal of the robotic scorpions that were the Palace Stingers' namesake. It sent a chill through him, but at least the technology was seemingly being put to good use elsewhere in the kingdom. Coal was leaning close to Ilio to ask who the man was, but the beaver's booming voice filled the air before he could get the question out.

"Welcome all to the third annual Soponunga Spiderback Showdown!" The audience cheered wildly. "What a beautiful day, isn't it? For those of you who do not know, my name is Jonka Bontrug. It is my pleasure as Soponunga's mayor to host all of you in our beautiful city. I hope you've enjoyed your time here. And I *know* you'll continue to enjoy it, because we've got quite a race planned for tomorrow!"

More roars from the crowd. Everyone was fired up or drunk or both. Coal imagined that, wherever he currently found himself, Garna Nomak was the latter.

"Every year we top ourselves, people." Mayor Bontrug said this with a wide, proud smile. "We've got eighteen racers signed up to compete this year! We'll have to start limiting the amount of entries if the Showdown keeps growing. But I'm pleased to say that we have several returning racers this year. Returning to the track is Dagosi Monsuo, with his tarantula Butolusko!"

The crowd went wild for Dagosi. Coal was busy worrying about there being seventeen other racers; he had not competed in a race with more than twelve before. But hearing that this guy rode a tarantula confused him, as the breed was not known for its speed or dexterity. They were brutes.

"And give it up for Cassallia Juj, with her jumping spider Wisp's Whisper!"

Even louder cheers for Cassallia. Jumping spiders were small and agile. She would be one to watch out for. More of a threat than a bulky tarantula.

"And finally, our last returning racer is..." The mayor trailed off, building anticipation. "...Manova Mandolat! With his wandering spider Night's Fang!"

The crowd went absolutely nuts at Manova Mandolat's name. He and his wandering spider sounded the most worrisome to Coal. The breed was famously aggressive, and they had a huge stride that could cover a ton of ground very quickly. Personally, Coal had never been able to tame one well enough to ride back in the day.

Bontrug went on, his bulky mechanical legs—similar to a spider's, Coal noted—clacking on the stage as he regularly turned back and forth to address each side of the crowd. "As I'm sure our biggest fans already noticed, last year's two-time champion Bandakla Hont will not be racing this year. We communicated recently and he informed me that he is taking the year off from racing to develop his own brand of wine. That is exciting, is it not?" The crowd affirmed. "So next year, look forward to that, as you can be sure it will be flowing freely throughout the fourth Spiderback Showdown!"

The audience lost their minds at the concept of drinking Bandakla Hont's wine in a year. Coal, however, was glad to hear that the reigning champion was sitting this one out. That meant his chances were slightly better. Though he was sure the other seventeen racers certainly weren't slouches.

Obviously the mayor wasn't going to go through all the other racers, he was just building hype for the returning ones. But it was good to know at least three people he was up against so that he could attempt to plan as much as possible. Six, if he counted Hiji, Noswen, and Yurzu, though he had no idea what breed of spider any of them were riding. He was still intrigued by the presence of the tarantula. That had to mean that the track was not solely about speed. Otherwise, why would the guy come back with a tarantula again?

The beaver droned on about the sponsors they had gotten for the race, about his "stunning" wife's latest initiative to improve certain parts of the city's infrastructure (though he spent more time rattling on about how gorgeous she was), and other mayorly things that sifted through Coal's perky ears without gaining purchase.

He was staring off into the distance, thinking about tomorrow's race. Ilio, sitting to his left, nudged him out of his stupor. "Getting worried?" he teased.

Coal winced in pain, drawing away from the man out of reflex.

"Shit," he muttered. Ilio looked concerned. "I hurt my arm last night," he explained. "I actually meant to ask if we could go see your sloth buddy for some medicine." Caught up in the whirlwind of his surprise date, it had completely slipped his mind. The arm actually had not bothered him much until Ilio pushed it. But it still needed to be taken care of before the race commenced.

Ilio nodded. "Of course," he said. "We can go now." He rose from the bench.

They did not make it far down Tucarumong Street before a familiar boisterous voice shouted Ilio's name and clapped them both on the shoulder, which nearly made Coal shout in agony.

Garna Nomak's long snout then appeared between their two heads and Ilio immediately let go of Coal's hand. He didn't know Ilio's reasoning for not revealing their affection to Nomak, but he was not going to question it. Truthfully, he too would like Nomak to know as little about his personal life as possible.

"Where've you been?" Nomak asked his assistant. "We've missed you over in the tent." He continued heavily patting Ilio on the shoulder.

"We were enjoying the festival," Ilio told him. "Eating food, playing games."

"Kiddy shit," Nomak laughed. "C'mon and have some drinks with us. You too, Lightbulb!"

Coal was getting sick of the nickname, but he forced a smile. His left arm ached.

"We actually were just—" Ilio began, but Nomak interjected.

"Don't matter! Come on over. Hiji's all alone with Mungrus, and I don't think no one can handle Mungrus on their own except for me." Without waiting for a response, he turned and marched back into the crowd, assuming they would follow.

Ilio gave Coal an apologetic look.

282 • *Travis M. Riddle*

Coal said, "It's fine. Really. My arm's not too bad right now." It was true. As long as he didn't have to wrestle Mungrus or something, he could easily keep the pain at bay. He had done so all day up to that point, after all.

They snaked through the crowd, the mayor's voice still blaring from the microphone with all of his P's popping harshly. Eventually they made their way to a tent set up among a line of others, all adorned with their racers' pennants.

Of course there was no such tent for Coal, but he quickly counted up the tents and saw there were only fifteen. Perhaps the other missing racers were Noswen and Yurzu. They seemed a strange bunch, and their entry was fairly last-minute like his own; they were only racing because they couldn't buy their way to the grand prize. He admired their temerity.

The pennant hanging from Nomak's tent was indeed not the one he'd seen yesterday with the long-antlered deer, so there had to be another deer entered in the race. Hiji's pennant was bright orange (seemingly Nomak's favorite color) with a blue square, and in its center was a cloven deer foot crossing over a spider leg, making an X.

Stupid, Coal thought with an amused grunt.

He entered the tent behind Ilio. Nomak was already pouring them each a glass of sparkling wine.

Mungrus was to their left, laying on the floor holding up a half-empty glass in the air, muttering to himself. Hiji sat in a plush chair on the other side of the tent, gazing morosely at the drunken beaver. He glanced over at the newcomers and flashed them a meager smile, raising his glass to them.

"Oi!" Mungrus groaned, sitting up to greet Coal and Ilio.

"He's started to say 'oi,'" said Nomak, setting down one glass and pouring another. "I don't know where he picked it up from, but it's annoying the absolute shit out of me."

Mungrus ignored him and stood woozily, managing to spill most of what remained of his drink. Once more he lacked a shirt of any kind, and bright pink wine splashed onto his brown fur. He went in to hug Ilio, who stiffened at the man's touch. He then moved on to Coal, who deftly maneuvered his body in such a way that the rotund beaver would not crush his arm, though he came away with a damp shirt. Just more stains to worry about.

Nomak shoved past his friend and handed the drinks to Coal and Ilio. Coal took a small sip and was surprised by how dry the taste was. Normally, he preferred his wine on the sweeter side, but it wasn't bad by any means.

The tent was shockingly modest, given Nomak's usual tastes. It consisted of a table at the back holding a bowl of ice with a couple bottles of alcohol. Next to it was a stack of glasses and napkins. There was also a cheese and bread platter, complete with assorted condiments to spread such as jellies and mustards and cream-based sauces. On either side of the tent were three lounge chairs, so it was a mystery as to why Mungrus was opting for the floor instead.

Ilio sat in the chair next to Hiji, and Coal sat in the next one over, closest to the entry flap. Mungrus stumbled backward into the chair opposite Ilio, while Nomak sat across from his racer.

Nomak took a deep swig of his drink, then addressed Coal. "Sorry you didn't do so hot at the table last night," he grinned. "It's a real shame. I thought Slapstick would be your game. I saw it in you. Or rather, I *thought* I did."

"It's alright," Coal said, putting on another convincing fake smile. "Everything turned out okay in the end."

"That so?" Nomak asked, intrigued. "Found yourself a spider, eh?"

Coal nodded but did not elaborate, and thankfully Nomak did not really care enough to pry.

"That's fantastic," the anteater said, sounding genuine. "The more the merrier, I say. As long as none of you beat Hiji here, I'm excited to see more people scramblin' over each other." He guffawed. "What kind of spider you got?"

"An orb weaver," Coal replied. He looked over at Hiji, who was sullen as ever.

Nomak flicked his tongue out and said, "Interesting. They're kinda tough to ride, aren't they?"

"They're on the trickier side," Coal nodded.

"But you can handle it, eh? Maybe I shoulda backed you after all!" He laughed again and gulped down more of his wine, polishing off the glass. He stood to refill it and Mungrus held up his own, shaking it and putting on a downright pitiful face. Nomak snatched his friend's glass and proceeded to fill it back up.

"What kind of spider are you riding?" Coal asked Hiji.

The deer seemed surprised that anyone was speaking to him. It took him a moment to reply. "A jumping spider," he answered.

"Those things are fast."

His own spider was remarkably quick on its feet, but jumping spiders might still have it beat in that department, and there were multiple to contend with. He would need to employ his *ingenuity and fortitude.*

"Damn right they are!" Nomak beamed. He carried Mungrus's glass back over, which was filled to the brim and sloshing around onto the floor. The two men clearly did not care about the state the tent would be in by day's end.

"Have you been riding long?" Hiji asked Coal.

Now it was his turn to be surprised by a question. Hiji had yet to initiate a conversation.

Coal said, "I haven't raced in several years, but I was into it when I was younger. It's probably been...I'd say maybe ten years since I seriously rode spiderback."

Not counting the previous night, of course. And it did not get much more serious than that.

"How about you?" he then asked.

"I've ridden all my life, since I was a kid," Hiji replied thoughtfully. "It wasn't until the past few years, though, that I started taking it seriously. Before, it was just a hobby."

As it turned out, Coal and Hiji grew up relatively close to each other. Both of them resided in towns up north, near the Houndstooth. Hiji's hometown of Quar'litu was only a two-day journey from Muta Par. Their racing backgrounds never overlapped, though, despite the close proximity. Neither had participated in a race the other was in.

"Did you ever go to Vala Tipar?" Hiji asked him.

Coal shook his head, but he knew of the place. Vala Tipar was a sanctuary built by the frogs that was somewhere between his and Hiji's homes. They dug out an enormous pond, filling it with flora and fauna to make it look more natural. Being shaped in a near-perfect square shattered the illusion, though. At each corner of the pond was a mossy statue, each depicting one of the four Lost Tiparuq, god-like beings that the frogs worshiped. In their native tongue, "Vala Tipar" roughly translated to "The Place of the Tiparuq." It was meant to be a place of worship for the frogs, where they could travel and submerge themselves in the pond's still waters, swimming from one god to the next and gain their blessing.

"My father was…odd," said Hiji, and by the tone of his voice Coal could tell he was putting it kindly. "He made me go to Vala Tipar before every race and pray to the Lost."

Coal laughed at that. "Why?" he asked. He had never heard of a deer praying to the Lost Tiparuq. Not that there was any strict rule against it, but it was peculiar.

"Believe me, we prayed to the Swift as well," Hiji said, referring to the deities that most deer, foxes, martens, and rabbits believed in. Coal had never really bought into it, though, and neither had his father; Coal was more concerned with the beasts lurking on the other side of the mountains than with whatever unseen forces some ancient scholar had dreamed up. "But my dad wanted me to gain every advantage I could, so he forced me to pray to anyone who'd listen."

Coal laughed again and said, "Well, whatever works, I guess."

"*That* didn't," said Hiji, cracking a smile for possibly the first time in his life. "I never won any of those times. I only started winning races after I was already old enough to decline doing any of that."

Mungrus bellowed some nonsense and Coal was about to ask Hiji what other traditions his father forced on him when they were interrupted by the tent's flap flying open.

In walked a jovial tapir, wearing a silver vest and black trousers, contrasting with the black fur on his upper body and white fur on the bottom. He scratched at his exposed chest with both hands, his nails circling around his nipples. He flicked his pointy ears, between which sat a green bowler hat. It was a much more casual look than Coal would have expected from Garna Dend.

Coal reflexively shied away from the man. Of course Dend would not know who he was, but still, he felt awkward suddenly being around the man whose office he had recently trashed in Vinnag.

"*Hahntsa toyv*, Tarrit!" the tapir grinned.

Nomak rolled his eyes and returned the greeting. Coal had not expected to learn the man's first name. He figured he'd always simply be "Nomak" in his mind.

Garna Dend was accompanied by two others. One was a menacing tapir with anger in his eyes, wearing nothing but dirty trousers and thick-soled boots. Probably the Garna's muscle. The other was a portly hedgehog woman wearing a smart pink blazer and a sunhat. Dend's wife, maybe? Or his racer, if he was sponsoring someone?

"Who's this ragtag crew you've got here?" Dend asked, scanning the tent and soaking each person in one by one. He gave Coal a sly wink.

"Fuck do you need?" Nomak asked, ignoring the question. "Here I was, foolishly thinking I wouldn't have to see your ugly face until the race tomorrow. I damn near made it, didn't I?"

Dend looked offended, placing a hand on his chest with eyes wide and mouth agape. "I'm just making pleasant conversation, that's all." He nodded toward Hiji and said, "This is your racer, yeah?" The man's voice was raspy, like he had a fruit pit lodged in his throat.

Hiji nodded and Nomak snapped his fingers at the deer to shut up.

Dend grinned. "I thought it'd be nice for you two to meet Meretta," he said, placing a hand on the woman's back. Her quills were covered by the blazer, though they poked out through the fabric ever so slightly. "I figgered it might ease the blow a bit if you knew who was beatin' you tomorrow, aye?"

"Oi," Mungrus responded with a burp.

"She's racing a funnel, isn't she?" asked Nomak.

This time Meretta nodded and garnered a snap from her own sponsor.

"Funnel weavers are big, stupid lugs," Nomak laughed. "Tough fuckin' luck with that."

"Easier to control than a fuckin' jumper," Dend practically spat. He almost dropped the front that this was banter between friends, but caught himself. He then turned his attention to Coal, eying the fox up and down. "What are you supposed to be?" he asked with a glare. "You this fat fuck's personal chef?"

"Nope," Coal replied, keeping his cool. He said nothing further and instead graced the man with a cheeky smile.

Dend stared at him a moment more before turning back to Nomak.

"Well, it was nice seein' you, Tarrit." It was very clearly not nice.

"Likewise, Rosch," said Nomak.

The tapir began to back up out of the tent and said, "Maybe I'll be seein' you later." He gazed at everyone in the room again, ending with Coal.

"I'm not so sure about that," said Nomak. "We like to eat at restaurants, you see. Not fish out whatever we can find in the toilets."

Dend smiled at the juvenile joke then followed his racer and bodyguard out of the tent.

Nomak leaned back in his chair, breathing out a sigh. "Just the sight of that prick gets my blood goin'," he grumbled. "I need another drink. How 'bout you lot?"

Everyone agreed, and so they drank.

THEY SPENT ANOTHER TWO hours in Nomak's tent while the festival raged on outside. The Garna had plenty of alcohol on hand, and he ordered food to be brought to them mid-afternoon: roasted vegetable sandwiches and salted, spicy chips.

A little while after they finished eating, Nomak told Coal it was time for Hiji and him to discuss tomorrow's race, so he needed to leave the tent. Couldn't have the competition listening in on their strategy. Coal thanked him for the hospitality and stood to depart.

Ilio followed him outside to say his goodbye. They walked away from Nomak's tent, the blinding orange pennant fluttering in the wind. A few tents down, in front of the one with the other deer pennant, they stopped and turned to each other.

Coal's heart was racing now that he was finally alone with Ilio again. He'd enjoyed hanging out with him even in the company of Nomak and the others, but he was glad to be rid of them. Even if only for a few moments.

He leaned in to nuzzle Ilio. Again, as he pulled away, he planted a soft kiss on the man's red feathered cheek. They stood apart and looked in each other's eyes.

"I had fun today," Ilio said.

Words were suddenly set to pour forth from Coal's mouth. He nearly couldn't stop himself. He grasped Ilio's hands in his.

What he wanted to say to the man was:

"Thank you for today. For everything today. I had fun too. Breakfast was amazing. Or brunch, or lunch, or whatever it was. And the festival, even though all the games were extremely stupid. The treats were good, though. I'd come again for those. This is a new thing for me, but I wanted to thank you for this as well. All of this. I've never done this with anyone before. That's kind of...why it was such a shock. But a good shock. A nice weirdness. It was the first time ever in my life I've shared something like that with somebody, and I think that's what made it feel so weird. I haven't had that before, so thank you for giving it to me."

He couldn't find the courage within himself to let the words out, though.

He swallowed them back down. Acid in his throat.

How would Ilio react if he had let all that word-vomit spill from his lips? Maybe it'd be fine, but maybe the woodpecker would stare at him stupidly, wondering how Coal had let himself get so heavily invested in such a short time span.

Afraid of ruining things, he fought the impulse and instead said, "I had an amazing time today. You know how to show a guy a good time." There was a slight quiver in his voice that he hoped Ilio did not detect. To mask his nervousness, he joked, "What's a better first date than dropping coins in a bucket?"

The woodpecker laughed. The sound was infectious, and Coal laughed too.

"Today was great," Ilio said. Which, in Coal's humble opinion, was selling it short. "I am incredibly grateful that I got to spend it with you. I am only sorry that it must come to an end already."

Coal shrugged. "Maybe it doesn't have to," he suggested. "I mean…I'm not doing anything later. Are you? You know where I'm staying. Maybe when you're done with this weird little meeting, you can come grab me and we can go for a walk or something. We can finally get me that medicine so that my arm doesn't fall off."

Ilio puffed his bright cheeks. "I think that sounds like an excellent idea," he said.

They brought their faces together again, rubbing fur against feather. Coal kissed him as they pulled away.

"See you in a bit?" said Coal, letting go of Ilio's hands and taking a step back.

"Indeed."

They waved goodbye, walking backwards to look at each other for as long as they could before Ilio disappeared into the tent.

There was noticeable pep in his step as Coal walked the streets of Soponunga. He immediately veered off of Tucarumong, which was still bustling with festivalgoers who he wagered would be partying deep into the night.

The side streets were empty, quiet but for the echoes of the party a couple blocks over. After a few hours spent with the rambunctious, incomprehensible Mungrus (with Nomak constantly gassing him up), Coal was grateful for a bit of peace.

The day's events flashed by in his mind. He replayed everything over and over as he walked, wanting to relive each moment. He tried to think of the last time he felt so elated, and failed. Everything about the day had been perfect.

Except for his utter failure to properly express himself a minute ago, but that was minor. And probably for the best. He did not want to scare the man off already.

Still, he knew that if things were going to work between him and Ilio, eventually he would have to tell him about his past. About what exactly had transpired with his father. His status as a Flesh Eater.

But perhaps it was premature worrying about such weighty things as that right now. They had only kissed for the first time today, after all. No one said they were officially in a relationship yet.

No reason to stress out about the Palace Stingers. Especially since there were no sign of them in Soponunga.

He closed his eyes as he walked an empty street, thinking about Ilio's soft cheek brushing against his own.

And then there was a rush of footsteps behind him and a harsh thud against the back of his head. His eyelids fluttered and he lost consciousness, collapsing to the ground.

21

*A*T LEAST I HAD *a good day with Ilio.*

That was the thought that entered Coal's head as soon as he regained consciousness. His eyelids were heavy and he could not keep them open for more than a second. He drank in the darkness, taking deep, steady breaths.

The next thing he thought was: *Bad.*

Bad, bad, bad, bad.

His head hurt bad. His arm hurt bad. His face hurt bad. The situation he was in was bad.

But his day had been good.

"You up?" came a familiar voice.

It was the harsh rasp of Garna Dend.

With great effort, Coal forced his eyes open, trying to blink away the drowsiness. Dend was standing before him, hands on his hips, sporting a scowl to go with his flamboyant hat. Coal coughed and the Garna jumped backward to avoid the spray.

"Disgusting," he muttered, wiping his snout with one hand and placing the other on his belly.

Coal took a moment to assess the situation. He was currently tied to a flimsy wooden chair with a rope (*Who besides gangsters would have a rope?* he asked himself) in what appeared to be a hotel room. It did not seem quite as luxurious as the Longowosk; it might be the one on Tucarumong Street where all the racers were staying, although it would have been quite a feat for Dend to carry his limp body through the heavy crowds back to the hotel. Perhaps it wasn't out of the ordinary seeing someone dragging a drunk, passed out friend back to their room. Or maybe it was just another more secluded hotel altogether. He had no idea. Whatever place they were in, Dend had surely rented out the whole floor just like Nomak. They were peas in a pod.

Accompanying Dend in the mystery hotel room were his bodyguard and Meretta, as well as two other men Coal had not seen before. Both were patchy-furred lynxes brandishing thick metal clubs. Considering the circumstances, he had to assume they would be used for bashing his head in rather than any sports activities.

Still, he breathed a sigh of relief. He was in a pretty bad spot, but this was possibly better than Stingers apprehending him. Dend had all the reason in the world to leave him for dead, though. The Garna had probably done worse for less. Vinnag was a cutthroat city.

Dend snorted and began ranting. "You prob'ly thought you was clever, huh? Sittin' in that tent with your prissy little drink, right under my nose." He snorted again for emphasis. "You think I didn't recognize you, you ugly shit? How many foxes with black faces you think there are out there, 'specially ones runnin' with Nomak?"

The "no killing" policy during their office infiltration was coming back to bite him in the ass. That macaw had gotten a good look at him, and even a passing glance would be enough to offer a helpful description given his exceedingly distinctive face. Once more, he cursed his namesake.

"I did not think I was clever," Coal said for some reason. "I was just enjoying my prissy drink and the company of friends."

"Ha!" Dend huffed. "Someone besides Nomak enjoying Mungrus Gagallo's company? That'll be the fuckin' day." He paced back and forth, never turning away from Coal. The fox fidgeted in his chair. The rope rubbed uncomfortably against his wrists, and having his arms tied behind the chair was putting a strain on his injured one.

The longer he kept Dend talking, the longer he could stave off further injuries or death. Although speaking also invited irritation, which could result in worse injuries or death. It was a losing battle.

"What's your plan here?" he asked the Garna, trying to maintain his cool. Not reveal how terrified he truly was. "I'm entered in the race too." Meretta's eyebrows raised at that factoid. "People are expecting me to show up. They won't just accept that a racer's gone missing."

He had no idea if that was true. It was entirely possible the beavers would not give one iota of shit about a racer dropping out or bailing at the last minute, but it was worth a shot. Anything to save his skin.

"Maybe," Dend nodded. "But you think I can just let what you did slide?"

Coal shrugged. "Could you?"

"No!" the tapir screamed. All his lackeys looked to him, and he took a second to calm himself down. "Do you even know what you did to Malley?"

Coal didn't know if Malley was the macaw or the fox, but either way, he was unaware of the person's fate.

Evidently Dend was not in the mood to expound on the matter, moving right along. "And of course Nomak thinks he's hot shit over there, with his two racers and two tiny balls."

So Dend thought Coal was one of Nomak's racers too. He did not have the time or mental energy to think through whether that was in his favor or not, so he neither confirmed nor denied it. He kept his mouth shut and let the tapir ramble on.

"Well, he ain't gonna feel like hot shit come tomorrow. No, no, no. We won't let him, aye, Meretta?"

The hedgehog shook her head, glaring at Coal strapped to the chair. He was taken aback by the sudden viciousness in the woman's eyes.

"He ain't gonna do too hot in the race if one of his team's too fucked to even climb up on his spider, aye?" Dend spat.

"He would not be too hot, no," Coal sputtered, speaking before he had actually formulated a thought, trying to find the words along the way that would help him avoid a massive beating. "It'll also piss him off, though. Super bad. He'll retaliate."

"This is retaliation for fucking up my office!" Dend half-yelled, catching himself before he raised his voice too much. His nostrils flared. "He can't retaliate on the retaliation! You can't just re-retaliate!"

Coal latched onto the man's strange logic and said, "But wasn't that retaliation for stealing his photos? Which would make *this* a re-retaliation?"

Dend was caught off-guard by this notion. He looked around at his crew, none of whom offered any advice or support. They stood idly by, waiting for orders.

"Shut the fuck up!" the Garna then shouted, not bothering to keep his voice low at all, which all but confirmed to Coal that the floor was rented out and there was no point in calling for help.

"Yeah, shut the fuck up!" Meretta joined in, ravenous. Her eyes were wide and glazed over, full of venom and violence.

Dend grinned at his racer's enthusiasm.

"Go ahead, Meretta," he said.

His use of the Garna's own logic had failed, and now he was going to be crippled the night before the race. After all he'd gone through to ensure he could compete. That diamond claw had been *just* within reach.

The biggest shock of it all, perhaps, was that Dend's racer would apparently be dishing out the punishment rather than any of his three hulking bodyguards.

Meretta lunged forward, landing in Coal's lap and knocking the chair over onto its back. He slammed into the floor with the woman on top of him, clawing at his chest and face. She cackled with glee. All Coal could make out in the flurry of movement was the pink of her blazer.

She proceeded to punch him over and over again in both arms. Unbearable pain shot through his left arm, setting it aflame, and he gritted his teeth to resist screaming in agony. But he had to give in and he yowled as Meretta continued pounding away.

Dend laughed at his pained shouts, huge belly-laughs that filled the room. His muscle joined in, the lynxes and the other tapir trying to match their boss's zeal.

"Get him, Meretta! Go on, girl!" Dend cheered once he controlled his laughter.

She cackled manically and moved on from Coal's arms to his stomach after forcefully pushing herself up off his body. Her blows winded him, cutting off his screams.

Soon the petite woman wore herself out and she stood, taking a few steps back from Coal's trembling body. He was covered in scratches, blood dripping down his limbs onto the carpet. Every part of him ached. His left arm felt like it was being gnawed on by the not-ventem in the dung tunnels.

Meretta wheezed at his side, exhausted from her bout of physical activity. When Coal could finally bring himself to open his eyes, he saw she was smiling, baring her tiny sharp teeth as she leered at him. He counted himself lucky that she had not jumped onto him quills-first.

"That's all you want?" Dend asked her. She nodded breathlessly. "Alright, then. If you're satisfied, I'm satisfied. How you feelin' down there?"

Coal tried to push out an answer—preferably a sarcastic or rude one—but he could not muster the strength. He had to focus on breathing in and out. His whole body quaked.

Even beyond his body being wracked with too much pain to speak, he had lost all hope. There was no point in spitting out some rude remark or trying to free himself from his bonds. He was already too beat up to ride spiderback tomorrow morning.

The race was lost. He couldn't afford Netraj's services. The Palace Stingers would track him down eventually.

He clung to his good day with Ilio.

"Well, it's a good start, but not quite what I had in mind, aye, boys?" Dend said, his tone jovial. Like he was playing a casual game with friends. "Pahb, go ahead and do what you'd like. Leave him untied when you're done. Give him a chance to make it down to the starting line and make a fuckin' fool of himself. I'd love to see him fall off that spider of his."

The whole room bellowed with laughter at the image.

"You got it, boss," said the other tapir.

"C'mon, dear," said Dend.

Coal, unable to turn his head, watched Meretta's feet disappear from view as she left the room with Dend. The Garna complimented her performance as they shuffled into the hallway, slamming the door shut behind them.

"Just us now," said the tapir, Pahb, as he took a foreboding step toward Coal.

He gave a slight nod, still unable to speak.

It would be better if I died, maybe, he thought. *Easier. Cleaner.*

That sudden thought scared him, and he immediately realized he did not earnestly believe it.

He felt hopeless, but even in these dire circumstances, he was able to experience a day like today.

He wanted that again.

He would have that again.

Suddenly Pahb hoisted him upright, only to flatten him again with a punch in the face. There was an audible pop as the man's fist connected with Coal's nose. The rickety chair splintered apart when it impacted with the floor. Coal was too battered to move, let alone with the speed required to escape the room. At this point the room was also spinning in his vision, so that added an extra layer of difficulty.

It was clear to him now why Pahb did not have a club of his own, like the lynxes. He absolutely did not need one. Nothing would be gained from using a metal club as opposed to his own fist.

Coal lay on the ground, the rope wrapped loose around his body and splinters digging into his skin. Miraculously, he turned himself over onto his stomach and began to crawl toward the window—simply because it was what was in front of him—but he made it less than half a foot before one of the lynxes kicked him in the stomach, hurling him onto his back again.

He was far past trying to keep his composure now and wanted to beg the men not to do anything else. To just leave him there. But his breathing was ragged and it felt like his ribcage was caving in. Tears stained his fur. All he could get out were single syllables that meant nothing.

Pahb lifted him up off the ground by his shirt as if picking up a sack of muffins. It was nothing to the man. He then threw Coal across the room, sending him crashing into a similarly shoddy desk that cracked in half with the collision.

There was nothing he could do. No way to escape, no way to fight back. He had to take it. He prayed he would lose consciousness again and not have to endure it any longer.

Each of the lynxes gave him a good wallop with their clubs, and then Pahb kneeled down before him. His body was slumped over in the wreckage of the desk.

The tapir wore a smug grin. He was having the time of his life. Let off the leash by his master.

Coal finally managed to say through his sobs, "Please—"

And then with one more punch to the head, his prayers were answered.

"IT ISN'T COLD HERE."

Coal sat in that ruined back room of the library, stone crumbled all around him, chewing on a piece of his father's thigh as the ghost of the man spoke. The trickle of the river outside was faint. He didn't know what time it was, only knew that it was dark outside.

Every time he ate part of his father, the man's glowing blue spirit appeared, which Coal had come to accept. Really what he had accepted was that he was losing his mind, hallucinating these conversations. His brain was trying to trick him, stimulate itself in a bizarre attempt to maintain his sanity by letting him speak to somebody.

It was not working.

The last several times the ghost appeared, Coal had ignored its attempts to converse with him, but this time he could not resist. It was definitely cold in that room. Nights during Brightmonth were always chilly. Coal asked the ghost, "Where?"

"Here," his father's spirit said again. He fixed his gaze on his son. "Wherever it is I am now."

Coal stared at the man, swallowed the bite of his thigh, shivered. While he was still convincing himself he needed to get a grip on reality, his curiosity was undeniably piqued. He said, "You can see the afterlife? You can feel it?"

"Of course," said Von.

Of course.

"What's it like, then?" Coal asked.

"It isn't cold, like I think many people expect, given that ghosts are always depicted as being cold in stories."

Coal knew the stories, of course, but had not deigned to test the theory on his father's ghost by running a hand through his chest or anything like that. He chose to maintain his distance.

"It's…hard to describe," Von went on. "Words can't do it justice because there's not anything to *see*, really. It is a feeling. I can feel myself existing in this space, and I can feel others, interact with them, but…I do not see anything physical until I am here, with you."

Coal tried to remember if any religion he knew of talked about the afterlife in such a way, but nothing immediately came to mind. He and Von had not really practiced any religion; his father would drag him along to the Lightmaker's Shadow ceremony every Pinkmonth, but that was all. That had only been three weeks prior, and now he wished he had paid more attention during the sermon.

"You can talk to other people there?" he asked Von.

The ghost nodded. "Not physically, but yes, we can communicate."

Coal took another bite of flesh and shuddered. It might have been from the act, or from the temperature, or both. For a brief moment, he wished he could experience the same warmth his father was supposedly feeling.

If any of this were actually happening, anyway.

He had already started talking to the ghost, which he previously told himself he wouldn't do. Didn't want to entertain the delusion. But the dam was broken and the water was gushing.

A tiny part of him bought into the fact that he truly was speaking to his father's ghost from the afterlife, somehow, and that part of him knew he wasn't going to get many more chances. If he wanted answers about who his mother was, about what happened to her, this was his opportunity. That small part of him felt compelled to ask.

The impulse needled him. Told him he should demand answers from his father. He had a right to know.

But maybe Von had a legitimate reason to keep it a secret from his son all these years. Something pretty drastic had to have happened for the woman to disappear from their lives entirely and for him to not offer even the vaguest explanation.

The answer might invite nothing but trouble into Coal's life.

Or, if not trouble, then at least it would color his perception of his parents in a way that he wouldn't be able to erase.

I want to know, though.

He reluctantly took another bite of Von's flesh, knowing that it would keep the ghost around a little while longer. The muscle and sinew tore between his fangs. Slid down his throat, slimy and wet with blood. He wiped blood and spittle from his chin with the back of his hand. The fur there was already matted with dried blood from the past few days.

His mouth hung open, the question on the tip of his tongue. Not a question; a demand. *Tell me who my mother was. Tell me what happened to her.*

Von could tell that his son wanted to say something, and so he stood there silently, watching. Glowing. Coal looked at the wreckage of the room through his father's idle, translucent body. Could see the man's corpse directly behind where his blue body stood. The juxtaposition made Coal want to vomit.

The words could not make it past Coal's lips.

He sat there, slumped against the wall, fearful of what his father's answers might be.

And so he remained silent.

The two watched each other, neither saying a word, until finally Von's ghost disappeared and left only his corpse behind. Bits and pieces torn off and consumed by Coal. Mangled.

That was the last time Coal saw his father's ghost. The last opportunity he had to ask about his mother. Wasted, because he had been too afraid of the reaction.

And now he would never know.

22

MORNING CAME.

Coal blinked his eyes open, bracing for misery. Girding himself to crawl miserably down to the hotel lobby, begging for someone to help him get to a doctor. He didn't know how he would pay, but he'd figure something out. He had to.

Sunlight shone in through the window, warming the blanket atop him. He shifted his head, digging the back of it into the pillow.

Wait.

A blanket and pillow seemed like odd accommodations to leave behind after beating the shit out of him.

Coal sat up and found himself in his Longowosk hotel room, tucked away safely in bed.

Stranger still was the fact that sitting up had not caused him immeasurable pain.

He twisted his neck left and right, and it felt completely normal. His chest no longer ached, and he could breathe just fine. He rotated his left arm, and even that had no issues.

Somehow he felt far better today than he had the previous morning.

"The fuck?" he couldn't help but mutter to himself. His eyes darted around the room, searching for any sign of what happened after he passed out. Something as mundane as a good night's rest could not be the cause for how reinvigorated he felt.

His body felt fantastic, but that did not stop the grogginess. He needed some coffee.

Coal pushed himself out of the bed, testing his legs. They were fine as well. Nothing ached, nothing was out of place, nothing was missing. He was worried for a minute last night that Pahb and his goons were going to lob off a limb.

Then he realized the race was today. He glanced at the clock in fear, but sighed with relief to see he had not slept through it. It was set to start in roughly forty minutes. Enough time to down a cup of coffee and get to the Tucarumong Street booth, as per the officials' instructions.

He was still wearing his clothes from yesterday, parts of which were stiff with dried blood. Glancing back at the bed, he was thankful to see he had not stained the sheets.

Next, he walked over to the brewer and examined the object, parsing out how exactly it worked. He was used to his father's ancient method of putting the ground beans in a pot, adding hot water, and letting the grounds infuse the water for a while before pouring it. Von always said that it worked for him, and that was good enough. These newish machines were introduced at least a decade earlier, made possible by the Dirt

King's electricity finally spreading throughout all of the kingdom, but Coal had never really worked with one. He'd gotten stuck in his father's ways, too.

As it turned out, operating the device was pretty simple. Soon enough, he had a piping hot cup of coffee brewed and he gulped it down eagerly. It had taken him a long time, but eventually he grew accustomed to the bitter taste of black coffee. Much like electric coffee makers, cream and sugar were too fancy for his father—plain coffee worked, so that was what he drank.

He sat down in one of the comfy chairs in the room's lounging area and tried to center himself, allowing himself to simply drink his coffee and relax. There was no need to rush this morning. He was fine.

Against all odds, he was fine.

Though that fact still nibbled at him. He could think of no reasonable explanation as to how he ended up back in his room without any injuries. Dend's people had certainly not held back.

Maybe I've been in a coma for a week, he thought. *Maybe I did sleep through the race and I've been asleep for so long, my body healed.*

But he brushed that idea aside. It was unlikely his body could recover in such a short amount of time, and it was unlikely that he would be allowed to just sleep in this hotel room for the amount of time it would actually take to heal.

So how had it happened?

It was a mystery he did not have time to solve. There was now twenty-five minutes until he needed to be at the starting line. He knocked back the last of his coffee and stood. He had all the time in the world once the race concluded to figure out what happened last night.

Speaking of which, he was suddenly reminded that he had technically stood Ilio up.

He swore and lurched toward the door, hoping to catch the man before he went down to the race and explain what happened. Ilio would understand; he knew how the Garnas operated.

Coal swung open the door and nearly screamed in alarm.

Stuck to the door was a slime. The creature was roughly the size of Coal's head and was a bright orange gelatinous blob affixed to the door, seemingly waiting for him to exit the room.

Hello, sir, said the slime.

Slimes were yet another strange creation of the Dirt King. No one in Ruska knew how exactly the creatures were born, or if they were "born" at all, rather than just manufactured. They were orange in color, starting out bright when they first entered the world and darkening as they neared the end of their lifespan, which was typically around two years. The oldest living slime was just shy of three.

They had no mouths, and instead communicated by vibrating their bodies, creating tones that could somehow be interpreted by people as speech.

"Hi," Coal said, steadying himself. Slimes were common in Ruska. His fright was due to not expecting to suddenly see one at all, let alone at eye level.

The slime crawled down his door, leaving behind a sticky residue that would evaporate within the next half hour.

I have a letter for you, the slime told him. **I was instructed to wait here until you awoke in order to confirm delivery. That is why I did not leave it unattended.**

"Okay," Coal said. Slimes were known to be overly verbose, offering elaboration and explanation when none was needed.

The slime stood before him, and Coal could see a sealed envelope within its body. The paper began to sluggishly course through the slime's orange jelly, finally jutting out from what would be its forehead, if it had a face.

Most slimes acted as couriers. That was their purpose when the Dirt King made them. At will, they could solidify their bodies, and no known substance could break through their shell. The residue on their underside could then plant them firmly on the ground, immovable. If one had a valuable item or an extremely important letter to deliver, it was best done by slime to ensure no one could steal it.

Coal grasped the letter, still halfway inside the slime, and yanked it out the rest of the way. "Thanks," he said.

You are welcome. Please confirm delivery.

"Uh…confirmed."

Thank you. Have a pleasant day. The creature then slid away from his door, heading back downstairs to wherever it came from. Coal had no idea if it was technically an employee of the hotel or not.

He stepped back inside and closed the door, momentarily forgetting what he'd been in a rush to leave for. He tore open the envelope and extracted the letter within.

First he looked down at the bottom of the page and saw that it was signed from Noswen and Yurzu.

These two are really persistent, he thought, remembering how pushy the raccoon had been trying to get him to speak with them yesterday afternoon at the festival. Now she was

310 • *Travis M. Riddle*

paying slimes to stick to his door to make sure he got their message.

He then proceeded to read the letter. It was succinct, which he appreciated.

Hello fox,

> *We hope you are feeling rested and ready for the race today. If we cannot win, we hope you do. As I tried to say yesterday, we have an urgent need to speak with you about important matters. We will be waiting for you at Tobulas Square at the ninth hour. From there, we will go somewhere more private.*

> *Regards,*
> *Noswen & Yurzu*

Coal knew where Tobulas Square was; he and Ilio had passed by it at some point over the past two days. But even if they were still waiting for him there, nearly two hours had already passed. He was sure whatever their important conversation entailed, it would not be concluded before the race started. He simply didn't have the time to talk to them right now. He had woken up too late.

And it was probably also too late to talk to Ilio. Knowing Nomak, he probably dragged his assistant down to the starting line over an hour ago, but Coal grabbed the paper he needed to give the beavers then shuffled out of his room and knocked on Ilio's door anyway.

Thirty seconds passed without an answer, so he darted down the hallway to head down to the officials' booth. He knew it would take about ten or fifteen minutes to cross the city and get where he needed to go. He'd woken up with ample time, but the letter had set him back.

It would have been nice to change into some nicer (or at least *not bloody*) clothes, but Coal had never been great with managing his time. In retrospect, he should have probably changed his outfit in between sips of coffee rather than sitting idly in a chair.

He darted through the streets of Soponunga, bobbing along with the sway of the river, sliding past people meandering across the city's many bridges.

Even in his hurry to reach the starting line, what he thought about most was Ilio. He desperately hoped there was no animosity there for failing to meet up with him.

Coal smirked to himself as he actually passed through Tobulas Square, though he did not see Noswen or Yurzu anywhere. Which made sense, given they needed to get to the race as well. They couldn't wait on him all day.

He made a point to avoid the alleyway where Garna Dend's cronies ambushed him. He did not want to go down there and find his blood on the ground or something similarly macabre.

Soon he arrived at Tucarumong Street, which was busy as ever. People milled to and fro, still partaking in the various food stalls and buying Spiderback Showdown merchandise to show their support for individual racers or the event as a whole. If he'd had more time, Coal would want to investigate whether Nomak had ponied up the tups to get some Hiji merchandise produced. The shy man would probably be mortified to have his face plastered on shirts and banners.

Coal hurried over to the beavers' booth and slammed his slip of paper down on the table.

The same two beavers were manning the booth today. "Good morning!" the woman beamed. She seemed to be the one in charge here. "Just under the wire!" she said, just like the first time they'd spoken.

"Yes," Coal nodded. "That seems to be my style."

She read over his paper and said, "We're glad to have you and White Rose, Mr. Rened. Please follow Sarya here to the starting line."

Another beaver approached him with a kind smile. She had long, fluttering lashes and wore a blue-and-silver outfit to match the race's color scheme.

"This way," she said, turning to leave.

Coal thanked the woman at the booth, then followed Sarya.

There had been no time whatsoever to theorize why a tarantula would be a good fit for this race. Coal realized he had no idea what type of race this would be, whether it was strictly treetop or ground or a blend of both. This was only the third year of the race, so he had not heard much chatter up north about its track. Regardless, most spiderback race tracks were altered in some way, whether minor or major, from year to year.

I really should have asked Hiji, he lamented, following Sarya down a back street, away from the gathering crowds. *Or Ilio. Ilio would've known. Idiot,* he chastised himself.

"Excuse me," he said to Sarya, who glanced over her shoulder as she continued walking. "What kind of race is this?" he asked.

The woman chuckled and said, "A spiderback race. If you're asking that at this point, you might be in trouble."

He laughed at the joke, but said, "I mean, is it grounded?"

"No, it is a hybrid race."

That was good to know. At least he had the bare minimum now. He was too embarrassed to press her for more details. She might not be at liberty to divulge them, anyway. He didn't want to put the young woman in an awkward position.

They were heading northeastward, to the edge of the city, where they could pass through the perimeter wall and cross a bridge to reach the tree line on the other side of the river.

Unprompted, Sarya explained to him some generalities about the track: it was located almost wholly in the forest, with the exception of a few sections, and circled around the northern side of the city before crossing part of the Lunsk River and finishing at Soponunga's main entrance.

It was hard for Coal to visualize, but he believed he got the gist of it. He would figure it out in the moment.

After crossing one more bridge out of the city, they approached the starting line.

Hundreds of onlookers were gathered around, already screaming in jubilation and anticipation. They waved banners depicting the icons of their favorite racers and munched on snacks, littering the grass with crumbs and other debris.

Sarya led Coal to the line of racers, positioning him three spots from the end, where White Rose was patiently awaiting him. The only spider that had been left without a rider.

Coal tried to get a good look at most of the racers as he approached his spot, though he missed a few.

The tarantula was impossible to miss, and was dead center in the line of racers. Its rider, Dagosi Monsuo, was a bear with overgrown fangs and scars covering his face. So maybe his use of a tarantula was less about the race's obstacles and more due to the fact that he needed a stronger spider to carry the bulk of his body. But still, Coal could not be sure.

He should have known Dagosi was a bear; they were usually the only people who gave their spiders real names, such as Butolusko for his tarantula, rather than foolish flowery names like White Rose or Wisp's Whisper.

He also saw Hiji with his jumping spider, as well as Noswen and Yurzu sitting atop hacklemesh weavers beside each other. That fact made Coal think the two were unskilled when it came to spiderback racing, and he suspected they'd been swindled by the Sculio Brothers. They had been offering to buy the diamond claw outright, so they had to have deep pockets, and no one who knew anything about racing would waste their tups on a hacklemesh unless it was their only option.

The last people he got a good look at were riding a jumping spider and a wandering spider, so he thought they might be Cassallia Juj and Manova Mandolat, respectively.

Cassallia was a bat wearing tight, white clothes that would not flutter in the wind and would keep her wings wrapped up so that they wouldn't either. Her jumping spider, Wisp's Whisper, scuttled forward and back restlessly.

She pulled a tiny vial from her pocket, uncorked it, and poured a single pink pill into her palm, which she then popped into her mouth and dry swallowed. It was Noctgone, stimulating her to keep her awake and alert for the race.

Manova was a bobcat who wore flashy gold and silver jewelry all over, earrings and necklaces and rings glinting in the sunlight. With just one look, Coal could tell the man was full of himself and was convinced every other racer was trash. The prize was his already.

Given their previous experience with this race, Coal expected the three of them—Dagosi, Cassallia, and Manova—to be his primary competition. Noswen and Yurzu, he was sure, had very little idea what they were doing here and only entered as a last resort because they could not buy the claw. He wasn't totally sure how skilled Hiji and the others were, but it would be a mistake to think of them as amateurs. He was confident in his own riding, though.

Sarya brought him over to White Rose and he greeted the spider with soft coos, rubbing its head gently before climbing up onto its abdomen. The lack of riding tack might prove to be his downfall, but he had a lot of experience riding without a saddle and did not feel he was at too much of a disadvantage.

To his right was Manova, who gave him a curt nod and a toothy smile. Even one of his teeth was gold.

And on his left was Meretta Noyles, who sat perched on her funnel weaver's abdomen in a plain white saddle with a shocked expression at Coal's arrival.

The last time he'd seen her, she was looking far more self-satisfied after viciously attacking him while strapped defenseless to a chair. Coal was pleased to see her so visibly disarmed.

"Hey there," he smiled to the hedgehog. "How you doin'?"

The woman gaped, not saying a word. She simply eyed him up and down, attempting to deduce how in the world he had managed to even get off the floor this morning let alone onto his mount. Finally, she managed to sputter, "How? How are you here?"

Coal shrugged. "Good question, isn't it?"

And one that he really needed an answer for at some point, but for now, it didn't matter.

Coal gave Meretta a smug grin before turning to face forward at the ominous trees ahead. But his pleasure from the hedgehog's apparent discomfort started to drain from his expression.

It was then the nerves started rattling him.

Everything he had worked for these past few days, everything he had gone through, came down to the next forty-or-so minutes. By the end of the hour, he would know his fate. He would either have the diamond claw, or he wouldn't, and it would have all been for naught.

He looked to the front of the crowd, hoping to spot Ilio somewhere among them. A smile from the man would help assuage his anxiety. But he saw neither Ilio nor Garna Nomak, who tended to stand out in a crowd. He could not even spy Mungrus anywhere, shouting gibberish and spilling drinks.

Coal gave the audience one last scan, flicking his ears to see if he could make out Ilio cheering him on at all, before giving up. He let out a resigned sigh.

Soponunga's mayor clambered out into the grassy field, perched on his mechanical legs. They pierced the earth below, kicking up clumps of grass and dirt with each heavy step. He stood before the racers to address them.

"Good morning!" he proclaimed. His voice was loud, but Coal was doubtful it carried all the way back to the audience. "The third annual Soponunga Spiderback Showdown is about to commence. Racers, are you ready?"

All the other racers reared up on their spiders' four back legs, so Coal followed their lead. White Rose hissed in excitement.

Mayor Bontrug beamed and readjusted his thick glasses. "Excellent! Now, on your marks…"

Coal was caught off-guard. He would have bet a hundred tups on the mayor diving into another lengthy, roundabout speech before kicking things off, but he was getting right to the point.

The crowd was going wild behind them.

Bontrug knew he had to give them what they wanted.

"Get set…"

Coal readied White Rose. He could feel the spider's body tense and shiver with anticipation. His own did the same.

You can win. You can win. You have to win. There's no other fucking choice.

Much to his surprise, hyping himself up was actually working. Only a little bit, but still, those simple words boosted his confidence.

Feeling suddenly brazen, he turned to Meretta and said, "Fuck you."

Bontrug then produced a gun from his coat pocket without warning and fired it into the air. *"Go!"* he screeched.

All eighteen spiders shot forward, scuttling toward the forest. The mayor sheepishly ducked down and narrowly avoided getting trampled by Dagosi's tarantula.

The race was on.

23

THE SPIDERS' SPINDLY LEGS were a blur as they all scuttled toward the forest as one writhing mass. White Rose barreled forward, gaining a good lead on the others. Once more, Coal was highly impressed by the spider's speed.

But Meretta's funnel weaver was fast, too. She sped up and came to their side, then steered her spider toward White Rose.

Coal reacted quickly and pulled back, allowing Meretta to take the lead but avoiding being knocked over by her mount. White Rose's body was thicker, sturdier, but funnel weavers were strong, and Meretta's looked as vicious as her.

The hedgehog hooted gleefully on the back of her great brown beast as they scurried ahead of Coal and White Rose.

No one had reached the tree line yet. Meretta was in the lead, with Coal following close behind. Cassallia and Hiji weren't too far back, which was no surprise with the agility of their jumping spiders. Coal risked a glance over his shoulder and saw that Dagosi was keeping an impressive pace considering the lumbering nature of his tarantula. He couldn't spot Manova, Noswen, or Yurzu, and the other racers he saw were unfamiliar to him. Plus, they were trailing fairly far behind, so at the moment they were of no concern.

Up ahead, Coal could see the fencing demarcating the race's route. It was the same type used to keep spiders in line at stables. The opening into the forest was fairly wide, but they would still be funneled inward a bit. Getting there first—or close to first—would be vital.

An idea came to him.

He veered around Meretta's left side and pressed forward. White Rose had no problem picking up speed. The wind was whipping at his ears, and Coal could feel the spider's body vibrating with delight as it ran.

Just a little more.

It wouldn't be long before they reached the trees. The world was rushing past in a vibrant green blur. Everything but the forest and Meretta faded away. He could deal with the other racers in a bit.

He had to get ahead of her. He urged White Rose on, and the spider came up to Meretta's side. She looked over at them and scowled. She spat in their direction, but the wind knocked it right back onto her own face. Coal would have laughed if he weren't so focused on the task at hand.

Meretta was still wiping saliva off her angry, pointed face when Coal pulled ahead of her. He grinned at the sound of her livid screech behind him.

Now he just needed to maintain the lead until they reached the tree line. The plan would work best there.

Every few seconds, he shot a look over his shoulder to see where Meretta was. When she swerved left, he did too. When she went right, that's where White Rose went. Coal mirrored every move, keeping White Rose's speed up, not giving Meretta and her spider even the slightest chance to get around them.

Up ahead he saw Cassallia Juj taking the lead, eliciting cheers from the audience that grew fainter by the second. She was nearly at the forest. It wasn't ideal, but it wasn't the worst thing in the world. Coal could handle her once he dealt with Meretta.

Even if all he accomplished today was ruining Meretta's chances of winning the race, that would be a victory for him.

Winning the entire race himself would be a *better* victory, but that was a wholly separate issue.

They were coming up on the forest and Meretta still hadn't managed to break through Coal's defenses. He watched Cassallia disappear amongst the trees, and next it would be his turn.

With only twenty or thirty feet between them and the forest, Coal glanced backward one more time to make sure Meretta was still directly behind them. After confirming she was, he gave White Rose a light tap.

White Rose leapt forward and into the air while simultaneously spraying webbing.

The sticky white substance splattered all over Meretta's lower body as well as her spider's face and front legs. Coal managed to look and saw the funnel weaver tripping over itself, tumbling forward and sending Meretta flying over its head—or she would have, anyway, if she were not stuck to the web.

As it were, her upper body was flung forward while her legs stayed in place, sending her face smashing into her spider's. Seeing as the spider's face was covered in web, she immediately stuck to the webbing there and let out a muffled scream, pounding her fists into the spider in rage.

Coal winced at her reaction, but quickly recovered and re-focused on the race. White Rose had jumped into the treetops and was darting across branches, leaping nimbly from tree to tree.

He could see Cassallia not too far ahead. Her jumping spider, Wisp's Whisper, was hopping over and weaving through the forest's obstacles. Fallen logs, scattered bushes, uncovered tree roots.

No one else was in the trees, as far as Coal could tell. Manova was now a short distance behind him on the ground, with Hiji in hot pursuit, followed by another deer and Dagosi. Meretta was nowhere to be found, likely still stuck to the grass right outside the entrance to the forest.

Coal finally let himself laugh at her misfortune. Garna Dend was going to be pissed.

White Rose was handling the treetops well. Some spiders took to the ground better, and Coal suspected that might be the case here since the spider was so damned fast, but its speed had not faltered.

Just as he was thinking about how great White Rose was doing among the branches, the tree line gave way to a small clearing in the forest. He held on tight as the spider lunged into the air—the trees on the opposite side of the clearing were too far away, and White Rose landed bumpily but swiftly regained its footing, not losing much momentum as it continued onward.

Ultimately, the hiccup had slowed them enough to allow Manova to overtake them. The bobcat wore a determined expression as he passed by on his wandering spider, not sparing a glimpse Coal's way.

Night's Fang was a horrific-looking beast. It towered above White Rose with its thick, powerful limbs. Its hair was a light brown that darkened at the tips of its legs, with nasty red fangs.

Coal had once seen an incensed wandering spider tear apart smaller spiders at a stable, and he did not want that same fate to befall White Rose. They had no trouble tearing a spider's leg from its body. He had no idea what Manova or his spider's temperament was, and Coal had no intention of finding out.

White Rose showed no signs of tiredness, so Coal urged the spider forward. He needed to make sure not to work the creature too hard and wear it out long before the finish line. There was still quite a bit of race to go.

The clearing was pretty, full of trilliums and violets that were squashed beneath spider feet. Night's Fang in particular tore through a huge bed of violets, sending vivid purple petals spraying into the air.

In front of Cassallia, Coal noted something odd. At first glance, it appeared to be another flower bed, a pack of violets. Approaching it at high speeds, it was nearly impossible to tell that it was actually a collection of petals on the forest floor.

But Coal caught it.

It was a trap.

He maneuvered White Rose to the left so that they would avoid the pile.

Cassallia, however, was moving too fast on the back of her jumping spider. The thing's intense speed was now a disadvantage for her and she let out a surprised scream as the ground gave way beneath them, sending her and her spider plummeting to the bottom of a wide, deep pit as the petals swallowed them up.

Manova guffawed heartily and commanded his wandering spider to jump over the pit, which it did with ease.

White Rose rushed past the pit, hot on Night Fang's tail. Down below, Cassallia grunted and groaned while struggling to get herself mounted on her spider and scramble back up the wall.

Coal realized his heart was pounding and he was breathing erratically. He tried to steady himself. He was pumped up by his minor victory over Meretta as well as Cassallia dooming herself, but he needed to stay focused and not get cocky. It was still anyone's race, and he wasn't even in first place yet.

He ordered White Rose to jump back up into the trees now that they were fast approaching the edge of the clearing. Hopefully staying out of sight of the others would grant them some sort of advantage, however slight. Leaves enveloping his vision somehow calmed him down as well.

There came a roar from far off to the right.

Coal could not identify the source of the sound. It was almost like a retno, but not quite. And he would imagine the animals, however few there actually were in this part of the forest, would have enough sense to steer clear of all these spiders. Thankfully it was markedly different than the sounds that Faranap's abominations made. Introducing those to the race would be catastrophic.

Whatever the animal, it was irrelevant. White Rose had proven it could take on even those abominations, so any normal forest animal would be a breeze in comparison.

For a moment he considered that it might even be Dagosi, letting out a violent roar like many top bear racers were known to do.

He spied Manova through the branches. They were gaining on the bobcat. Behind, he could not see any other racers, but they might be close; his vision was obscured by tree branches, and it wasn't aided by how fast they were moving.

Then he heard a heavy rustle a good distance behind them. Someone else had joined them in the treetops. Coal was thankful for his adept hearing.

As a precaution, he steered White Rose closer to the perimeter fencing. He gave the spider an instruction, and it began to spit out some web. It continued to do so as Coal moved them toward the other edge of the perimeter—carefully jumping from branch to branch while doing so—and repeated the process, going back and forth a few times, creating a tricky barrier behind them. A rude surprise for whoever was trailing them to get tangled up in shortly.

He leaned down and half-shouted praise to White Rose. A smile spread across his face.

They were suddenly jostled as the tree branches shook. White Rose managed to save itself and continued on, and Coal looked down to see that Dagosi had caught up to them.

The brute was slamming his tarantula into trees on either side of him, going back and forth across the path like Coal had been doing with White Rose's webbing. Rather than slowing down Butolusko, the action seemed to energize the spider.

They slammed again and White Rose lost its footing this time. The spider tumbled down through the branches, sending Coal tumbling off its back and crashing into the underbrush. He narrowly avoided slamming his face into thick branches on the way down.

White Rose swiftly righted itself, and Coal stood, not caring to brush off the leaves and dirt clinging to his already ruined clothes. He rushed over to the orb weaver, grimacing at Dagosi's laughter growing distant as the bear increased his lead on them.

Coal climbed up onto White Rose's abdomen, catching a glimpse of Cassallia in the distance. She had not lost a terrible amount of time escaping the pit, it seemed.

He ushered White Rose on and the spider shot forward like a bullet.

Manova was out of sight, but Coal could still see Dagosi around forty or fifty feet ahead. If not for being atop a giant spider, he might have mistaken the massive brown bear for one of the forest's tree trunks.

White Rose deftly dodged errant tree roots that were snaking out from the earth, creating tricky footholds to get caught on. The spider scurried past tree trunks, the fur of Coal's face blowing wildly in the wind. Another unfamiliar roar sounded, closer this time. Coal's ears flicked to determine where they were coming from and pinpointed the animal somewhere on his right.

Not close enough to worry about just yet, but certainly something to be cognizant of. He was unsure if it was another obstacle set by the Soponunga race officials, or if it was a wild animal out on the hunt.

In the end, it did not matter which was the case. The outcome would be the same.

Hopefully it would encounter Manova or Dagosi before him.

Cassallia screamed something behind him, but to Coal it sounded like Buatang, a language which he did not speak. She sounded invigorated, though.

He sped White Rose up and was glad to see the spider still had a ton of energy. Cassallia angrily yelled something else in Buatang, and he looked over his shoulder to see that Hiji was passing her on his own jumping spider. Another problem to think about later.

For now, Coal gained on Dagosi, whose pace was impressive but no match for his orb weaver.

The tarantula lumbered through the forest, still ramming into nearby trees as it went along. Coal briefly pondered how much of that was strategy and how much was just a result of the tarantula's bulk. Dagosi let out a hellish roar, throwing a fist up into the air triumphantly.

Coal did not know what the man was celebrating, but he was getting close and knew White Rose would be unable to slip around the hefty tarantula. They had a relatively wide berth in the forest, but it would be tough to get around the bear's mount, factoring in all the trees.

He commanded White Rose to scurry to the left and climb up a tree. He did not want to risk jumping to the tree and having the spider miss or collide with a branch. His spider was skilled and probably could have pulled it off, but the race was tight right now. No room for even the slightest mistake.

Taking the extra time allowed Cassallia and Wisp's Whisper to get closer, but they still had some ground to cover. White Rose darted through the treetops, pulling up on Dagosi.

Coal braced himself for the tarantula to hit the trees again, and it seemed White Rose was expecting it as well. As they landed on the next nest of branches the tree shuddered, but White Rose did not miss a beat and scurried along, leaping to the next tree and then the next.

A few seconds later, they were ahead of the bear and his hulking mount. There was no time for self-congratulations, though, as Manova came into view.

He brought White Rose back down to the forest floor, diving through branches that scratched at both him and the spider. They were only surface-level, though, and did not even draw blood.

Dagosi bellowed furiously at the sight of them. The tarantula's footsteps pounded on the ground, kicking up leaves and dirt.

It had worked the first time around, so Coal decided to employ the same trick he'd played on Meretta.

He tapped White Rose and the spider jumped forward, shooting its web behind them and scuttling on.

But Butolusko was much tougher than Meretta's funnel weaver. The tarantula burst forward, tearing through the meager webbing that flew through the air and brushing it aside with ease.

"Nice try!" he could faintly hear Dagosi yell. The bear's voice was hoarse and ragged, accurately reflecting his scarred face.

Shit, Coal thought. Having to contend with an aggressive wandering spider was bad enough. Adding a pissed off bear riding an even-bigger-than-usual tarantula to the mix was troublesome.

All he could do was urge White Rose to hurry, but he did not know how much of the track was left.

In the middle of the path was a tall stack of freshly-chopped logs towering high, almost to the trees' lowest branches. White Rose jumped up and over them, having to scramble up the side for the last few feet. They ran atop the stack and jumped back down on the other side. He expected Dagosi might try to pummel his way through the obstacle, but who knew. Coal did not think that even the tarantula could break through it easily.

There was a light footfall behind them, and Coal saw that it was Hiji.

Fire lit the deer's eyes, glaring straight ahead at Coal.

This was not the same Hiji he'd shared so much time with over the past few days. All timidity had sloughed away and left behind a rabid, ferocious beast who wanted nothing more than to win.

The man's jumping spider scuttled forward, halving the distance between them in mere seconds. Coal yelled *"Shit!"* and pushed White Rose forward, but Hiji quickly caught up to them.

Interestingly, he held back, trailing shortly behind Coal rather than maneuvering around. He could have passed them easily at the speed his spider was capable of.

Coal was in the middle of trying to figure out the deer's plan when suddenly it went into action.

Hiji ordered the spider to jump into the air, and it landed forcefully on top of Coal and White Rose. The comparatively diminutive spider came down hard, shoving Coal down onto his spider and pushing White Rose's body into the dirt. It propelled itself off the orb weaver and landed gracefully on the path ahead, hurrying toward Manova in first place.

White Rose stood up shakily. Coal held a hand to his chest, coughing. He gave White Rose a moment to recollect itself, with Dagosi still in the distance behind them, but he lamented that he couldn't give the spider more time. They needed to get a move on.

The spider got off to a rough start but quickly regained speed. Its gait was a little lopsided, and Coal feared something was wrong with one of the front left legs. It did not seem to be giving White Rose much trouble as of yet, and hopefully the spider could stave off the pain for the race's duration.

It was not the best time for another animalistic roar to echo through the forest, closer than ever. It definitively did not belong to Dagosi. Coal had a feeling they would all know what animal it belonged to pretty soon.

Luckily he still had his eyes on Hiji, for now. The deer had pulled a clever trick and put a lot of distance between them. Coal needed to make up for it somehow.

They were coming up on another clearing. Manova was surely already in it, and Hiji was about to pass into it.

Coal and White Rose entered the clearing, which was totally devoid of any greenery except short-cut grass. There appeared to be no traps or obstacles set up for the racers, which

was peculiar. They had almost fully crossed the clearing before Coal saw a retno carcass over by the tree line. The animal's belly was torn open and one of its antlers was snapped
off its forehead. There were no flies buzzing around the mangled body. It was freshly killed.

That did not bode well.

The retno disappeared from view as they reentered the
thicket of trees. There then came the rushing of water. They
must be coming up on the part of the Lunsk that passed
through the forest.

From up ahead, he heard a loud tumble intermixed with
someone yelling.

And then another roar.

He was struck by fear, too stunned to even swear.

He and White Rose powered through and quickly came
upon the scene of violence.

Manova had been knocked from his wandering spider and
had collided with a tree trunk, which was smeared with blood.
He lay slumped on the ground, his skull caved in and blood
pooling in his lap.

Nearby, close to the water's edge, Night's Fang was rearing
up on a nightmarish creature that would have been right at
home with the not-ventem Coal tangled with in the
Houndsvein.

Just like how that monster shared some visual similarities
with a ventem, this thing looked like a retno, but at the same
time didn't. Its body was thin and graceful, walking on four
long, muscly legs that curved into sharp points like scythes. It
sported two crown-like antlers that jutted off into all directions, tangling up in each other, ending in pointed spikes ripe
for impaling. But unlike a retno, it had no fur, and instead its
skin was a mottled dark greenish-yellow, constantly moving,
as if it was made of a viscous waterfall. The creature's face

330 • *Travis M. Riddle*

bore a single tusk sprouting out from its uneven mouth, and too many eyes—five, with four of those being on one side of its face, trailing down to its cheek.

The not-retno and Night's Fang circled each other, waiting for someone to make the first move. The spider bared its fangs, hissing at its enemy, while the monster remained silent. They peered at each other through breaks in the trees.

Coal had brought White Rose to a stop, as had Hiji with his spider only a few steps ahead. The deer was overlooking the area, trying to determine the best route through. Coal did the same, but he recognized that any sudden movement would potentially set the monster upon him rather than Manova's spider.

He knew this could not be a part of the Spiderback Showdown. There was something unnatural about the not-ventem in those tunnels, and the same was true of this thing before them. There was no way someone would be willingly introducing these creatures to the world, let alone placing them in the middle of a huge competition.

Though he *had* seen those abominations in Faranap. If creatures such as those were being manufactured, then maybe anything was possible.

But something was happening, and Coal did not have time to work through the possibilities. Hiji seemed to notice it the same time he did.

More of the not-retnos were stepping through the forest, leaves crunching underfoot, approaching them. They had made it through the race's perimeter fence. Coal counted at least ten. No one was the same, but all had similar malformed features: melting skin, tangled antlers, the wrong number of eyes.

Coal gulped. He readied White Rose to move, but he did not yet know what he was going to do.

The monsters had them surrounded.

The atmosphere was tense as they both watched Night's Fang and the monster taking stock of each other. The other ten stood still, waiting for something to happen.

It was then that Dagosi burst onto the scene, screaming madly while his tarantula's feet pounded the earth and shook the trees.

And so the creatures descended upon them.

24

FOUR THINGS HAPPENED ALL at once.

The first was that the not-retno squaring off with Night's Fang charged forward, head down, intending to impale the spider. Night's Fang crawled up the tree trunk beside it, avoiding the monster by only a second, then leapt on top of it, smashing the creature's face into the ground and digging its fangs into the not-retno's neck.

The second was that Hiji urged his spider forward, hoping to break through and continue with the race, but one of the monsters was upon him immediately. Its antlers were less spiky, more curved like a shovel, which it used to slide underneath the spider's thorax and flip it onto its back, upending Hiji, who tumbled toward Manova's body.

Third, Dagosi let out another furious bellow, sounding like his throat was set to rip apart. This attracted the attention of several not-retnos, which all charged his tarantula. Butolusko reared up and came down hard on the first creature to reach them, slamming its head into the dirt and crushing the monster's skull, though not without severely damaging its own leg on the not-retno's horns in the process. Dagosi then hopped off his mount's back and stormed toward one of the other monsters, ducking to the side out of the way of its antlers and tusk, then jumping onto its back, bringing it to the ground.

And lastly, one of the (many) not-retnos ran at Coal. He let out a terrified scream and had White Rose scramble up the nearest tree, where he thought he might wait in the branches for things to blow over. He was then horrified to learn that the creatures could climb, piercing the ends of their legs into the trunks and hoisting themselves up.

He screamed again. The not-retno pulled itself up into the branches, swinging its chipped tusk at them. Coal was startled and lost his balance, falling from White Rose's abdomen. His head smacked against a branch on his way down before landing flat on his back.

His body was the one screaming now. He slowly pushed himself up, the fastest he could move being not nearly fast enough. When he finally opened his eyes, he looked and saw White Rose up in the branches, backing away from the not-retno which was still swiping at the spider.

Nearby, Hiji was shaking Manova by the shoulders. It seemed clear to Coal that the bobcat was dead, given the massive crater in his skull and the lake of blood in his lap, though he understood the impulse. The man looked like a formidable fighter and would be good to have in the fray, but it wasn't happening.

Which confirmed that this could not be an official part of the race. There was no way the mayor or anyone else involved would sanction monsters that could kill the racers. The idea was ludicrous.

They were on their own out here.

Hiji's spider was nowhere to be found. It had either scampered off or leapt into the trees somewhere.

The deer finally conceded that Manova was dead. He tossed the body aside and stood, staggering away into the trees, diving behind a bush.

Cowering in fear was one way to approach the situation, Coal supposed. That was another impulse he could relate to.

A not-retno then charged toward Coal, letting out one of those warbled screeches he had been hearing throughout the race.

All three of its pus-brimmed eyes were on the right side of its face, so it had to turn its head to the side to see where it was going. This created a very lopsided charge, with no conviction in its direction.

But Coal was still sitting on the ground, which put him at a stark disadvantage. The thing's horns were barreling toward him, and out of foolish instinct he put his hands up to block them.

The not-retno almost missed, but at least a few of its spikes would have connected with his body if Coal had not grabbed them out of the air first. They pierced his palm, blood running down the rough yellowed bone. He held on tight, trying to break the antler, but he lacked the strength.

His actions angered the creature. It bucked its head, sending Coal tumbling to the side as he let go of the antler. The thing then pierced the ground with its tusk, barely missing Coal's arm. Its horrible vision once again worked in his favor.

Meanwhile, the not-retno that Night's Fang had bitten was thrashing wildly while the spider pinned it to the ground. It screamed, slamming its head on the ground repeatedly with more and more force, snapping its antlers and tusk, which only caused it to scream in more pain.

Dagosi had not yet managed to kill the one he was fighting, but he had punched it in the side and neck numerous times and the beast was stumbling around in a daze. The bear slid off its back behind the creature then grabbed its hind legs, yanking them out from underneath it, its chin crashing into the ground and breaking its tusk in half.

His tarantula was faring just as well. None of the not-retnos had done any damage to it, though few had actually tried. It had taken down one more in addition to the first that had attacked it, and now three more circled the husky spider, waiting to pounce. Butolusko hissed and scuttled around, keeping watch on all the monsters.

Coal then noticed that more of the creatures were emerging from beyond his vision. There was no telling how many were lurking in this part of the forest.

The not-retno's tusk was still stuck in the ground next to him. For some reason he rolled into it, his body stopping as he collided with the ugly bone. Nothing happened. He did not know what he expected to; perhaps that the tusk would break, like what Dagosi had done to his opponent?

But Coal was nowhere near as powerful as the bear. He pushed himself up off the ground just as the not-retno freed its tusk from the earth and reared up on him. He dodged out of the way of its scythe-like legs, crouching under the thing's body. Then he pushed himself upward, heaving against its stomach, shuddering at the touch of its cascading, rotten flesh. He heaved with all his might and threw the monster aside. It rolled on the ground and into a rock, which was not enough to kill or even seriously harm it, but Coal hoped that it hurt a little bit.

Coal was finally able to stand again and took a moment to assess the scene. It was a nightmare.

Night's Fang's prey had ceased moving, and so the spider moved on. It was currently prodding Manova's corpse, trying to wake its master. When there was no response, it hissed in anger and attacked the closest not-retno.

The three not-retnos leapt at Butolusko simultaneously. The tarantula batted away the one in front, but the other two pierced either side of it. Butolusko shook them off, dislodging their horns easily, but the tarantula started to bleed profusely. That fact seemingly did not bother it much, as it then swatted at one of the creatures and bit into its torso with vigor.

Coal did not know whether the tarantula's venom would be as harmful as Night's Fang's, but he couldn't imagine it was a pleasant experience for the not-retno regardless.

But for every monster one of the fighters eliminated, it was replaced by one or two more. There was a seemingly endless supply of them seeping out from the forest, blocking the path in all directions.

One thing was certain, and it was that Coal was no fighter. Even equipped with a gun he could barely do any damage, let alone unarmed. He lacked both the might and the finesse that Dagosi, Butolusko, and Night's Fang possessed. His best bet to get out of here alive was to flee across the river.

He could not do it on foot, though. There were too many of them, and they were too fast. One would impale him in an instant if he made a run for it. Hiji had recognized that, and that was why he was hiding instead, with his spider missing.

White Rose leapt to another tree and was safe from the not-retno that had followed them up. The monster could scale trees easily, but jumping from one to the other was out of the question. Coal was glad his spider was safe for the time being, but he desperately needed a ride out of there.

All told, only a minute or two had passed since they all first encountered the not-retnos. Time was moving in slow motion for Coal, like dragging his hand through mud.

Dagosi suddenly stumbled backward into him, sending him falling onto his ass again. His palms scraped against dirt and rocks, dirtying the wound he had received from the not-retno's assault.

The bear turned with ferocity, ready to pummel the creature he'd run into. When he realized it was a fellow racer, he yelled, *"Come on, then!"* and jumped back into the fight, punching one of the not-retnos attacking Butolusko in the hind quarters.

Another not-retno took the opportunity to rush forward and pierced Coal in the back. It tore through his shirt and sent him lurching onto his stomach, sprawled helplessly on the forest floor.

Suddenly more racers bounded into the area.

The first thing Cassallia Juj did was cry out in fear and confusion. Coal could not see what she did next, but he could hear her *not* stop screaming.

A spider bashed against the monster that had attacked Coal, sending it careening into a tree trunk, breaking its spine with the impact. It lay limp at the base of the tree.

Coal could not roll onto his back. It had six holes punched into it, which were all gushing blood. In his stupor, his first thought was, *This shirt is so fucked.*

But he craned his neck and in the corner of his eye could make out who had saved him. Noswen was riding atop her hacklemesh weaver with a strained expression. The spider was shit for racing, but it evidently packed a powerful punch. Powerful enough to topple a not-retno, in any case.

The raccoon slid down off her mount as Yurzu came to a halt shortly behind her.

"What the—?" the bat muttered softly, absorbing the chaos.

Noswen hurried over to Coal. He huffed a greeting, but that was all he could manage. His breathing was haggard and he could not move.

"Don't speak," Noswen instructed him. "Hold on a second."

It was an easy order to follow. He clamped his eyes shut and focused on breathing.

"Noswen, what—?"

"Shut up," Noswen cut Yurzu off.

She ripped Coal's shirt, which tore away easily with six holes already torn through it. Then she placed both her hands on his bare back, running her fingertips across the wounds. His orange fur was matted with blood and he cringed at her delicate touch.

"It'll be fine," she told Coal. To Yurzu, she said, "Keep them away!"

The bat let out a terrified yelp but did not voice any defiance.

A few feet away, Dagosi was shouting with every swing of his fists. He had been smart to dismount Butolusko; they were wreaking far more havoc separately than together.

"This is going to hurt," Noswen then said. "I'm sorry. But trust me."

Coal wanted to ask what she meant, but then it happened.

Noswen dug a finger into one of the holes in Coal's back. It helped him find his voice, which he used to scream in anguish. It hurt too much to even cry.

It was like fire filled the hole in him. He squirmed beneath Noswen, but she held him firmly to the ground, keeping her finger inside him.

"Stop fucking—" she grumbled.

The intense heat then gave way to coolness, and Coal could feel her slowly pulling her finger out. As she did so, the hole was filled with a substance that was viscous and sticky, clutching to Noswen's finger as she extracted it, before coming loose from her fingertip and snapping back to the hole and solidifying. There was a mild itch at the surface of the wound, but it went away after a few seconds.

He could not see his back, but Coal could tell that the wound was healed. There was no more pain, no more leaking blood. Noswen had done something to him.

"What the fuck?" he breathed out. What had she done? "Was that—"

He was about to say *magic*, but he knew it was a ridiculous notion, and anyway she dug her finger into another wound and his sentence was cut off by his own earsplitting shriek.

Noswen was certainly not lying when she warned him it would hurt.

But like the first time, it soon cooled and the pain faded away. Before Coal could say anything, she moved on to the next hole and repeated the process (him unable to control his shouts every time) until all six wounds were sealed.

The raccoon then rolled him over and looked him gravely in the eye before trailing down to examine his bare chest. As she did so, she asked, "Are you hurt anywhere else?"

"Just my palm," he panted, "but I'll be alright there." It was not a deep cut, and he did not want any more of that intense pain inflicted upon him, even if it resulted in healing.

"Good," she said, standing. He did the same.

Yurzu had done an admirable job of fending off any approaching monsters. Coal was impressed by the young bat's fortitude. After fainting back at the signup booth, he would not have expected the guy to have so much spirit. Yurzu was clearly unable to control his hacklemesh very well, but he could at least make the beast circle around to block the not-retnos' advances.

Noswen climbed back up onto her spider and shouted something at Yurzu in Buatang. He nodded and had his spider climb up into a tree.

Nearby, Cassallia was high in the treetops, her spider leaping out of the way of a monster's swipes as it climbed and lunged toward them. She had yet to stop shrieking. Coal couldn't fault her.

He still hadn't seen Hiji since the cowardly deer went to hide. He looked over in that direction and saw a curious not-retno sniffing around, obviously on the man's trail. If he didn't get out of there soon, he was done for.

"Hey!" Coal shouted to Noswen atop her spider. She turned to look down at him, visibly irritated by him interrupting whatever plan she was about to enact. He pointed over at Manova and asked, "Can you help him?"

What she had done to his back was otherworldly, unnatural, and he had no logical explanation for it. Maybe something could be done to revive the bobcat, too.

"No," Noswen said immediately upon seeing Manova.

She then turned away and rushed her hacklemesh weaver into a group of not-retnos that were beginning to surround Dagosi. The bear was going to have a number of new scars in his collection after today.

There was no way to explain how Noswen had healed his back, and Coal realized the same could be said of his injuries from Meretta and Dend's men that disappeared without a trace overnight.

With Noswen having wanted to speak with him that morning, it could not be a coincidence.

There was a rustling in the leaves above, and suddenly White Rose was plummeting to the earth. The spider righted itself in the air and landed on its feet, sending up a flurry of dead leaves in its wake.

Coal smiled at the sight of his spider, unscathed but for a few scratches from stray branches. A not-retno then roared and lurched toward him and he jumped out of the way, keeping his footing and remaining upright for the first time in this whole battle.

Given how poorly it went the first time, he was not going to attempt breaking the thing's antlers or trying to kill it. Instead, he ran around the creature and darted toward White Rose as the monster turned to face him again.

This was his chance to get away. His path to White Rose was clear of any not-retnos for now.

But the one that had charged him was in hot pursuit, and its stride outpaced his own. Soon it would be upon him, cutting him down with its horrible scythes.

He whistled, and White Rose came to attention. The spider spotted him and scurried his way before bounding into the air, vaulting over both Coal and the not-retno. It landed on the other side, skidding into a turn, then sprang forward again and tackled the creature to the ground. White Rose quickly started spraying webbing, climbing over the not-retno to cover the entire thing in a sticky white cocoon.

"Yes!" Coal cheered. He was instantly embarrassed, and was glad to see no one else in the area was paying him even a modicum of attention.

Yurzu and his spider then crashed down on top of a nearby monster. Upon seeing Coal standing there stupidly, the bat yelled, "Go! Finish!"

He couldn't argue with that.

Coal climbed up onto White Rose's abdomen, complimenting the spider on a job well done. In front of him, he could see more racers approaching their position, being led by the other

342 • *Travis M. Riddle*

deer and Meretta Noyles. They were about to have a truly awful time.

He rotated White Rose and charged ahead.

To his left, he saw that Hiji's jumping spider had reappeared at some point, probably fallen from the trees. Hiji was racing toward the spider with a not-retno nipping at his heels. The man was yelling at his spider to meet him halfway before the beast got to him.

Coal veered White Rose in that direction and rammed into the monster chasing Hiji. It was thrown aside into a tree trunk, but it was not dead. It was already standing shakily to continue its hunt when Coal turned his spider away.

He passed by Hiji, who let out a distressed thank you as he mounted his spider. Coal didn't reply, needing to focus his attention on dodging the multitude of not-retnos ahead.

Thankfully, it seemed they had depleted their supply of backup. Now, when Dagosi, Butolusko, Night's Fang, or Noswen took out one of the monsters, their numbers dwindled and were not replaced. They were winning. All of them were still in great shape, except for maybe Butolusko, with no signs of slowing down. They should be able to take care of the rest of the beasts, Coal was sure.

White Rose did not need to be told what to do aside from which direction to go. The spider was clever and, despite the minor injuries it had incurred, still lightning fast.

It weaved through the line of trees and monsters, shooting web as it passed them to stick the not-retnos to the ground, trees, or each other. When necessary, the spider leapt onto trunks and propelled itself off to surmount the obstacles, living or otherwise, in its way.

Coal's body swung back and forth, but he clutched the spider tightly and refused to let go. He maintained his position on its back as the spider cleared the last of the not-retnos.

He held on tight, watching as they barreled toward the Lunsk, and he instructed White Rose to climb into the trees. The spider obeyed, and they leapt through the branches, from tree to tree, until they shot out over the water.

More trees hung over the river, and Coal could only pray that the spider would get them there.

Suddenly White Rose began to rotate in the air, pointing its spinnerets toward the other side of the river. Coal was nearly knocked off the spider's back and into the water below.

White Rose then shot a burst of web from its body, connecting with a distant tree branch. The string snapped taut and Coal grasped the spider's thick hairs, holding on for dear life as they swung through the air.

Coal screamed as they came to a rough landing on the other side of the river, tumbling over each other.

They both stood shakily and Coal glanced over his shoulder, out across the river, from where they had escaped the massacre.

Are we really okay? he asked himself, scarcely believing they had left the monsters behind.

None of the not-retnos were following them, but others were: Hiji, finally reunited with his jumping spider, as well as Cassallia Juj and her jumping spider, were quickly formulating their plans to cross the Lunsk.

Oh yeah, fuck, Coal thought with an audible groan. *We're in the middle of a race.*

For a few minutes there, he had completely forgotten.

He hopped back onto White Rose and gave the spider a congenial rub on its thorax. "I know that was fucked, and I'm sorry, but can we go a little faster?" he asked the spider.

He gave the command, and White Rose took off. He smiled at the spider's resilience.

And, admittedly, he smiled at being in first place.

25

W HITE ROSE WAS ASTOUNDINGLY
fast for an orb weaver, but all jumping spiders
were naturally gifted in that regard. They would
need more than speed to win.

They tore through the forest. Coal hardly even needed to
give White Rose any commands; the spider's instincts were
great, and he let it follow them. There were times when a trap
went undetected by Coal, and he was left wondering why
White Rose suddenly veered off-course or jumped into a tree,
only to watch Hiji or Cassallia nearly plummet into a pit or
unleash a swinging log, the latter of which was one of the more
brutal traps Coal had seen used in a spiderback race.

Spiderback races were as much races as they were obstacle
courses. Traps were set everywhere, as well as nature and
other objects being arranged in such a way to provide shortcuts
to those clever enough to spot them—or delay those foolish
enough to fall for a trick.

It was why Coal momentarily entertained the idea that the not-retnos were planted by the race officials. He had once participated in a race that placed ventems in the path, stomping around and using their sturdy bodies to block the way, ramming any spider that irritated them. Later in that same race, there had been lines of qualls set up with their backsides facing the race's route, defecating uncontrollably and creating slippery hazards in the path.

Thinking back on it, he wasn't sure if that or the not-retnos were a more appalling thing to encounter.

Hiji had been the one to suffer the log's wrath. His spider tripped a wire somewhere, and a thick log suspended by a rope suddenly dove out from the treetops and slammed into the man's chest, sending him flying off the spider's back.

Coal and Cassallia rushed onward while Hiji recovered, apparently more angry than hurt. He quickly hopped off the ground, hand to his chest, swearing loudly.

The bat was neck and neck with Coal. He attempted the strategy he'd used on Meretta earlier, trying to move White Rose in front of her to block her advancement, but Wisp's Whisper was too agile. Cassallia edged forward and swiftly feinted right before shooting off to the left.

Her trick worked. He swore as Cassallia and her small white spider pulled ahead. To her credit, she did not mock or taunt him after besting him. She wore a determined look on her face, locked on the path ahead.

They broke into an area riddled with thorny bushes and vines draped from tree to tree, making it near impossible to leap over the bushes. Cassallia tried, and her spider instantly got tangled up and fell down into the jagged greenery, cutting up its legs as well as its rider.

Coal had seen the spectacle and slowed White Rose to a trot. Then he backed up a little and made the spider climb up into a tree.

Most obstacles were primarily an issue when speeding through recklessly and crashing into whatever was set up there, such as the flower petal-covered pit earlier. Cassallia was clearly not one for caution, having fallen for the ruse multiple times now.

Though Coal came to discover that the treetops had problems of their own. As he and White Rose climbed up, he found dozens of geigexes lounging amongst the branches.

On its own, a geigex was not a big issue. They were small tree-bound creatures, somewhat apelike in appearance but with thin, gangly limbs and long oval heads with snouts that hung limp past their bellies. They sprouted wings from their backs in adulthood, and the older they were, the longer and sharper the bones jutting from their elbows and knees became.

In groups, geigexes tended to rile each other up. If one grew agitated, the others usually followed suit, building on that angry energy until they destroyed whatever was nearby.

So, needless to say, a whole pack of them turning their ugly, distended faces toward Coal was not something he wanted to see after the ordeal with the not-retnos. Geigexes were Ruska's most plentiful animal species, but still he was taken aback discovering so many huddled together.

Down below in the clearing, Cassallia was still having a rough go of it. Wisp's Whisper's limbs were too short to easily climb over the bushes and avoid their thorns, while jumping almost always resulted in hitting a vine or two and plunging downward back into the aforementioned thorns. Coal could hear her shouting irritably in Buatang. All he could recognize were the curse words.

She would not be delayed for long, though. He had to break through the geigexes if he wanted to gain the lead.

The animals were calm right now, simply staring him down, but in a second it would be a different story.

Coal squeezed his legs on either side of White Rose's abdomen, and the spider lunged forward.

The geigex nearest them let out a wet bellow, spraying snot and phlegm everywhere as its snout lashed wildly. It jumped forward, reaching its twig-thin claws toward the spider.

White Rose clung to the branches with all its legs but one, which it used to swat the geigex away. This one was young, its wings underdeveloped, and it crashed through the canopy, falling into the thicket of bushes below. Coal chuckled after hearing Cassallia yelp in alarm.

Assaulting one of their brethren understandably caused unrest among the other geigexes. One by one they each unleashed the same phlegmy scream. Some banged their fists against the branches, rattling the leaves. Those who were older extended their wings in a display of dominance.

Before any of them could move, Coal told White Rose to rush forward.

The spider scuttled across the web of branches, dodging swipes from the beasts and ramming those that it could not avoid.

A particularly feisty one grabbed on to White Rose's back left leg, digging its claws into the flesh and gumming the limb. White Rose had to stop moving and shake the thing off, allowing the others to move closer.

The geigex on White Rose's leg refused to let go. Blood mixed with thick saliva from the animal rubbing its mouth all over. Coal couldn't fathom what it was doing, but he reached back and punched it in the head. The geigex immediately let go, clutching its head in its hand and yelling at him.

"Go!" Coal shouted at White Rose, urging the spider onward before the rest of the animals could reach them. He could hear some flapping their wings while others' claws scraped against tree bark.

He glanced down to see if he could spot Cassallia between the branches and mark her progress, but the branches were too tightly packed. Which was good for White Rose's traversal, but bad for his visibility.

It only took a second to realize that White Rose was not moving at its typical speed. The spider was limping along, doing the best it could, but the geigexes were getting too close for comfort.

Coal looked back at the leg the geigex had latched onto. White Rose was dragging it along weakly. It was not bleeding much, but it was covered in the animal's spit. He then remembered something that should have been clear from the start: a geigex's saliva contained a numbing agent. That was partially how they captured their prey.

"Shit," he murmured. He prayed the finish line was close. They had crossed the river already, so it couldn't be far. Thankfully, White Rose would recover just fine after a couple hours of rest.

A flying geigex swooped by overhead and landed on a branch in front of them. Coal wished he still had that gun so he could blast the thing away, but he immediately felt guilty about the thought.

White Rose was undeterred by the geigex. It screeched at the spider, but White Rose barreled on as if it wasn't there. They would collide in only a few moments.

Coal decided to expedite the process.

One leg out of commission wasn't too bad, all things considered; the orb weaver had seven more. Well, six, if he counted the injury from earlier in the race. So maybe two legs out was not fantastic. But still, he thought the move would work.

He was relying on it a lot, but it had proven effective thus far. No reason to quit now.

Coal tapped the spider and White Rose surged forward, spraying webbing on the trailing geigexes. The animals were unenthused about the turn of events. They halted their pursuit, planting themselves on the branches and trying to tear the web off of them.

A few that had lagged behind were able to swing around the mass of tangled allies, but they were of no concern to Coal. He and White Rose should be out of the trees before they had a chance to reach them.

Which only left the lone geigex ahead.

White Rose wasn't slowing down, and the animal was standing its ground. The geigex yelled again, a warbled, high-pitched sound. It flared its wings in an effort to intimidate them.

It was unsuccessful. Geigexes were inherently stupid-looking creatures.

But it unexpectedly leapt forward, over White Rose, smashing into Coal. He was unprepared for the assault and his legs loosened from the spider's abdomen. For whatever reason, he clutched the geigex's shoulders, wrapping himself up in the animal's body as they both smashed through branches, plummeting to the ground. Its slimy snout rubbed against his face, wetting his fur with mucus. He retched.

Luckily he was cognizant enough to turn in mid-air so that when he and the geigex came crashing to the earth, the beast was the one taking the brunt of the fall. But unluckily, he had miscalculated, and instead they both landed on their sides while still holding on to each other.

Coal groaned in agony and willed Noswen to appear out of thin air to heal him again. If she could magic up his wounds and bruises, why not teleport too? Evidently anything was possible.

They were still laying on the ground together when Cassallia and Wisp's Whisper stumbled out from the clearing and tumbled over their bodies.

"Fuck me!" Cassallia screamed, careening over her spider's head and landing face-first in the dirt. Whatever she tried to say next was muffled but equally irate.

Wisp's Whisper did not fare as badly as its rider, regaining its footing quickly after tripping into another (non-thorny) bush. It hissed. The spider had to be positively sick of bushes by now.

Coal untangled himself from the geigex's grip, leaving the thing writhing on the ground. It did not seem injured, but rather pissed off that it had not killed him. It lay on its back, pounding its fists in the dirt like a child throwing a tantrum.

A few feet ahead, White Rose gingerly climbed down a tree trunk and awaited him. The spider looked more banged up than he'd thought. Nothing that some rest wouldn't fix, still, but he felt pity for the beast.

He rushed past Cassallia, who was spitting dirt out of her mouth and uttering more Buatang swear words. Wisp's Whisper stood idly by, watching the livid bat trying to compose herself.

Coal hoisted himself up onto White Rose and ushered the spider forward.

Once again, he zig-zagged White Rose across the path, sending out webbing to craft a barrier for Cassallia to overcome. It seemed to slow people down before, given how long it took some of them to reach the not-retno massacre.

With White Rose's leg in its current state, they would need any advantage they could get. Coal suspected that Wisp's Whisper might be in bad shape now too, with all those cuts from the thorn bushes. They might be evenly matched.

All he could do was keep racing.

White Rose was putting up an impressive effort. He could swear its gait was improving, and he wondered if the spider was as determined to win as he was. Or maybe just determined to end this race as soon as possible and go sleep in a web somewhere.

His thoughts turned to Ilio. He hoped to see the man at the finish line, preferably away from Garna Nomak. He also hoped that there were no hard feelings about him missing their nighttime date. He wanted to hug him, kiss him. After all this, he just wanted to disappear in Ilio's embrace.

There were butterflies in his stomach at the image. Ilio's red-feathered cheeks puffing when he saw him. His beautiful orange eyes.

Coal was yanked from his daydream back into reality as Cassallia appeared from the leaves above, crashing back down to the ground ahead of him and surging forward. She and Wisp's Whisper had entirely avoided his web trap, it seemed.

They weren't far ahead, but any gap was too wide. Second place was not good enough, not after he'd come this far and done so much.

He needed that diamond claw.

Sorry, Coal thought before encouraging White Rose to run faster.

The spider obeyed, scuttling along the underbrush.

He observed Wisp's Whisper carefully and noticed the spider faltering every few steps, though it was keeping a remarkable pace nonetheless.

And then he could see the tree line.

They were almost out of the forest.

The bridge into Soponunga would be just beyond that.

The finish line was near.

He needed to overtake Cassallia.

In a flash, they were clear of the oppressive trees and open air enveloped them. There was an expanse of grass between them and the finish line.

Hundreds of people were congregated around a tall sign erected near the city's southern bridge, which was painted blue with silver letters spelling out FINISH. They cheered and hollered at the sight of the two racers.

Their cheers filled him with hope and energy. White Rose sped up a little, and he could tell the spider was reinvigorated too.

He kept a straight, steady path, hoping White Rose would gain some momentum by not having to weave side to side. Cassallia was doing the same, but Wisp's Whisper was starting to lag.

"Hurry, hurry, hurry!" the bat screamed to her mount. But no matter how much she yelled at it, the spider was unable to obey. It was leaving behind droplets of blood, a trail leading all the way back to the forest.

White Rose was no longer dragging its back leg, but Coal could see the spider was having trouble moving it. The limb was undeniably slowing them down.

Cassallia ordered Wisp's Whisper to jump, but its leap came up short. Additionally, the spider had to take a moment to recover after it landed, which angered her even more. She was on the move again before Coal and White Rose could fully catch up, but they had shortened the distance between them a bit.

But it gave Coal an idea. Cassallia's jumping spider couldn't jump, but his orb weaver could. White Rose had demonstrated that time and time again over the past several days. The spider should be able to use its other legs to propel itself and land without the use of its numbed leg. It was possible they could cover more ground faster that way.

He gave the command, and White Rose followed it without hesitation. They soared through the air, coming back down beside Cassallia. She looked over at them with a grimace then made Wisp's Whisper jump again, and this time it took the spider even longer to regain the strength to keep running. So much so that even without jumping again, White Rose caught up with no trouble at all. Cassallia glared at them again as they rode beside her.

This will work.

He knew it would. And it would be satisfying to beat Cassallia using her own strategy. Coal instructed White Rose to jump forward again, and they came down several feet ahead of Cassallia, who screamed in frustration. As they landed, White Rose broke into a sprint without missing a beat, never losing a moment like Wisp's Whisper did every time it carried out the order.

They repeated the process over and over, putting more and more space between themselves and Cassallia. The crowd was losing its mind at the spectacle.

Coal didn't dare hope that he had the race in the bag. There had been too many races he'd seen in the past where someone was seemingly in the clear before losing it all at the last second.

But the finish line was so close. He was now able to make out individual people in the audience. They were no longer amorphous, colorful blobs in the distance.

They continued jumping, running a short distance, then jumping again. Sometimes Coal even had White Rose spray some webbing behind them as they lunged forward, just for fun.

He looked over his shoulder and grinned seeing how far back Cassallia was. Again, he did not want to assume first place was his, but…he had to admit, it seemed unlikely Cassallia would surpass them with Wisp's Whisper so roughed up. Far behind her, he also spotted another figure emerge from the trees. The dark splotch was pretty big, leading him to suspect it might be Dagosi. He would be mighty impressed if the bear had somehow passed up Hiji after his intense, bloody bout with the monsters.

Up ahead, Coal strained to find Ilio in the crowd. He squinted, scanning back and forth among the onlookers. He spotted several woodpeckers cheering and jeering, but none were Ilio.

As they grew closer to the finish line, the figures behind it came more and more into focus, details etching into their faces.

A beaver's chipped front teeth.

The wrinkles of a tapir's weathered face.

A double-hooped earring dangling from a lynx's pointed, perky ear.

Suddenly Coal was upon them, and he had to pull White Rose to a skidding halt. Everyone around him screamed madly. His instinct was to shrink away. They were all losing their minds.

He looked up and saw Soponunga's massive wooden structures set against clear blue sky. Then he looked over his shoulder and saw the back side of the finish line banner.

His mouth hung open, staring dumbly at the banner. His gaze drifted downward and he watched Cassallia approach, fury in her eyes. Behind her, still quite far away but coming up third, was Dagosi and Butolusko.

"I won?" Coal muttered to himself. He dismounted White Rose and placed a hand on the spider's back, taking it all in.

Then a beaver was jovially smacking him on the back, shouting, "Congratulations!" He grabbed Coal by the wrist and shot his arm into the air. To the crowd, he screamed, "I present to you your winner of the third annual Soponunga Spiderback Showdown!"

There were a few boos from people who had placed bets on someone else or had a favorite racer, but a majority of the crowd cheered excitedly at the declaration.

Coal stood there in a daze, his hand held aloft by the beaver. He stared out into the crowd, all their faces blurring together, their cheers forming a wall of sound.

A smile snuck onto his face.

It was all over. Everything he'd gone through had paid off.

The diamond claw was his. He could sell it and use the money to pay Netraj.

He could buy back his future.

He joined the crowd in celebrating. He let out an ecstatic cheer, pumping his other fist in the air.

Cassallia was unamused.

26

THE TOP FIVE FINISHERS were Coal, followed by Cassallia, then Dagosi, then Hiji, and finally Meretta. The hedgehog had to be a truly formidable racer to have still finished in fifth place after being bogged down by Coal right at the start.

Apparently the race lasted forty-eight minutes, but it had felt like five in Coal's mind. Everything had gone by in a blur out in the forest. Encountering the not-retnos still seemed like it occurred only a moment prior. He was also told that in its three years, that was the longest it had taken the first place rider to complete the course. If not for the awful attack in the middle of the race, that factoid would have embarrassed Coal.

Once the astonishment of winning the race wore off, Coal immediately informed the mayor of what transpired in the forest. Dagosi chimed in with his own violent details. The bear was also able to provide a more exact location within the forest where the incident took place.

Mayor Bontrug wasted no time in sending people out to investigate the scene and retrieve Manova Mandolat's body. There was no sign of Night's Fang at the finish line, so Coal had to assume the spider fled deeper into the woods. With the search underway, Showdown officials began ushering the crowd back across the bridge into the city and toward Tucarumong Street, where there would be a closing ceremony. The city's frog stablemaster, along with his apprentices, set to gathering up all the spiders to corral them back to the stable and patch them up if necessary.

As Coal navigated the streets, brushing shoulders with the other racers at the head of the pack, he tried looking around behind him for Ilio. All he did was trip over his own feet and make himself look like a fool. Among the crowd, he was also suddenly acutely aware of the fact that he no longer had a shirt.

For the duration of the walk, he garnered disdainful looks from both Cassallia and Meretta—the latter especially. Even Hiji seemed irritated with him, but the man was already transitioning back into his regular aloof demeanor.

He could hear murmurs from the crowd behind him, people wondering where Manova was. Only seventeen racers had returned. Some were already correctly guessing the man's unfortunate fate. Coal's stomach twisted and the joy of winning was fading away fast, replaced by guilt and sadness.

During the race, officials had set up short platforms on Tucarumong's main stage for the first, second, and third place racers to stand on, set in front of a velvety blue curtain. All the racers were brought around to the back side of the stage, behind the curtain, to wait for the ceremony to start.

While they waited, someone mercifully came over and provided Coal with a plain white robe to cover himself in lieu of his ruined shirt out in the forest.

Coal stood by Dagosi, the sole person who seemed to harbor no ill will toward him for winning. He saw Noswen and Yurzu standing together and was glad that they were both okay after the scuffle. The bat definitely did not seem like a fighter. But they were next to Meretta, who had fixed Coal with a skin-crawling scowl, so he did not approach them. Every so often, though, the pair cast a glance his way.

Mayor Bontrug paced a few feet away from the group. His mechanical legs clacked against the ground, whirring as the gears and pistons worked to move the stiff limbs. They now reminded Coal of the not-retnos' scythe legs. The man was muttering to himself and occasionally consulting one of the race officials, planning on how to break the sad news to the excited audience. He frequently removed his glasses and rubbed the top of his nose in frustration.

Finally, he took to the stage and approached the microphone with no small amount of trepidation.

"Good afternoon, everyone," he began. Even these simple words wavered in his throat. "Once again, thank you for joining us for the third annual Soponunga Spiderback Showdown."

As was customary when he said the full name of the event, there were cheers, though they were noticeably less enthusiastic this time around. Rumors about Manova were spreading.

Bontrug cleared his throat and continued addressing the crowd. "Before we crown the victor, I'm afraid I have some rather sad news to share with you all. I am sorry to say that Manova Mandolat—skilled racer and dear personal friend to many—has passed away." He allowed a moment for the information to sink in.

Hushed cries from the audience, followed by whispers as they began to discuss amongst themselves what may have happened.

"I am told that there was an incident in the forest. There was a vicious animal attack, resulting in Manova's death and injuries for many other racers. While it is true that we do incorporate animals into certain sections of our race, I have been assured that these were *not* sanctioned by anyone involved with the Soponunga Spiderback Showdown and were instead wild animals that somehow forced their way through the fence and onto the track. We are already working to retrieve Manova's body from the site of the incident as we speak."

A dark pall was understandably cast over all of Tucarumong Street.

Mayor Bontrug said, "Let us all observe a minute of silence in honor of our fallen friend."

The whispers quieted down. Many people closed their eyes and bowed their heads, while others blankly stared ahead or at the ground.

Coal looked to the other racers, who all shifted uncomfortably. Some were shedding tears at the loss of their friend. The racing community was more tightly-knit than he had known.

A minute passed, then Bontrug said, "Now, while we mourn the loss of a great racer and an even better man, let us also celebrate the accomplishments of our other racers today."

It was not the most graceful segue, but it could have been worse. Still, Coal felt like a fraud having to go up on that stage in front of so many people and accept his prize after such a horrific event.

"In third place," Bontrug started, "Dagosi Monsuo, riding his tarantula Butolusko."

To Coal's surprise, the crowd mustered up some enthusiasm for the bear as he trundled up the wooden steps onto the stage. He smiled and waved at the clapping audience and assumed his position on the Third Place platform.

360 • *Travis M. Riddle*

"Next, in second place, was Cassallia Juj, riding her jumping spider Wisp's Whisper."

There was even wilder applause for Cassallia as she took the stage. The mournful tone of the event was not totally gone, but it was no longer as dour as it had been only a minute before. Even the mayor's tone was lightening.

Cassallia took her spot on the platform, smiling for the first time since finishing the race. Coal knew that inside she was still boiling over at the thought of him beating her.

"And finally..." Bontrug trailed off, building unnecessary suspense, provided most everyone had seen who crossed the finish line. "In first place, newcomer Von Rened, riding his orb weaver White Rose!"

Coal almost didn't move and was momentarily confused by the mix-up before he remembered he had given them a fake name. He hurried up the stairs, waving cordially at the crowd. They politely cheered for him, but clearly would rather have someone they were already fans of as their champion.

He nervously stepped up onto the intimidating First Place platform and gazed out at the audience while Mayor Bontrug spoke.

The beaver droned on, his words not registering in Coal's ears.

He had found Ilio.

The woodpecker was standing on the left side of the crowd, in a closed-off area reserved for those associated with the racers. He was wearing a bright orange suit to match the one Garna Nomak was wearing. A bizarre order on the Garna's part, to make his assistant match him, and one that Coal would tease Ilio for later. And, of course, Mungrus was chugging a beer next to them.

The suit looked *much* nicer on Ilio than Nomak. But that went without saying.

Coal gave Ilio a small wave, smiling optimistically. He still did not know how the man felt about his disappearance the night before.

But Ilio puffed his cheeks and waved back, a mild movement detected by neither Nomak nor Mungrus. Not that Mungrus ever really picked up on anything that was going on. Nomak wore an irritated expression due to the distinct lack of Hiji up on the stage. With Coal taking the deer's place.

He breathed a sigh of relief. Ilio was happy for him. He did not seem mad. Coal couldn't wait to see him and talk to him after all the pomp came to a conclusion.

At some point, Mayor Bontrug's speech ended and some other beavers motioned for Coal, Cassallia, and Dagosi to exit the stage. The mayor followed them hurriedly, wanting to end the ceremony as quickly and cleanly as he could under the circumstances. He scuttled off hastily once they were off-stage, his robotic legs working overtime to get him far from Tucarumong Street.

But Coal did not have the diamond claw in hand. There was no way he had been in so much of a daze staring at Ilio that he missed being given the sought-after prize.

Back behind the curtain, Coal awkwardly mumbled to one of the beavers, "Uh…the prize?"

The woman gave him a confused look. "What about it?"

"I…want it?" He recognized how rude he sounded, so he amended, "I was just wondering when I'd be receiving it."

To him as well as Cassallia and Dagosi, she said, "You can obtain your prizes from Mayor Bontrug's office at your convenience. Congratulations on your victories." She then shuffled away in a huff.

He was all too aware that Cassallia wanted nothing to do with him, but he thought he might ask Dagosi if he wanted to accompany him to the mayor's office. Dagosi evidently had other plans, though, and walked away by himself before Coal got a chance to speak with him.

But Noswen and Yurzu hurried over, eager to speak. Maybe he would finally get to know what it was that Noswen seemed so desperate to discuss.

"You won," Noswen said, amazed.

"I won," Coal nodded.

"Thank the skies," Yurzu groaned, smiling by the raccoon's side. He was quite a rotund, fuzzy guy, and he looked relieved by Coal's win, which was odd given that they were fellow competitors.

Noswen allowed herself a brief smile too. "Good. That's good," she said.

Coal didn't follow, but said, "I got your note this morning, but I woke up too soon before the race and had to rush straight there. Sorry." He then recalled their letter stating that if they couldn't win, they hoped he would.

The woman waved his words off. "That's fine, it doesn't matter. There's still time for us to talk. Not here, though. Somewhere private."

"Maybe the Longowosk Hotel deck?" Coal suggested. There was always a loud racket covering up quieter conversations there.

Noswen blinked. "You're a dim bulb, huh?" she asked flatly. Coal was definitely growing weary of being compared to a lightbulb. "Somewhere *private*. Not in the middle of an outdoor bar. We'll talk in your room there. That alright?"

Coal nodded.

"Okay. We can meet you there after you get the claw."

Coal asked, "You're not gonna, like…mug me, are you?"

"Yes, we're going to beat the shit out of you and steal the claw. I thought it'd be better to warn you so that you'd be totally prepared for it," Noswen said sarcastically. She rolled her eyes but said nothing else.

She certainly had some bite to her. Coal felt a little foolish having asked the question. The woman had saved his life, after all. And Yurzu had been the one urging him to finish the race. They were invested in him obtaining the claw, so why would they want to steal it now? After all they had done for him, they had earned some level of trust.

So he told them his room number (to which Noswen replied that they obviously already knew considering they had left him a message there), and then said he would be heading to the mayor's office right away. The duo told him they were going to grab a bite to eat and would meet up with him after. He recommended the Crookery.

The two of them disappeared down the street, and when Coal came around the side of the stage to be absorbed back into the city's throng, Ilio stood there waiting for him.

Coal rushed into the man's arms and wrapped him in a tight hug. They nuzzled, with Coal kissing Ilio's cheek before pulling back.

"Are you okay?" Ilio asked, looking him up and down. Coal was self-conscious about his chest being visible with the loose robe fluttering open. "What happened out there?"

"I'll explain later. It was…not good," he said, and Ilio frowned. "But I'm okay, don't worry. Not a scratch on me. Well, I mean, a few scratches, but those are from falling out of a tree. Not being attacked by monsters."

"Monsters?" Ilio said, panicky. "The mayor said it was animals!"

"He might've downplayed things a bit," Coal said, "but I'm fine! Really!" He went in for another nuzzle.

364 • *Travis M. Riddle*

"Good," said Ilio. "Speaking of being fine, the Garna is not. He is positively livid about you beating Hiji. Ruining his big bet and snatching the claw out from under him...it was quite funny," the man sniggered.

Coal grinned. "Another funny thing is you two looking like Papa and Baby over there in your matching suits. What the hell is *with* that?"

Ilio let out a long, exaggerated groan. "Do not get me started on this. Please forget you ever saw me like this. I beg of you."

Coal laughed at him. "I am never going to forget," he said. "But I need to go collect my winnings real quick. Then I've gotta talk to some other racers back at the hotel, but after that, maybe we can have that date we missed last night?"

Ilio's face lit up. "I did not want to pry, but yes, I would love to make up for the time we missed."

"That's another fucked up story that I'll tell you later. But I swear, I would've been there if I could have."

"I believe you."

They brushed their cheeks together again. Every time, it warmed Coal's heart and made his chest swell. All the stresses of the past twelve hours melted away in the man's embrace.

He planted another kiss on Ilio's cheek then said, "I'll meet you at your room in a bit." They bade each other farewell, and Coal started toward city hall.

The smell of river water was refreshing after a harrowing hour in the forest, surrounded by dirt and leaves and blood. Coal took his time walking through Soponunga. Part of him was anxious to hold that diamond claw (as well as the cash portion of his prize), but he also needed to take the time to slow down and appreciate the victory.

And more importantly, appreciate the fact that he had made it out of there alive. No one could have predicted what happened today. He shuddered at the image of Manova's crushed head filling his mind.

He made it to city hall and entered the massive, daunting building. The structure contained all the intricacies, sturdiness, and durability that a building in a more advanced city such as Vinnag might possess, but was still built entirely of wood. The beavers' ancestors were highly skilled craftsmen.

Coal was awed by it, inside and out. The interior design was very traditional as well, sticking to classic beaver architectural motifs like a wide, open floor design and intricate etchings in the walls themselves. He did not know whether the images depicted anything literal or metaphorical, but he enjoyed the swirling, complex patterns that covered every inch of the walls. They had beautiful, striking depth to them. He felt the urge to run his finger along the grooves, letting his nails get stuck in the recesses.

He spoke to a receptionist, who had him wait for close to half an hour before finally bringing him to Mayor Bontrug's office.

The beaver was flustered, wiping anxiously at his brow while he welcomed Coal into the modestly-decorated room. "Hello, Mr. Rened," he greeted him.

"Hi," said Coal. "I hope this isn't a bad time. It's just that I was heading out of town soon, so…" He didn't know if that was actually true or not, but it might as well be.

"I understand. It's not the best time, I'll say, when someone dies on your watch. Especially a public figure," he added, as if that was markedly worse than a "normal" civilian dying tragically.

"I'm sorry," Coal said sincerely. He wished he could have done something to save Mandova.

Bontrug waved away his useless condolences. "Here, let's get you on your way. Come, take a seat."

Coal moved toward the man's desk and sat in one of the two velvet chairs opposite his own. In each corner of the room was a plant with wide, flat fronds in a purple clay pot.

Bontrug caught him eyeing the plants and said, "Imported them from the Mudlands. The pots, I mean, not the plants. Those tacuses wouldn't last a day in the Mudlands."

Coal feigned interest in the pots, nodding along and sporting an expression like he was impressed. The boars up in the Mudlands were renowned for their skill with clay, but it was not a subject Coal could say he cared much about.

Bontrug's machine carried him around behind his desk and stopped at the chair. He pressed a button near his waist and there was a soft *click* like gears locking into place. Then he slowly lifted himself out of the metal seat and plopped himself into the desk chair.

Coal had noticed something peculiar about the man's body while he shifted into the desk chair. His lower half had been cut off at the waist, and his shirt rode up as he hoisted himself. Coal saw that his torso ended in a long, green scab that appeared to be dripping ever so slightly onto the rug. As if it were a fresh wound.

But he did not want to prod or shame the man, so he buried his morbid curiosity about the peculiar injury. He patiently waited for the mayor to input the code to a safe embedded in the side of his desk.

"Ahh, here we go," the man smiled, popping open the safe. Before he reached inside, he said, "What did we say for first place again? Ten tups and a watch from Yette's Jewelry?" He chortled at his own joke, and Coal joined in out of politeness. It felt like he was doing that a lot lately.

The beaver rummaged through the safe, out of Coal's view, and soon pulled out a stack of tups. He slammed it down on the desk with vigor, and Coal smiled. Three thousand tups was nothing to scoff at, especially after going without more than only a couple hundred at any given time for the past year.

And then Bontrug finally pulled it out: the diamond anteater claw.

It was housed in a glass cube, the dull end nestled into some dark blue velvet to keep it in place. The claw arched like a bridge, its pointed tip resting atop the velvet just at the edge of the case.

It was a deliriously beautiful piece of art. The claw was dazzling, and the realism astounded him. It curved perfectly smoothly into a sharp point. There was no denying that it was a genuine diamond, but there were no rough-cut facets typical of a diamond that one would find in a ring or a necklace. Certainly not something one would find at Yette's Jewelry.

"Wow," Coal uttered, staring wide-eyed at the claw. "It looks so lifelike."

"Aside from being so glittery?" said Bontrug.

"Aside from that, yeah."

The claw was the same size as Nomak's biggest one. After seeing the craftsmanship of it, Coal could understand why the man and Noswen were both willing to pay such an insanely high price to own it.

Just then, the thought occurred to him that he could potentially sell it to Noswen for even more than Nomak had originally offered the Eorpu Naro anteaters.

How much had Zank said the Garna ponied up? Twelve thousand tups?

The number almost dazzled him even more than the claw itself.

Whether he sold it to Noswen in his own hotel room or walked down the hall to Nomak's, soon he'd be rid of the claw and far richer.

"Congratulations again," said the mayor, pushing the glass box toward Coal. He sighed heavily, staring wistfully at the diamond claw.

Coal pulled the box the rest of the way toward him, then asked, "Is there a…a bag, or something, that I could put this in? I'm not sure it's the best idea to walk around with it in plain view."

"Of course, of course," said Bontrug. He swiveled around in his chair and pulled himself toward a nearby drawer, from which he fetched an unassuming burlap sack. He tossed it to Coal.

He gently placed the box inside the sack and thanked the mayor. "I'll get out of your hair now," he said, rising. The man was obviously preoccupied thinking about the nightmare he had to deal with now after losing a racer.

Next year's race—if there was one—was guaranteed to have a lot of new precautions in effect.

And on that note, Bontrug asked him, "Shall we be expecting you in next year's race? Defending your title?"

It was impossible to know what Coal's life looked like a day from now, let alone in a full year. "Maybe," he replied, thinking it unlikely.

"Ahh. Well, we would love to have you. I'm sure you'd fetch some great sponsors the next time around, now that you've proven yourself a fine racer."

"I'll consider it. Thank you."

Bontrug nodded and reached his hand out for Coal to shake. In order to reach him, he had to use his other hand to push against the desk to boost himself up higher, and Coal caught another glimpse of his bizarrely mangled lower half. He forced himself not to stare, but had to confess he was captivated by it.

He shook the beaver's hand, then departed. He smiled and nodded a goodbye to the receptionist as well on his way out.

Back on the street, he breathed in the fresh river air and held the sack close to his side. Then he set off back toward the Longowosk Hotel for his meeting with the strange raccoon and bat.

The future was within his reach.

His heart swelled with excitement and hope.

27

NOSWEN AND YURZU WERE awaiting him in the lobby of the Longowosk. The raccoon was drinking a cocktail at the bar while the bat sat in a nearby armchair, scratching at his chin, deep in thought.

Coal greeted them, and Noswen polished off her drink in one gulp so that they could head upstairs. She told him they thought it would look weird loitering around his door, and they wanted to draw as little attention to themselves as possible.

Noswen whistled low as they entered Coal's room. "Fancy place," she muttered, walking through the whole space. "The Rened pockets run deep."

Her statement was doubly wrong, seeing as his name wasn't Rened and also the real Rened in Muta Par was pretty far from wealthy. But he still didn't truly know who these people were or what they wanted, so he decided to remain concealed behind the moniker Von Rened for now.

"Actually, I'm staying here for free," he said, which after hearing it out loud he realized did not sound any better. "Garna

Nomak bought a block of rooms, and this one was left over. His assistant let me stay."

"Who is Garna Nomak?"

He had been so deeply involved in the Garna's insular world, he forgot that the man's name (and the title of Garna) wouldn't mean anything to a non-Vinnag resident. "Doesn't matter," he said. "Rich guy." He took a second to remove the robe he'd been given and slipped on a proper shirt.

"May I sit?" Yurzu asked. His voice was quiet, barely a squeak. Coal guessed that he himself might only be a few years older than the bat, but Yurzu still seemed like a kid to him. He nodded, and Yurzu nestled into one of the room's many comfortable chairs.

Coal stood near the doorway, silently watching the two strangers. Yurzu had settled into a chair and was once again scratching at his chin while Noswen sauntered around, inspecting the room's amenities.

She pointed at the coffee brewer and said, "Nice. I got one of these last year. Made my life much easier. You need a lot of energy when you're dealing with six kits running around, all wanting attention from Mom." She then stood over by Yurzu.

They both stared at Coal, who stared right back.

Finally, he said, "So what is this about?"

The raccoon sighed and nodded. "We should get right down to it," she said. "It's not going to be your favorite conversation, so just…gird yourself."

Coal's brow furrowed. He didn't have the faintest clue what these people wanted with him.

Noswen's eyes flicked toward Yurzu, then she nudged his shoulder.

The bat was visibly uncomfortable having to initiate whatever this conversation was. But he cleared his throat and said, "We know you're Blighted."

Coal had no idea what that term could possibly mean. He said, "That sounds kind of rude. What are you talking about?"

"You have magic in you," the bat clarified.

For a few seconds Coal said nothing, looking back and forth between the two of them. Of all the things in the world Yurzu could have said, that was perhaps the last thing Coal would've ever expected.

He didn't really know how to respond. It was hard to come up with a reply to someone accusing you of possessing a quality that does not exist in the real world.

What he settled on was, "Excuse me?"

"There's no reason to act dumb," said Noswen, rolling her eyes. "You know about mine already. My healing."

"So that *was* magic?"

"Of course it was fucking magic," she groaned. "How else do you think I healed you without medical supplies?"

"I just…" He trailed off, at a loss. Magic was not a thing. It was just something out of books. Why would they think he possessed magic?

Noswen sensed there was not a second half to his sentence. "My ability is healing. You're welcome, by the way."

"Thank you," he mumbled. Then, "So are you the reason I wasn't a total wreck this morning?"

"Yep," she confirmed.

"How—?"

"We were following you," she cut him off, knowing what his question would be. "Once Yurzu confirmed it was you with the magic, we needed to have this conversation with you. You blew us off, though, so we were waiting until you were alone. The idea was to get your attention when you were away from people. But those goons got to you first. We kept following, and once they cleared out of that room they took you to, we broke in to help."

"*After* they beat the shit out of me," said Coal. "I wish you'd maybe intervened a bit sooner."

"Sorry. But look at us. Neither of us is really the fighting type. We barely made it out of that scrape in the forest, and that's only because we had those spiders."

She was right. Maybe they could hold their own if needed, but Dend's men were nasty brutes twice their size, if not more. They would've been pummeled just as badly as he was.

Noswen continued. "So once again we tried to have this conversation with you by leaving that note to meet us before the race. We wanted to explain everything so that you knew the situation going in."

"That slime scared the hell out of me," Coal said with a dry laugh.

"Sorry," she apologized again. "That was my idea. I figured subtlety was ill-advised. Didn't want to leave it on the table or something and risk you missing it. I thought a slime stuck to the door was unmissable."

She wasn't wrong.

With that mystery solved, Coal then asked, "So what's he do, then?" He nodded toward Yurzu.

"His blight is a little more subtle."

She nudged the young bat again, and he spoke. "I can detect sickness in people." His words were rushed, all smushed together.

"We could make a hell of a team if we wanted to, huh?" said Noswen.

"Are you *not* a team?"

"Not a medical life-saving sort of team, no," Noswen shook her head. She looked to Yurzu again.

"A side effect of my ability," Yurzu continued, "is that I can feel when someone has magic in them. It feels like a sickness. Like an intensely powerful disease."

"That doesn't sound good," said Coal. "You sensed that in me? A *blight*?" Their terminology felt weird on his tongue.

"Detecting magic takes a lot out of him because of how strong it is," Noswen explained for Yurzu. "When it hits him hard enough, it can even make him faint."

That explained the incident at the signup booth a few days before. Yurzu had seemed totally fine until Coal and Ilio approached.

But it had to be a mistake, and Coal told them as such. "I've never done anything magical. I can't heal anyone, I can't shoot fireballs from my hands, I can't grow ten sizes bigger. I'm a dud. Your power's wrong. Maybe *you're* not really magical, either."

"My power is never wrong," Yurzu shot back, his tone firm for the first time. There was a story hidden behind his words.

"You might have just not experienced it yet," Noswen cut in, trying to soothe the sudden tension. "But has there ever been something…I don't know, *unexplained* in your life?"

There was one glaring incident.

Speaking to his father's ghost would probably qualify as "unexplained" to most people.

He had long since written that off as some kind of hallucination brought on by severe dehydration and starvation. That was the only thing that made any sense.

And yet part of him didn't believe that. Part of him knew he really had been speaking to his father, somehow. Part of him always believed it had happened.

It was getting harder to deny.

"Maybe," he ventured, not wanting to provide any further detail just yet.

But Noswen's next question was, "What happened?"

Coal shook his head. "First, I want to know what the fuck this is all about. Even if I do have magic in me, what does that have to do with you two?" It was a massive *if.*

"That's where the team comes in," said Noswen. She took a step toward Coal, who instinctively backed away, so she stopped. "There are three more of us. Magic users, I mean. And we've been looking for you."

He wasn't sure if she was waiting for some kind of reaction from him, but he offered none, so she went on.

"Here's the short version: every few hundred years, a group of people are born with magical abilities. Not sure why, it seems random and based on nothing to determine who is born with it and what the ability actually is. It's not usually the same each time. But it always coincides with the Houndstooth starting to…I suppose *crack* is the best word for it."

Coal frowned. "What do you mean?" he asked. "The Houndstooth's bark is impenetrable."

Noswen nodded. "And that's not by accident, or some force of nature. There's a darkness inside it. The Dirt King has been working for hundreds of years to keep it contained. If it was unleashed on Ruska, it would be catastrophic. All the plants, all the animals, all the people—we'd be helpless to stop it. It would infect everything."

"How in the world could you possibly know that?" asked Coal.

Noswen glared and said, "It's what the Dirt King told us."

"And that darkness is seeping out," Coal ventured a guess.

Another nod, from both Noswen and Yurzu. Noswen said, "Exactly. And you saw an example of it today. Those monsters in the forest were a result of the Houndstooth's disease. It creates those creatures like it's some fucked up factory. Pumps them out into the Houndsvein. As you can see, they're starting to emerge topside."

"I saw one of them in the tunnels," Coal blurted out. "It looked like a ventem, but…not."

"It's like it's trying to produce recognizable animals but screwing up the process," Noswen said. "Again, there's a lot we don't understand, but we know that much. And the Dirt King also knows how to stop it. Like I said, this happens every few hundred years, and he's always able to stave it off. That's where we come in."

Coal did not like the sound of that. He had worked so hard to secure his future, and now that he had met Ilio, he wanted to see where that went. He didn't owe the Dirt King anything. He was repulsed at the prospect of being roped into some grand mission that he had no say in.

"Six people are born with magic. The Blighted. And there are six ancient artifacts in Ruska, each kept safe by their respective species. The Dirt King has recruited us to seek out the artifacts and bring them back to the Houndstooth, combining our magic with the artifacts' innate power to re-seal it."

Coal blinked.

He said, "That sounds absurd. You realize that, right?"

"Yes," Yurzu piped up.

Noswen ignored her companion and said, "It might sound absurd, yes, but it's what the Dirt King told us. I'm not the guy's biggest fan by any means, but I find it a little hard to refute an immortal being who's seen it all and lived through this multiple times. Plus, you've seen the evidence yourself. There are vicious, unnatural creatures infecting Ruska. They killed that bobcat today."

He could not dispute that aspect of her story.

Something she had said earlier was nagging at him. He asked, "What did you mean by wanting me to know the situation going into the race?"

"I wanted you to know that all three of us were on the same team. That if any of us won, we all won. Are you really that dense? Have you not pieced this part together yet?"

He took a second to think about it, then felt the weight of the sack slung over his shoulder.

"The claw is one of the artifacts," he said.

"Finally," said Noswen.

That was why Yurzu had urged him to flee and finish the race. And it was why they were trying to buy the claw before the race even started, so that they could guarantee their possession of it and not let it slip through their fingers by losing. Which was smart, because as he had noted, neither of them were skilled racers.

"You should've gotten something better than hacklemeshes if you wanted to win," he said. "Especially with all that money you've got from the Dirt King, I assume. And you said *I* had deep pockets."

Noswen shrugged. "It worked out just fine, I think."

Coal carefully placed the bag on the floor and pulled out the glass cube encasing the diamond anteater claw.

There were still parts of Noswen's story that weren't adding up. He said, "If this thing is some ancient, powerful artifact that the anteaters were supposed to safeguard, why did they sell it to the beavers? Shouldn't it have been too important to give up?"

"I can't speak for the anteaters," Noswen said, "but that thing is hundreds of years old. The other two leaders we've spoken to had no idea what the actual significance of their items were. One of them didn't even know they had it or where it was, they had to send someone scouring through their archives to find it. The anteaters probably didn't know either and just thought it was a valuable piece of art or jewelry or something."

Coal carried the claw over to the bed and sat on its edge, staring down at the transparent cube in his lap. The diamond within glistened.

From the sounds of it, with the addition of the claw, that would make three artifacts they already possessed. Three down, three to go.

Countless questions raced through his mind.

"Who are the others on your team?" was the next he asked.

Yurzu was still letting Noswen take the lead. She answered, "An orangutan named Lop, a boar named Biror, and a saola named Jatiri. Oh, and a slime name Zsoz to safely transport the artifacts for us."

Some of those surprised Coal. The boars were famously reclusive, primarily keeping to themselves in the Mudlands. And the saola population had dwindled drastically over the past decade. There were not many of them left.

"Why aren't they here?" Coal asked.

Noswen sighed. "Well, we thought this one would be easy. When we learned the claw was being used as a prize in a race, we figured we could just buy it off them and they'd replace it with something else. We did not expect such integrity from the officials. So they sent me and Yurzu to handle that, while the others stuck around Sadatso. Time was of the essence, with the race starting soon, so we thought it'd be faster if only two of us went."

Sadatso was a small village within the territory of the deer. "Was one of the artifacts there?"

"Not there, exactly, but housed in a temple nearby. A silver antler. They thought it was a sculpture, so they sold it to us for the right price."

"Why not just tell them the Dirt King needs it?" Coal asked. "Surely he could demand they hand it over. He could give you decrees or orders or whatever it is he'd give you."

"It's not exactly meant to be public knowledge that the Houndstooth is shattering and letting loose horrific beasts," said Noswen. Her tone suggested that he was an imbecile. "The Dirt King instructed us to not mention our task or that we are on official Palace business."

That sounded a little shady, but he could also sort of understand the reasoning.

It all still sounded unbelievable, and what he could *not* understand was why the Dirt King didn't already own all these artifacts if the same thing kept happening every few hundred years. One would think it'd be wise to keep all the artifacts together and close by.

But it was impossible to ignore the monsters he'd seen in the forest and the dung tunnels, as well as Noswen's ability to heal him. And the fact that he had allegedly spoken to a ghost. If that wasn't proof of magic, he didn't know what was.

Even if everything Noswen said was true, though, it didn't change matters.

"I'm not interested," he said.

"Doesn't fucking matter," Noswen said bluntly. "You're one of us. One of the six Blighted. You have to do it."

"Why?" he growled, still staring down at the claw. He wanted to sell it to her and be done with the whole thing.

"Were you not listening? We have to channel our magic into the artifacts. Six people, six artifacts. It doesn't work if there's only five of us. We won't be able to seal the Houndstooth, and then all of Ruska will be fucked. Do you really

380 • *Travis M. Riddle*

want to be the person solely responsible for fucking the kingdom?"

Put that way, it did sound highly unappealing.

"Look, I won't lie, it's a fucking mess, and it's a huge ordeal," Noswen said. "I have six children back in Holluwak.
I've got a husband that I left behind. You think I want to be
here, competing in some dumbshit spider race, risking my life?
I could be at home, cooking stew or watering flowers or teach-
ing my youngest to read or doing whatever the fuck else I
want. But I'm not. I'm here, competing in a dumbshit spider
race and risking my life. And I'm doing it so that the kingdom
isn't fucked. I'm doing it for them, for my family. So that they
have a future."

Her words sent a pang of guilt into Coal's stomach. He
looked up from the claw to her face. She was glaring at him.
Yurzu looked immensely uncomfortable.

The guilt was exacerbated when she then said, "None of us
want to do it, but we need to. Don't be fucking selfish."

It was another argument he couldn't fight against.

The future he was constantly telling himself he was
fighting for would be lost if the entire kingdom succumbed to
whatever the Houndstooth's bark was holding back.

He could still have that future.

He just needed to fight a little longer.

Coal sighed.

"If I did this," he started, "I need some guarantees."

Noswen groaned. She was clearly not one to put up with
anybody's nonsense. "Like what?"

This meant he would not be able to sell the claw to Nomak,
and he clearly couldn't sell it to Noswen and walk away, either. Without that money, he could not pay Netraj. But if he
did this for the Dirt King...

"There is…I've been marked, and I need my record erased. If the Dirt King can do that for me, no questions asked, then I'll agree."

"You have to agree no matter what," said Noswen, "but calling in that favor shouldn't be a problem. Others are asking for more, and the Dirt King agreed to their requests."

He sighed again. If anyone could erase his record, the Dirt King could. Saving the kingdom seemed like a more than fair trade.

In the span of ten minutes, his entire life had been upturned yet again. Thrown into an epic trial, complete with ancient artifacts, magic spells, and unknowable monsters. It was a lot to wrap his head around.

Once more, he felt as if he was helplessly fighting against a current dragging him thrashing through the violent waters of his disastrous life. Unable to do anything about it. Being directed wherever the waters wanted him to go.

Realistically, what choice did he have?

"Alright," he resigned. "I'll join."

"You were always going to join, because you had to," Noswen pointed out again. "But good. I'm glad we've come to an agreement." She clapped Yurzu on the shoulder and said, "Honestly, things seem to be progressing at a faster rate than we anticipated. There were far more monsters out in that forest than we were expecting to see."

"How many were you expecting?"

"None."

A faster rate indeed.

The raccoon said, "We'll leave tonight to head back to Sadatso and meet up with the others. There's no sense wasting any time lounging around here, as nice as the room is."

"What did you do?" Yurzu suddenly asked him. Coal almost jumped at the unexpected sound of his voice. "What mark do you need erased?"

Coal stared uncomfortably at the bat. "I'd rather not say," he replied.

Noswen butted in, unsurprisingly. "Don't pull that card. We're a team now, and we need to trust each other." She grinned. "What better way to build trust than to reveal a deep, dark secret?"

She was right, he knew. Coal stood and walked over to the raccoon, handing her the cube that held the diamond claw.

"I'm a Flesh Eater," he said dryly.

Neither of them knew how to react. Their expressions betrayed their shock.

Noswen faltered, then asked, "And what is your blight?" She knew better than to pick at the scab that was his Flesh Eater status.

Coal stepped away and returned to the bed. He sat himself down, bouncing lightly on the mattress. "They go hand in hand, actually. I thought it was all in my head, but I guess you've confirmed it really happened." He took a deep breath, then said, "I can speak to a person's ghost if I eat their flesh."

Again, he had stunned them into silence. The bat's face scrunched up in thought, and Noswen's mouth hung open, trying to formulate a response.

"I...well, that's a new one," she finally said.

Coal agreed. "Shooting fireballs from my hands would be a lot more useful in a fight."

He stood from the bed. If they were going to leave tonight, he needed to go see Ilio. There was absolutely no way he would abandon the man without an explanation for the second time. He explained to the two that he had some business to take care of before they left, and that he would meet them later at the city's northern bridge.

"By the way," he said, showing them to the doorway, "my name's not Von Rened. It's Coal Ereness."

Yurzu was unfazed, but Noswen chuckled as she stuffed the claw back into the bag, which she then slung over her shoulder.

"You're just chock-full of secrets, aren't you?" she grinned.

28

THERE WASN'T AN ANSWER at Ilio's door. He was probably still with Nomak, unfortunately. Coal dreaded the thought of marching down to Garna Nomak's room and having to confront the anteater, but it was inevitable.

Down the hall, he rapped his knuckles on what he knew to be the Garna's door. There was a shuffle of feet inside, a darkening of the peephole, and then the door swung open to reveal a smiling Ilio, still sporting his flashy orange suit.

Coal's stomach fluttered. It took all his willpower not to lean forward and kiss him right there in the entryway.

"Five minutes," Ilio whispered.

Coal nodded, and Ilio moved to shut the door, but in the background Nomak shouted, "Who is it?"

Ilio mouthed an apology before pushing the door open further and saying, "Coal."

"Ah!" Nomak boomed, coming into view at the back of the room, sprawled in a lounge chair. "*Von Rened* himself. Come on in, Lightbulb." As Coal acquiesced, Nomak grinned and said, "You sure do got a lot of names, don'tcha?"

"I suppose so," Coal agreed.

Ilio waited a moment, not wanting to leave Coal's side, but the Garna urged him to continue his job. He disappeared into the bedroom to do whatever it was the man had tasked him with.

So it was just Coal and Nomak left in the lounging area. There were plenty of places for Coal to sit, but he did not make for any of them, and Nomak did not invite him to sit.

"You're just the guy I was wanting to talk to," said Nomak, drumming his fingers on his fat belly.

"Oh, yeah?"

He knew where this was going. If this conversation had happened an hour ago, he would have been thrilled. Now, though...

"First of all, congratulations on your win."

"Thank you."

"That was *mostly* sincere. I *am* impressed, although I'd be a liar if I said I wasn't pissed, too. I had a lot of money put into Hiji. You know that. Fucker couldn't even crack the top three, though, so maybe it wouldn'ta made a difference even without you there."

Coal shrugged. "Hiji's good," he said. "I was impressed by his performance out there. He's a formidable racer."

"Well, being formidable doesn't win me prizes," Nomak scoffed, waving a hand lazily. "Winning does."

"Fair enough."

"But anyhow, you won. You've got the claw. I'm not sure how much you know about it, but...it's a pretty valuable piece of anteater history."

Coal cocked an eyebrow. "Oh, yeah?" he said again, playing dumb. He was curious to find out how much of the truth

Nomak knew about the artifact, or if its true history really was lost to time, as Noswen had theorized.

Nomak nodded. His tongue slowly emerged from his mouth, flicking around in the air before settling on his chest. He dribbled a little saliva, seemingly lost in thought about the diamond claw. Coal made an effort not to appear visibly disgusted.

Then the man slurped his tongue back into his mouth and said, "Yes, yes. It's quite a beautiful piece of work, isn't it? Assuming you've seen it?" Coal confirmed that it was indeed beautiful, and Nomak went on. "I don't want to bore you with the full history of it. I'm sure you're tired after a long, exhausting day. The race alone I'm sure would tucker anyone out, not to mention whatever happened back there to kill that bobcat."

The Garna seemed to be egging him on, wanting him to elaborate and describe what exactly had transpired, but Coal did not want to give him the satisfaction. He simply nodded again.

"But what I'm getting at is that it's been passed down from generation to generation of great anteater leaders. The story is that it was crafted by Eorpu Naro's finest jeweler hundreds of years ago. Have you heard of the Vaksura family?"

"No."

"They're practically anteater royalty at this point. A long line of jewelers, the best in Ruska. What I've heard is that it was crafted by one of their ancestors and given to Lady Totsia as a gift."

Coal had no idea who Lady Totsia was, but he did not really care and did not want to ask. Apparently some story about the claw's origins had been fabricated however long ago and effectively spread throughout society.

Or maybe the Dirt King is wrong about the claw, Coal suddenly thought. But that was a notion to entertain later.

"So you can see why this would be a highly valuable item to me, as an anteater," Nomak concluded.

"Of course," Coal said. "If it was a gift for Lady Totsia, then..."

"Exactly," Nomak said, pointing at him.

It was quite possibly one of the flimsiest arguments Coal had ever heard, but he was already about to disappoint and anger the man, so he did not want to provoke him.

"I'm prepared to offer five thousand tups for the claw."

Coal almost laughed. Zank had mentioned the Garna offering twelve thousand to Eorpu Naro for the artifact before they sold it to the beavers instead, but he should not have been surprised given how he'd been manipulated into wasting his own money on that Slapstick game. Nomak never had any respect for him before, so why would he now?

"That's a very generous offer," said Coal, making an effort to erase any trace of sarcasm from his voice.

Nomak smiled, convinced he was about to get what he wanted, like he always did.

"But I can't sell it to you, I'm sorry."

Again, he almost laughed. This time at the abrupt, drastic shift in Nomak's expression. His face scrunched up like he had just caught a whiff from a bucket of rotten food.

"Why not?" Nomak demanded. He sat up in his chair, scowling.

"I am just not in the market to sell it," Coal replied. Obviously he couldn't explicitly say why, but what he said was not untrue.

"Why not?" Nomak repeated.

"You just made a pretty good argument for why I should hold onto it," Coal said, suppressing a sly smile.

"I offered you *five thousand tups*," Nomak said.

"Yes. I will have to respectfully decline."

The anteater was fuming as Ilio reentered the room. The woodpecker looked from his boss to his—(Coal didn't actually know what he was to Ilio, he realized)—*friend*, confused as to how things had so quickly soured.

"Why the fuck'd you even come here, then?" Nomak snarled, clearly furious but not fired up enough to actually push himself up out of the chair.

It was a reasonable question, and one that Coal had not considered the optics of, considering that he and Ilio were trying to keep their relationship (was "relationship" a word with too much connotation?) a secret from the Garna.

Coal was about to sputter some nonsensical explanation before Ilio cut in and saved him.

"As I told you, I offered one of our extra rooms for him to stay in while he was here. I told him to come by when he was getting ready to leave so that I could assist him with the checkout process, since it was all arranged by me."

Steam was about to billow out from Nomak's nostrils. He was growing angrier, now not even getting the claw as compensation for a free room, but it was too late to change that. Coal had undoubtedly tipped over onto the man's bad side, just as he had been trying to avoid.

"Are you ready to depart?" Ilio asked Coal.

"Yes," he responded before the question had fully left Ilio's mouth.

The Garna lunged out of his chair, stomping toward Coal. He stopped only a few inches from his face, breathing his sour breath into Coal's snout. He lamented his keen sense of smell.

"I want that claw," Nomak muttered. Coal could taste every syllable.

Coal, almost choking on his words, said, "I'm sorry."

The two stared at each other for a few seconds, as if Nomak thought his threatening expression and tone might cause Coal to reconsider.

When the gambit failed, Nomak threw himself back into his chair, sending it scooting an inch or two. "Are you done?" he growled to Ilio.

"Yes."

The anteater pondered a moment, trying to cook up an excuse to keep Ilio there instead of going off with Coal, but he came up short. Instead he grumbled and waved the two of them off, like swatting at flies.

Ilio gave his boss a curt, polite nod and turned to exit, ushering Coal along through the doorway. When they were back in the hall a safe distance from the Garna's room, Coal said, "Nice save back there."

"Thank you. I have come to find it best if the Garna knows as little as possible about my personal life and thinks of me strictly in a business sense. I doubt he cares very much at all about my life outside of how it affects his own, anyway."

"Understandable. Do I actually need your help checking out, though?" he asked.

"No," Ilio chuckled. "You were never officially on the books. Perhaps you have noticed your room was not being cleaned each day?"

"Can't say I did," Coal confessed.

"Well, that is why. And even so, since I am the one who booked the block of rooms, I will be performing the checkout for all of them in any case. You have nothing to worry about."

Except for saving the entire kingdom, maybe.

But he did not need to burden Ilio with that. Not so early in their—

"Relationship" *was* a word with too much connotation behind it. They had gone on a (very nice) date, and they had

390 • *Travis M. Riddle*

kissed a few times, but that was it. Neither had agreed to any sort of commitment. It was far too early for anything like that. Far too new.

He *did* need to break it to him that he was leaving, though.

Before he could broach the subject, Ilio said, "I have something for you."

Coal realized he had followed Ilio back down the hall toward the man's room. He unlocked the door as he spoke, and he held the door open for Coal to slip past him.

"You do?" he asked, stepping inside. Ilio's room was identical to his own, but flipped. And also much cleaner, since it was apparently being attended to each day by the hotel staff.

"Yes, let me fetch it," said Ilio, scurrying off to the other side of the room while Coal seated himself.

Now was as good a time as any to break the news to him.

Coal said, "There's something I wanted to tell you."

"Hmm?"

He sighed heavily. No part of him wanted to cancel his plans with Ilio again, even if last night it had been out of his control. Stopping a darkness from spreading and infecting the whole valley was probably the only thing that could get him to do so. And even that was a toss-up.

"I need to leave Soponunga tonight. Pretty soon, actually."

He heard Ilio stop in the other room. "Oh," he said, resuming moving things around. "So no date, then?"

Just hearing the word *date* sent Coal's heart racing.

But he said, "Sorry."

There was a pause, then Ilio said, "It is okay." He emerged from the other room, holding a plain paper bag. "I am sorry for the lack of decoration," he said, glancing down at the paper bag. "I did not have time to spruce it up. It has been a busy day."

Coal smiled. "I'm no fancy boy, I don't need pageantry. And you didn't have to get me anything at all. They already gave me a diamond claw, you know. Sets a pretty high bar for you to clear," he joked.

Ilio laughed and walked forward, taking a seat in the chair next to Coal. He handed over the bag.

"I did not intend for it to be a congratulatory gift. Although I did not expect it to be a parting gift, either." His smile faltered, but he recovered. "I simply wanted to get you something."

Coal smiled at the man's thoughtfulness, then dug into the bag.

The object inside was a book. He pulled it out and examined the cover. It was written by Danai Loroto, an author he had never heard of. The title was *A Popular Bargain*. The cover was an illustration of two shadowed men seated at a table, each holding a hand of cards.

"Is this some kind of jab at my shitty Slapstick skills?" Coal asked, grinning. "Will this teach me how to gamble better?"

Ilio laughed. "No," he said. "Well, I do not think so, anyway. It is a mystery novel. A new release, actually, so I hope that it is good. It is the author's debut work, so perhaps the mystery will be pedestrian enough for you to solve it."

Coal's mouth hung open in faux offense. "Wow," he said, looking from the cover to Ilio then back again. "I cannot believe you said that. Not only insulting *my* intelligence, but—" he checked the front cover again "—*Danai Loroto's*, too. But I hope you're right," he chuckled. "I could use an easy win. Thank you." He slipped the book back into the bag and leaned over to hug the woodpecker. "That was very kind of you. Aside from the insult," he tacked on.

"You are welcome," said Ilio. "I hope you will be able to find time to enjoy it wherever you are going."

"Sadatso," Coal said. That much was safe to reveal.

"What is in Sadatso, if I may ask?"

That part was *not* safe to reveal. Coal tried to quickly concoct a lie. Unfortunately, since he had spoken so freely about his familial situation before, he could not offer the classic "family emergency" excuse that everyone always accepted without question.

But none of the lies that came to mind sounded convincing at all. Maybe it was because he did not actually want to lie to Ilio, so his brain wasn't allowing him.

"I can't say," he finally sighed, looking back down at the bag guiltily. "Sorry. It's—"

"One of those complications you and I seem to be so familiar with," said Ilio.

Coal nodded. "Exactly."

Even if Ilio understood, it did not make Coal feel any better about having to conceal what was going on from him. The fate of the kingdom in which he lived was probably something that would interest the man.

"I hope White Rose has rested enough for the journey," Ilio said. "The race seemed grueling for the poor thing."

Coal actually didn't know what method of transportation they would be using; Sadatso wasn't particularly far from Soponunga, but it wasn't close, either. It would be at least a few days if they walked.

But what Ilio said gave him an idea.

"You know, I don't have to leave just yet," Coal said. "And you're right, the race was shit. Faranap was shit, too. White Rose deserves better." He stood, smiling, and said, "Let's go release them."

"Really?" said Ilio. "You aren't riding them to Sadatso?"

Perhaps Noswen was expecting him to ride the spider out of town, but he didn't care. With the Dirt King funding their quest, she could afford to buy or rent him another spider.

White Rose was bred and raised in that awful, cramped stable surrounded by those abominations. The forest would treat the spider well. Plenty of places to stretch its legs, jumping from tree to tree, testing out its speed and crafting enormous, breathtaking webs.

"Let's do it," said Coal, resolute. Then, quieter, "I want to spend a little more time with you before I go."

Ilio's cheeks puffed. A sight that Coal did not think would ever grow old. He rose and said, "I like that idea."

NOSWEN AND YURZU WERE waiting for him on the northern bridge out of Soponunga. The raccoon leaned back against the railing with her arms crossed, staring down at the wooden planks, while the bat peered over the edge at the water. They had overstuffed backpacks at their feet, and no spiders.

Coal was admittedly relieved at the sight of them. Part of him was worrying he'd been tricked and that they were grifters stealing the claw from him, sending him spiraling into ruin.

It was hard to decide which would be worse: having his highly-valuable prize stolen, or it being true that the world might be ending.

The sky was dark, the moon peeking out over treetops in the distance. The Lunsk flowing beneath their feet created soothing music.

Coal was still a few feet away, lugging his few possessions on his back, when Noswen looked up and saw him approaching.

"Sorry for the wait," he called. Though he was apologizing, there was still a faint smile on his face from the time he'd spent with Ilio. The disappointment of leaving him had not yet set in, though he imagined it would not take long. For as long as he could, though, he wanted to hold on to that joy.

"We've only been waiting an extra, what? Forty minutes?"

"Sorry," Coal said again.

"It's fine," said Noswen, unable or unbothered to hide the mild irritation in her voice. Coal could sense that she was a good person deep down, just somewhat prickly.

"No spiders?" he then asked.

"Nope. Going on foot," she replied. "For someone who was expecting to ride a spider, you sure did show up without one."

"Sadatso is a long walk," said Coal. He had spent so many months walking south through Ruska, he was certainly not looking forward to traveling all the way back up to the Houndstooth. If they didn't own one already, the first thing he planned to advocate for when he met the rest of the team was purchasing a wagon.

"Yes, it is," Noswen said. "That's why we're leaving now." She shouldered her pack, and Yurzu did the same.

Coal still felt awkward around the bat. The next few days on the road might give them an opportunity to open up and get to know one another more as they grew more comfortable around each other, but he suspected the guy might just not be a talker. Noswen did not seem to push him to speak up often, after all.

"Is the claw in there?" Coal asked, pointing at the raccoon's bag.

"Yes. It's safe," she assured him. She turned to depart without another word.

As the trio trundled across the bridge, Coal said to Yurzu, "Sorry for making you pass out the other day."

The bat was surprised by the apology, raising his eyebrows. "It's okay," he said. "It happened every time I met a member of the team."

"Does it bother you now, being around me? And Noswen too?"

"I've gotten used to Noswen's by now, but your energy is still...kind of hurting," Yurzu admitted. "After being around you guys long enough, though, I'm able to acclimate."

"I'm glad you found me before the race, then," said Coal with a smirk. "Imagine if it had happened during the race. Ouch."

That brought the shadow of a smile to Yurzu's fuzzy face.

Heading out of Soponunga, leaving behind any sense of normalcy—in spite of how decidedly *ab*normal the past few days had been—Coal still felt trepidation about the quest thrust upon him.

How could he not?

Nothing about this made sense. Not only were there still gaps in Noswen's (or rather, the Dirt King's) story that didn't add up, but he was also undeniably ill-equipped for this mission.

He was just a librarian from Muta Par.

Even taking into account he was born with some magical ability, all he could do was speak to ghosts. How would that help? How would that keep him or anyone else safe?

Noswen could stick her finger in someone's bleeding holes and patch them up. Yurzu looked like an even less-skilled fighter than Coal, but at least his magic had some useful functionality.

But despite that trepidation, he felt good about what he was doing.

He wanted to be with Ilio. They had only spent a few days together, and it would be foolish—insane, even—to call it love, but he was definitely infatuated with the man. He wanted to explore that further.

This was just an obstacle he had to overcome in order to do so.

Once he sealed the Houndstooth and saved all of Ruska, he could go on another date with Ilio.

He smiled, thinking about the novel in his bag that Ilio had given him. He wished he had the foresight to buy a gift for him as well, but he had not exactly been expecting to leave on such short notice. He figured he would be riding back to Vinnag with Ilio and Nomak, on his way to paying Netraj and spending time with the peculiar woodpecker who he could not get off his mind.

All of a sudden, Coal was craving a bag of vegetable chips from a shitty vending machine. They were fast approaching the tree line, and far off to their right was where they had entered the forest for the race. He could still see the fencing set up amongst the trees.

It would be several days before he could satisfy that snack craving. The Dirt King's technological gifts were many, but even he had not yet uncovered a way to provide electricity in the middle of the forest.

"I expect you've planned a grandiose feast to celebrate finding me," said Coal. Yurzu chittered by his side. Had that been a laugh?

Noswen replied, "I guess you're sleepwalking, because if you think that's true, you must be dreaming."

Coal laughed, and he confirmed that Yurzu was definitely laughing as well. Already breaking through the bat's defenses.

They soon entered the forest, Noswen leading the way with confidence.

None of them could replace Ilio, but Coal was looking forward to spending more time with Noswen and Yurzu and the rest of the team. Especially Jatiri; he had never met a saola before.

"Well, if there's no feast, do either of you at least have any vegetable chips?" Coal ventured.

"Are you going to be like this the entire time?" Noswen asked, ignoring his actual question.

Yurzu laughed even louder.

EARLIER, AFTER GAINING ASSURANCE from the stablemaster that White Rose's wounds were patched up and doing fine, Coal and Ilio checked the spider out and led it through Soponunga, then out the southern exit. From there, they had turned right, heading west and away from the direction of the Sculio Brothers' shack. The last thing Coal wanted was to release White Rose into the wild only to be captured by those unscrupulous deer.

Ilio told Coal he'd never ridden spiderback before, so Coal gleefully helped him up onto the spider's abdomen.

"This is extra hard," he explained to the man. "Orb weavers are notoriously a little trickier to stay upright on, and without a saddle, it's even harder."

"I feel like I am going to fall," said Ilio, swaying a little on the creature's backside.

"Here, let's do this." Coal told him to scoot back a little, which Ilio did with extreme caution, and then Coal hoisted himself up in front of him. "You can hold onto me to keep yourself steady," he said.

Ilio's arms slid around Coal's waist, fingers interlocking at his stomach. He pressed his chest to Coal's back and said, "This is better."

Coal spurred White Rose on, and Ilio's grasp tightened. They both laughed as they bounced on the spider's abdomen, gripping with their legs to not be bucked off by its gait.

The breeze had felt nice, rustling the black and orange fur on Coal's face. He perked his ears up and listened. The only sounds he could hear outside the city were White Rose's gallops and Ilio's breathing.

Ahead, the sun was beginning to sink down below the treetops to wait for morning. Purple sky exploded into orange as it struck the leaves. Scant starlight twinkled mischievously.

Coal slowed White Rose to a stop at the edge of the trees, then disembarked before helping Ilio down. The spider stared straight ahead at the forest, but obediently stayed put at Coal's side.

He took a minute or two to walk around the spider, inspecting all its limbs, ensuring he would not be making a mistake by releasing it into the wild. But the stablemaster's assessment appeared correct; White Rose was a little bruised, perhaps, but there was nothing seriously wrong. Nothing a night of rest wouldn't cure, as he had predicted.

Ilio watched silently as Coal rubbed the spider's head. Its many eyes blinked curiously, none at the same time. It rubbed its bristly fangs together and gazed at its rider.

"Thanks for all your help," Coal told the spider. "I couldn't have won the race without you. I doubt any other spider would've gotten me there." In his head, he added, *You'll never know it, but you may have helped save the kingdom.*

Ilio took a step forward, then another, and Coal turned to him.

He said, "Come on, give ol' Rose a pat."

The bird walked to the spider's head and placed a wary hand on it, near Coal's. White Rose barely reacted. The spider did not flinch, and it only gave the woodpecker a brief glance.

Watching Ilio with the spider, standing there with his red cheeks puffed up in delight and the feathers on top of his head disheveled by the wind, there was a lot stirring inside Coal that he left unsaid.

He did not want to dive into some grand, romantic speech, even if that was how he felt in the moment. For one, he thought it would make him look crazy given how little time they had actually known each other.

And besides that, he did not want the evening to be defined and remembered by his words. He wanted it to just be remembered for how they felt there with each other, breathing in the crisp forest air, holding each other's hands, enjoying each other's company. Nothing more than that, nothing less. Let them remember how they felt this night, rather than thinking about and analyzing whatever words would spill from his guts. Second-guessing their sincerity, or regretting something said or unsaid.

The speech he had wanted to make back at the opening ceremony festival still held true. It still roiled in his chest. But for now, he would keep it inside.

Better not to risk tarnishing the moment, if his words didn't go down well with Ilio.

That was what he was most afraid of. The fear of *what might happen* quelled him, as it had when presented with the chance to ask his father's ghost about his mother. As it always did.

Instead, they would hold on to the feelings they felt tonight. Give him something to chase across Ruska. Something to come back to, when all the madness ended.

"This is the only way I can think to repay you," Coal said to the spider, momentarily turning his attention away from Ilio. "I hope you enjoy your new life out there."

Then he started to lead White Rose forward into the forest, guiding the spider and eventually letting go, standing back as it continued deeper into the trees without him. It crept forward on its long, skinny limbs, stepping over logs and bushes. Twenty or so feet into the forest, it rotated its body to look at its rider. Former rider.

Coal clicked his tongue, issuing a command to the orb weaver that equated to "go" or "forward."

White Rose considered the order for a second, then turned back around and continued into the forest. It picked up speed and leapt onto a trunk, scurrying up and disappearing amongst the leaves.

With White Rose gone, Coal wasn't sure what to do next. He felt good about giving the spider a new life. The spider had granted him the opportunity to secure his own future; it was only fair he return the favor.

He grabbed Ilio's hands, weaving their fingers together as they walked a short way into the forest.

"What are we doing?" Ilio asked.

"I thought we might sit a little while," said Coal.

"Don't you need to go?"

Coal shrugged. "Yeah, but who cares?"

He brought Ilio over to a particularly thick tree trunk and leaned against it, sliding down to rest on the forest floor. The bark scraped against his back, pulling at his shirt, but he didn't mind it. On the ground, he tapped the fingers of his free hand on brittle dead leaves. The other still held Ilio's, who now sat beside him. "I thought we might watch the sunset," he said, knowing all too well how corny the idea was. And yet he wanted to do it. "I said we could go on a date tonight, and I'm trying to make it so I'm not a complete liar," he laughed.

"If the sun is down, then technically we are on a date at night," Ilio grinned.

"That's my thinking."

"Clever. I will allow it." Ilio looked out into the woods, densely packed with trees, and said, "Hard to see it from here, though."

"True. It'll still be pretty, though."

The sun was already starting to shine between the tree trunks, blasting yellow light like an explosion in the distance. If they looked behind them, they would be able to see the darkening sky, but Coal did not want to move.

"It will probably be at least another twenty or thirty minutes until it has fully set," said Ilio. "So at a minimum we have to wait half an hour for you to not be a liar."

"That's true too," Coal nodded, resting his head on Ilio's shoulder. He squeezed the man's hand.

Ilio squeezed back. "What would you like to talk about while we wait?" he asked.

"Anything," Coal answered truthfully. "You pick."

What he wanted to do until nightfall was talk to the man about anything at all. Just absorb each other. Chase those feelings.

It was another good day with Ilio.

THE STORY CONTINUES IN...

MOTHER PIG

ACKNOWLEDGMENTS

Part of me thought I'd never write a series. It seemed too daunting. I was reading other fantasy series, some written by friends of mine, and I could not fathom how these authors were keeping so many plates spinning and so many threads untangled in their heads. It still baffles me. I also swore I would never write a romance because I didn't feel like I could do it justice, but...Coal and Ilio started talking to each other and how could they not end up together? Even though I still don't know how these other authors write such complex multi-volume epics, I had a story I wanted to tell, about a fox embarking on an epic quest that he wants nothing to do with. There's a lot more to it, but you'll learn that in the rest of the series.

It's been a whirlwind writing the Houndstooth series. Not only did I never expect to write a trilogy, but I definitely did not expect to write one during lockdown for a global health pandemic. But it's given me a lot of time to sit with these characters and this tale, and I'm excited to share the journey with all of you. I can't wait for you to meet the rest of the Blighted in book 2.

I want to thank my trusty crew of beta readers: Emily Atwood, John Bierce, Tyler Gruenzner, Jenna Jaco, and Tim Simmons. They helped whip into shape parts of the book that weren't working quite as well and also gave me a confidence boost mentioning parts they loved.

Thank you to the bloggers who have supported my work. Calvin Park from Fantasy Book Review, Ella from The Story Collector, Jordan from Forever Lost in Literature, Phil Parker from The Speculative Faction, Alex from Spells & Spaceships, and Peter from The Swordsmith. Your words of encouragement have made me feel like perhaps I'm not a total fool bumbling around after all.

And thank you to the community of authors I've found myself enmeshed in throughout the past couple years. Jon Auerbach, John Bierce, Angela Boord, Josh Erikson, Barbara Kloss, Devin Madson, Steven McKinnon, Richard Nell, Kayleigh Nicol, Carol A. Park, Clayton Snyder, Aidan Walsh,

Phil Williams, and Dave Woolliscroft. Your insight and support has been immeasurable, and it's always a treat getting behind the scenes looks at your upcoming projects!

Special acknowledgment for Dave Woolliscroft for showing me how to do a proper acknowledgments section even if he doesn't know it. I'm just looking at the back of your books to see how to be classy and following your lead.

Last but not least, thank you for buying this book. For taking a chance on an indie author. Without your support, we'd be nowhere. If you can, please leave a rating or review on Goodreads and Amazon, and if you think your friends and family would like these strange stories of mine, perhaps gift them a copy. I'd truly appreciate it.

See you next time.

RECOMMENDED READING

ROSEWATER by Tade Thompson (The Wormwood Trilogy). Set in a near-future Nigeria in a city that surrounds an alien dome, this book has been one of my favorite recent reads. The main character, Kaaro, is one of my favorites in sci-fi. This whole series has such a distinct voice and atmosphere that feels unlike anything I've read before. It's funny, it's thrilling, and it makes you think.

INTO THE LABYRINTH by John Bierce (Mage Errant). One of the most dizzyingly complex magic systems I've come across in a series. This is about a young guy entering a magic school and learning how to master his abilities while trying to make friends along the way, but the series goes on to...well, to say much more would spoil the surprises in store. But suffice to say, the world Bierce has crafted is one of the richest and most unique ones I've ever had the pleasure of reading.

THE WOLF OF OREN-YARO by K.S. Villoso (Chronicles of the Bitch Queen). If this book doesn't grab you with the first line, I don't know what to tell you. A fantastic opener for what promises to be an incredible trilogy set in a Filipino-inspired world with a complex, fascinating, and sympathetic main character. This first book feels personal in scope while still hinting at huge, epic stakes with a fully fleshed-out world. You're not going to want to miss out on the Bitch Queen's story.

KINGSHOLD by D.P. Woolliscroft (The Wildfire Cycle). One of the best fantasy series out there, self-published or otherwise. The first book involves a city where the king and queen have died and how it makes the shift from a monarchy to a democracy. It has an experimental style, with a short story collection coming in between each regular novel, but every book is vital to the full experience. Each book just gets better and better, and I can't wait to see how this thing wraps up.

THE TRAITOR BARU CORMORANT by Seth Dickinson (The Masquerade). Baru Cormorant is possibly the most interesting, complicated protagonist I've ever read in a fantasy novel. Dickinson's characterization of her is fascinating, as is the history of this world and its various cultures. Every piece of this series feels believable no matter how dark and weird it gets. And trust me, it gets very dark and weird.

RICE BOY by Evan Dahm. An epic journey through a beautiful, surreal fantasy world with one of the cutest and most charming characters I've met in a graphic novel. The first of many stories Dahm has crafted set in the world of Overside, all of which I love. The whole thing is available to read for free online, as well as in a print edition.

ABOUT THE AUTHOR

TRAVIS M. RIDDLE lives with his pooch in Austin, TX, where he earned his bachelor's degree in English Writing & Rhetoric at St. Edward's University. His work has been published in award-winning literary journal the Sorin Oak Review. He is the author of such works as *Balam, Spring* and *The Narrows*, which Publishers Weekly praised for its "intricate worldbuilding and familiar but strong narrative arc."

Find him on Twitter and Instagram @traviswanteat or at www.travismriddle.com